THE
SECOND
WOMAN

LOUISE MEY

THE SECOND WOMAN

TRANSLATED FROM THE FRENCH
BY LOUISE ROGERS LALAURIE

PUSHKIN VERTIGO

Pushkin Vertigo

An imprint of Pushkin Press

71–75 Shelton Street

London WC2H 9JQ

THE SECOND WOMAN was first published as *LA DEUXIÈME FEMME* by Éditions du Masque in France, 2020

First published by Pushkin Press in 2021

This book is supported by the Institut français (Royaume-Uni) as part of the Burgess programme

ROYAUME-UNI

1 3 5 7 9 8 6 4 2

ISBN 13: 978-1-78227-715-6

Designed and typeset by Tetragon, London

Printed and bound by CPI Group (UK) Ltd, Croydon, CRO 4YY

www.pushkinpress.com

THE
SECOND
WOMAN

1

SOMETHING HAS CHANGED.

Sandrine stares into the mirror, tries to identify the shift, pinpoint what is out of place. Although, conversely and for the first time, she feels that some unknown thing is exactly where it ought to be.

She stands naked in front of the glass, dripping from the cool shower she ran, not to get clean as such, more to relieve the oppressive heat that sticks her feet to the floor.

Normally, she hates showering in summer. In winter, she is not afraid to step out of the bath: the filter of steam blurs her contours and spares the details when, despite her best efforts, she catches sight of herself in the mirror. Then, she can ignore the sluggish, sagging shape of her own body. Ignore her own existence. In summer, she washes in cold water, and the dread of her reflection stiffens her movements, hunches her spine, forces her to stare at the floor.

But something has changed, and for the time in ages, perhaps the first time ever, she examines her reflection without loathing, only curiosity. Objective, even kindly enquiry. This envelope of flesh is the same as every other day and yet something has changed. But what, she cannot say.

Strange to look in the mirror and not feel the urge to holler and scrub herself out, cut herself into tiny pieces, dissolve. Not to mutter fat cow, *fat*, fat and ugly, stupid, *stupid* bitch. She searches inside for the scorn, the cutting words that have coursed in her veins for as long as she can remember looking at herself, but they are nowhere to be found. She gazes anew at her narrow, sloping shoulders; her small, pear-shaped breasts, flat and elusive from the first; her stomach, which has never been flat; her too-fat thighs that inflict suffering with the onset of warm weather, their skin rubbed raw by the first steps of summer, so that skirts are banished or she must end each day waddling grotesquely from her flesh-wounds. She is one of those women who wear jeans on the hottest days of the year, who quake when the season for fine, lightweight fabrics comes around. If she could, she would live in endless winter, hidden under layers of discomfort and shame. Concealed inside clothes, because that's what you do with fat cows like her, *fat*, fat and ugly, stupid, *stupid* bitch. You hide them away.

She is still the same. But something has changed.

She puts on the nightdress he gave her. He insists she wear it. And she wants to please him. She doesn't tell him the nightdress is too short, cut for a body that will never be hers, that the synthetic fabric sticks to her skin, that by morning the too-thin straps have cut into her shoulders. He insists, and she puts it on.

She comes out of the bathroom and feels the linoleum under her feet. It's not late, but already the upstairs corridor is dark. September takes her by surprise, every time, with nights that nip at days still scorching with heat.

The boy's door stands open. Invariably, he closes it – he's a dormouse, a vole, a slow-worm, forever curled and coiled out of sight. But his father comes to check on him and leaves the door open. A silent dialogue. Sometimes, at night and through to the pink light of dawn, she hears the tiptoeing of feet across the floor, the sound of the door closing, but his father always wins and the light-footed boy retaliates by retreating to his nest, enfolding himself in his quilt, curled into a tiny ball, shielded by a fortress of duck down and soft, pastel-coloured toys. She is very fond of the boy, and the sight of him hidden among the printed trucks and footballs of his bedsheets, even on the hottest nights, brings him so terribly close, as if they were one and the same. As if he were hers.

That's not how it is. He is not hers. He's his father's son, and she, Sandrine, came later. When she moved in, each time she thought of how he had come into her life with his little boy, into her fat cow's life, fat, *fat* and ugly, stupid, *stupid* bitch, her heart would melt in her throat, at her sheer good fortune.

The corridor light is on, now. He has pressed the switch at the bottom of the stairs. A conquering shaft of yellow pushes its way into the boy's room.

She looks at the bed. Nothing peeks out from under the sheet. The intrusive light fades into darkness across the floor. The boy likes to have a night light, but his father thinks he is too old. If Mathias doesn't want to lie in the dark, he can leave his door open. They always leave the corridor light on. The cover rises and falls; he is breathing softly. She pulls the door delicately towards her, leaves it neither closed nor ajar. In their tiny war, she takes no sides.

She walks on, and her shadow glides along the wall to the top of the stairs. She knows the dark imprint of her body can be seen from below, from the sitting room; that if, downstairs, he wants to know what she's doing he has only to look at the wall. She found it both strange and comforting at first, and sometimes she wondered if this was his night light, of sorts – the knowledge that she was there and what she was doing. He showed such concern: for her movements, where she was from one minute to the next. She felt she was eagerly awaited, protected, needed. A new, warm feeling that pulsed in her veins after so long alone, living for no one but herself.

A floral shirt lies over the stair-rail. He bought it for her at the market. She never buys clothes on a whim; decades of fitting-room catastrophes, emotional landslides swallowed down in silence, have left her immune to shopping on impulse.

But he liked the shirt. It was pretty, he insisted. That summer, he wanted to see her in delicate, lightweight fabrics. She resisted, said nothing, but often she gave in.

She pays careful attention to her clothes. Her soft, lardy silhouette allows no margin for error. She needs no one's advice now, not even the wardrobe experts who say figures-of-eight should cinch their waist, and pear-shapes should emphasise their neckline. A heap of slush, that was her body-shape, not one you see in the pages of a magazine, and she had learnt slowly, painfully, to choose things that corrected her defects as best they could. She wore structured tops with sharply defined shoulders to compensate for her neck that slid straight down to her too-fat arms. Loose-fitting blouses to hide the fat that rolled in waves over her stomach, a tide that refused to turn, however obstinately she exercised, however violently she starved. High-waist jeans that she ordered specially and got adjusted by hand. They were expensive. She had only a few pairs.

She had tried the shirt on; decided she looked repulsive. That was yesterday. She had left it there, on the wooden stair-rail, not daring to touch it again. He didn't want her to give it away, and they couldn't take it back. She looked nice in it, he said. It's a present. I'd like to you have it. Wear it.

And so she picks up the shirt to take it down to the utility room – you never know who's tried it on, where it's been. Best to wash it first.

Normally, the feel of a hostile garment would floor her completely. She had composed her daily uniform with such care all these years because dressing was torture, the one thing worse than being naked. The day her mother persuaded her to try a skirt that was too small, she had dug her nails into her hips until she drew blood. Her mother knew the skirt would be tight, she just wanted to see her daughter bent double, red with shame at the unbreachable barrier of her pudding thighs. Clothes were enemies to watch for and hold at bay. She had wept, and binged, and vomited and drunk over the trying-on of clothes that did not fit. But he has insisted she wear the shirt, since yesterday, just as he insisted all summer that she wear 'something different'. 'Something different' from the uniform body-armour she had developed for so long. He told her over and again the shirt would look pretty, until she agreed to try it on. She had looked at herself in it: a fat, ugly cow. That was just after coffee, but the shame of being herself had gnawed inside until evening. And yet he said it suited her.

He doesn't like things left lying around, so she will wash the shirt and see. She takes a deep breath, picks it up by the yoke (too narrow, too shapeless) and holds it at arm's length. Ordinarily, she would rather die than put the thing on. But no. Because truly, something has changed. She doesn't know what, but she wants not to think about it, with all her might.

She comes downstairs, concentrating on the feel of the floor against her skin, the soft, dry wood that prints its narrow grain on the soles of her feet. So as not to think about the mirror she hadn't wanted to smash, the shirt that is just a harmless piece of fabric dangling in her grasp. So as not to think about what has changed, the thing she doesn't want to frighten away. She thinks, instead, that the stairs are dusty, she should have taken the vacuum cleaner out when she got home, she'll do it tomorrow.

She knows she will see him as soon as she reaches the ground floor, his gaze turned expectantly towards her, every time. At first, his eager anticipation had flooded her with warmth, tingled the top of her stomach, almost between her breasts.

But he has not turned around. For the first time, he is not looking out for her.

He is sitting in the same armchair as always, in front of the TV, but he hasn't turned to watch her come downstairs. Night has fallen and the sitting room is bathed in the blue light emanating from the big screen.

The melody of the evening news, voices whose song follows no known logic, placing full stops where they're least expected, framing questions that are not. The sound is low, but she can hear the voice of a journalist who says that *More rarely? As well as patients suffering from Alzheimer's and other degenerative memory disorders? Paris's Pitié-Salpêtrière hospital treats people who have. Quite simply. Forgotten who they are. People like this woman?*

She draws nearer. The voice continues, says that *Madame X arrived at the Pitié just a few days ago. From Italy, where she spent more than a year. During which she never spoke, until suddenly, she began to speak in French?* And when Sandrine stands beside the armchair, he turns to her, his face gleaming with sweat, though it's not warm in the sitting room, they had closed the shutters against the sun. Now is the time to open them and let in the cool night air. She is about to ask if that's what he wants, if she may open them. This is his home, and she always asks, despite the bowl decorated with her name in the breakfast cupboard, her shoes in the hallway. She doesn't dare say 'our home, my home'. But his mouth is open to speak, so she says nothing. He says: It's her. It's her.

His voice is toneless, unfamiliar. Sometimes, when he disapproves, his speech becomes strained, even alarming, as if a horrid, stiff rope is strangling his words. But this is something different.

'Who? Who's "her"?' Sandrine asks.

On the screen, a woman's face. She has dark brown hair and regular, neatly drawn features. She smokes a cigarette and leans against a pillar in a tree-lined courtyard. The place looks old and imposing. Her long, slender neck casts a shadow that catches at her collarbone, her thin shoulders. Her breasts are round. She lifts the cigarette to her lips, showing the finely delineated muscles of her forearm.

The woman on the screen is everything that Sandrine is not, but she has known that for a while now. The woman on the screen is framed in yellow, in a photograph on the dresser.

Shipwrecked, drowning, Sandrine glances wildly back and forth, from frame to screen, screen to frame, clutching at one last hope, perhaps it's not really her, it's impossible, she's dead, she disappeared, melted into thin air, she's the empty space in the bed, the absent mother.

'Who?' Sandrine asks again, as if pretending she doesn't understand could change anything, cancel the moment, as if acting like there's nothing wrong can help her now, even as she sinks to the bottom, even when it's too late; and already, she pictures herself alone again, in the small apartment where she had waited to come alive, preserved in readiness through the long, slow absence of a man, her man.

No, worse than alone. But what could be worse? She knows what: rejection and exile. He will throw Sandrine out, because the other woman is alive. If she is alive, she will come back. If she comes back, he will leave her. Leave Sandrine. There had been one vacant post, and she has lost it now. He will get rid of her, the fat, ugly cow.

'Her.'

He doesn't dare speak the name.

Neither does Sandrine.

But on the screen and in the yellow picture frame, the same dark eyes devour the light, the boy's mother, the woman who was there before, the woman who was there first.

The first one. The first woman.

2

WHAT WILL HE DO? What should they do?

The journalist's voice says that *Anxious to discover her identity? The woman has been assisted since her return to France. By the police. Who are searching the accessible data on persons reported missing in suspicious circumstances in recent years. And of course. The team at the Centre for Cognitive and Behavioural Disorders is constantly. At her side. Helping her to recover the memories her mind has suppressed. The mystery should hopefully, soon? Be resolved. Join us for another Tale of the Unexpected tomorrow – a journey to the heart of the Paris sewers.*

What are you going to do? Sandrine asks.

He says nothing at first, sits as if drawn into the screen. The subject is closed, and anyone entering at that moment would see a couple as if turned to stone in front of the evening weather forecast, outlook fine for tomorrow, temperatures above average for the time of year.

She stares at the top of his scalp. She remembers the first time she told him she loved his head, his hair, that she loved all of him. That she moved to press her lips into his hair, breathe its smell, kiss his head; she doesn't do that any more, he doesn't like it. He's losing his hair, a slight bald patch on top, and thanks her not to talk about it, not to mention it, dislikes it when a breath of evening air, a kiss, reminds him of its existence. But it touched Sandrine to see the delicate skin laid bare, little by little. She explained that she wished she had known him before, that she had always known him, and that she loved to watch him change.

To observe the passage of time in this man, whom she loved. It anchored her to a point on his lifeline, into which she had come so recently, so late. The small, warm, naked patch told her over and over again that she was really there, they were really together, that she really lived in this house, with this man and his little boy, both of whom had been missing a woman's touch.

Sandrine had met him because a woman was missing. His wife.

The first woman had disappeared. She had seen it on TV, heard it on the radio: when the first woman had failed to come home, he had appealed for help. He was with the woman's parents, the woman's son, the four of them grouped around an empty space. He was crying and the sobs in his voice had touched Sandrine deeply. A man who cried. She had felt a wave of sorrow sweep over her, she thought, poor man, poor man, and his poor little boy, and those poor parents who had lost their daughter.

The pain she felt for them was lesser, because she had no knowledge of the sort of parents who would plead for their daughter's return. No one had ever pleaded for her. She had always been awkward, an embarrassment, too soft and feeble, too slow. They hadn't thrown her out, but they never liked the sight of her around the house either – something she had always known. He with his loud voice and brusque gestures, whenever Sandrine got in his way; she with her sinuous, serpentine way of talking, her staring eyes and dry skin, like some species of reptile. Sandrine had never known loving parents, and so she could not imagine their distress.

But he, the man who cried in front of the cameras – he whose heart had been torn out all at once, who found himself suddenly missing the other half of his universe – she knew exactly what he was feeling. Straightaway, she had recognised her twin in pain and sorrow, she who had so much love to give, to a person unknown; she who felt the void that gnawed at the pit of her stomach. She knew someone was missing in her life, and when she saw him, she knew he was that someone, the man who cried. Their sorrows were reflections in a mirror.

He was devastated, he fought and stifled his sobs, and the parents-in-law had stepped up to the microphone. The family was organising a White Walk, they had to do something, the inaction was killing them, and they invited anyone who wished to join them. He had stepped back as they spoke, his broad, heavy man's hands on the shoulders of the small, expressionless boy.

She had taken part in the Walk. Even now, she has no idea where she had found the courage. The shy one, the spare wheel, the one her friends put up with and asked along, the one you remember when you need help moving your stuff, the one you forget on the guest list for a party. When she saw him cry on TV, it had been years already since anyone had needed her help moving house, years spent with no one but herself, nothing but her work, her small apartment, her car. Years when she had been unable even to embrace the cliché and surround herself with cats, because they made her throat sore and her skin itch.

She filled her life carefully, swimming on Saturday morning, then the market, meals to prepare for the week, plenty of fresh vegetables – she was watching her weight – then books, lots of books, until it was time to go to bed.

On Sundays she always got up too early. She would have loved to be one of those people for whom sleep is an activity in itself, who could spend all weekend snoring in a semi-coma – but no. At eight o'clock in the morning, sometimes earlier, very often earlier, she was awake, in the empty apartment that echoed with nothing but the cries of the children from the floor above. She hated the noise. She would get straight out of bed and put on the radio, loud, a music station. Then she would take the car to some unlikely event, a bric-a-brac sale where she would find nothing to buy, some obscure museum. She had gone into a pet shop once, but ran out moments later with the urge to vomit, the animal reek of despair was so strong she could taste it.

On Mondays she would return to the office, mimicking her colleagues' yawning reluctance, concealing her secret delight at the prospect of five long days at work that would shield her from the unbearable tête-à-tête with her own self. Weekday evenings were easier, she often arranged a trip to the supermarket, then there was her shower, and her lengthy, meticulous grooming, the nightly, acrobatic contortions so that she could shave her legs. She applied cream, too, with great diligence and care. Anti-cellulite cream, belly-fat cream, stretch-mark cream, blackhead cream, cream to prevent bags under the eyes. There were things to be dissolved, melted away, and things to be encouraged: a separate shelf was devoted entirely to magical potions that would firm the flesh of her breasts, tone her neckline, plump her too-thin lips. Then dinner, lots of fresh vegetables – she was watching her weight – and then she would watch a film, chosen with care and precision. She had watched romantic films until she felt quite sick, she detested their nauseating sentimentality, preferred films that smashed things up, explosions, battle scenes, films where the love interest was a pretext or a reward, not the journey itself. She had lost patience with the path to romance, the one she could never find, never take, and so she would curl up in front of a mindless action movie, and that would see her through to bedtime.

The woman's disappearance had not caught her attention at first, though it had made the regional TV news. Sandrine had half-heard it and permitted herself some mildly wicked reaction: 'So much for having it all,' as if a woman's abduction was somehow the price for her perfect life, husband, child, house. Or 'How stupid, to go running alone in the woods,' though she knew it was unfair to judge. She knew, too, that life was turning her sour.

She watched out for that now, because she had noticed it more than once, the petty, snake-like cruelty, the slow pulse of her tainted bloodline. She had discovered it by chance. The car had broken down one day, and she had taken the bus to work. The one time she had no need to fake the show of tiredness and irritation on arrival at the office, because the bus had taken an hour to cover the journey she made in twenty minutes by car. A couple had sat down in front of her. He was very short, overweight, and the rolls of fat around his neck were coated in thick brown hair that sprouted from beneath his shirt collar. The synthetic fabric had bobbled, and was tucked carefully inside his trouser belt, worn too high. At his side, his companion. She, too, was overweight, and flaccid, sitting with her breasts resting on her belly, which rested on her thighs, clad in a flowered skirt that clashed with her striped polo-necked jumper. They smiled at one another and exchanged small, kind words as they stroked one another's hands. They were ugly, hideously dressed, and happy; she had hated them from the very depths of her soul, bolt upright in her seat, her mouth twisted in disgust, and when she rose to get off the bus, she had shot them a reproachful, scornful look, as if they were doing something wrong – as if they themselves were wrong. The girl had sensed it and looked up at her. Instinctively, the young man at her side had gripped her hand more firmly, and the hate had almost escaped from Sandrine's mouth, she had almost done what had been done to her so many times, when strangers called her Fat and Ugly ('You should go on a diet, young lady', 'Sure you need that ham sandwich, Piggy?'). She had almost said something nasty in turn, after all why not, the two of them were far uglier than she was and no one had ever thought twice about hurting her. But she had stopped herself just in time. That's not you, that's not you, don't do it, you're a nice person.

And with difficulty, she had summoned a thin, polite smile that reassured the girl with her ugly skirt and her pasty face spilling out over the polo neck. The ugly, happy girl with her ugly, happy young man. Sandrine could have slapped her. Stepping down from the bus, she took a deep breath, but her acid saliva provoked a grimace that stayed with her until she reached the office.

And so Sandrine had added nastiness to the list of things she needed to watch. Because she knew she could not be nasty, no one can afford to be nasty as well as ugly.

So it was that when she first heard the news – the news about the woman who had disappeared, the woman who had gone running and never returned – she had thought bad things, and corrected herself, and let the news item pass unnoticed. But people had talked about it for a long time, the parents had gotten involved – in fact, they were the ones who had reported the woman missing and alerted the media. The man who cried was too broken.

Unless he did it. Killed his wife… her colleague Béatrice had suggested one day during their lunch break, as they all ate the contents of their Tupperware boxes in the communal kitchen.

Forty-five minutes, not long enough to go out, not long enough for a shy person to form any real connection. Sandrine never spoke much at lunch, there was barely room for girls like her, the quiet ones, unused to spouting their opinions unabashed, the way men did. That morning, the day of the family's press conference, a week after the woman's disappearance had found its way onto the regional TV news, they had all been given their first sight of the tearful husband, the desperate parents, the little boy with his crumpled features.

No! The word had burst out of Sandrine's mouth, before she could do anything to stop it, and her face had turned scarlet, embarrassed by her sudden conviction. How would you know? her colleague retorted when the moment of surprise had passed.

Nothing. Sandrine didn't know anything. She felt it, was all.

And on Sunday, the day of the White Walk, she had woken up, and without a second thought she had taken the car to the town where the missing woman lived, not wanting to admit that she was going there to find the man who cried.

There were a lot of people. Family, and friends. Busybodies, too, and people who were genuinely concerned, and others, like her, whose motives were less clear – and Sandrine thought to herself that it was strange to come and share this desperate anxiety that was not her own. She felt like a thief, a sham.

Dressed in white, the parents of the missing woman were handing out photographs. She hadn't seen the husband at first, the man who cried and who had touched her so deeply. Only the parents, and she remembered that expression, one she had read a hundred times and never understood, the look of 'urgent despair' that she noted now in the couple's tense animation. They were in their early sixties, perhaps slightly younger. They moved about constantly, from one group to the next, holding photographs of their daughter, and Sandrine understood that they were looking for her. That they were still looking for her. It was four weeks since their daughter had vanished as she ran on the path through the forest, the path she ran along every day. But they were still looking for her. With the urgent energy of despair. That was before the woman's clothes had been found, and her shoes. For them, the White Walk was not a commemoration, it was a search party. Sandrine heard them tell someone beside her that the cops had stopped searching. Or weren't looking in the right places. That people were giving up, that already, the story was getting less coverage in the papers and on the news.

Sandrine had stood, hesitant, shifting her weight from one foot to the other. It was cold, and her breath sent timid clouds into the air. When she caught a stranger's eye, she showed a small, kind smile, concerned and compassionate. I'm here to help, she told herself. I'm here to help.

At last, they all set off, walking away from the cul-de-sac of small, neat houses. There were about sixty people, maybe more, quite a crowd. That was what it looked like, she told herself – a protest. Sluts, her father used to say, during her years at the lycée; sluts walking the streets with filth and rabble, you can watch your face, my girl, if you start running with that crowd. And so, when the other students were skipping class, waving their makeshift placards, hating the system, Sandrine had been the one who stayed behind, alone in the room set aside for study periods. One evening, on TV, a close-up shot had showed some of her classmates, girls out in front with the word 'NO!' scrawled in lipstick across their cheeks, the boys marching either side. Her father had said, Just look at those filthy little sluts, if I catch you doing that one day you just watch your face, and she had felt relieved and furious to have missed the march, because she was already watching out for her face, some evenings, when he'd been drinking and she had breathed too hard, so she might just as well have gone along. But no, Sandrine had stayed huddled all alone in the study room, and when the controversial government bill had passed into law and things had gotten back to normal she was the girl who never went on the marches, the *manifs*. She was the traitor, the reactionary.

On this Sunday, the day of the White Walk, she had hesitated until the very last minute: should she follow the column threading through the wood that began at the end of the cul-de-sac, or turn around? It would be almost lunchtime when she got home, and half a Sunday vanquished. She shifted on the spot, uncertain, until she was almost alone in the cul-de-sac, unsure which way to walk.

And then the door of one of the houses opened and the little boy came out, the same little boy she had seen on the television, and behind him, emerging from the shadows, his father, the man she had seen cry and who had broken her heart.

That evening, in bed, she had tossed and turned. Sandrine the shy one, the quiet one, asking herself how she had found the courage to go and speak to them, to walk towards the man who cried and his son, but she had done it, she had done it, she told herself over and over, cheeks still burning, her skin strangely electric. She had spoken to them and they had taken the path through the woods together. She said, I came to… to offer my support. And he had said, Ah, that's kind of you, in a toneless, indifferent voice as he locked the door behind him. Then she had said, It must be terrible for you, I'm so sorry.

And he stopped staring at his hand as it fiddled with the key in the lock and he had *looked at her*, at Sandrine.

That night, Sandrine had tossed and turned in the warmth of his gaze, until finally she stripped naked between the sheets. He had *looked at her*.

She knew two kinds of look, just two kinds of male gaze: the one that checks you all over and tosses you aside, and the one that checks you all over and decides it feels hungry. Indifference, or a predator's threat, nothing else, all her life.

The indifferent eyes were many, looking her over like a master butcher assessing a carcass, quick to decide, lingering at her breasts, her thighs, then up to her face, then sliding away to another place, something in the distance – a shop window, or another woman. She would be judged inadequate, insufficient, or too much. Those stares left her wounded and relieved in equal measure. Sometimes, the men who didn't like what they saw made a grab for it nonetheless, felt her with hard, greedy hands; pinched her, caught hold of her, worked her flesh like dough; and then her heart would race in her chest, and she would be overcome with fear and panic. If she was lucky, the men behaved like that only in passing, then forgot all about her, while she was left in a fevered, exhausting state that lingered for days after. One day, she had seen a woman turn on one of those men who had touched her without asking, heard her scream the words WHO THE FUCK DO YOU THINK YOU ARE? I DON'T GIVE A FUCK, YOU SAY YOU'RE SORRY RIGHT NOW OR I'M CALLING THE POLICE! and Sandrine had watched the scene, open-mouthed; could you, could they do that? Could women react, lash out, object? Could they resist the barbarian hordes, refuse their bodies, defend themselves? Sandrine had stared at the woman, with her tiny, mouse-like frame, and she had been afraid the man would hit her. He almost did, but the woman refused to shut up, she had stood her ground, and her cries had drawn people out from the shops onto the street. Two elderly ladies were walking towards them, with their poodles, the dogs had barked, and other men had arrived on the scene. The man said OK, OK, shut your mouth, and walked away. The woman had trembled all over, but she held her head high, she must have been one of the girls Sandrine's father told her about, the sluts who made trouble for everybody, and Sandrine had learnt never to make trouble in her world, she was a good girl.

Her father was not a part of that world, anyway. Her father was the first to teach her that indifference was a blessing, even as a child. When he peered into her face, he was looking for something she should spit out, and she always did. He hated her vacant expression, her mouth always full – you're fat enough – her school marks in literature and writing, Who cares about that, fucking waste of time, what about the school teams, you get fucking nowhere in sport and you expect us to clap our hands? He would rumble on like that for hours, often ranging far back over the course of her life, while buttering a piece of bread, leafing through the TV schedules, keeping up the brutal stream of words. She would listen, huddled tighter and tighter into herself, learning never to answer back, never to object, balled tightly around that part of her that was not entirely broken, trying to keep it intact, though it shrank, year after year, until now there was almost nothing left.

She had managed to get away. She hadn't tried that hard, it was pure luck: the job she had found after completing her training was too far away to commute each day. She had feared her father would not let her accept the offer, but his expression had reverted to indifference, at last. Well… er, go then. Go. Think we'd try and stop you? You raise them up and then off they go, just like that. Fuck it. He told her she'd be off 'strutting about', which meant 'acting like a whore', and her mother nodded silently, as always. Sandrine said nothing, she just wanted to leave, and leave she did, at exactly the right time, because since her breasts had begun to form, too late, too flat, too small, her father's eyes had turned hungry, too, and he hid it less and less and Sandrine dreaded things so terrible she could not put them into words.

She encountered plenty of hungry men, there was something in their scavengers' eyes, something cruel, a craving, nothing more. They would grab her in the street, on the bus, make wet, squelching sounds, get out their sex, gorged with violence. She would freeze, speechless, like a frightened animal, or walk faster to get away, tearing her feet from the ground, heavy with shame, each step a superhuman effort.

At the supermarket she had met a cashier who seemed nice, who had long conversations with her, flowery words, soft-spoken. She had agreed at last to go with him to the cinema, and he had fucked her like a sack, in the car, exactly as her father had said they would, it had been painful and dirty and he had buttoned himself up again straightaway and left her alone in the cinema parking lot. The next day she had gone to his checkout, just to know, to understand, and he had ignored her, but two shelf-stackers had whispered as she walked by. She had changed supermarkets after that.

She had let other guys try their luck, she was prepared not to mind what they did to her body if they liked her as a person, in exchange, even though in the romances she watched back then, it was always beautiful and gentle, and the sheets were always fresh. One of them had told her, eventually, that he wouldn't introduce her to his friends because she wasn't his type, what he really liked were beautiful women. Another had ended it after two ugly nights when he had called her late, and drunk, and then nothing.

But on that Sunday, the man in the blue shirt had looked up and into her eyes. Neither hungry, nor disgusted – something new. And he had smiled.

Later, she told him she had fallen in love with him then and there, the moment he smiled, though perhaps that wasn't true, perhaps it was just beforehand, when he looked at her first; or perhaps that was wrong too, perhaps she had loved him forever, he, the first man to look at her with kindness in his eyes, before breaking into a smile. She never kept anything from him, he was so worried she might be hiding something, he needed so badly to know that she was telling him the truth, the whole truth, keeping nothing back, it made her happy to feel that he wanted to know everything. What she told him was no lie, it was just that she honestly didn't know, and anyway it really didn't matter.

It must be awful for you, I'm so sorry, she had said, again, that Sunday, encouraged by his smile. He said, That's kind of you. And his voice was exhausted. His eyes were sunk deep in their sockets. The face of a man who had reached rock bottom.

The little boy stood silently on the doorstep, scratching his elbow with thin, sharp fingers. Sandrine saw the marks gouged in his soft skin. He stared at his feet and made no effort to hold his father's hand, and when Sandrine spoke to him, he gave no reaction.

What's your name? His father said, The lady's asking you a question, and the little boy was startled out of his thoughts and mumbled: Mathias. Hello, Mathias, said Sandrine to the little boy, who said nothing more in reply. Have you come for the Walk? asked the father, walking towards her, stepping down from the porch, his hand around the boy's wrist.

Suddenly, she panicked: what should she say? 'No, not really, I came because I saw you cry on TV and I felt so sorry for you.' Her body behaved as usual: fingers twisting together, hiding her stomach, forehead flushing deeply, voice stammering. She hated moments like these. Each time, she dreaded the sound of her father's voice: 'Say something, dammit, no one's going to eat you, how hard is it to answer a simple question, eh? Huh?

Stupid girl. Unbelievable. Shut up then, if you've got nothing to say for yourself.'

But no. No, he looked at her again, her hands all knotted with shame and embarrassment, the red flush rising from her neck, descending from her forehead, while she said I... It's... because... and he had saved her, with a small gesture, an arc of the palm of his hand, as if wiping a slate clean. He had saved her with two words: I understand.

For the first time in her life, she was glad that someone had spoken in her place, happy for someone to interrupt her hesitant words. He's kind, she told herself, with a feeling of relief that broke over her like a wave, he's kind. They had walked together, the three of them, through the wood, the last link in the chain, while up ahead, the band of do-gooders wound its way through the trees and along the path.

The weather was fine that afternoon, rays of pale sunshine touched the dead leaves that shone like heaped treasure. The boy walked in silence, followed by Sandrine, and lastly his father. He had asked her about herself, her work. She said, Oh, it's not very interesting, but he was sure it was, he asked in detail about what she did, her colleagues, their names, were they nice? He enjoyed hearing about it. She understood that he was desperate to talk about something other than his wife's disappearance: tiny considerations, insignificant things, and she had confided in him with disconcerting ease, how the law firm was organised, the other secretaries, the room they used for breaks, the conversations, her own silences (a little), her lunch boxes and salads, she liked cooking. She broke off frequently, ashamed of her misplaced babble on this search for his wife, but each time he urged her to go on, in the woods that rustled with the careful passage of the people walking ahead of them.

They had come full circle, and when they emerged at the opposite end of the cul-de-sac, an odd-looking couple had stared at them. A woman and a man, silent, possibly hostile. She was thin, almost gaunt, wearing a leather jacket and a woollen sweater; she had a thigh gap, and she stood bolt upright, her feet in lace-up boots that Sandrine thought rather manly. She was carelessly but very comfortably dressed. He was good-looking, with a touch of grey at the temples, high-rise trainers, filthy now with the damp soil of the wood. Ordinarily, Sandrine would have had thoughts. Jealous, small-minded thoughts: a figure like that and all she does is dress like a man. But this time, nothing. She thought nothing at all. Even the persistent stares directed by the two strangers at their unlikely trio left her unscathed. She was so happy, and so busy hiding the fact. Her joy was like an insult hollered aloud in the middle of the anxious crowd.

He had grasped the little boy at the neck, his big hand comforting on the puny shoulders. He excused himself and walked off to join his missing wife's parents, the couple she had seen handing out flyers earlier that morning. She turned and walked back to her car. She was happy, and ashamed.

At home she had taken off her shoes, her jacket, and put on her softest things. Her everyday pyjamas were not soft, she chose shapewear: leggings designed to flatten the stomach, padded, structured bras, all carefully chosen and matched. Armour against the dread of an accidental glimpse of her reflection, the very thought of which filled her with horror.

But that Sunday, she had dug out the soft, indulgent fabrics that normally she allowed herself only when she was ill. Long, shapeless jogging pants that made her flat, broad backside sag even further, a big T-shirt that hid her flaccid chest, a huge gilet in soft wool that had come to her from her grandmother, a dear, gentle woman, sweet as honey, whose memory comforted her when a small voice whispered sometimes in her ear that there was no escaping the bonds of blood, that her nasty comments and cruel thoughts were no mistake, but the expression of her innermost nature, which would gradually, inescapably reveal itself over time, however hard she tried to block the slow transformation. She had curled up on the sofa, snuggled in the gilet, like a warm, soft embrace, and watched the films she had banished, romantic comedies, dripping with misunderstandings and kisses on station platforms. Her stomach rumbled but she wasn't hungry, and finally she went to bed without eating, pressing her hands to the warm flush between her legs, imagining the caress of soft palms, the long embraces that would make her feel like a queen.

Next day, her alarm sounded, and the state of grace lasted just a little bit longer, a tiny bit longer, until she saw herself in the mirror. And all at once, her body had slumped, her shoulders slouched and weary. She was still herself, still ugly, and fat, a great, big, fat cow, fat and ugly, stupid, *stupid* bitch. She was just herself, and he had smiled and talked to her because he was kind, and nothing more.

She had pushed the memory away, like an old piece of clothing you never want to see again, pushed to the bottom of a drawer. Padlocked. She had imagined things, it was an illness, a disease, cause and effect, it had unleashed images that fired more than her imagination. She felt pathetic, pitiful, an old maid who let herself get carried away because a man had spoken to her once, and smiled. And so now you're going to marry him, adopt the boy and God knows what else, you stupid, fat bitch, poor cow, poor ugly cow, you poor, stupid bitch, staring for hours at stupid, mindless films, fingering yourself to thoughts of an almost complete stranger just because he cried on TV and happened to give you a smile. Stupid, stupid, you're nothing, nothing, nothing at all. She had locked it all away and for days, weeks, whenever she saw his face, the face of the man who had come out of the small, neat house, a bolt of shame would leave her rooted to the spot. The memory had gripped her several times over, bursting obstinately from its locked drawer, while she was sitting on the toilet, or standing in front of the fridge in the break room at work, or at home chopping vegetables. And she had groaned under the burden of shame.

The following week, the case of the missing woman took a new turn, and when she arrived at work the secretaries were all standing around one computer screen, watching blurred video footage of dogs making their way over a field surrounded by police officers and yellow plastic tape. A farmer had found the woman's clothes in the middle of his beetroot field, half-burnt and soaked with diesel and rain. It had rained continually, in fact, since the day of the Walk, as if that sunlit Sunday had been somehow fake, a manufactured memory. As if the clouds themselves were spitting a reminder that she had made it all up. Everything the woman had been wearing when she disappeared was there in the cold earth of the field, from her shoes to her bra, and the women watching the video in the office had pictured themselves naked, at night, in a cold, muddy field of beetroot; there were no flippant comments, no jokes now. Only Béatrice spoke: What a sick bastard. Shit.

And at that moment, Sandrine had thought of the parents she saw on the day of the Walk. So she could stop thinking about the husband and son, keep their images at bay. And she had thought to herself, Poor people.

The field stretched in all directions around the jumble of clothes, and at the far end of the field lay a ravine, a muddy ravine that had set the dogs barking, but there was no one there, and the reporter had adopted a suitable tone as he gave the viewers to understand that someone had very probably stripped the woman, killed the woman, burned her clothes, disposed of her body – like some ghastly nursery rhyme – and everyone had prayed deep down inside that the list ended there, that someone had not taken the woman's body somewhere else, and done things to her, terrible things, everyone had seen enough TV series, enough films, to know that there were monsters who would do such things to the bodies of dead women.

For days, no one talked of anything else. People went home and locked the door tight behind them and told themselves, Thank goodness it isn't me, thank goodness it's the monster, thank goodness it's not the monster and me.

And then it all subsided, once more.

There were other things, a terrible road accident, football, everyone had moved on to the latest news. Sandrine too, though it was an effort, and some evenings her hands forgot that her head wasn't allowed to think about the man, the man's smile, the man's sorrow, the warmth that awaited him, there in her belly, the warmth that would make everything right.

It was winter, then spring.

That first mild day came, the one that comes around each year, the one that feels like an awakening. The one that ends with a spiteful inrush of cold, like a bad loser, but whose sunlit afternoon reminds us that the sun is still there, and that there is a world without cold and damp, without boots against the rain, without a scarf; that a gentler, kinder world exists.

That was always one of the worst days of the year for Sandrine. Often, when it fell during the week, there would be a movement, a plan, a first *apéritif* after work, on a café terrace, to which she was never really invited because she was too shy, but which would be organised around her, rather awkwardly. And she would say that she had something else on, an appointment. The others would pretend to invite her along: Oh, shame! Another time! And they would continue their plans in a flush of relief and finally set off all together, all the firm's secretaries. Sandrine would wait long enough to be sure, she didn't want to run into them downstairs, smoking outside while they decided where to go for drinks. And then, when she finally left the office, the street was filled with the scent of rebirth and warm tarmac. She seldom felt more alone than on that day. Every year, she told herself she would be ready, that things would have changed by then, that she would have learnt how to be interesting, to be worth inviting, and that she would have met someone, that she would go down and out into the street to meet that someone, that she would no longer need to lie, that the soft, mild air would whisper a promise. But every year, there was the same tightening of her heart, and every year she went home alone while the others went out, still not knowing what was wrong with her, still not knowing why people found her unapproachable, while her brain whispered: But yes, you know perfectly well, stupid, fat bitch, fat, ugly cow.

That evening, that year, Sandrine had gone home, and she held her breath as she walked from her car to the hallway of her block. It had never been so hard, and she *refused* to smell the aroma of spring when her own heart was set to a winter that would likely never end. In her apartment, she drew the curtains against the world outside. It was colder indoors than out, and that suited her fine, she would stay by herself in her own private dead season. She made everything cosy, lit the lamps, and outside in the street the melody of family life was heard, because everyone had opened their windows wide. The sounds

33

of children's bath time. Sandrine had clenched her teeth, so as not to holler out loud, Well not me, what about it, fuck right off, all of you, just piss off with your happy fucking families and your fucking children.

She had taken a long shower, longer than usual because she had to sit down on the floor of the cubicle and cry.

Next, she had dried herself, turning her back to the mirror, and taken out her creams, her bottles, her potions, like a witch's rite, to take care of the body that weighed her down to the ground, to appease her private tormentor, like feeding a detested inmate on death row and asking yourself, Really? What's the point? Every now and then her nails encountered a spot on her fine skin, a hair dimpling the epidermis, and she dug them in, hard and cruel, before she remembered to stop, that she was only making it all worse, though the painful picking was the only thing that relieved those moments when she was sinking and felt she might drown. For years she had dug into her pores, eviscerated hair bulbs and ripped out stray hairs, drawing red welts on her pummelled skin, and then, when the frenzy passed, she would survey the damage, guilty but soothed; at least now she looked exactly the same outside and in, tortured, repulsive. She had managed to space out these crisis points, with the move away from her father, work, the car, her meticulously planned evenings, she managed to resist the need to make herself bleed, but that evening the floodgates opened and she had sat herself comfortably down on the bathroom floor with her eyebrow tweezers, their edges razor-sharp, and she had picked and pecked at anything that was pickable, anywhere on her skin, blackheads, ingrown hairs, hidden sebum, she had scrutinised all there was to scrutinise, all the revolting things her body tried to hide from her, everything that made her repulsive and unworthy of love, and every painful

34

pinch of the tweezers had helped to calm the raging seas. It had taken hours, but the calm returned. And then she got to her feet and took out the disinfectant, the healing balms; checks and balances, assault and atonement, a silent, self-administered pardon, It's OK now, it's over, what have I done, forgive me. In those few moments, when the vertigo subsides, when the fever breaks, she doesn't even know to whom she's saying sorry.

The body she inhabited so reluctantly was painful to the touch. She wrapped it up as best she could, then curled into a ball on the sofa, phone in hand, ready to drown herself once and for all, swept away on the tidal wave, the spectacle of other people's lives, the ones standing safe on dry land, the ones who told her about their *Lovely after-work drinks with the team!* Or that they are the *Happiest man alive! She said YES!!*, or that *Bump No. 2 is on its way!* She had journeyed far, far back into other people's photos, all those pictures of sunny days and happy, hugging groups, and she had wanted to fucking end it all right there, and then the message popped up.

The man who cried. It was a sign, the thing she needed to stay alive.

He wrote that he'd been looking for her, with the name of her town, her workplace, that he was happy he'd found her. That he wanted to thank her for her presence that day, for being there, for her lovely smile.

She had burst out crying all over again, for joy, for relief, for having come through. And the messaging had begun. She hoped that the end of the investigation had brought resolution, that he could begin to grieve, how was his little boy? Yes, he was very relieved that things had finally been brought to a close, it was still very hard at times but he had to put the past behind him and try to build a new life, the little boy was well.

35

They had begun living together even before they met a second time, his messages would be waiting when Sandrine woke, after a short sleep and long nights spent writing to one another. In his words, she heard the voice of the man who cried, she felt his pulse beat in the hollows of her body, she even smelt his fragrance, the scent that had intoxicated her in the woods that Sunday, fearing she might keel over, all these things bundled up on her sofa, curled in a ball in bed, distracting her at work. When they saw one another again, she was already living for him alone.

They had to wait, because what was happening was not easy to explain, not easy to talk about to other people. They felt no need to tell anyone else, everything was crystal clear, they were in love, they knew straightaway, for certain, nothing could change that, and Sandrine, who had expected nothing, asked for nothing, received notes and words she did not know, about kindred souls that had found one another, impatient, miraculous. He had come to see her several times, on the pretext of important meetings that necessitated an overnight stay, leaving the little boy with the missing woman's parents, who redeemed their loss in the dark wells of their silent grandson's eyes – even before she kissed him for the first time, Sandrine had worried about the little boy.

She had welcomed him to her small, ordinary apartment, the man she had waited so long to find, and suddenly everything became real, palpable, just as she had imagined, and more. He had touched her, devoured her, told her she was beautiful, he said You're mine, her very own film, and in the morning he was still there, all around Sandrine, enfolding her like a protective armour. They had made love again, standing up, against the washbasin in the bathroom, she had trembled with fear, half resisting, toothbrush in hand, telling him she was fat, that she didn't want to, but he had taken her, just like in the films, and she had let herself go, a little distant, as if in a dream. So this was what she had longed for, what he was doing to her, the life of people who loved one another. Afterwards, he had hugged her tight. From the outset, that was what she liked best, that moment of abandon when, trembling, he huddled against her body, his breathing short and hard, his voice hoarse. You're mine, the words reminded her of the first time she had seen him, the man who cried, and she held him tight, he needed her, she had someone to live for, and it filled her with an electric heat.

Eventually, he had invited her to his house, and introduced her to the little boy who said a polite Hello. Mathias's eyes were so dark and still, like twin lakes. In the sitting room, on her first, uncomfortable visit, Sandrine's eye had fallen on the yellow picture frame on the mantelpiece, and in the frame, the first woman, and in the first woman's face, the same dark eyes that said nothing.

It all happened very quickly, in the end. Too quickly for the parents-in-law, who remained rather awkward, stand-offish, which was perfectly normal, all things considered. But it was the child who mattered to them, now, and Sandrine felt an unforced affection for the little boy, no need to pretend, she liked Mathias and waited patiently for him to like her in turn. She owed him that.

Mathias was a timid creature. He was startled by loud words and unexpected noises. Often, he would curl up and stay still as a mouse, wary of the world. Sandrine knew his father was afraid that Mathias would stay that way – Cowering like a little scared girl! OK, his mother had disappeared, but still. She, Sandrine, had no opinion on the matter, not being the little boy's mother meant she was free simply to feel fond of him.

After a few months, Sandrine came for weekends, and then one day, he asked her to stay. She had answered, Until when? Always. He wanted her to stay forever and like a good girl, eager to please, she had stayed through Sunday night and called work early on Monday morning, faking a hoarse voice and pretending she was sick. No, nothing serious, just feeling a bit knocked out, it's just for today, I'll feel better tomorrow. Then, together, they had dropped Mathias off, the three of them together on the school run, so very like a proper family, a family she had borrowed and didn't want to give back. She had put off the inevitable, and returning home on Monday evening was lonelier and more miserable still than if she had gone back the day before. She ordered the removal boxes the minute she arrived.

Now, every morning, she wakes in the bed of the man who cried, in the first woman's place. On the first morning of her new life she had opened her eyes and looked around her in the semi-darkness, at the curtains, and at him, still sleeping beside her. She felt hot, as she always did when sharing a bed. The man beside her radiated heat and she pushed back the duvet, exposing her damp skin to the cool air of the bedroom. She would get used to it, she told herself then, but she never has. She wakes up stifling, even on winter mornings; perhaps she's not made for happiness or perhaps her oh-so-lonely body needs time to get accustomed to this all-enveloping, animal warmth. He is never far away.

Mathias said nothing when she moved in. She supposed his father had talked to the boy, taken the time to announce the news, to ask him. She didn't know. When she arrived, anyhow, Mathias had said nothing. He was so quiet. And yet she sensed a secret life in him, febrile, held in check. He remained on his guard and she waited. On the first day, Sandrine promised herself she would be patient. She had dreamt of this miraculous family for so long: she, the second woman, the father, the son, and a space in the bed – though she still felt she had stolen it, usurped it like an ugly, fat-bodied cuckoo. She couldn't pretend with Mathias, she could never have produced such a delicate, dark little boy. Mathias was a raven-child, sallow-skinned, with bottomless eyes that watched from their hiding place, clever, knowing eyes that she sometimes caught staring in her direction.

Her suitcase had lain open in the bedroom for a few days, and then he had emptied the wardrobe, the chest of drawers, and taken the first woman's things downstairs. It was time. It was the right thing to do. He wanted her to have space to put her clothes away. The parents-in-law said nothing but Sandrine had sensed their silent condemnation, on her first Sunday living at the house, when she waited in the kitchen as they arrived for lunch, when Mathias's father opened the door to greet them. That day, the little boy's presence had kept the peace. Silent Mathias, always so discreet at the end of the table; so long as he was there, so long as she was fond of him, he was the thing she held in common with the grandparents, her residence permit. She knew it had all happened so quickly, she knew it was offensive, the happiness born of their grief, the life she had begun, timidly, to lead, not daring to move the furniture, nor the yellow picture frame from which the face of the missing woman kept watch. Not even daring to claim a little more space.

She had come with one suitcase, a few bags, the boot of her car barely even full. She had moved into the first woman's house and waited impatiently for the day when she would feel at home. She had made mistakes. When she tried to put her books on the shelf, for example. He had taken it badly, and that was normal, she understood. The bookcase on the ground floor was reserved for his books, his work, arranged in a special order. She had wanted to surprise him, and he had flown into a rage: Where do you think you are? She had thought she was at home, just a little, and she had been upset, and then he had said he was sorry. He said sorry for days, he was tired, of course he would make some space for her if she wanted. Upstairs, where the first woman had made her own space for sewing and ironing, in the third bedroom. There's a nice set of shelves there, they're all yours, and it's time we cleared out that room anyway, what do you want to keep? He had asked her that question, asked what she, Sandrine, wanted to do with the first woman's things, and she knew that the storm had passed, that she had not made a mistake, that he was kind.

She had kept the sewing machine, the big, round basket full of fabrics, the decorated cigar box where the needles and bobbins were stored. The shelves were full of books and ornaments; she had left the books and put the ornaments in a box. Among the first woman's books were crime novels, feel-good novels, and classics – great literature, *A Room of One's Own*, *The Count of Monte Cristo* – and she thought she might read them later, one day. Now, on the empty, painted wooden shelves, in place of the ornaments, she arranged her own books, not all of them, she had left some things in the garage too, just because. And then everything was all right.

3

S ANDRINE SEES THE FIRST WOMAN on the TV screen and
in the eyes of the man seated in front of it. She glances
around the sitting room, at the shoebox under the glass coffee
table, in which Mathias keeps his toys so they aren't left lying all
over the place. Sandrine realises that if he sends her away, she
will not see the little boy any more, and her stomach clenches as
if to hold something tight. She doesn't dare ask what will happen
now, what he's thinking, how he feels.

She waits for him to speak.

For several long minutes, he says nothing. He says again, It's
her, it's her. And then, They've found her. And then nothing.
He is often restless, and nervous, the type of man who finds it
hard to sit still in one place, who paces nervously like a guard
dog, constantly alert, never allowing himself to relax. Always
asking where she is, what she's doing, why has she come home
later than usual, he's been worried. Why were the toys left lying
about? And what about schoolwork? Mathias has to get it done.
And supper, he's hungry. And Sandrine would soothe him with
careful gestures, tokens of her love, pick up the toys, put the *gratin*
to warm in the oven, explain the traffic jam, the diversion. She
does these things, and she tells him all this, because she loves him,
loves and is moved by the man who cried, his fretting is an endless declaration of love, we worry about the people we cherish.

But here, now, he says nothing, he sits motionless, as if stunned,
and he stays that way for a long time. Long enough for Sandrine

to sit on the arm of the chair because her feet are beginning to ache from the heat and the silent wait. She senses that she must not speak, there are times like that, moments she has learnt to recognise, when his answers snap and bite. You just need to know, so that you get the best of him, and here, now, Sandrine keeps quiet.

The silence endures.

Finally, she asks, hesitantly, if he wants to go to bed, and he shakes himself, turns to her with oblivious, expressionless, owl-like eyes, and sees she has been there, sitting beside him, all along. She is about to get up but he catches her by the wrist and pulls her towards him, bends forward, buries his head in Sandrine's stomach, and she strokes his head, waiting, murmuring a hesitant lullaby, It'll be all right, it'll be all right, though she knows that's not true, that everything is collapsing around them; but that's all she has left, the man's face buried in the synthetic satin nightdress, and the lie she repeats to them both, that everything will be all right.

Long minutes pass, and then he moans, What will happen now? And his voice is hoarse with tears. Sandrine holds the man who cries in her arms, the man who is breaking her heart. And she holds him tighter still against her, her throat aching with relief at the obvious truth: he is overcome, profoundly disturbed by the first woman, he doesn't want to her to come back, and Sandrine clutches him, massages him, presses her fingers into his flesh, his warm, pulsing scalp, this is her man, her house, hers, it's her family, she will not let the first woman steal it all away, she will not let her break it all apart, she will protect them, she will protect herself, it's all hers, hers, hers. She takes the remote control from the hands gripping her waist and turns off the TV. Suddenly, she feels almost self-assured, emboldened by the promises she has made herself. This is all hers, and he doesn't stop her. She likes that, likes the thought that she is the one protecting him, guiding him. She leads him upstairs and into the bedroom, puts him into bed like a child, then lies down and takes him in her arms, shelters him. He says nothing, but his breathing is calmer, and he falls into an agitated sleep. She watches over him through the dark, unable to sleep herself.

Twice during the night, he thrashes about in the grip of a nightmare and she cradles him, holds him until he relaxes once more, snoring softly like a big cat whose fur she strokes.

Just before dawn, she is still awake, her eyes wide and sore, but she will do anything to defend her family. That woman will steal nothing from her. For all anyone knows, she organised her own disappearance, took some time out, went off to Italy with another man, that would be it, and then what, changes her mind after all that and decides to come back, scheming and plotting to take back the things she had decided she didn't want? Well that's not how it works. Finders keepers, you step out of line and you lose your place.

4

T HE ALARM SOUNDS and Sandrine is startled, enough to realise she has slept a little, in spite of everything; she dozes fitfully in the bedroom, waiting for daylight; it is still very early, and the sun comes later in mid-September.

All summer, he has insisted she find something else, a job nearer to home, so that she can get up later, not have so far to travel, and if it takes her a while to find a new job, that's not a problem, he can look after her. I'll look after you, he says, for as long as it takes. Sandrine has done nothing about it for the moment, though she does everything else he tells her to do, because his ideas are good, he's a brilliant man. But not that. She's reluctant to give up her job, without really understanding why. Perhaps, if she thinks about it, she can see her mother, pale as an insect on the forest floor, shut up at home, her skin white as a maggot. Or perhaps not, that can't be it. Surely this is nothing to do with her mother, there must be something else, but what? What she knows is that she wakes very early anyhow, so what does it matter if she sets off at dawn to drive to work? She's always the first up, padding around the house in her bare feet. She makes the coffee, sets out the cereal, then wakes them up, her men, with tender gestures and whispered words. Precious moments when she feels most at home, in this house where her things have yet to find the space they need. But early each morning, her feet tread a familiar trail. From the toilet to the kitchen, from the kitchen to the bedroom, from the bedroom to Mathias's room, she could

44

find her way with her eyes closed, and she likes that. A shy animal criss-crossing its terrain, silent, unobtrusive. And she tells him it doesn't bother her, working there, such a long way away, and he darkens, and stops insisting, until he can't stop any longer and the conversation restarts. As if she had offended him by refusing to become financially dependent. All that summer, the subject had buzzed overhead like a cloud of storm flies, and finally she had said OK, I'll think about it.

But this morning, when she hears the alarm, she feels it has sounded too soon. And now it's Tuesday. That's impossible, she thinks, unbearable. That something so terrible should happen, that the first woman should come back, perhaps even come back here, to their home, and that it should still be Tuesday morning, in spite of everything. Time should adapt to our inner storms, keep pace with our private catastrophes, our intimate disasters, but no, it's Tuesday morning. It makes no sense, it's practically an insult, but it's Tuesday all the same. This is the first thing that enters her head, her anger at the day that breaks no matter what, shamelessly, inappropriately. And then a second thing, the thought that kept her awake until the small hours: perhaps everything will be all right. All it will take is for the first woman's parents to have seen nothing. For them to be told nothing. For the police not to discover where the woman is from. That could happen, sometimes the police fail to find things: they searched for the first woman when she disappeared and didn't find her, so yes, it's possible, and then everything will be fine, she'll be stuck in Paris, far away, caught in her own web of lies, shut up in a psychiatric hospital, and everything will be all right for Sandrine.

In bed, in her feverish, half-waking state, after an almost sleepless night when her mind churned over and over, Sandrine's logic veers through absurd twists and turns. If she were to leave her body there and then, rising up as she so often does, Sandrine would see herself sinking through emptiness, pedalling frantically, a tiny, frightened mammal running on its wheel. But she does not wander, for once, and lies powerless to interrupt the wild race of her thoughts, to erase the brutish insomnia that dulls her senses until she is convinced that yes, all it will take is for no one to talk about it, no one to find anything out, no one to say anything, and everything will be fine. When no one says anything, everything is always all right.

She still believes this when she gets out of bed, her head heavy with the mixture of clarity and dazed emptiness that accompanies every sleepless night. And as she sits on the toilet, listening absent-mindedly to the flow of urine released after the painful urge she contained all through the night, for fear of waking her man, she remains certain that all it will take is for everyone to keep quiet, and everything will be all right. She tears off a sheet of toilet paper and wipes her sex. Unthinking, automatic gestures. And she begins to pray. Though she believes in nothing, and certainly has no faith as such, more a complex, meticulous system of equivalences that kept her head above water, gasping for breath, throughout her childhood, adolescence, and early adult life. If I can hold my breath until the lights turn green, Papa won't be there when I get home. If I don't walk on the cracks in the paving stones, I'll pass my history test. If I get to the car park before it starts raining, they'll give me a job. It's a system she has carried everywhere, with her creams and potions, her suitcases. If the evening meal is ready when he gets home, if Mathias has tidied away his toys, if the washing is dry, we will all be very happy. She does not put this last equation quite so clearly into words, but she has never truly relinquished the secret, convoluted mechanism.

46

Get the apple tart right, help Mathias with his homework, satisfy the man who cries, sweeten his homecoming, anticipate his needs, and we will all be happy. Avoid the creaky step when you come downstairs, and there should be some orange juice left, if there's some orange juice left, then no one knows, no one will have seen the news report, no one will know Caroline is alive. The coffee machine has been playing up recently, you need to press several times to get the percolator started. But if I can get it started first time, we will all be very happy.

She does everything exactly right, the step does not creak, there's some orange juice left. She presses the button on the coffee machine and waits.

Nothing happens.

The telephone rings.

Sandrine stares at the coffee machine, at the button that ought to light up red. She waits for the *rprprprpshhhhhtfffffrrrt* of the percolator as it starts, but there's nothing. Nothing.

The telephone rings again, twice, three times.

She has ruined everything. Filthy stupid, fat, filthy, ugly, stupid filthy bitch, you've fucked everything up, stupid fucking fat cow, it's your fault, your fault, all your fault, your fucking fault, all this, it's all because of you.

She takes the call and it's the first woman's mother, with the voice of a person who's had no sleep, who dares not believe, who cannot allow herself to believe, a voice that sounds the same as Sandrine's, for reasons that are so opposite to her own it's almost funny. Each of them has suffered a white night, telling herself no, no, no, no, impossible, no, it can't be true, but the night is over now, and day has come, and with it, into this world where Sandrine now lives, the first woman. And when the mother asks, her voice fringed with sobs, Did you see? Sandrine wishes very hard, very, very hard, harder than anything she has ever wished, that she could say No. And that would be an end to it, that one word could cancel everything out, that reality could be wiped away, and the telephone call cut, and that the mother would choke and her fucking slut of a daughter would die for real this time, but Sandrine cannot do that, Sandrine is incapable of that, because Sandrine is nice and kind, and only knows how to sink while others swim and so she says Yes, and it's all over.

First, she must go and wake the man who cries and that alone is against everything she knows, everything she wants. The man who cries is never so completely hers as when he's asleep. When they were first in love, she would spend hours watching him sleep. Silent, vulnerable, the cleft that splits his forehead eased at last, his skin pulsing to a soft rhythm in secret hollows that she alone knows. He is soft and warm and she can see the pulse in the vein below his ear, at the corner of his jaw. Each time, the revelation of his beating heart seems to her like a brutal, raw gift, as if the thing itself had been torn out and placed on a table, as if his body lay open, its intimate, crimson flesh suddenly exposed. This is more precious than the sight of him naked, of his sex. Because here, he controls nothing, decides nothing, here he is like a vulnerable child.

He is there in bed and she is sorry, sorry and sad as a beach in winter, desolate, like scorched earth, desolate and sad as a marble tomb glistening in the rain. Because she is going to wake him up, because the first woman will always have come back, and because Sandrine will always be the second woman, one woman too many. She places her hand on his shoulder, the pads of her fingers turn white as she presses them into his warm flesh, he grumbles and turns over. She insists, louder, It's her mother. On the telephone. Her mother.

He takes the handset and shuts himself in the third bedroom, where Sandrine has arranged her books. He speaks to his mother-in-law, no, to his almost-ex-mother-in-law (what do you call the mother of a woman you married, but who disappeared, and was declared dead, and has now come back?). She has no proper title, just her own name: Anne-Marie, wife of Patrice, mother of Caroline, the ex-mother-in-law of the man who cries.

Someone had called Anne-Marie, someone saw the news, someone from the infernal army of do-gooders, and the knowledge that Sandrine came so close to being left in peace fills her with a sudden gust of spite. Then she thinks of Mathias, Mathias with his silences and his eyes like bottomless lakes, and she tries to think only of him, to tell herself this is good for Mathias, good for Mathias. For Mathias and his silences, the silence of an orphaned baby bird, a tiny, timid mouse. Mathias will know that his mother is still alive, and beyond Sandrine's misery, and her dread at the prospect of a reunion, she knows that this is a good thing, that she must tell him, that because she has made a place for herself here, because she is so fond of Mathias, the little boy will save her again, anchor her somehow, somewhere. She, the tiny, pathetic boat lost in the storm. Mathias's happiness is the rope that will keep her in port, her lifeline.

She stands planted outside the door to the third bedroom, then manages to unstick her feet from the floor. That's better, she should move, he doesn't like her spying on him – no one does. She unsticks her feet and walks to the bathroom, performs her morning wash, her cat's toilette – crotch, face, armpits – before her clothes and perfume. Then she dresses, carefully.

She cherishes the uniform she has put together over the years, her interchangeable, structured, rigid clothes. And never more so than now. She puts on her high-waist panties, the corset-like bra, close-fitting trousers that compress her stomach, a burgundy shirt and a jacket with square, padded shoulders. Everyone is still in their summer clothes, while she dresses for autumn. She applies make-up to her imploring eyes, evens her tired complexion. The make-up saves her, gives structure. She looks at herself in the mirror and says, Ready. Like every morning, except that usually she means, 'There, I'm as present-able as I can be, as not-unpleasant-looking as possible, ready to bother the world as little as possible.' And this morning she means: 'I'm ready, prepared – for the worst, to lose everything I have.' She's lost everything, already, but there she is with her hair parted straight and her clean-cut shoulders, squaring up to the disaster foretold. She glances at her phone, it's late, Mathias has slept longer than usual. In the third bedroom, the voice rumbles on, uninterrupted, never rising, never thundering. Like listening to an engine ticking over quietly, like watching a demolition from a distance, the violence of the huge, monstrous machines as they tear everything down, relentlessly eradicating and undoing, but silent, as if she cannot quite hear the roar of the engines, cannot quite grasp the scale of the annihilation, is unable fully to realise that the destruction is irreversible, how completely non-existent the thing they are tearing down will become, how completely and definitively beyond all hope of reconstruction. Finished.

Mathias is startled, as always, when she wakes him up. But she is ready, as always, with gentle, cocooning words. Hello mister, it's all right, it's only me, I've come to wake you up, it's time for school; your cereal's ready. Did you sleep OK? Sweet dreams?

He never answers the litany of questions. Sometimes, Mathias shows signs of giving in, a vague urge to trust and confide in her, but he always checks himself, guards his dreams fiercely, allows a show of affection but pushes intimacy away, as if he has always known, from the beginning, that Sandrine is not here to stay.

Mathias gets ready for school. She stands outside in the corridor while he rubs his face with a flannel, then puts on his blue T-shirt. He had worn a white one on the weekend, a little too short, and Sandrine saw that he was growing fast, that his missing incisors were growing back, already he was so very different from the little boy she had met that day, the day of the White Walk, the day of the outing into the forest.

In the kitchen, the coffee machine is working at last, and the boy eats his cereal, watching the untouched breakfast bowl set opposite him on the table. His eyes move from the bowl to Sandrine, in mute questioning, and Sandrine says, He's on the telephone to your grandma. Mathias looks down into his own bowl and munches his cereal. Sandrine looks at her watch and fills her bowl with hot coffee. Usually, she waits until they are all together before eating her breakfast, but this morning the clock is ticking and she must get on.

She lifts the bowl to her mouth, and her nostrils are filled with a damp, acid reek of tinned tuna that forces her to put it back down on the counter in a hurry, with a quiet puff of disgust. She feels slightly sick. What a vile smell. She opens the fridge, takes out the Tupperware box she must use for the ground coffee, opens it and lowers her face hesitantly, to sniff it. The coffee smells of tuna. There's no reason why it should, but the coffee smells of tuna, cheap tinned tuna. Hurriedly, she tips it into the recycling bin then goes to the pantry to find another packet. There is none left. She returns to the kitchen, checks the store cupboard again. Nothing. And she panics. The lack of sleep, Mathias sitting opposite her with his black eyes and his vampiric expression as he opens his mouth to receive a spoon loaded with cereal. She loses her balance, stumbles. She looks ridiculous, she knows, but she stumbles, her eyes brim with tears, and she bends down to hide and look for the coffee where it cannot possibly be, among the saucepans and the floorcloths. The clatter of metal covers the boy's quiet munching.

When Sandrine stands up empty-handed after searching the very last cupboard, Mathias is watching her with an anxious frown – what's the matter, why is she afraid – and she tries to calm herself and explain: There's no more coffee. Mathias is worried too, he's not indifferent, she can see that. He shares her concern. She blames herself for her lack of self-control, she's the grown-up and clearly, if she is in distress, the boy knows there must be some reason, though the apparent reason is absurd. He peers at the cafetière full of black liquid, asks, Isn't that coffee OK? And Sandrine says No, it smells funny, I need to make another pot, but we've run out. Mathias slips from his chair, his feet touch the tiled floor, and he lifts his chin to rest it on the countertop, next to the full pot of coffee, trying to understand. He says, But it's the same as always? Sandrine rubs her eyes, she doesn't want to cry in front of the boy, she can't understand what's come over her, and her failure to understand makes her feel even more lost. Upstairs, a door snaps shut and the sound makes them both jump, as if caught red-handed. They stare at one another like children in a fairy tale, caught in the ogre's lair. Sandrine gets a grip, fights to calm herself, yesterday's news has turned her world upside down but that's no reason to make the boy panic, she forces a smile and says, It doesn't matter, don't worry, I'm just tired, that's all. But the footsteps coming down the stairs, the creaky step, are like shovelfuls of earth tossed into her open, moaning mouth, *shit, what is wrong with you?*

As he walks across the sitting room to the kitchen, she is surprised to feel Mathias's hand reaching for hers, his tiny, sharp fingers squeezing her fleshy palm, he is sweet and kind, poor thing, he can feel she's losing it, that something's different today, he probably thinks she's gone mad. Perhaps he's right.

Across the table, her man holds the cordless house phone in his hand. He places it on the tabletop then sits down. Sandrine pours his coffee like a person jumping off a cliff, but all he says is, Some friends of theirs were watching television, they called them. He speaks in a low voice, he plays with the telephone, clumsily, unaccustomed to its size, his fingers are used to the small, slender shape of his mobile phone. Who uses their house phone these days? It never rings except for nuisance calls and bad news, one thing at least that's still true, as reality unravels. The house phone only rings for funerals, accidents, apocalyptic occurrences. Sandrine knows she should feel something, something else, but for the moment she feels relief that the coffee tastes OK to him, and absolutely nothing else. Everything is upside down, the coffee should be unimportant and the first wife's resurrection utterly overwhelming, but everything is muddled, Sandrine's brain is capable of holding two things only: relief about the coffee, and a nagging question. Should they tell Mathias? What should they say to Mathias, they will have to explain everything to Mathias, should they try and explain to Mathias what has happened, and in any case Mathias is not hers and it's not up to her and she cannot be the one to decide.

He drinks his coffee, carefully, thoughtfully. One swallow, two. He doesn't seem to want to talk to the boy. Not yet. She must guess what to do, and she says Go and clean your teeth, Mathias, hoping she has guessed right, because they mustn't make themselves late, on top of everything else.

He drinks a third mouthful of coffee and that's it, stupid of her to have gotten herself into such a state, she really doesn't know what came over her. She doesn't want to push him, hurry him along, but it's getting late so she says, What do you want to do? And straightaway, in his face, she sees the tension tightening his jaw, the source of the nightmares as he lay in her arms. He has no idea what to do either, poor man, how could he know, he still hasn't digested the news. I have no idea, he hisses. Shit! And she is relieved, in a way, that something has shattered the funereal silence. She would rather know how things stand, and how things stand is that he has no idea, perhaps he doesn't know what to do because he wants to keep her, the second woman, the replacement. He says, I've got to get to work.

She drops Mathias off at school and arrives at the office just in time. It's not like her to be late, and her colleagues stare. She hopes nothing shows.

Sandrine has said nothing, in fact she never tells anyone anything. Her parents never call for news and she lets them be, wishes they were even further away; her friends don't think of her any more, nor she of them. In any case, she hadn't wanted anyone to know, about her new house, her new life, her man. At first, she wanted to keep it all to herself, warm and safe like a delicate sapling; and then it was too complicated to tell, she just wanted to say I've found someone, but people would have asked Who? And how could she tell them it was the man who cried, the one her girlfriends and workmates had seen on TV, so she kept her secret – in the break room, the distance between them grew. Her colleagues guessed she was in a relationship, maybe, but each time she thought she might confide in them, she remembered how her man had cautioned her, and the comments at lunchtime, when Béatrice had spoken up and said, Unless he did. Killed his own wife. You can bet it was him. And yet Sandrine would have liked to tell them, even now, she longs to do what other people did, take a picture of her feet beside his, and the little boy's, and show it to the whole world; she has been so happy, twinkling with new joy, like a shower of confetti. She loves everything, the tough early mornings, the tailbacks on the drive home, the lasagne burnt a little on top, getting the house in order. One day she was surprised to find herself chuckling in delight as she cleaned the toilet, wiping bleach over the trickles of urine down the outside of the bowl. Men! Will they ever learn? Mathias prefers to sit down, but that's not how men do it, and now he's learning clumsily, adding his droplets to those of his father. My man, she says, my men, and she likes the sound of the words.

Before getting down to work she texts to let him know she's arrived safely. She thinks perhaps he will answer, tell her what she wants to know, what's happening, what he's decided to do, but he doesn't reply and she lets it go, conscious that if she insists, it will come to no good. He will tell her once his mind is made up. At lunchtime her phone rings and she hurries to take the call but it's not him, it's the first wife's mother. It's Anne-Marie.

Anne-Marie never calls her directly, unprompted, just to chat. They only ever discuss practicalities, like when her son-in-law has failed to hear his own telephone ring. What time is lunch on Sunday, should we pick up some bread, bring a dessert? But Sandrine knows her man dislikes them being in touch, so she always keeps it short, and after all, the woman is nothing to her. She's Mathias's grandmother, and that's important, but not enough to spoil her own love story. But now Anne-Marie is approaching her directly, up close, she needs to talk and Sandrine has no idea what to do, what to say, so she says nothing and lets her talk. Anne-Marie refers to her telephone call that morning, apologises for waking Sandrine up, then pours everything out in a confused torrent of words.

At length, Sandrine understands that Anne-Marie is asking whether she and her man both knew Caroline was alive, before she called them that morning. Sandrine recoils briefly, distances the telephone from her ear for an instant. She dislikes second-hand conversations, circuitous, indirect approaches. She thinks that if Anne-Marie has something she wants to ask her son-in-law, then she must ask him directly. She doesn't say so, of course, she does her best to dodge the question, repeats several times that she's at work, that she can't quite hear, that she doesn't have much time. Sandrine knows how to slip between people's fingers, the best way to duck issues as they arise. It's a skill she learnt when she was very young. After a few awkward moments, Anne-Marie sighs the disappointed sigh of a woman who cannot break a bond, who recognises another's loyalty, and so she stops asking indirect questions and says simply that she is going to try and call the Pitié-Salpêtrière hospital, in Paris, but that very early that morning it was she who was called by the police, to say that they had identified Caroline; that they knew, that it was really her. Anne-Marie leaves a moment's silence, to catch her breath or perhaps to give Sandrine a chance to congratulate her, but Sandrine says nothing and so Caroline's mother continues, tells her that she will go with Patrice, go up to Paris to meet their daughter, with family photographs, Caroline as a little girl, Caroline as a student, and Mathias of course, she forgot to say, but they would be taking Mathias with them. Though his father doesn't seem favourable, says they aren't sure yet, that they need to take things step by step. Anne-Marie speaks the words as if Mathias's father has suggested something absurd, but Sandrine puts on her sensible, getting-everyone-on-board voice and says, Yes, he's right, that is the best way to proceed. For you, Anne-Marie, and for Mathias of course, and doubtless for— she cannot speak the first woman's name. For your daughter. Anne-Marie says, Yeeeessss... and Sandrine stays silent. She wants no part of this questioning, she does not want Anne-Marie to able to declare, later, that 'Sandrine said...' She almost resents Anne-Marie for putting her in such an awkward position. She finishes by telling her, I'll let him know you called. She doesn't want that to sound like some kind of threat, she just wants to show that she knows her place, that she will not add to the confusion. But Anne-Marie is nettled. She says, As you wish, then cuts the call. With inevitable, unjust logic, the edifice crumbles around her. Everything crumbles as she knew it would. For Sandrine, there is comfort, of sorts, in this avalanche foretold. Guilt is a made bed that knows the contours of her body already, because this is her fault, of course. She should have stopped herself from believing, she should have avoided the creaky step.

Anne-Marie called me at work, she says cautiously when he gets home that evening. She sets the news down on the table with the rice salad, and waits, and watches. Where's Mathias? he says in reply. Is he not coming down to say hello? And already, the tone is tense. He must have had a terrible day, she sees it in the way he throws his briefcase onto the table, dislodging one of the place settings.

She says, You must have had a difficult day, I'm sorry. He softens, regrets his action already, smiles, she forgives him. When that fluent exchange, that silent conversation, slips between them, Sandrine feels the she-wolf's impulse again, that urge to defend what they have. Mathias is upstairs, she says. I didn't know whether you'd want him to hear or not. What you've decided to do, she adds.

He washes his hands, she moves the briefcase aside, puts it in its proper place, straightens the scattered plate and cutlery. He leans in behind her, puts his arms around her waist. He smells her hair, her neck, and his breathing is calmer. What did Anne-Marie say to you? Sandrine tells him, carefully, calmly. It's important that he should believe her, it's important that he should know she is keeping nothing from him. It's the two of them, the two of them and Mathias, against the unknown, against everything that is uncertain. At that moment, everything that is uncertain is barrelling up the motorway to Paris, with the booklet of official family records, the *livret de famille* that will tell the hospital that Anne-Marie and Patrice are indeed related to the woman whose memory has been wiped clean. They have no doubt whatsoever, they have seen their daughter and they have gone to fetch her. And here she is, in the kitchen, with their daughter's husband, waiting for the assault, uncertain whether to pull up the draw-bridge and sharpen their weapons, uncertain what to do at all. He squeezes her stomach and asks, She didn't say anything else?

Anything else? What else? Nothing, no, nothing at all. Sandrine waits, it takes all her strength to keep silent, she who since last night has wanted nothing but to holler and scream fit to burst. He says, Well, listen, for the moment, we can't be certain, I don't know what the cops have got, their tests, their files, but sometimes they get things wrong. I know Anne-Marie is dead certain, but I'm not, and I won't have the kid mixed up in this while I'm not absolutely sure.

Sandrine turns around, twists her body in his grip and looks into his face, studies the face of the man from yesterday, the one who said, It's her, it's her, in that toneless voice. She doesn't understand, but OK, if he's not sure after all, that gives her a chance. For once, uncertainty has a faintly protective, comforting aura. Fine, he's not sure. He adds, And then we'll see.

We'll see. 'We'll see' means: 'We don't say anything to Mathias. Do not talk to Mathias about this.' And that's how it is. They eat supper while talking about something else, about the bland, rather tasteless salad dressing, about the test Mathias passed with good grades, which is just as well. Above all, he talks about the contract he's negotiating at the moment.

Later, when Mathias has gone upstairs and she has finishing loading the dishwasher, he is still on his feet in the sitting room, trudging around and around, hands thrust deep into his pockets, as if he's trying to anchor himself to the floor, force himself to stay in one place and contain the nervous pacing. Time and again he passes in front of the yellow-framed photograph, frowning with concern.

The kitchen is clean. Sandrine folds away the tea towel in the small cupboard under the sink and joins him. He pauses mid-circuit and says, We'll see what happens. If it's her. I don't trust them. Imagine if it's somebody else? Mathias— he adds, again, but leaves the name hanging. Sandrine is thankful. At least his instructions are clear. This is what they will do, protect the boy. She stares into his face, and nods. This is why he didn't hurry away with his parents-in-law, to join the woman. He doesn't believe it. Or he dares not believe it. He's afraid to go there. Afraid to leave. Afraid to leave Mathias. Afraid to take Mathias with him. He's afraid it will be her. Afraid it won't be her. He looks so upset because he does not know what will happen. She understands, she really, truly understands. She does not want Mathias to suffer, either. But each time she tells herself that, she cannot help but think that if he is no longer a motherless child, then she is no longer the second woman, she is one woman too many.

They get into bed in silence. He lies down, tense and rigid on the mattress. When he turns out the light, she sees furrows of uncertainty wrinkling his forehead in the purple half-light; deep, glistening. He thinks of nothing else. And that is why he has set a bubble around the three of them this evening, a fragile membrane of 'We'll see' and 'Perhaps it's nothing' and she goes to sleep thinking about their sham, everyday supper, their conversations on the brink of the abyss, picturing the delicate lie with its soft, shiny outline, watching it spin gently in the air and struggling with all her desperate might to convince herself that it will never burst.

5

THE BUBBLE BURSTS at noon the next day. Sandrine returns to her desk, after washing her hands, to a deluge of emotion in a message from Anne-Marie. She and Patrice have been able to see her, to see the woman, it's really her, it's Caroline. Anne-Marie's voice in her ear is loud with sobs and floating with happiness, it's her, it's their daughter, it's, it's, they are so relieved, they're talking to the police and the doctors to see how they can sort things out from here. Sandrine doesn't understand why she has been chosen to receive the news. It seems cruel to her. Like telling your washing machine, in some grand, official announcement, that it's about to replaced by a different model. But when Sandrine tries to call her man and reaches his voicemail, several times, she understands. Anne-Marie needed to voice the words. She must have called them both, in turn, until finally – overwhelmed with relief, unable to resist the overpowering urge to tell them what has happened – she poured out the news in recorded messages.

She sits down and listens to Anne-Marie's words one more time. That's it, it's over, it's starting, the war has reached her door. Her mind is a blank. She opens her Tupperware box, looks at the salad, feels suddenly sick, shuts the lid and breathes slowly, deeply through her mouth, fighting to keep control. Béatrice overtakes her, cutlery in hand, heading for the break room, throws her a glance, she must look like some huge gaping carp, a dumb-faced fish. Are you OK? Béatrice asks. She looks genuinely concerned, but Sandrine doesn't answer, mutters Uh-huh. It's none of her business, in any case. They're hardly going to become friends now, Sandrine thinks. Rebuffed, Béatrice shrugs her shoulders and continues on her way.

She called you too?! Who the hell does she think she is?! *Shit!*

Sandrine curls tight inside at his words. That's unfair, she never encouraged Anne-Marie to contact her directly, still less to confide in her. She says, But you weren't picking up! To explain, to defend herself. He makes a sudden, brusque movement, like an automaton: throws out an arm and tosses his plate aside, fingers outstretched, shoulder stiff.

Sandrine is startled, her shoulders stiffen too. She stares at the spot where the plate had been. The tablecloth is barely ruffled, the fork scarcely out of place, but the plate has gone.

Sandrine doesn't move. She dislikes loud cries, sudden movements; she dislikes what they do to her body, how it freezes like terrified prey, but she cannot move, the gesture of the man sitting opposite has petrified her. He rubs his temples, roughly. She sees the folds of skin rolling beneath his fingers. He says he's sorry. Sandrine makes no reply, her mind is filled with the image of herself, sitting hunched and tense at the table, and him facing her, minus his plate.

He apologises once again.

Then he comes closer to her, repeats once more that he's sorry.

Confusedly, she tells him it's OK, it doesn't matter. She knows she hasn't been herself these past few days, and neither has he. She knows that this is all completely out of the ordinary. She must try her hardest, or she will ruin everything. He places his hand on her neck, warm and dry. She closes her eyes for a moment, remembers the first time he touched her that way, the sensation of belonging, of finding a place in the world, how that simple gesture had resonated through her entire body. She summons a sweet memory of them walking together in the street, when he closed his fingers around her and she had felt slender, tall, desirable. Because a man could hold the nape of her neck. A man wanted to keep her at his fingertips. A man wanted to show the passers-by, the store windows, the trees, that she belonged to him. *Try your hardest, try your hardest.* The skin of his fingers is soft. Sandrine recovers herself. She inhales deeply, awkwardly, and she wonders how long she has been holding her breath.

I'm sorry, he says again, and he bends down, kneels, puts his head on Sandrine's knees and clutches her legs, he is lost, too, they are both lost, together; it's appalling but it's what matters.

There is a tiny, mouse-like noise. Mathias is making his way cautiously across the tiled floor. He had been sent upstairs to do his homework in his room, so that the grown-ups could talk; Sandrine hopes he hasn't heard anything, then remembers the plate, the jagged shards scattered over the floor, and she pulls herself together and says Watch out, don't come any further, there's a broken plate. She gets to her feet, taking her man with her, and busies herself sweeping everything up with the dustpan and brush. Put your slippers on, Mathias, there may be some bits left. And so that the boy will not worry she adds, It was me, it slipped out of my hands as I was laying the table.

The debris is dispatched in seconds and order is restored, Mathias quiet and discreet at the far end of the table and his father who smiles at Sandrine, a tender smile, touched no doubt by her proffered white lie, her desire to spare him the explanations, to accommodate him. He says, So what have you made for us? It smells good! And while they eat their supper, everything is not all right but everything is better than it was.

Night falls and she gets into bed, wearing the nightdress. She holds a book but cannot focus, reads the same page twice, ten times, thirty. He waits until Mathias has gone to bed to return Anne-Marie's call, and from the sitting room she hears one half of the conversation, a low rumble, and she tells herself that's what people hear when an earthquake strikes, the people sunk beneath the surface, those who are about to die, just before the end.

When he comes to bed, at last, she keeps her eyes on the page because she understands now that asking questions only complicates things further, that she must wait until he is ready to talk. And so Sandrine waits, scratching furiously at her knee under the sheets.

He takes off his trousers, his socks, his T-shirt, comes and sits in his trunks on the edge of the mattress. She sees only his back. Sandrine's nails dig into the skin of her knee and she realises she can feel blood on her fingers. He waits for a moment before speaking: They're going to come back up with her. Sandrine doesn't understand, but she translates: Anne-Marie and Patrice are going to bring Caroline, the first woman, back.

They are going to come back with their daughter, their daughter whose memory is still a blank. Because Caroline remembers almost nothing. He says this in a neutral tone, with a hint of pity. Perhaps the parents thought that when she saw them, everything would come back, but no. Finally, they have been allowed to take her with them and now everyone knows that it really is Caroline, and what Caroline herself wants to know about is the child. The hospital that treated her in Italy sent a file with her to France, and the file stated that she had had at least one baby. So when Caroline saw two strangers arrive, their eyes red with emotion, her first question was: And the baby? Anne-Marie and Patrice said Yes, the baby is a little boy and his name is Mathias.

They showed her photographs. Nothing. Caroline and her blank memory looked at the photographs for a long time, her eyes tracing the shape of Mathias's face, his biggish ears, his round nose, the brown arc of his eyebrows, and the colour of his eyes, raven black. Nothing. And so Caroline is coming. Caroline is on her way. With Patrice and Anne-Marie, Caroline is coming here, she is coming back to see her son, to remember her son. The first woman is coming back. Sandrine feels suddenly very hot and her heart beats wildly, and then he adds They'll be back tomorrow. Anne-Marie wanted her daughter to talk to Mathias over the phone, but that was nonsensical, they must proceed carefully, see how it goes when they get back, and Sandrine feels calmer, just a little, understands that the first woman is not coming back here, to their house, she will stay with Patrice and Anne-Marie.

Sandrine waits a few seconds for the pounding at her temples to subside, just a little. She wants to know, but doesn't dare ask, if he suggested she come here, if he has spoken to the first woman. Dangerous questions, she wants to keep clear of them. But she needs to know what's happening, she needs to be ready. She thinks of a way to formulate the question. Then finally she asks, gently, What do you want to do? I said I'd see this weekend, he says. I'm at work all day as it is, and Mathias has school. So we'll see this weekend. His voice is calmer than it has been over the past few days. He must be relieved that she's alive. That's normal, perfectly natural, she's alive and he's relieved, what else could she expect, but when Sandrine imagines the relief felt by the man lying at her side, turning out the light with the tip of his finger, she feels her whole body turn to ice.

She closes her book in the darkness. And turns to face the window, settles her head on the pillow. She feels him turn and hold her close. She wants to turn and hold him in her arms, but he's squeezing her so tight she cannot move. His hands are hungry, avid. He plants his fingers in the skin of Sandrine's hip, rubs himself briefly against her panties, then pushes the fabric roughly out of the way and enters her. She is very dry, she would have liked enough time to reach for the lubricant she keeps in her bedside table drawer, for the times she can't get wet. It's very quick and after a few grating thrusts, he groans like an animal and releases her. At last she can turn around, touch his arm, his shoulder, ask with small, silent gestures for him to give her the reassurance she needs in return, to hold her close. They don't always want the same things at the same time, it doesn't matter, but he turns his back and Sandrine is left there in the hot, clammy night, semen trickling in her hot, clammy, sticky sex. She gets up in the dark and walks to the toilet, to let the last drops of his ejaculation trickle out. Her knee is raw, the blood has run down her leg. She takes a warm shower, her sex burns a little, then she dries herself and searches in the drawer for her healing cream. Finally, she goes back to the bedroom and puts on clean panties, a slightly too-tight bra, pyjamas. Reassuring, familiar, protective things. And she curls up with this thought: that he desires her, he wants her, he wants to keep her. She ought to feel comforted, she repeats to herself that she is reassured. But her night is broken by repulsive, anatomical dreams in which the first woman is there inside her, a parasite that bursts out of her body, tearing everything apart in its wake.

6

THE FIRST WOMAN is to come on Sunday. For the moment, she is staying with her parents. Sandrine does not know what has been arranged with Anne-Marie and Patrice. Only this: that the first woman will come back to her home on Sunday. No, to *her* home. Sandrine's home. Who does this house belong to? This man? This child? What are they supposed to do? Take turns, fight, cut everything in half? Sandrine feels more sure of herself at night, when her man is inside her, drowning his distress in her soft, comforting flesh; then he falls asleep and she tosses and turns through the night, her stomach knotted, her sex warmed, feeling like a person struggling in quicksand. On Saturday, she wakes slowly, with difficulty, but too early. She takes stock, draws up a shopping list. She emerges from the pantry into the kitchen and closes the door behind her. There are screw-holes in the wood, the memory of an additional latch he had removed when Mathias grew taller. The thought of the little boy calms her slightly. She goes out to do the shopping. The raw light details the roads and traffic circles, giving them the exaggerated quasi-realism of a film set. At the supermarket, she wanders up and down the aisles, touching familiar products with the tips of her fingers. She reads the labels, the brand names: partially hydrogenated vegetable oils, free-range chicken, 3 for 2: empty, familiar, harmless words that weave a web of habit and normality all around her.

When she gets back, he's still asleep and Mathias is playing quietly in a corner of the sitting room. She starts to put away the shopping and asks the little boy what he would like to eat tomorrow. Mathias could ask, 'Why? What's happening tomorrow?' but instead he thinks about it and says he would like chocolate cake. His father comes downstairs. The step creaks exactly when it should. Fleetingly, Sandrine thinks of that morning, when she had avoided it to keep bad luck at bay, and failed. It seems like a very long time ago to her. It was only yesterday. She is about to make coffee, but he waves the racket he's holding in his hand and says he's going to meet Jean-Jacques at the courts. Then he looks around at the kitchen, the sitting room, frowns. Something is wrong. Mathias, put away the toys you've left all over the place.

From his corner, with his two plastic dinosaurs, Mathias mutters something. What did you say? Mathias, what did you say? Yes, the little boy pipes again. Yes. Sandrine watches the boy and his father. Mathias doesn't know yet, he's going to talk to him this evening. As for her man, his eyes are puffy despite the cold water he splashes on his face each morning. His features look gaunt, his mouth thin and tight as a tripwire. He has slept badly, too, he's worried. She knows now, she has understood. He loved Caroline, he has told her that, but he finds it hard to talk about the first woman, though he told her one day that she, Sandrine, had mended him, that thanks to her, the heart he had thought was broken was beating again. He loved her, the previous woman, she knows that, he doesn't need to say more, she remembers his tears, that day on the television news. He loved her but she had gone missing, presumed dead, and he had grieved and moved on. And now he loves her, Sandrine, and nothing can ever be simple and straightforward again. Don't worry, she reassures him, we'll clean up. Won't we, Mathias?

He goes out, his sports bag slung over one shoulder. She doesn't make coffee. The mysterious reek of tuna emanating from the Tupperware box is still there, though she seems to be the only one who can smell it. She pours the hot water over a herbal teabag and watches as Mathias eats the two croissants she had bought for him and his father. She isn't hungry; fevered anxiety tightens her throat.

After breakfast, Sandrine plugs in the vacuum cleaner. It's Mathias's job to take out the waste bins, dust the lower shelves of the big, serious-looking bookcase that furnishes the back wall. They get organised, Mathias completes his tasks diligently, the tight knot loosens a little in Sandrine's throat. Several times, for a few brief seconds, she even manages to forget why they are so busy cleaning the house, taking greater care than usual.

The morning goes by, the sky clouds over, a few drops fall, she's glad she hadn't got started on the windows. She shows Mathias how to programme the washing machine, and after a few moments' hesitation, he turns the dials and shares a conspiratorial smile with Sandrine – his father doesn't want him to grow up 'a housewife', but Mathias enjoys cooking, the ingredients, everything in its place. Lunchtime approaches and she prepares a salad and a toasted sandwich for the little boy. For once, she doesn't text her man to ask if he's coming back, if she should keep something out for him to eat. He stays out most of the day when he plays tennis, grabs a snack, eats out. It's his time, it does him good, she won't bother him.

When the doorbell rings at about 3 o'clock, she tells herself he must have forgotten his keys, glances all around, satisfied: the house is spotless and tidy. Mathias is on the sofa, knees tucked under his chin, slippers off, socks on, watching a cartoon on TV. A well-deserved treat. She opens the door, duster in hand. It's not him.

A couple stands outside, the woman slender in a mannish outfit, the man with greying temples and stubbled cheeks. They say something. She has seen them before. They stare at one another. Intrigued by the silence, emboldened by his triumph with the washing machine, Mathias comes and peeks out from behind Sandrine's legs.

She searches her memory, while they ask if Mathias's father is at home? That's it, it's coming back to her. The day of the White Walk. No, he's not at home, Sandrine answers. They would like to come inside for a few minutes and she doesn't know what to say. Or rather, she knows she should say no. She knows she's not the mistress of this house. That she cannot make such decisions. For the past few days, the first woman's imminent return has been a cruel, insistent reminder of just that fact. Since this morning, the thought has scarcely been out of her mind. They step inside nonetheless, and Sandrine cannot quite understand how they interpreted her hesitant silence as an invitation. All she can find to say is, 'The floor! I've just done the floor!' They stand still, puzzled. A moment's hesitation, then Mathias hurries off and returns with two clean floorcloths. He hands them to the police officers, who use them to waddle and slide over the clean tiles like emperor penguins, until they reach the sofa. She didn't want them to come in, still less to take a seat, and yet here they are, indoors and sitting comfortably. What now?

They ask, When will he be back? About 4 o'clock, perhaps later. Sandrine watches the woman first and foremost, her slender arms in the black jacket. The faint drizzle that hesitated to turn to rain has left droplets on the smooth leather, she must be feeling hot. The unknown woman introduces them both. Judicial police officers. They have been investigating a disappearance – Caroline, the wife of the gentleman... Could they perhaps talk somewhere else? The woman interrupts herself, glancing at Mathias. The little boy unfolds his spindly frame from the sofa, where he had curled up once again, and climbs the stairs. Sandrine waits for the creak of the step before answering the woman. And so? And what? And so we were informed that she has been found alive, says the woman. The Pitié contacted us first. We called the Marquezes. And Caroline's husband, of course. You didn't know we spoke to him that morning? The woman insists on this point and Sandrine can't quite understand why. It hadn't occurred to her, but of course he would have been informed, Caroline is his wife. What are they trying to get her to understand, what do they want her to say? It's all perfectly normal.

The woman cop says again, We were the ones who called him, he's well known to us – Caroline's husband. We questioned him at the time of her disappearance. As a suspect. Did you know that?

Sandrine doesn't know anything any more. Sandrine can't speak. Sandrine can't hear. She can't quite understand what these people are doing, sitting on the sofa; on whose authority they lean back against the cushions and say such things, say that her man is, was, a suspect, look at her quite so intently, gaze around, openly and unapologetically, at the coffee table, the bookcase, the freshly dusted TV cabinet and, in the background, the kitchen. They are making everything dirty. At that moment, she hears the car in the driveway, and his hesitation. He must have spotted the unfamiliar car in the cul-de-sac, asked himself who it was. The sound of the door handle turning is noticeably slower than usual, and when he comes inside, Sandrine knows. He is boiling with rage. The visitors rise, taking their time. The woman, especially, is slow to get to her feet, very much at home, pushing herself up, palms pressed to her knees, adjusting her jeans. She proffers no handshake.

Mathias's father has changed since tennis, he's wearing freshly-laundered trousers and a pale blue shirt, he looks smart – smarter by far than the two cops with their dark T-shirts and fraying jeans; Sandrine knows he likes to take care of his appearance, well-turned-out, respectable, not like the rough types you see about, his loafers polished and not a crease out of place. He walks towards them and Sandrine, who knows him off by heart, reads the anger and loathing in his eyes. He is scrupulously polite, greets the two officers, but she can tell by the vein pulsing at his temple, the clenched fists thrust deep into his trouser pockets. She has not the slightest doubt: he hates them, the pair of them, and especially the woman. And Sandrine understands. She understands perfectly. They have come into his house with no hesitation whatever, and now they are glaring at him, hard. They have no respect for him, especially not the woman, you can feel it, she's shorter than him but it seems as if she is staring down at him from above. Whereas, Sandrine knows, she is absolutely not his type, not the kind he approves of at all, she's so unfeminine, hasn't even done her hair, he scorns women like her, despite their shapely arms and their flat stomachs, and Sandrine is perfectly OK with that, one less thing to worry about, a little less competition for her, the one with every handicap in that particular race. He flinches an elbow and Sandrine stands up, uncertain what's expected. He's giving her a sign, but no clear instructions – certainly not to go and make coffee. And so she hesitates, standing awkwardly, before finding an excuse in Mathias. I'll go and see if he's finished his homework.

She climbs the stairs, taking her time, making sure to press all her weight on the creaky step. She looks up. Mathias has poked his head around his bedroom door, to see who's coming. She smiles conspiratorially, but the smile is a façade. She pauses briefly. If he doesn't want them to hear, they mustn't hear. Especially Mathias, he's just a small boy, and what are they saying downstairs? She cannot bear for him to hear vile things, thinks that will make him afraid. She puts her finger to her lips with a knowing *Sshh!* then walks towards him and takes his hand. She won't leave him standing in the corridor. She closes the bedroom door on them both and glances distractedly through his exercise book. Mathias does well enough at school, he's not brilliant but he works hard, concentrates, the only problem is his imagination, his openness to ideas. Mathias takes excellent dictation, his writing exercises are grammatically faultless – but so impersonal that his teacher had called his father in one day. The boy says nothing, she told him. Well, maybe he has nothing to say to you, his father had retorted crossly. We can't all be super-imaginative. But clearly the boy is, he draws birds, huge and sleek, birds of prey, always with a few, small teeth showing. You know, Sandrine told him gently one day, birds don't have teeth. Yes, the small voice replied, but it would be good if they did. Oh, really, why? He gave no answer.

He has a poem to learn for Monday. Sandrine asks if he knows it and Mathias rattles through Baudelaire's 'The Albatross' while he sorts his toys. Like something he's eager to offload. The recital is interrupted only when he pauses for breath. She doesn't insist. He ought to like it, though – the huge bird. She asks if they can play together and hesitantly, as if confiding a secret, Mathias shows her a big Lego base supporting the walls of a house, solid and even-sided. A house with one room, a bed, a kitchen, a table, and a single chair. Sandrine asks, Is it a house for one person, all on their own? She thinks of her old apartment, the solitary cup waiting for her in the sink each evening, from breakfast, and she shivers. That's a bit sad, isn't it? Mathias doesn't answer, he is fixing an outer wall all around the house, he needs to concentrate. I mean, it was a bit sad for me, when I lived all by myself, Sandrine blurts out, then bites her lip because she knows that children should not have to carry the burden of grown-up doubts and fears, it said so in the book she bought before coming to live here with Mathias and his father. Minutes pass, with the soft clatter of plastic bricks and a *click* from time to time as the little boy pushes a piece of the wall into place. Then he asks, But are you still sad? No, Mathias, I'm very happy to be living here with you. With both of you. Another silence, scarcely broken by the indistinct rumble of voices beneath them in the sitting room. She gazes around the bedroom. It had taken them some time, this morning, but it is neat and tidy now. Mathias is well brought up. His father doesn't like to see toys lying around, and the little boy has several boxes for his plastic dinosaurs, his colouring crayons. I'm just going to the toilet, Mathias, I'll be right back. She pushes herself up, one hand on the bed, then sits down heavily on the freshly changed duvet cover, with its pattern of airplanes. Are you OK? asks the boy. I got up a bit too quickly, Sandrine tells him. I'm seeing stars! She stands up and this time everything is OK, she makes it to the bathroom. The Velux window is open, with a view of the small driveway and the road. A delicate scent of summer wafts in from outside, fluttering the white window-blind. She pushes her jeans and panties down, and sits. She hears the front door open, footsteps on the driveway. The police officers are leaving. The door closes, hard and loud, he has slammed it shut. She hopes everything was all right.

The female cop's voice floats up from the driveway, through the bathroom window: I could have done without seeing him again. How he found himself a replacement so fast is a fucking mystery. Plus, she's pretty. You never know, said her colleague, he's probably charming with her. It'll never last, the woman's voice answers, punctuated by the thud of a car door closing. And then: I know men like him. They don't change. Last time, we didn't manage to get him to—

The second car door closes, cutting off the sound of her voice. Sitting on the toilet, Sandrine stares at her knee, the ugly brownish scab that has formed over the wound.

She's afraid he'll be furious, but the police officers' visit seems to have left him stunned, as if in shock. He calls to them both in careful, measured tones, and when they come downstairs he settles them on the sofa then sits down facing them, on the coffee table, and explains what is going to happen. Tomorrow, a lady is going to come with Nini and Papi Patrice. She's going to spend some time here with us. Because she wants to see you. Your grandparents and the— the police think it's your mother.

Sandrine has placed her hand around Mathias's shoulders, and when the word 'mother' slips out into the room, like a great, wobbling bubble, his entire body shudders with a kind of hiccup. This is a very big piece of news and Mathias sinks deep into the sofa, as if crushed, almost liquefied. He turns his head to look at Sandrine. She says, Yes. He opens his mouth and a torrent of quick-fire, chirruping questions pours out. Sandrine has never heard him talk like this. But so, she isn't dead? But so, where was she? And is she going to stay, is she going to stay afterwards? Why can't we see her now, why did she go, why has she come back and where is she now, and where was she before, have Nini and Papi Patrice seen her already, and are they going to come with her and— His father lowers his head, presses his face into his hands, and Sandrine sees that he is overwhelmed by the questions, by the news he has

75

delivered against his better judgement, by the consequences of his words; she can tell that he knows he has released something he himself cannot quite grasp, and which he is now powerless to change, like trying to catch a river, or unbreak a mirror. Impossible. But there it is: the first woman has come back, he has said it, and now she has returned to life, and there is no going back. Outside, the patter of raindrops has ceased. He says, We'll see tomorrow, then gets to his feet and goes outside to mow the lawn.

The afternoon is quiet, like the sky before a storm. Unsure how much she is permitted to say, Sandrine tries to explain to Mathias what has happened. Your mama— everyone thinks she had an accident. She was found a long way away from here, in Italy. And because of the accident, she can't remember anything. She didn't say anything when they found her. She was looked after in a hospital, and then she went to a place where she could rest and get better. She stayed there for a long time. And then a few days ago, she started talking. And because she was talking in French, the people at the Italian hospital contacted the Italian police, and they contacted the French police. And she— well, she asked to come back to France as soon as possible. She came back last week. And the French police started looking through their... files, like a sort of great big dictionary, and inside it are the names of all the people who have disappeared. Nini and Papi recognised her on the TV news, but the police recognised her, too, from their files.

She thought it would take a long time, but finally, the story was told in just a few minutes. The resurrection of the first woman, and everything it means for them, for Sandrine and for Mathias, is contained in a few short sentences. Mathias says 'OK' and hurries upstairs to his bedroom. Sandrine fetches her ironing, turns on the radio. Outside, her man rides the tiny tractor obstinately back and forth over the grass that is already mown. She wants to go to him, tell him that everything will work out, but she cannot be sure that it will, and she sees him clinging desperately, just like her, to everyday habits, pre-planned tasks.

Tomorrow the first woman will be there. Here, at his house, at their house, at her house. *Her* house. Sandrine cannot believe it. It's all so strange. Should she treat her as a rival, an enemy, an ex-wife? She feels suddenly hot. Bittersweet saliva rises in her throat. Quickly, she replaces the iron and runs to be sick in the kitchen sink.

Outside, the noise of the mower is interrupted. A few seconds more and he comes back inside through the patio door, looks around for her. She has just rinsed her mouth with a glass of water and is afraid he'll come close, smell the acrid stench of vomit that she can still taste on her lips. Fortunately, all he says is, Don't leave the iron unattended like that. Then he crosses to the pantry, where they keep the slug pellets – not in the garage because the box might get damp and come apart and they'd have to throw the whole lot away and money doesn't grow on trees.

When he emerges, she smiles reassuringly, says they can eat a vegetable *gratin* tonight, if he likes. He stares at her, empty-eyed, then nods and heads back outside to the garden. She watches him through the kitchen window, his bare forearms and the small bald patch at the back of his skull. She goes upstairs and brushes her teeth.

Passing in front of Mathias's bedroom door, she hears noises inside, and knocks softly. She doesn't ask if she can come in, but waits outside for his answer. Mathias knows it's her, his father never knocks, he just reminds Mathias about the open door rule.

77

His father thinks a child has no right to refuse, but Sandrine understands, and so she waits, a little, then knocks again.

Mathias says Yes! in a trembling voice and when she enters, the cute, immaculately tidy bedroom resembles a debris-strewn beach after a storm. There are clothes on the bed, on the desk, on the floor, and she doesn't for one second think to be angry with him, though they had tidied everything away just a few hours earlier. She is caught by surprise because Mathias is usually so meticulous and neat. He has changed his clothes since coming upstairs and now wears a yellow, long-sleeved T-shirt with a dragon motif in faded colours. It's too short for him.

But— But Mathias, what are you doing? Sandrine asks gently.

There are photographs on the bedside table, photographs of Mathias when he was smaller, with his mother, and in them he is wearing the brand-new dragon T-shirt. Sandrine recognises the photos, she saw them once in an album, before they were stashed in the garage after a sort-out. At the time, she had wondered briefly why the slug pellets had to be kept away from the damp, in the pantry, while the family photographs were left in the garage. She had told herself that Mathias's father didn't want to come upon them by chance in the house, didn't want to see them, didn't want to suffer. Mathias must have been hiding the photographs in his room for some time. She looks at the little boy, at his soft mouse-like muzzle, his thin arms accentuated by the too-tight sleeves. He must have gone to the garage, climbed up to reach the shelves, the photo albums, and removed the pictures without anyone seeing him. It took a degree of skill to do something like that, so that no one in the house would notice. She is proud of him, even if the book she bought, the book about young children, said that hiding things was never a good sign. Mathias stares at his feet, shifts awkwardly. He had panicked and let her into his room, and now it's as if he wants more than anything for her not to be there. Yet she has never shouted at him; she doesn't understand why he would be afraid of her, and then she sees that he is trying to position himself between the photographs and her, that he forgot they were there when he told her she could come in. Is he trying to make sure she does not punish him for taking them and keeping them with him in his room?

The photos are nice, Sandrine says, as if nothing at all is the matter, and the tension escalating so visibly in the little boy's body is suddenly released. He calms down. She isn't angry. She moves towards him and a soft rustling sound tells her she has stepped on a rubbish bag. The clothes Mathias has strewn about are the ones from the corridor cupboard. Too small, washed and folded, they had been waiting for the next charity collection, before Mathias exhumed them. She says, Don't you think that T-shirt is a bit short? Mathias twists his hands, whispers something. Hm? I can't hear what you're saying, speak up, mister! Mathias answers, very quietly, It's so she will recognise me.

Sandrine kneels beside the boy, hesitates. OK. OK, but—have you found what you want to wear tomorrow? Mathias nods, points to the dragon.

If you like. Fine. So, can we put the rest away? Your papa… It's very hard for him, too, and perhaps it's better if there isn't a big mess as well as everything else? And perhaps your mama will want to see your room? Wouldn't you like your bedroom to be all nice and tidy, if your mama comes to see it?

Together, they fold everything away. Mathias finds it difficult at first. Normally, Sandrine folds his laundry, but he soon learns, his gestures are careful and precise, and eventually, two piles of T-shirts are neatly folded in front of him. They can be put back in the dark green rubbish bags, and the rubbish bags can be

79

returned to the cupboard outside in the corridor. As if nothing has happened, says Sandrine, and she goes downstairs. It's time to get started on the vegetable *gratin*.

He is still outside, trimming a box tree with painstaking, measured snips. Sandrine glimpses his face in profile, sees his deep frown, the stiffness in his neck when he bends down. When Mathias comes downstairs and stands beside her, she realises she has drifted away and been staring into space, motionless in front of the kitchen sink, for several long minutes. He has put on the T-shirt he was wearing before, a T-shirt with no dragons, one that fits him. It takes a keen eye to detect his small signs of impatience. Sandrine wants to cry. She knows them both so well, now, her men. She wants so much for them to be happy. But she wishes that did not mean the end for her, her repudiation, like a faulty model sent back to the shop. She is treading a fine line, she wants to be nasty, and selfish, she wants to think of no one but herself, but each time Mathias comes and stands beside her, each time she smells his aroma of washing powder and pastries, she cannot. The thing she wants more than anything is that he should not suffer.

Supper is strange, like an ordinary Saturday evening, except that tomorrow they will open the door and let her in, unforeseen, unknown, the end of their fragile happiness. Sandrine glances continually at Mathias. Nothing can be cancelled, nothing can be unshattered. For months, he was a motherless child, more than a year, almost two, how can that be repaired? And this homecoming will open his wounds, stoke the anxiety in his nervous, bird-like movements, the fear he half-admitted to her: what if she doesn't recognise me? If she doesn't recognise him, will she still be his mother? Can so small a heart survive the loss of a mother, twice over? Sandrine talks about the chocolate cake for tomorrow lunchtime. She hopes Mathias's father will take up the thread, tell them his thoughts, or his fears, about tomorrow, but he says simply, They should be here around midday. Nothing more.

The evening passes slowly, painfully, in front of the TV. Outside, the rain has held off, but the sky is overcast once again. He has the remote control, and none of the programmes suit him, nothing is to his liking. Bored by the documentary that interests Sandrine and Mathias, he flicks through the channels, giving less and less time to each. Mathias sits between them, his knees tucked under his chin. When his father dismisses the 'pain-in-the-butt' documentary, the little boy hugs his legs closer still to his chest, and Sandrine sees from his empty eyes that he is somewhere else, deep inside, a place where he can tell his own secret stories. She watches his tiny fingers mechanically tracing the weave of his socks. They stay that way for an entire programme, until his father says All right, then – have your damned documentary. He finds the channel, the voice-over says '... and for many years to come', and the theme music signals the roll of the closing credits. Great. See? Now it's finished! says his father, as if it was both of their faults. That's enough, get off to bed, Mathias. And the little boy unfolds himself quickly, retreats to his room.

Don't we get to say Good night? Her man's voice interrupts his exit and the boy freezes, stares once more at his socks, says, Yes. Good night. Off you go, says his father. He is deeply troubled. Everyone is troubled, even the sky outside, bearing down with all its might upon the house that stands poised to break apart. Sandrine searches for something that might soothe him, but can think of nothing. His silence, his avoidance of the subject, tells her loud and clear that he does not want to talk about tomorrow, about yesterday, about the day when the television showed them the first woman, and Sandrine does not insist. She ventures a

81

question, Would you like a tisane? His answer is short and curt: Who are you talking to, me?

Sandrine hesitates. Outside, on the stone-tiled terrace, she thinks she hears a drop of rain. At last, perhaps. She says, Yes, of course! She attempts a small laugh, as if the exchange was a joke, when she knows perfectly well that something is wrong. Oh, so you do know I'm here. Here, in my own house. Remember? He lets fly the words, like the remote that he tosses to the tiled floor as he gets to his feet and climbs the stairs. Sandrine stands speechless, asks, What do you mean? Wait, wait, don't go, tell me! But he doesn't stop. He reaches the upstairs corridor, she hears his footsteps pause, and his reminder to Mathias: Leave your door open! How many times? Then a few more paces to their bedroom, then nothing.

Sandrine feels suddenly tired. Exhausted by the tension. Outside, the storm has not broken, there is only a faint, warm breeze. She slides from the sofa to the floor and picks up the pieces of the remote, slides the plastic cover over the batteries that sprang from their compartment when he threw it to the floor. Then she must get up, plump the cushions, empty the dishwasher that has finished its cycle. Her legs feel like lead weights, but she completes her tasks, numbed and comforted by the enforced routine, telling herself that when she goes up to bed he will have calmed down, they can talk. But when she has finished at last, and showered, he is lying motionless, facing his side of the bed, and she falls asleep waiting for the storm.

7

S HE WAKES AT DAWN, the sky is still dark and the garden still parched. It did not rain in the night. Lying half awake, she had sensed the flicker of distant lightning, and sharp flashes closer to home, and she thought of the sky as a great belly, barren and silent, bringing forth soundless screams, and nothing more.

She goes downstairs, lifts the lid on the coffee, retches as she remembers the vile stench of damp tuna. Perhaps she should see a doctor. Perhaps she's caught something? Something serious. What could alter her sense of smell? A brain tumour. There: she will sicken and die, emaciated, pale as a heroine in a classic novel, on her hospital bed. They will come to see her, both of them, their loving hands pressing her weak fingertips. Her men. They will tell her, I love you, I love you, don't die, and she will whisper, with her dying breath, Be happy. And leave them to the first woman. But they will never forget her, they will soak the sheets of her deathbed with their tears, thinking but not saying out loud that there can be no happiness without her, and the first woman, who has returned to take possession of the house, and the men, will be forever second, and she, Sandrine, will be the one they miss and mourn, she will be the one in a yellow picture frame on the bookcase in the sitting room, the one whose inscrutable gaze follow Caroline everywhere, every day. And the first woman will shiver, and feel uncomfortable, an imposter, a lifelong guest in her own home. And then, only then, will they be equals.

Sandrine drinks her herbal infusion, pulling at the bra that cuts into her flesh. She must have put on weight, again. The thought ruffles her mind like a breeze on the feathers of a swan. She should curl up tight at the very idea, panic and stumble, but how can a person fall when they're already on their knees, flailing with slow, clumsy gestures against the sly undertow of quicksand? So this is what it takes for her not to feel ugly: the world has to crumble around her, everything must come to an end, so that she can feel indifferent at last to the space her body has stolen from the world around her. A joyless release. She remembers watching her grandmother retreat from the world in the same way, adrift somewhere far out at sea, her body still present, but her gaze more and more distant. Perhaps Sandrine is dying, simple as that, dying of a failed love affair. She indulges more morbid fantasies: a stroke, perhaps. He'll come down in a while and find her collapsed on the kitchen floor, he'll call the emergency services but it will be too late, what time is it, 7.52 a.m., it's still very early, if she has her stroke right now, she can be dead and buried by the time the first woman comes knocking at the door. She sighs and places her cup in the dishwasher. The china holds the smell of liquorice, something she hates as a rule, but it's the only tisane she has been capable of swallowing for the past few days. Yes, definitely a stroke. Stop it, that's enough. She takes the butter out of the fridge, gathers her ingredients – flour, sugar – and by the time Mathias comes downstairs the cake is in the oven.

The little boy points his nose over the edge of the kitchen sink, looks to see if there is any unbaked mix left. Sandrine loves to cook for him and she knows how he likes to lick the spoon, the bowl. He stops her from eating it herself, it's easier to hold back if Mathias can enjoy it, but this morning, the traces of cake mix hold no appeal. She barely notices the rich aroma of melted chocolate, preoccupied with the vision of herself, deathly white and still, laid out in a fine casket, in a perfectly cut jacket and silk shirt. She hasn't put the bowl to soak, so she reaches into the sink and lifts it out. Here you are, Greedy! But you can't just eat raw cake mix for breakfast, now, can you? He nods, a finger loaded with mix already in his mouth. Sandrine sees that the hair framing his beaky baby crow's face is damp at the ends. He has washed his face and dressed already. Usually, on the weekends, he comes down in his pyjamas. Sandrine recognises the yellow T-shirt with the dinosaur motif, the one from yesterday, the one he had prepared so that his mother would recognise him. Her throat tightens, and even Mathias's proffered smile, between two lavish licks of his finger – Mathias, whose marks of affection are scant and sparing as a rule – even that cannot console her.

The morning wears on. Outside, the raw glare of daylight stings the eyes. The sky is still threatening. Perhaps he'd like her to set the table on the terrace for drinks before the meal? He likes that sometimes, a chance to show off the immaculate garden, the neat rows of flowers and box hedges that he snips and slices every weekend until the leaves give up the fight and fall into line. When the small hand approaches 10, she makes coffee and asks Mathias to sniff the cup. What does that smell of, do you think? He's not sure. Umm, coffee? As if she is asking a trick question. OK, I just wanted to be sure. She places the coffee on a tray with two slices of baguette, butter and jam, and carries it upstairs.

He is sitting on the edge of the bed, his feet on the rug, his back hunched. As if he had managed to get that far but no further, paralysed by doubts, crushed by what lies ahead. Slowly, he turns his head to look at her. An unexpected shaft of sunlight, so sudden and violent it seems almost artificial, shines through the windowpane and defines strange hollows in his features, dark craters that speak of an abyss of anger and dread. She recoils, steps back, says, I've made you some coffee. He rubs his hand over his forehead, as if to wake himself up, emerge from the nightmare. Outside, the sun disappears and when his face emerges from behind the big, coarse contours of his hand, Sandrine recognises the anguish of the man who cries, and she puts down the tray on the chest of drawers and steps forward, arms open wide. He clings to her stomach, in the pose of a lost child, the pose that touches her so deeply, and he says, It's a nightmare, a fucking nightmare, I just don't know what to do.

She holds him tight against her, strokes his head, his shoulders. Like her, he is staring ahead, to the moment when all this will become an unquestionable reality, when the first woman can no longer be kept silent, in a box, tidied away so that they can get on with their lives. The first woman he is no longer waiting for, whose return to life he has accepted, of course. But when she enters his house, she will be real, unavoidable. Perhaps, like Sandrine, he sees the first woman as a thick, dark cloud drawing ever closer, a tempest ready to be unleashed, ready to blast everything they have made, everything they had rebuilt together, the three of them. Again, she caresses him, without answering. He hates to appear weak, and she knows it. Anything she might suggest is a risk, she will not impose, no decent woman does that, and Sandrine is already a virtual exile in the borderlands of this family; she knows he loves her but she can find no comfort, no reassurance here, she knows she is perched on a fragile branch that threatens to break and take her down as it falls, far, far away from her man, her mainstay, the trunk of the tree. Well, he has recovered himself, the panic has subsided, they will say no more about it.

She says, I ironed your shirts yesterday, they're in the utility room but I can bring them up now if you like, if you want to choose which one to wear? Do you want me to set the table outside? He detaches himself from her and stands up. Naked, he always looks shorter, and each time she is reminded, as if her brain cannot quite process the fact, that she is a hand's breadth or length taller than he is. He swallows a mouthful of coffee, passes his hand over her cheek. She shivers, folds her arms across her breasts. It's as if she has passed a test, taken the lead. The coffee, the shirts, and above all making no show of deciding for him, giving him time to get back into his man-suit and pretend she never saw him naked, and plagued with doubt. Yes, he says at last, the smell of coffee on his breath. Is the blue one there? Yes, the blue one, I did it with the rest. Wait, I'll fetch it. She is at the top of the stairs, one foot extended to go down, when he says loudly, No, lay the table inside, it's going to rain.

The table has been laid for well over an hour when they hear a car in the road, shortly before midday. Sandrine absorbed herself in the task of placing and straightening the cloth, aligning the knives and forks, trying hard to create a table for an important occasion, though not a celebration, telling herself that something vaguely along the lines of a funeral lunch would do the trick. Which is near enough the truth, finally. Since first thing that morning it has seemed to her that everything she does, every small household task she completes, is a nail in her own casket. Sandrine is standing at the kitchen sink when the doorbell rings and a streak of white lightning tears the sky apart, just above the lime tree at the bottom of the garden.

She removes her apron, she's wearing her office clothes, the ones that make her stand up straight and feel structured, sharply defined. Often, he complains when she wears them on a Sunday. He prefers her in other clothes, bright colours, flowery shirts, but this morning he said nothing, probably didn't even notice, preoccupied with choosing between two different bottles of wine, pacing all over the sitting room, looking for dust where there is none to be seen, while Caroline watches silently from her yellow frame on the shelf in the bookcase.

At the sound of the bell, Mathias jumps up straightaway from his corner – a favourite spot between the armchair and the window, where he has been staring at, but not studying, the drawings in a book about birds – and races to the door. Another flash of white illuminates the sitting room, where the deepening gloom, over the past hour, had them wondering whether or not to turn on the lights. Sandrine watches Mathias spring to life and thinks, Quick as a flash, of lightning, the true meaning of the expression she has never properly understood until this morning, until the sight of a little boy running to his mother, who has come home at last.

WAIT! his father hollers and Mathias stops dead, one hand on the front door. The boy is trembling with eagerness, all over. He turns to look at them, and his face wears an expression of utter, transparent pleading – but already his father has caught hold of him and moved him brusquely to one side. He is the one to open the door, and Mathias utters a small boy's cry, an AH! of surprise and excitement, with both hands pressed to his mouth.

Framed in the doorway, Sandrine sees not Caroline but the two police officers who called the other day. She thinks, they must have had an accident – perhaps the car bringing Anne-Marie, Patrice and Caroline has overturned on its way to the house. That must be it, a far preferable scenario, though she likes and respects Mathias's grandparents. A terrible accident, but the police will tell them: They were killed outright, they did not suffer. It happens like that sometimes, in films and books, the police officers tell everyone 'They were killed outright, they didn't suffer.' Sandrine hangs her apron on the hook inside the pantry, everything in its place. She feels extraordinarily calm, disembodied; she feels nothing at all and it's better that way, no doubt. The police officers are talking, she sees Mathias fidgeting impatiently, and his father's hand on the front door, and she thinks, It will be so much easier if they are all dead, but he steps back to let them come inside. Following behind the two police officers are Patrice, and then Anne-Marie who turns and gestures to the slender silhouette of a woman, standing on the drive.

Everyone stands in the hallway that leads into the sitting room, then steps back to let the woman through, like a wave spreading slowly over a beach. And the wave carries her inside. Caroline.

She is thin, dark-haired, in jeans and a white T-shirt, with black ballerina pumps. She advances into the room, looking around for something, and her gaze falls on Mathias, working his pointed fingers into the flesh of his little boy lips, and Caroline says, uncertainly, You're Mathias… and he doesn't answer, he just takes a few quick steps and clings to her, violently, and so tightly that the skin of his knuckles whitens against his mother's jeans and his whole face disappears into her thighs, and the woman bends over the child and runs her hands through the crow-black down of his hair, over and over again.

Sandrine looks at the man in whose house she is living, her man, Caroline's husband. She sees his back, his shoulders, his arms, and observes his stiff, awkward movements with sudden, unwelcome detachment, telling herself that if he steps forward, if he takes her in his arms, then perhaps she, Sandrine, will drop to the floor and die instantly, right there on the spot. She thinks these thoughts, in a kind of daze, but he shows no sign of affection, doesn't even hold out his hand to the woman who makes no gesture towards him either, he simply lets her pass, makes way, and closes the front door. People move about, uncertain where to put themselves, the police officers shift their weight from one leg to the other, even Caroline's parents, who have been to the house a thousand times, are unsure as to whether they should take a seat. Caroline, for her part, is unable to move because of Mathias, a human graft, a whimpering parasite. At length she manages to twist herself around, bends to whisper something in her son's ear, a question. She we all go and sit down together? Hm? Mathias? The child loosens his grip very slightly, barely enough for her to move to the sofa, and even then he clings to her, sitting on her lap. Sandrine is glad she feels nothing, she was prepared for the worst, told herself for days on end that it was all over, otherwise the sight of Mathias overflowing with love would certainly have reduced her to tears, she who after all this time had secured nothing but polite indifference – at best, his silent consent to a caress that was seldom returned. In all this strangeness, Sandrine decides to fake it… She lifts a tray of sliced bread, toasted and cut into canapés, and joins everyone in the sitting room. Anne-Marie gives her a kind, gentle smile, recasts her in the role of the nanny, the help. She prepares to stand up, Hello Sandrine, wait, let me help, but Sandrine says, No need, Anne-Marie, it's no problem, and sets the tray down on the coffee table. Then she waits in silence to be introduced to the first woman, who watches her with an indecipherable expression.

There is a long pause, too long. Patrice looks at Sandrine, Anne-Marie looks at Caroline, Caroline looks at Mathias. The police officers stare at his father. At last, he recovers himself, unfixes his gaze from a point in space, somewhere behind the sofa, turns his head to look in the direction of the kitchen. She— it's normal you don't remember her, that's Sandrine. She's… I met her after your— After you were… She's been living with us for a while, then he hesitates and says, She's very good with Mathias, very kind. At which Anne-Marie and Patrice both nod vigorously and Caroline says simply, Ah, well, hello Sandrine. The awkwardness persists, but Sandrine ignores the heaviness in the air and sets about transforming the moment into something ordinary, as if that were possible. She goes back into the kitchen to fetch another tray with glasses, fruit juices, wine and beers. It's raining hard now. Sandrine makes a third return trip, with little bowls of peanuts, sausage rolls. Laboriously, the conversation begins.

They talk about the strange weather and the rain that was forecast for that morning but nothing and then here it is. Finally, Caroline speaks up, I'm sorry, I suppose you're looking for an explanation, and especially you, Mathias, but I can't remember anything, and the investigation into what happened to me is still ongoing.

Mathias looks up at her and says, But you recognise me, don't you, Mama? Caroline strokes his cheek and shows him a very kind smile, broad and warm, but she gives no answer. She turns to look at the police officers.

The woman cop looks at Mathias and suggests the boy goes to another room, but Mathias is oblivious to everything except his mother. Caroline nods. Do you want to show me— she corrects herself, Shall we go and play in your bedroom?

She doesn't remember the house, thinks Sandrine. Does she remember Mathias?

The two of them climb the stairs and Sandrine begins serving the drinks. Now, it's the turn of the woman in the leather jacket to speak. Sandrine is free to scrutinise her at leisure, while she addresses the group. She's not as young as Sandrine first thought, but there is an energy about her – the set of her jawline, her movements. She wears a pale grey T-shirt and through the opening in her jacket, Sandrine sees patches of sweat darkening the fabric under her arms. She cannot bear anyone to see her sweat, never wears T-shirts because her soft, shapeless body cannot take the unstructured look, the lack of support. Yet the woman is very self-assured, with a kind of assurance that she, Sandrine, will never have. Caroline and Mathias tread together on the creaky step and clumsily, she opens a bottle of fruit juice, as if her body has decided to corroborate her self-diagnosis, reinforce what is plain to see.

The female cop refuses a glass of wine, takes some sparkling water, tells everyone that the investigation into Caroline's disappearance had been closed but that Anne-Marie and Patrice have encouraged Caroline to file a complaint against persons unknown, for assault and attempted murder. And to request that she and her partner take charge of the case once again, because they worked on it at the time of the disappearance. She looks Sandrine in the eye as she says this, firmly and insistently. Not in an aggressive way, but Sandrine isn't used to eye contact, she's one of those girls who was always taught to lower her gaze, like a timid herbivore, vulnerable to prey, and she does not know how to handle this direct, unflinching gaze. The cop seems to be weighing her up, perhaps even warning her. Outside, the rain is falling in sheets on the stone-paved terrace, and the lawn. When the policewoman finally shifts her gaze to Caroline's husband, Sandrine feels released and takes a few moments to watch the heavy curtain of drops that shatter to a fine mist as they strike the concrete slabs incrusted with tiny pebbles, drench the carefully mown grass. In Italy, Caroline was treated by someone on the hospital's psychiatric team, Anne-Marie explains. She saw someone here in France, too, during the few days she was at the Pitié-Salpêtrière, and they – the team at the Centre in Paris – advised her to find someone, to continue the treatment until her memory returns. Anne-Marie speaks the words as if she has no doubt whatsoever that her daughter will be restored to her intact, with her memory intact. Patrice seems less certain. He passes his hand over his mouth and chin, stares at his feet. Oh yes, one other thing, says the woman cop's voice, followed by a small, slight creak. Sandrine turns back to look at the little group in the sitting room. The woman cop is leaning forward to hand Anne-Marie a piece of paper. The names of the therapists we talked about, she says. All of them recommended by one of the psychiatrists they work with. Of course, it's Caroline's choice, Patrice is careful to point out. We're discussing this for her now but it's just in case she can't decide for herself. There's nothing mentally wrong with her, really, is there? Just that she can't remember what happened.

His words die on the silent air, Anne-Marie nibbles a fingernail and Patrice takes her hand, says again, That's all it is. They say that it might… that it could very well come back, it's just her memory. Then Patrice looks at the man who is once again, wholly and completely, his son-in-law. She doesn't remember, he says. Nothing at all? asks the man who cried. She doesn't remember anything at all?

Anne-Marie says, One or two little bits and pieces have come back to her already, since we went to join her in Paris – childhood memories. And one memory, very clear and precise, of the day she came home to us, at the apartment, after she passed her driving test. That's why she came back with us, she knows we're her parents. But I'm so, so sorry, she doesn't remember you at all.

93

Everyone turns to look at Sandrine, and she realises that she has spoken aloud, Not even Mathias? Anne-Marie says, No, and her voice breaks. Not even Mathias. The hospital that examined her in Italy said she had had at least one child. She absolutely wanted to see him. She thinks that is what will come back to her. Something... the maternal instinct.

Sandrine turns her head to the garden once again. She doesn't believe in the maternal instinct. She watched a documentary with Mathias one day that showed how a mother animal can abandon her cub, fail to recognise it, mistake it for another, or leave it to die if she doesn't recognise its smell. She didn't need a documentary to tell her that. Her own mother was proof enough. Mathias had listened to the voice-over, wide-eyed, and when the screen showed the image of a female monkey cradling the baby of another dead female, Sandrine said, Look at that, Mathias. Not daring to add, It's just like us.

Do you think she recognised him? That she recognised her son? the male cop asks. He doesn't say much. His voice is rounded, warm, comfortable. No, I don't think so, says Anne-Marie, and then she begins to cry and Patrice holds her close and says, It's OK, everything's going to be OK, my Nini, she's back, she's here, that's a miracle in itself, isn't it? Huh? Huh, Nini? If she's recognised us then anything's possible.

Patrice and Anne-Marie sit together as one on the sofa, a single body crying double. Sandrine is perched on a stool, there aren't enough seats and at that moment she would like her man to take her in his arms and tell her, too, that 'Everything's going to be OK.' But he is too stunned for that, and sits staring at his feet and his clasped hands. Another small creak, and everyone looks up. It's Caroline, coming down the stairs. Anne-Marie blows her nose and the two parents compose themselves, while their daughter takes the last few steps down into the sitting room. When she sees every face turned towards her, she lets go of the handrail, crosses her arms and says, He fell asleep almost in the middle of a sentence, I think it's a lot for him to deal with.

Sandrine says, Yes, he didn't get much sleep last night. Caroline shows the glimmer of a smile and says, Me neither. Then she uncrosses her arms, fishes in the back pocket of her jeans for a crumpled pack of cigarettes and asks, Is it OK if I go for a smoke outside? Followed by silence. Caroline's husband remains in shock, saying nothing, and so Sandrine says, Yes of course, go ahead, if you stay under the awning against the wall you'll be dry. The woman cop gets to her feet, one hand in her jacket pocket, and says, I'll join you. The glass door slides open, and then shut. Sandrine gets up to see to the oven, warm the chicken. She cannot see Caroline and the woman cop from the kitchen window, they're standing further away along the wall, but she can see their hands, raised and lowered, each to its own rhythm, the cigarette lifted to the lips, the glow at the tip, the breath of smoke, the finger tapping the filter. Caroline's hand is small and leathery, her fingers are short, her nails bitten. The woman cop's hand is bigger, more muscular, her nails are bitten too, and yellowed slightly with nicotine. The kitchen window is ajar and Sandrine hears the women's voices. Inside, the policeman's smooth, rounded tones summarise things she already knows, the day of Caroline's disappearance, the fruitless weeks that followed, the empty ravine at the bottom of the field. He says they followed every possible lead at the time. Sandrine knows all this, her man told her everything and she doesn't need to hear it again. She prepares the salad, and it's the voices of the two women outside that sidle into earshot.

How do you feel? asks the woman cop.

95

OK, just very strange, says Caroline in reply. I hoped that when I saw him, everything would— Everything would…

Her voice breaks and the cop speaks a few words of comfort, tells her everything will be all right. Today, everyone is telling everyone else that everything will be all right, because nothing is right at all.

Nothing whatsoever? the woman cop asks once again, after a few moments consoling her fellow smoker.

Nothing, says Caroline. His face, his smell, nothing. I mean, he's my son, I believe you, it's just that I don't know it myself, but it's as if— I'm not making sense, I just mean…

Yes, I understand, says the woman cop, I understand. This is just the beginning of very complicated process, Caroline. I'm no shrink but I spoke to people at the Centre when we came to fetch you with your parents, and they say nothing's guaranteed, that it will take time. But that if one memory of life with your parents has come back to you that's a very good sign already. How do you want to arrange things in the meantime?

A moment's silence follows, a long exhalation, a cloud of smoke, and Caroline says, I'm going to stay with my parents, anyway. I mean— quite apart from what you're thinking, I don't recognise him either, and then there's another woman here now.

That's her. Caroline is talking about Sandrine. They're talking about her. Sandrine waits. Caroline speaks again: And he hardly says a thing, it's almost as if he doesn't recognise me either.

The woman cop has nothing but kind words for Caroline, her voice is softer, gentler than the voice she uses indoors, and Sandrine tells herself, once again, that the woman cop will find the right words to soften the blow. She'll say: It must be a shock for him, too, I can understand that, he was profoundly moved when we told him we'd found you. Or words to that effect. But no, the cop says nothing. Several smoke-laden breaths. Still nothing. Then at last, she says, We've already talked about this, Caroline. I've been very clear with you, about everything that happened when you... disappeared. You know what I think about your husband. Ex-husband. I think it's better, too, that you keep your distance.

Caroline never said she thought it was *better* to stay at her parents' place, just that that was what she wanted to do. So who else thought it was better *too*? Caroline's parents? The other cop? The shrinks at the Centre after they found her? The lettuce is clean. Outside, there's an uncertain exchange about what to do with the cigarette butts. Finally, the patio door slides open, and the two women step back inside, Caroline holding the stubs in her hands. She moves towards the kitchen, her smile forming the question. Sandrine says, Ah yes, and shows her the rubbish bin next to the fridge. Caroline throws away the stubs and moves across to the sink, asking, May I wash my hands? And Sandrine says, Please, go ahead! And she steps aside, pulling the salad wringer towards her.

Caroline soaps her hands, carefully, deliberately rinses, then pulls open the door to the cupboard under the sink where they keep the tea towels and the hand towels. She dries her hands. Sandrine watches the manoeuvre, speechless. The tea towels and hand towels are never left lying around, he hates that. They are always put away in the cupboard and when his friends come for dinner, there is always one who ends up with wet hands and asks Where can I...? But Caroline knows, she knows where to find the towel to dry her hands. She closes the cupboard door, smiles at Sandrine who stands rooted to the spot, then returns to the sitting room. She slips between the sofa and the coffee table, and again Sandrine notices her sinuous allure. This woman who says so little, supple as an eel. She's lying. She has something to take, something to steal. She watches as Caroline sits beside her mother. Sandrine watches as she stares at her husband, tries to catch his eye. At last, he looks up, sees her, wrings his hands, turns his head to the kitchen and calls out to Sandrine, Let's eat. She nods. She tries to smile at him but a grimace is perhaps the only expression her mouth can form. She feels suddenly very hot, and puts down the salad bowl she has just filled, to clutch the edge of the kitchen worktop. She reaches out to the sink. A drink, drink, it'll do me good, and then everything goes very, very white.

She wakes up months, or just one second, later. The cop has placed his hand under her head and at the far end of her legs there is Caroline, holding her feet up in the air. Caroline was a nurse. Had begun training as a nurse. Had begun training as a nurse before meeting her husband and moving away. After that, she hadn't resumed her training because she loved taking care of the house. And then after that, of course, she had Mathias. Sandrine knows all this, her man told her right from the start, so that she would know and then afterwards they would say nothing more about it because, as she understood perfectly well, it was painful for him. Sandrine knows, too, that Caroline could have been a vet, ought to have been, but she lacked self-confidence, Anne-Marie had told her that, one day, when they were drinking coffee after lunch and the men had gone out to the driveway to look at the new car, and Mathias was playing tenderly with his toy soldiers. Mathias has his own very special way of playing soldiers, he treats the little plastic figures like other children treat their dolls. His soldiers spend a lot of time wounded because they've been defending themselves from attack. And so he lays them down, tucks them in, sings them lullabies.

Anne-Marie watched him that day, and shared her memories of her daughter: Caroline's generosity, her empathy, her careful nature, her love of animals. Anne-Marie said, What that little pup needs is some dolls, see how he plays with his soldiers! And Sandrine had laughed, His father would never agree to that! And Anne-Marie said, Yes, that's— But she wasn't smiling any more.

The same with the dog. Mathias and his big eyes, like saucers, whenever he meets a dog in the street. Mathias loves dogs and dogs love Mathias. It's astonishing to see: *all* dogs love Mathias. Tiny little pugs and huge guard dogs alike. They can smell him a hundred metres away, and they wait for him behind their garden fences, look out for him at the window, come up to him in the street. They lick his hands, butt him gently with their heads, begging to be stroked. When Sandrine is out walking with her two men, it's almost comical. A dog will turn its head to Mathias and grin, then look at his father and growl, its hackles rising. Love, hate, love, hate. When she saw this for the first time, Sandrine thought they'd make a great circus act. But of course it meant no dog at home. Though Anne-Marie and Patrice were prepared to pay for the dog and its upkeep, even to buy a pedigree animal because at first Mathias's father had said No, we're not adopting some mongrel, you never know where they've been. And what if it's sick? And so the grandparents had suggested a spaniel, a setter, something with a good pedigree, up to date with its jabs, all that. They were ready, and Mathias's father had said No. He won't be the one to look after it, it'll have to be taken out, leaving hairs all over the place… it'll make more work for Sandrine. Sandrine had raised an eyebrow, surprised to be used as an excuse. Perhaps she would have liked to talk it over between them, but on the other hand if they found themselves with an expensive dog that showed an aversion to the head of the family, things could get complicated, for sure. What if you got a dog, at the apartment? she had suggested to Mathias's grandparents, looking for a compromise. And so now Anne-Marie and Patrice have a dog, who – exactly as expected – demonstrates an all-consuming love for the little boy and detests his father with all its might. The dog stays at Anne-Marie and Patrice's apartment. Whenever Sandrine takes Mathias to his grandparents' place, he comes home brimming with joy, reeking of mutt, his knees grubby from playing on the floor, brought out of himself for a time by endless licks from a half-German-shepherd-half-goodness-knows-what, all mixed-up and jumbled like a portrait by Picasso, because Anne-Marie and Patrice chose an unidentifiable cross-breed at a rescue shelter, and haven't regretted it for a moment. All this passes through Sandrine's mind in a series of bright, quick-fire images as she opens her eyes in the kitchen.

Around her, as she comes to in the bright, dazzling light, she sees the anxious faces of the cops and the older couple, and in the background, upset or annoyed, her man, who says, at length, All right, give her some air, let her breathe. Caroline brings Sandrine's feet back down to the floor. The cop says, I can't feel a cut anywhere, in any case the scalp always pisses blood, we would have noticed. Gently, he removes his hand and steps away from the patient, he has no place beside her, he's a stranger, the man with whom Sandrine lives is the one who should be there; and he comes, and kneels beside her, asks if she's all right. Sandrine likes that he's concerned, she likes that he has shaken himself out of his torpor for her sake. He helps her to sit up, says, There's no cut. She feels her scalp, can't find any bumps, only her elbow hurts a little. She says, No, it's OK, we can eat if you like, and she holds out a hand for him to help her up. The policewoman says No. Sandrine thinks she's just being polite, like when people refuse to accept the last slice of cake and say no, really, honestly. But she sees the woman cop take out her telephone and call an ambulance. Sandrine feels her man's fingers closing tight around her own, and she knows, as sure as the rain has stopped outside, that he's asking himself, Who the hell does she think she is? He says, But she's just said she feels fine! And his tone is perfectly controlled, and the woman cop replies calmly: Any blow to the head and it's straight to the doctor. Or I'll take her to Emergency myself, whichever you prefer, Sandrine. Sandrine hesitates and more than anything she finds it impossible to think because he's crushing her fingers and it hurts, more and more. The woman cop says, Let her go, sir, and in a fraction of a second the strange, shifting, uncertain atmosphere veers sharply towards open hostility. It's a relief, in a way, like the storm that has broken. He doesn't like the woman cop and she doesn't like him. She's humiliating him, giving him orders in his own home, and she may even be doing it on purpose.

Sandrine recovers her fingers, her breath, her thoughts. Her priority is not to anger him further, to find the best solution, and she decides that a trip to the emergency room is the least bother for them all, that Anne-Marie can serve lunch, that if she, Sandrine, ruins their reunion, she will be the sort of woman he detests, a troublemaker, always disagreeing, talking too loud, the hysterical kind, always complaining. She says OK, if you really think it's best to go to the hospital for a check-up? It sounds like a question, a last chance for the woman cop to say, You're right, let's stay here if you really feel OK. But no, the woman in the leather jacket just nods and reaches out to help Sandrine to her feet.

Stepping outside the house, she feels an escalation of panic, as if she has been evacuated, expelled, precisely the thing she dreaded: the first woman has come back and she, Sandrine, the second woman, is out on the street. She swallows and tries to reason with herself. He watches them from the door, signals with his hand. Sandrine waves back, forcing a smile. The woman cop says, Seatbelt. With luck, we'll be back in time for dessert. Then she fires the engine, manoeuvres expertly out of the parking space and sets off in the direction of the hospital.

The estate houses slide past, then the traffic circle and the link road to the motorway. The hospital's only fifteen minutes away, says the woman cop. Yes, I know, says Sandrine. Then, searching for something to say: Do you live around here?

No, but I came here very often when Madame Langlois disappeared. Madame Langlois is Caroline, of course, though Sandrine has never thought of her in those terms. For her, it's Caroline, or the first woman, or his ex, or Mathias's mother. She has sometimes pictured herself as Madame Langlois, allowed herself a few, idiotic moments scribbling *Sandrine Langlois* on a scrap of paper. Like a love-struck girl, she knows that, but she never had a boyfriend as a girl, from whom she could borrow a new name, just for a moment, to doodle on her school book, and so she had indulged herself, while at the same time refusing to believe it, and how right she had been.

You knew about that, didn't you? the woman cop asks, and Sandrine realises she has been spoken to, though she heard nothing. Perhaps she really is unwell – and those phantom smells that follow her around. Perhaps it's best if she sees a doctor after all. She had thought about it that morning, it wasn't the best time, but at least it would be out of the way. When she tells him tonight that she has had other moments feeling faint, and sick, perhaps he will feel less angry at the woman cop who insisted she be taken to hospital, and at her for agreeing to go. I'm sorry?

Sandrine asks, after trying for a moment to pick up the thread of the conversation.

I said, your partner was a suspect at the time of Madame Langlois's disappearance, you knew about that, didn't you? Sandrine nods. She does not want to be reminded of that. Yes, she knows, it was on the news, but that was also the moment she fell in love with the man who cried, and she does not want to be reminded of the disgusting comments Béatrice made back then. The lies. All the people who had no idea and said bad things. But she, Sandrine, she knew: a man who cries is incapable of hurting his wife. She hopes the woman cop will stop talking, but no, she carries on, and Sandrine is already imagining what she will tell him tonight, the man she set about loving when everyone was saying bad things about him. What an awful woman, she will say, what a wicked person, to say such things, to say such vile things about you, to me, she was talking utter nonsense.

The clothes Monsieur Langlois was wearing on the day of his wife's disappearance have never been found, says the woman cop. Witnesses saw him dressed in grey and white in the morning, and blue and white in the evening. He went to collect the little boy from school, something he never did normally, though he still hadn't reported his wife's disappearance. And he never did, in fact. It was the parents – Anne-Marie and Patrice. Their daughter was meant to go and see them with Mathias after school, and she never came. Did you know that, too?

Sandrine concentrates on staring at her fingers, she pushes at the cuticle of a nail with a nail of the opposite hand, then moves on to the next one, and so on.

He didn't go to work on the day she disappeared. The absence was unplanned. He told us he was ill, that he had stayed at home with a bad cold. He said his wife dropped Mathias off at school,

103

then came home to change and went for a run in the wood that surrounds the east side of the housing estate. What man fails to call anyone, to report anything, even after several hours have gone by, when his wife doesn't come back from a run that usually takes thirty or thirty-five minutes? He said he thought she'd gone shopping. Did you know that? Did you know that, too? And that when we called that evening, he was perfectly fit and well? No sign of a cold at all?

Sandrine wishes the woman would stop talking. She knows she must be polite. But she wishes the woman would shut the fuck up. Finally, to cut her short, she says, Yes. He told me all that when we met. He has nothing to hide.

Really? the woman cop persists, and her tone suggests an angler who feels a bite. Did he also tell you that his explanation makes no sense, because he had stopped Caroline from driving? For almost two months, she had been forced to go everywhere on foot. Mathias's school is half an hour's walk away. She had been making the journey on foot with the boy every day, morning and afternoon, for at least six months.

Sandrine rubs her temple. Her head is beginning to hurt now, a lot. It was definitely a good idea to go to the hospital.

The woman cop finds a space in the car park, near the entrance to the emergency service. She kills the engine, sits in silence for few moments, then says – in a quite different voice, kind and concerned – Sandrine, Monsieur Langlois wasn't simply questioned as part of this investigation, two years ago. He was our prime suspect, the most likely perpetrator. He puts on a convincing show, we had a very, very hard time getting anything on him from the neighbours, but we found out some things eventually. My colleague and I do not believe Caroline just *disappeared*. Do you understand what I'm saying?

Sandrine says only, Please, can I get out of the car? And the woman cop heaves a sigh.

Sandrine gets out. Everything the woman cop has just said is buzzing in her head, like a great, black insect, a deafening, unbearable roar. This woman is lying, why is she lying, she's telling Sandrine the story she already knows, but in a horrible, ugly version. Sandrine knows it's all untrue, her man has told her, he told her everything. He cried and he told her everything, he poured his heart out to her, clinging to her knees, and she stroked his face, wet with tears, for a long time, swearing to take care of him, because she loves him, because he loves her, and people who love one another don't tell lies. The woman cop isn't in love with her man, she's the one telling lies. Sandrine takes a deep breath. The fresh air does her good but it does not ease the pain that is clamped like a vice around her temples. Fortunately, the woman cop says nothing more. That isn't why they're here, after all, Sandrine reminds herself as they walk the short distance to the hospital entrance and go inside.

The waiting room is quiet. The policewoman glances around at the patients lining the walls, then takes out her badge and heads for the reception desk. Her tone is friendly but authoritative as she asks for Sandrine to be seen as quickly as possible.

The woman doctor is pleasant. Then she establishes that the policewoman has accompanied Sandrine here purely by chance, and not in the line of duty. Unhurriedly but firmly, she escorts her from the room. There is some discussion in the corridor outside, the two women seemingly each as obstinate as the other, and several times Sandrine hears the words 'I perfectly understand, but', which mean 'You're pissing me off.' Finally, the police-woman waits outside. Their exchange has endeared the medic to Sandrine, though she has never had a woman doctor and she cannot quite rid herself of the idea that men know best. She must follow the woman's index finger with her eyes, try not to blink when a too-bright light is shone into her pupils.

Frequent episodes of fainting?

No, but a feeling as if I'm about to black out, several times recently. And nausea – no, the problem isn't so much the nausea, but the coffee that smells of tuna, bizarrely.

Tuna? the doctor asks, raising her eyebrows, and Sandrine feels embarrassed, takes back what she said, apologises. She doesn't like doctors, she doesn't being the centre of attention, being a bother, talking about herself. Besides, they're always in a hurry and she's always the one who's done something wrong: she needs to sleep more, drink more fluids, walk more, eat this way or that. Sandrine never tells them the whole truth any more anyway, not since the old guy her mother took her to see on occasion, when she was delirious with fever, the one who saw the bruises and said nothing, did nothing, except examine her tiny breasts on the pretext of checking for something, she never understood what. She never said anything about it, of course, there were worse things, but a small voice inside her – the furious voice that she buries deep down because it might spell trouble for her one day – had hollered loud and clear: *For fuck's sake, you don't need to handle the breasts of a fourteen-year-old girl with sinusitis...*

Sandrine denies her own words, about the tuna, with a slight wave of the hand, as if she had got mixed up, as if she was joking, but the woman doctor smiles, waits patiently, asks, Tuna? You mean, you were making coffee and one day there was a smell of tuna? Or the coffee itself smelt of tuna?

Sandrine tries to give the right answer, though she wants this to be over quickly. She hasn't forgotten that all this time, at home, Anne-Marie is serving the meal. Mm-hm, says the doctor. May

I ask you to lie down? What a strange way to put it, Sandrine thinks. That's not how you talk to a patient, it's Take your clothes off, open your legs, and This is where it hurts. Thought so. Well it's nothing, you're just stressed, put your clothes back on. Sorry, no cheques. And so she hesitates, unsure what to do. I'd like to examine you, your lymph nodes, your tummy, says the doctor, a second time, to the motionless young woman.

Sandrine pivots on the trolley covered with a sheet of coarse tissue paper. The woman doctor asks her to lift up her T-shirt, rummages in a drawer, tells her she's about to examine her stomach. Sandrine feels a rush of relief. Good. She never likes to show her legs, if she doesn't have to. She's ashamed of her little girl's knees, all covered in scabs. She hears a clatter of metal as the doctor searches through her drawer then says, Damn, they haven't stocked up the— OK, wait there, I'll be right back, and she leaves her lying on the trolley. Through the closing door, Sandrine sees the policewoman glancing nosily at her recumbent shape, at the black vest top she's wearing under her shirt, her exposed belly. What is that woman's problem, what's she looking for? Really, she's weird.

The woman doctor returns, and Sandrine sees the police officer stop her, tell her things, ask her questions. The woman in the white coat nods, irritated, and finally says something like 'Go and wait in the waiting room, please.' And when she pushes open the door she looks a little concerned, like the other woman, and Sandrine catches her staring harder than before at her exposed skin. There's a small blind over the glass panel in the door, and the woman turns the slats so that they cannot be seen from outside. I'm so sorry, it would probably be easier if you took off your vest top? Sandrine does as she's told, and the woman looks her all over. She's searching for something. Something she can't find, apparently, because the cleft in the middle of her forehead softens a little, and she begins to feel Sandrine's neck, then says, I'm going to feel your lymph nodes now, and then your stomach. Does it hurt here? And here? Does that feel sensitive, or not? Finally she says, Now, the police officer who brought you in is insisting we take some X-rays, but you're showing no sign of a bad blow to the head. Your pupils are dilating normally in response to a light source, your speech is clear and coherent. But, are you— You may be pregnant, so we won't be doing any X-rays.

Pregnant.

Sandrine can't seem to hear anything any more, the doctor's words are covered by a sudden ringing in her ears. She can hear, but it's like overhearing a conversation in another room, she can make out the words, vaguely, but she's not really paying attention.

…In the absence of any sign of trauma, I mean. I'm going to write you a prescription for a pregnancy test. You'll need to bring in a urine sample. The test will confirm whether or not you're pregnant. And it would be a good idea to see your gynaecologist. Do you have a gynaecologist? *Madame? Madame…?* Sandrine?

The woman places her hand on Sandrine's wrist, as if pressing a doorbell. The ringing stops and Sandrine turns to look at her. You… Is this unexpected? A surprise? the doctor asks, and seeing Sandrine's broad, goofy grin, she breaks into a smile herself, and opposite her Sandrine nods her head vigorously like a delighted child. Yes, yes, absolutely! The doctor says, Well then, I hope the results confirm everything for you.

The woman leaves her alone in the consulting room, goes off to find some form or other, Sandrine neither knows nor cares. She sits pressing the belly that has always been too soft, the breasts that have always been too flat. At last this body can serve a purpose, achieve something incredible: it will make a person, how extraordinary, unhoped for, crazy. Completely crazy. She who has always fought this hideous husk, felt the burden of this weight at every step, is suddenly thankful, brimming with gratitude for this flesh-and-blood machine that has succeeded, will succeed, in making something so huge and wonderful. She, Sandrine, is going to have a baby, a child. Of course, of course that's what it was, she can feel it now, inside her, no need for tests, a baby, a child, she'll look after it so well, he'll be so good, she'll dissolve the very last drops of bad blood in this tiny, brand-new creature. This room is so pretty, the doctor is so nice, what beautiful clouds outside the window, nothing can touch Sandrine now as she smiles all the way down to her belly.

In the car, on the way back, the policewoman tries a different strategy. Or perhaps she's given up. She talks about anything and nothing, about the weather and the house where Sandrine lives. Barely an hour has passed, they must still be eating, she'll be able to serve the chocolate cake. Suddenly, Sandrine feels hungry. The vague, numbing sickness that paralysed her jaw and made it so hard to eat over the past few days has disappeared, she could eat something now. But what? What does she feel like eating? Fennel. She wants to eat fennel. When the car reaches the traffic circle that leads to the estate, Sandrine asks if they can stop for a minute at the supermarket. She hurries to the vegetable section; there are bulbs of fennel from Italy, each round base like a single white buttock marked with translucent stripes. Sandrine smells their fresh aroma, tinged with aniseed, it tingles her nostrils and tortures her stomach. She passes the checkout and opens the bag, strips off the outer layers – they may be dirty – and begins to nibble like a rabbit. The flesh is crisp, and each bite releases the delicate, fragrant juice. She's delighted, eats two large pieces

with careful, rodent-like concentration. Really? asks the policewoman, smiling. Just like that, no sauce or anything? Sandrine
has finished the fennel by the time they pull up in front of the
house. She releases her seatbelt and is about to open the door.
The woman cop reaches out to stop her, places a hand on her
elbow and gives her a card. Here's my telephone number, OK?
If you feel... if something's wrong, whatever it might be, you
can call me. At any time, Sandrine, I mean it. Sandrine takes
the small, glossy card, says Yes, yes, and slips it without a glance
into the back pocket of her black jeans. Outside, the tarmac is
still damp, the light is grey, the weather is anything but fine, but
to Sandrine it's a beautiful day. She has no idea what's going on,
what will happen next in this house, where the first woman has
been all this time, but it doesn't matter. We just don't care, do
we, little bean? she says silently, to her belly.

Inside, they're on the cheese course. Anne-Marie is tossing the
salad in its bowl. Mathias is talking, a lot. His piping voice greets
them as soon as they open the door. He is always more talkative
when his grandparents are there, but Sandrine has never heard
such a light-footed, tripping torrent of words. He is talking
to Caroline, explaining, telling her things, about school, and
birds, and Papi-Nini's dog whose name is Picasso, and Caroline
asks questions, shows genuine interest, as if making up for lost
time – a heartfelt pretence. The scene is almost normal, even
with a cop and a woman back from the dead sitting at the table,
and everyone plays along assiduously, says, Ah yes, well when I
was at school... And everything is rolling along, with no apparent difficulty. Everyone plays along at family lunch gatherings,
to a greater or lesser extent, if you think about it. It's just that
here, everyone is playing that little bit harder. Sandrine enters

and assumes her role, reassures everybody. Just a dizzy spell. She takes her seat at the table, passes the cheeseboard with its curved, two-pronged knife, thanks Anne-Marie for taking care of lunch. The conversation resumes, around tales and memories of severe or kindly schoolteachers, and through it all, Sandrine wears a smile she cannot quite keep hidden. She has a secret, a well-guarded secret. Of course she won't declare the news at the table in front of Caroline and the two police officers, she won't say anything now, she'll keep it in a safe, warm place. Several times, she catches the eye of the father-to-be, an anxious furrow between his eyebrows. She answers with a smile each time but it does nothing to soothe him, poor man. He doesn't know, and so he does not yet have – as she does – this ultimate, sparkling reason to be happy, a reason that sweeps everything else aside, a reason to decide that none of this matters, that Caroline… Well, they'll just have to see, but that's not what matters now, not any more.

The chocolate cake is served, and the coffee. The empty bottles are standing beside the sink. Caroline suggests the outline of a plan: she will come back from time to time and try to recover some images from the past, some memories. Anne-Marie cuts in, Yes, well, we'll have to see what the psychologist says… Caroline continues, talks about having the boy over to her parents' apartment, where she'll be staying for a while, and no one objects. Mathias's father stares at his hands, his feet, the woman cop, her partner, his hands, his feet, and says, If you like, why not, from time to time. His words are slow and laboured. There we are, thinks Sandrine, it was pointless to make a mountain out of this, after all. We'll just see. And with that, he pushes away his plate and says, So…

Sandrine knows the signal, his end-of-meal ritual, it's over, they can get down from the table. Anne-Marie says, Yes, perhaps we should be getting back. Mathias is quiet and discreet, content to keep close to his mother, their two chairs pressed close together, her arm around his shoulders. Suddenly, he understands that she's about to leave once more. His face twists in an expression of sheer terror. He throws his arms around Caroline and says NO! No no no no! No, why why? And it's hard to find the right answer. Because in the grown-up world, no one houses their revenant first wife and their new partner under the same roof. Sandrine ought to retreat into her shell, apologise for the bother she has caused, apologise for existing, but no, she is the second woman, she too is carrying a child fathered by this man, her place is at his side, now. And so she stays where she is, says nothing, she has earned this seat at the table.

Mathias insists. Everyone tries to reason with him, the cop mutters to his colleague, I told you we should have come with the social worker. Sandrine cannot see what difference a social worker would make to the little boy's reaction. She rises, curls her fingers around the stems of the wine glasses and carries them, *gling, gling*, over to the dishwasher. Anne-Marie has already loaded the plates from the main course and Sandrine thinks, she really is a kind lady. She arranges the glasses in the top rack, lining them up with care. At her own apartment, she did the washing-up by hand and when she came here she was given endless lessons on how to load the machine so that it would wash everything properly, because if a thing's worth doing it's worth doing well. At the table, Mathias is whimpering uncontrollably now, and Sandrine hears his father's voice, slightly raised, That's enough, Mathias. Which is usually enough to send the boy racing straight up to his room, but today is no ordinary day and even the menace in his father's voice cannot quieten the boy. Sandrine makes another return trip to the kitchen, carrying the dessert plates. The cops have got up and are standing slightly apart from the group. The only people left at the table are Mathias, entangled as one body with Caroline, his grandparents, bending over him, remonstrating and reassuring him gently, and his father, of course, who clearly would have preferred things to turn out differently. When Sandrine enters the room for the third time, to take away the empty coffee cups, he turns to her, overwhelmed and unsure. Why not let him sleep at theirs tonight? She whispers the words very quietly, as she bends to slip her fingers through the narrow cup-handles, so that Mathias will not hear. She has no wish to fan the flames. Too late: Mathias has heard her though his sobs and cries out, begging, Yeeessss, yesss, pleeeeaase! It's unclear whether he is pleading with his father, his mother, or both of them, but Sandrine's attempt at discretion has failed. Mathias's father crosses his arms, uncrosses them, pinches the bridge of his nose, and says finally, OK, very good, but only for tonight, Mathias.

At the granting of this night of freedom, his son's wailing subsides, then stops altogether. A few more sobs, proof that this was not play-acting – as if anyone doubted that – but true despair. Mathias is trembling, thin and puny in his dragon T-shirt a couple of sizes too small, while Anne-Marie takes a napkin and wipes his cheeks, says, *Oh là là*, such misery! But everything's all right now, Mathias, it's all right… Now, if you're sleeping with us tonight, you'll need a change of clothes and your things for school tomorrow, how about going upstairs with your mama, to get everything ready?

The table is cleared. Caroline utters something like an apology. She says, I understand it's— that it's difficult for… For you. Both. She covers her dilemma. *Tu* or *vous*? How best to address the husband she doesn't remember? She turns her eyes to Sandrine. I don't want to destroy what the three of you have made. Just give me a chance to, to remember, OK? Then she gets to her feet and, unsure what to do, holds out her hand for him to shake. Their skins touch, and Sandrine sees something pass through Caroline, a start of surprise, no, more subtle, like a shiver of wind over a still lake, but so furtive, so quick that she decides she may have imagined it. Then Caroline holds out her hand to Sandrine, who does her best to fight the sinking unease invariably provoked by a stranger's gaze. The first woman looks at her keenly, as their fingers grip. They cannot help but look into one another's eyes, and so Sandrine tries to read the face before her, to understand, but there is nothing there, only Caroline's dark eyes that draw everything in. Sandrine has been letting her thoughts run away with her again. Anne-Marie says, We'll try to find a psychologist, so that we can all see where we're at. We must make sure Mathias is not traumatised further. Thank you... it's kind of you to let us have him tonight.

He composes his face, gets a grip, recovers his smile, says, Of course. We need to get organised. It's just that he's used to life without his mother, now. Caroline stares at him, her face as inscrutable as the photograph in the yellow frame. On the end of her arm, Mathias tugs and pulls. She turns and allows herself to be dragged away. Everyone stands awkwardly, waiting for them to come back downstairs with his things. Sandrine goes back to the kitchen, hesitates to start the dishwasher. In the sitting room, the awkwardness grows. He does not invite anyone to sit down while they wait.

The kid's place is here! His words roar like thunder, as soon as the sound of the cars pulling away has faded into the ordinary afternoon that continues outside their door. Sandrine is hand-washing the little cognac glasses she had taken out to serve with coffee, glasses brimming with goodwill, determined like her to give the impression that everything was perfectly normal. She jumps, startled by his unexpectedly loud voice. A glass slips and shatters, she feels a prick in her finger, and a trickle of blood appears along the bone. She reaches for the kitchen paper in its wall dispenser, improvises a bandage on her forefinger, the tip sticking out like a swaddled baby's head, all of which takes a few seconds – time enough for him to add, And that other stupid bitch, coming here, ordering everyone about! Where you should go, where you shouldn't go, it's not up to her! He draws nearer, visibly angry.

Sandrine thinks of the neighbours. The house is semi-detached, she closes the window. It's turning colder outside, anyway. The movement draws blood from her finger, a red stain spreads over the wad of coarse paper. She hopes it's not too deep, the last thing she needs is another trip to the hospital. She undoes the temporary bandage. He calms down immediately at the sight of the blood. I'm sorry, I'm sorry I shouted. Show me that.

The blood soothes him. He is transformed – a concerned, attentive nurse. He sits her down at the kitchen table and goes upstairs to look for the first-aid kit, dresses Sandrine's finger with deft, expert gestures. She wonders if this is the right time to tell him, but she doesn't want to do it any old how, she wants it to be— to be, she doesn't know, but meaningful at any rate, and he scared her just now, and that's spoilt everything and she thinks that the best thing is to wait for the test results. That's it, she wants to wait to be absolutely certain before telling him the news. That's it, she'll wait. And so she talks about something else, takes advantage of his tender mood, pacified by the cut, to say gently, You know, I don't see how you could have settled things otherwise. I mean, how you could refuse to let him go with his mother, for tonight at least. You said yourself, we're going to have to find ways to work this out, it's bound to be complicated.

He pulls the gauze too tight around her finger, he's irritated again. What's with the cod psychology? Suddenly you're the shrink-in-chief around here? All they can talk about is fucking psychologists, it's all nonsense if you ask me. No shrink alive is coming anywhere near my son to mess with his head!

Sandrine says Ouch! He's pulled the bandage too tight, they need to change the gauze, the cut is bleeding again. Again, at the sight of the blood, he softens, apologises profusely, kisses her wounded finger.

He puts away the bottle of disinfectant. She inspects her finger, the fresh, clean bandage. Did she say anything to you when you were in the car? The question is gently put. He puts the white gauze bandages in the bin. Sandrine wrinkles her nose. She'd prefer not to answer, prefer it if the question hadn't been asked, but it's there on the kitchen table now, between the first-aid bag and the fruit bowl. She told me she questioned you at the time of the disappearance. I told her I knew about that, that you'd told me.

Is that all?

She said you wouldn't let Caroline drive. That she took Mathias to school on foot. That was all.

And what did you say to that?

Nothing, my head was hurting, I just wanted her to be quiet.

He smiles. Sandrine has given the right answer. He places a hand on her shoulder, at the base of her neck, and sighs. He kneels beside her. His expression is very serious.

Listen to me, Sandrine. I… I've never spoken to you about this and I don't want Mathias to know. But she… She drank. She drank a lot. I didn't let her drive because I was scared there'd be— I was afraid for her safety, and for Mathias. Sandrine watches his face, he's close beside her, deadly serious. Do you understand? Sandrine nods automatically. They make things up, he adds. The cops, especially that one, but that's the truth of it, she drank. Caroline drank. She was here all day, drinking. I tried to help her as much as I could but I… I didn't know what to do. She would hide bottles all over the place, I couldn't keep up. Do you understand?

Sandrine nods again. It makes sense. He's right, that explains everything. The woman cop who tried to mess with her thoughts. It all makes sense. Suddenly, Sandrine's eyelids feel heavy, he sees them droop and flutter, says, Come and watch TV. You can finish this later.

The rest of the afternoon passes quietly. She curls against him on the sofa while, on the screen, cars hurtle around a Formula 1 racetrack, round and round. Usually, she would open a book, but not today. Today, it's enough for her to lie there, her head on his knee, warmed by the thought of the little bean growing, perhaps – definitely – in her belly. They are interrupted by a text from Anne-Marie that makes both their phones vibrate at once. He reads the messages: they got back OK, everything's going fine, thank you again. Sandrine daydreams and finally falls asleep. The doctor warned her that if she is pregnant, she'll doubtless feel tired; encouraged her to get the blood test done as soon as possible and meantime to eat whenever she's hungry and sleep as much as she can. The prescription is stowed at the bottom of her handbag, carefully inserted between the pages of a special buys leaflet she had picked up at the supermarket checkout, rolled into a tight tube so as not to get crumpled.

He wakes Sandrine up at 7 p.m. The news has taken the place of the cars, and he's beginning to feel hungry. There's some chicken and salad left, she prepares a big cold platter that she barely touches, still sluggish from her nap. When she has cleared everything away and turned on the dishwasher, she goes upstairs to take a shower.

She wants to feel very hot water this evening, the first to hint that the heat of summer may be at an end. Stepping out of the shower, she deliberately wipes the steam from the mirror with a broad sweep of her towel and looks at her breasts, her belly. She was right, nothing shows but something has changed. She places her hand on her sex, explores, slips her fingers between her labia, wonders how she will get a human being out through there, tells herself she isn't the first and that what will be, will be. She puts on leggings and a vest top, but not her usual nightwear, especially not the bra that digs into her now. She gets into bed, takes the book she has begun from the bedside table, reads one page, and falls fast asleep.

He shakes her awake, clearly alarmed. It's only half-past 9 and she's asleep already? She hasn't even emptied the dishwasher. She mumbles sleepily: At the hospital they told me it was due to tiredness, stress. That I need to sleep. Then she turns over onto her side, lets the book fall to the floor, and without even pausing to ask herself why she has told him a lie, Sandrine sinks down once more and sleeps like a root in winter.

8

THE ALARM RINGS for a long time before she manages to open her eyes. A minute goes by, then he slides his foot over to touch her calf, says, Your alarm.

He still has almost another hour to sleep. She pulls herself up, sits on the edge of the mattress, her feet touching the woven rag rug. It's Monday morning, she's exhausted, and then she remembers the little bean and gets to her feet, plodding heavily but light in her heart. She performs her cat's toilette, chooses her clothes. From the chest of drawers, she takes out things that are a little too big, she always has several sizes in reserve, never throws them away when she manages to lose a little weight, convinced that failure stalks her: not only will she never reach the ideal weight she calculated one day from the method in a magazine, but she will, inevitably, recover one day all the weight she has lost. She thinks about that word, 'recover'. It sounds like someone claiming what is rightfully theirs. Perhaps that's what it is, perhaps her broad, flat bottom, her pudgy stomach, are exactly what she needs, because since she's been living here she has put on weight, and he encourages her, asking for more bread at the table, full-fat cream on the pasta, and with all that she has made a little bean, despite the pill she swallows so carefully each morning. In the bathroom, when she has evened her skin tone and done her eyes, Sandrine stares at the pack she started this month, lying in wait in the medicine drawer. She punctures one of the tiny blisters and pops the pill out into the sink. It makes a tiny *tic* as it lands on the porcelain. She has never kept even one single secret from her man. Invariably, waves of uncertainty and guilt engulf her, so that even the tiniest pretence looms like a mountain. And that's without the little bean, whose existence he knows nothing about for the moment. But that's something different. It's not a lie, it's a surprise. She opens the fridge with a light, guiltless touch. Eat whatever you like, until your appointment with the gynaecologist, the doctor said. Never has Sandrine opened a fridge door without that feeling of shame, and guilt, in the hollow of her ribcage. Without hearing, far off in the distance, her father's voice that says, Look at that great, fat, stupid lump, she knows how to eat all right. But this morning, everything is different. She eats four radishes, half a pot of vanilla cream pudding, and one of the orange-flavoured biscuits she usually loathes. Then she goes back upstairs to clean her teeth, and leaves for work.

The drive to the office is uneventful, until her telephone interrupts the playlist to signal a quick-fire burst of messages. He's awake, and worried. On any other day, she would grab the phone and tap a reply, *On my way to work*, and if he persists, asks for further details, she gives her location: *Leaving the motorway. At the Valeyre intersection. Just passing the hypermarket*. But she will not touch her phone in the car today, out of the question, it's dangerous. What if something was to happen to her? Not to her, Sandrine, but to the mother of the little bean. At a stop sign, she shuts down her phone and tugs the lead from its socket with her right hand, then pulls away. She turns on the radio. When she parks outside work, there are three missed calls.

Sandrine kills the engine, then calls him back. He picks up instantly, yelling into his phone, Where the hell were you? Where are you?

'In the car, I was driving.' She senses something out of the ordinary in the voice hollering at the other end, something she cannot identify or explain. The last few days together have been so strange, their everyday routine familiar but distant, like a currency no longer in use. And the little bean will change everything, too. She can't wait to do the test, to know for sure, and then to find the right occasion, the perfect moment, to tell him. She has not the slightest doubt, but showing him the paper that will make it official seems like a good way to announce the wonderful news. A succession of joyful scenes unfolds before her eyes: the test results placed on the coffee table, or inside a card, with a teddy bear, a baby's bottle? The time is not now, over the phone, in a car park, at any rate. And there's a small part of her that enjoys the secret. She has something for herself alone. Something important. She strokes her stomach and smiles.

'Everything's fine, absolutely fine. My phone was in my bag, I didn't see it buzz. But I got to work OK. What about you? Did you get back to sleep? Are you OK?'

He tones it down slightly, perhaps she's reassured him.

'I need to be able to reach you, you know that.'

Yes, she knows, and if he cannot, his reaction is always precisely the same, as now. She was surprised by his acute, perennial anxiety, at first, but then she reminded herself that the first woman had disappeared, and she understood the root cause of his insistence. But nothing can encroach on her happiness this morning and she says, I'm sorry. I can't wait to see you tonight. Silence at the other end, then, You forgot the coffee, and it's true, she hadn't given it a thought, she had made her tisane and left the tuna-coffee in the fridge, hadn't touched the coffee machine. Oh, that sort of thing can happen, the doctor had told her, too. All sorts of things can happen, some women become short-sighted during pregnancy, and only then. Others find their noses get bigger. There are some, too, who spend six months being sick, so believe me, if the only problem is that the coffee smells of tuna, then all you need to do is steer clear of coffee and everything will be fine… And so Sandrine hadn't made the coffee, and he's right, she just very simply and completely forgot about it. She says again, I'm sorry, really, I'll make it up to you tonight, I'll make a rice pudding, just the way you like it, OK?

The day goes by, like any Monday, and everyone arrives at the office and says, How are you? That Monday feeling! At lunchtime, Sandrine goes out to buy a sandwich. Everyone stares as if a horn was growing out of her forehead: she who always, every lunchtime, gets out her Tupperware box of vegetables or lettuce leaves, and sits nibbling like some miserable rabbit, because she's watching her weight, and never leaves the break room. She says *Bon appétit!* to everybody and goes out to the bakery. But nothing appeals, apart from the big shortbread biscuits filled with jam. She buys one and eats two mouthfuls before putting it away in her bag, then stays where she is, sitting on a bench, enjoying the cool temperature, the pleasure of wearing a jacket and basking in a ray of sunshine that brightens her day without making her sweat. She takes out her book and finishes the chapter during which she fell sound asleep yesterday evening. She is just at the end of her break, slipping a bookmark into her book, when a man stops in front of her and says something, something unwarranted and brutish, the same sort of thing as usual, it's always much the same, and it always means much the same thing: You're out in the street without a man, and you're all mine. Sandrine says, Leave me alone, can't you see I'm pregnant? And the man apologises and moves away. It's as simple as that, and as miraculous, and as stupid, because in reality nothing is showing at all. But it works.

When she sits back down at her desk, Béatrice comes to see her and asks, Are you all right, Sandrine? But the true answer is too complicated and so Sandrine smiles and says, Yes, fine, how about you? It always works, people don't like to insist. Béatrice says, Fine, thanks. And goes back to her place.

The telephone buzzes a great deal over the course of the afternoon. He's had news from Anne-Marie: Mathias has gone to school, everything was fine, and when Caroline and Anne-Marie dropped him off in the morning he understood that last night was an exception, that the grown-ups are trying to find a solution, how best to get organised. She can go and fetch him as usual. What did she eat at lunchtime? What did she do this morning, and what's she doing now? She's leaving at 5 p.m., right? Sandrine reassures him, reassures him, reassures him. The days of silence had been so unbearable, symptoms of such profound disturbance, that today she almost delights in his never-ending concern. When her workday is over, before turning the key in the ignition and beginning the drive home, she lets him know, as usual, and he's happy. That's how you repair the damage done by the first woman: by giving yourself time to take a deep breath, and swallow. Everything will be fine. Taking time is what matters, the time to say, I'm on my way back now. What matters is Mathias, and the little bean.

Mathias sits quietly waiting for her, as usual, in the hallway at school. The young woman who oversees the after-school period smiles when she sees Sandrine and says, Well now, this one! Always so quiet, but we couldn't get him to stop talking today!

Sandrine tries to smile back, but it comes out slightly twisted. All the patient, unspoken care with which she had surrounded the boy had never brought him out of his habitual reserve. She swallows down her disappointment, because it's a mean, petty feeling and she really wants to be careful, to be even more careful than usual, because whatever she feels now, in her veins, is feeding the little bean, too. When Mathias reaches up to take her hand, there is no nastiness left in her at all. He talks a little, says he drew a picture after school, she asks if she can see it, and they stop to take the sheet of paper out of his school bag. It's another bird, huge, its beak bristling with teeth, and she asks, But why do you draw birds with teeth all the time, Mathias? And he says, as if it was obvious, Because then they can fight, and get away. And he tucks the picture safely out of sight, to give to his mama.

So did you have a nice time? At Nini and Papi's? Sandrine asks, attaching her seatbelt, and in the rear-view mirror Mathias nods his head vigorously. He says that Picasso the mongrel dog likes Caroline a lot, that she let Mathias sleep with Picasso in his bedroom, that the dog isn't allowed up onto the bed but that as soon as the grown-ups leave the room, of course he lies on the duvet, on Mathias's legs, and Mathias goes to sleep feeling very happy and it's like his legs are paralysed. Sandrine listens to this enthusiastic account with some surprise. Of course, Mathias is still quieter than children who chatter and trill and who you can hear from a long way off, but he tells Sandrine more in these few minutes, on the car journey home, than in all the months they have spent together.

Back at the house he falls silent once more, asks to go upstairs to his room. Sandrine climbs the stairs a few minutes later. Mathias is carefully stacking his favourite books on his bedside table and when he sees Sandrine watching him, he huddles like a tortoise in its shell, becomes the same Mathias as every other day, timid and just a little sly, with his silences and his sidelong glances. She asks what he's doing, and he whispers at last that it's in case he goes to live at Papi and Nini's, with Mama. Then he bites his lip and begs her, But you mustn't say so, promise you won't say so? Sandrine nods, flattered by his show of trust, though she doesn't dare tell Mathias that very probably, things will not work out like that, at least not straightaway. Given the way his father reacted on Sunday evening. She doesn't explain this to the boy. One thing at a time. Instead she says, If you like, but it's probably best if you put them in a special bag. So that everything stays tidy. She pulls the door to, behind her, without closing it completely, giving him some of the privacy he cherishes, by way of thanks, a virtuous circle. And she goes off to fold the pile of clean laundry she's carrying, then tidy it away in the chest of drawers in the bedroom.

She has just put the trunks in the drawer when she hears the car pull up outside. She goes downstairs, her cheeks suddenly pink with impatience, seized with an urge to tell him. Never mind about the test. She will tell him today. Perhaps not right this second, but this evening, she'll tell him. Perhaps she'll serve them an *apéritif*, and when he asks what they're celebrating... She treads firmly on the creaky step, pays no attention. She places a hand on her belly. No, no *apéritif*. She'll tell him now.

He has already closed the front door behind him, dropped his briefcase on the floor, and is standing with his nose pressed against the little glass window in the upper part of the door. He doesn't turn to look at Sandrine, just mutters his greeting: Filthy bitch.

She freezes at the bottom of the stairs. He says it again, Stupid bitch, she stuck it out for weeks last time! *Fuck.* Parked outside the house in that clapped-out piece of junk for months on end.

At least he's not talking about me, thinks Sandrine, but then, who? She stands there, stupidly, then moves towards him, one hand on her belly, asking herself what he's talking about. When he turns to face her at last, he looks her up and down with a reproachful air and says, You've put on weight again.

Sandrine is twelve years old. He speaks the words and straight-away she is twelve years old. Too fat, her bottom too big. Her body spilling over – the enemy – but an enemy that can make her invisible, keep her safe. The men in the street, who insult her and touch her. Her head sunk into her shoulders. He loves her as she is, she knows that, she knows, he always tells her. He's the one who serves her more cheese, forbids her from eating the low-fat kind, but sometimes, occasionally, he makes comments about her weight, and today is one of those days. She lowers her head. She doesn't know how to respond, she never knows how to respond, and in any case when he's like this it's best to say nothing at all. He adds, And would it kill you to wear something differ-ent for once? It's true, she does always dress the same way, he's right. She concentrates on her feet, counts the floor tiles within her field of vision, waits for it to pass. I bought you a shirt, I buy you clothes, but no, you prefer your own things, so you can go out and parade yourself, is that it? Six, seven, eight floor tiles. She doesn't understand what she is being accused of: dressing too plainly, or too much the same, or too much with clothes he hasn't bought for her himself, but she's knows there's no point even trying to ask the question. Nine, ten, eleven. The doorbell rings and Sandrine addresses a silent 'thank you' to the person outside, whoever it is.

It's the woman cop. That's who he was talking about. She's the piece of grit irritating their return to normality, she's the one who's got him so worked up. He's right, the woman's a stupid bitch, she's ruined their evening. And she doesn't even try to come inside this time, no, the intruder stands outside on the doorstep, one elbow propped up high against the brickwork, next to the doorbell, scratching the top of her head and running her fingers through her hair. She's on the lookout, alert and spry. There's another word Sandrine doesn't use every day: the woman cop looks spry. Too much at ease, provocative. She says Oh, I just came by to see how things are going. Hm? The kid, all that. Then she pokes her head in through the door and says solemnly, politely, Good evening Sandrine. I hope you're all right?

Sandrine gives no answer. He has turned around and stares fixedly at her, like the policewoman, and she senses that she must show hostility, back him up, show him she's on his side. The woman cop gives a little nod of the head, as if letting it go, and says, I understand. Then she asks, And the boy, is he here? I called in at the Marquezes' apartment, they said you'd taken him back tonight.

He keeps calm. His hand tightens on the door handle, his knuckles are white, but he keeps calm and asks Sandrine, in a detached voice, Can you ask him to come down? And the order is called back up the stairs. Mathias appears, treading lightly. He stops on the last step, bends forward, sees the policewoman.

She asks, So you slept at your grandma and grandad's, huh? He nods. Was that nice? Another nod. Good, well I won't keep you any longer, then. I was just passing.

She walks back to her car but doesn't start the engine. And he stays behind the door, watching her. They stay like that for a long time. He says nothing.

'Hasn't that fucking woman got anything better to do?' says Sandrine, almost an hour later, as she puts their dinner on the table. He doesn't like her to be vulgar, but she's on his side, it's a proof of her support, and that's the most important thing. He leaves his post at the front door, at last, clasps her waist as he walks by, and kisses her. He heard what she said, the misplaced expression of loyalty, and he presses her to him. She rests her head against his shoulder, there's nothing more they need to say, she is with him, he's here with her, the weight pressing down on her shoulders eases a little. He releases her, sits down and says, It smells good.

They call Mathias.

So how was it? he asks his son. Mathias says nothing, the question is asked a second time. Finally he whispers, It was nice, we ate chocolate ice cream. And your mother, what did she say to you, eh? Mathias, look at me. What did your mother say? Does she remember anything now? What does she remember?

Asking Mathias to 'look at me' is like asking a fish to walk. He's so timid, always averting his gaze from the grown-ups, slippery as water. He tries, forces himself. LOOK AT ME. The words ring louder in the kitchen, where the atmosphere is tense now. This is the woman cop's fault, Sandrine tells herself. It's her fault, another evening ruined. She asks, Do you want some more ratatouille? And he hollers, KEEP OUT OF THIS, THIS IS NOTHING TO DO WITH YOU!

This is the woman cop's fault, her fault, everything was fine, everything would have been all right. He's shouting at her in front of Mathias, and Sandrine is angry with herself that the little boy should see that. It's the first thing that crosses her mind after a moment's blank, a burning flash of white in which she focusses her entire self on sitting motionless, being invisible, and her memories: lingering memories of a tiny creature, naked and vulnerable, this is how a mouse feels under the gaze of a cat. She hates it when she freezes in terror like this, but she cannot help it, she is a guilty little girl all over again. Mathias whispers something they cannot understand. He insists, What does she remember, huh? You spent the evening with her, she must have spoken to you. The boy's impossible! MATHIAS, LOOK AT ME. The little boy begins to cry, says he doesn't know, that she didn't say anything. Finally, his father understands and says, She doesn't even remember *you*, is that it? That's it. Huh.

Mathias is shocked into looking up, his eyes brimming with tears. He looks at his father.

'No one ever talks straight to this boy. Me, I'm talking to you like a man, Mathias, so you listen to me: your mother doesn't remember you and men don't cry.'

The little boy knows what 'men don't cry' means. He stifles his sobs. Sandrine has seen him do this before, it's like watching an earthquake, the opening of a great rift. Mathias rips something open – an act of violence – and hides his tears deep inside. Each time, it's like watching him swallow his own self. Under the table, Sandrine places a hand on her belly and tells herself No, not tonight. The little bean will stay hidden a while longer. There's no hurry.

9

THERE IS NO HURRY for the next several days: he is irritable and sometimes says nasty, unkind things. The days are unexceptional, but in the evenings everything is sour, and dangerous. He comes home seething with rage. The woman cop is parked out on the road each evening. She shows up just before he gets back and leaves late, not always at the same time. Sandrine wonders why she comes. Can't she see that she's ruining everything? Can't she see that her presence is the source of all this anger? If they could have a quiet evening, the three of them, she could tell him about the little bean. She could—they could… it would, she doesn't know. Things would be different, better. The week drags on for years.

On Thursday evening, she is overcome with nausea and struggles to stay at the table, faced with a plate of mashed potato and its unbearable, bitter smell that reaches her in waves. She is saved by a call on the house phone, trilling its announcement of bad news. He says, What, again?! and gets up to answer. With his back turned as he walks towards the phone, Sandrine seizes the moment to empty her plate into the sink with a sweep of her hand, then sits down again quickly. She wipes her dirty hand on a piece of kitchen paper and smiles at Mathias.

With an empty plate in front of her, she can breathe better. When he returns to the table, she feels just a little more comfortable. That was Anne-Marie, he says. They're coming on Saturday.

He doesn't say so, but she gathers that he had no choice in the matter, and silently she tells her belly, once again, Not this evening. He doesn't like it when visits, and times, are imposed on him in his own house. He told Sandrine, one evening. He said, At any rate, the house is in my name, this is my place. Like a goblin in a fairy tale, terrified his treasure will be stolen. Sandrine knows he doesn't have to agree to the visit, but he's doing what's required of him, because he's a man of principle. Because how would it look otherwise, huh?

Mathias knocks his glass against his plate. Not on purpose, but the shiver of joy is the only outward sign that he has heard his father, who clenches his jaw and says, Careful, Mathias. Will they have lunch with us? Sandrine asks. He snaps back, We're not running a restaurant, what do they think? The social worker's coming too, anyway, and God knows who else. And Sandrine understands: the cops. They will be there, again. That evening, in bed, he takes her roughly, as if he senses that something in her body has changed, as if he wanted to push her into telling him, into revealing the secret, but she holds back because now is not the right time, not the right way. She is scared, a little, afterwards, when she goes to the toilet and wipes herself and sees blood. But after the third wipe of her hand, holding the tissue that she scrutinises carefully, she calms down. Nothing unusual, nothing dangerous. She repeats the words to herself before falling asleep, tells herself that she's seeing the gynaecologist tomorrow, anyhow.

The surgery is white with touches of mauve. The gynaecologist is Black, and dressed with touches of mauve. The place smells of eucalyptus.

She had picked the number at random, thought that 'Claude' would be a man. She hasn't been to the doctor for a while – apart from the hospital trip. The one she went to see when her man insisted she take the pill, because it's so much easier, was supercilious and cold. Now that she's moved in with Mathias and his father, she gets the old prescription renewed at the pharmacy. The pharmacist is supercilious and cold, too. He addresses her as if she's stupid, she hates their brief exchanges. But it's just an awkward, unpleasant moment to be endured, and then she's all set for another few months. She feels guilty that she hasn't gone back to the first, dark-haired, bespectacled doctor, but she tells herself that if Mathias's father finds out, she can reason she needs someone close to her work. She searched on her office computer, erased her history, small, secretive acts that feel like the preparations for a big surprise, something huge. At the testing lab, she asks for the blood to be taken from her leg, but they refuse. And so she takes care to get rid of the little pad of cotton wool and hide the tiny bruise in the crook of her elbow, before going home that evening. She is lucky, the injection was skilfully done, there's almost nothing to see now.

The doctor with the deceptive first name comes to find Sandrine in the waiting room. Her hair is loose, and Sandrine – who hates her own lank, stringy, tow-coloured hair – looks enviously at the cloud-halo that frames the doctor's face, like a million tiny black butterflies.

Sandrine sits down and the doctor smiles and says, So! As if they know one another but haven't met for a long time. As if she is burning with curiosity to hear everything Sandrine has to tell. Sandrine doesn't know how to answer, she was never the brightest spark. She takes the lab results, freshly printed at work, from out of her bag.

OK, says the doctor, reading the sheet. And so what do you think? Sandrine doesn't understand. Opposite her, the woman is still smiling. I mean, you're six weeks pregnant. Is that good news, or a problem?

Sandrine stammers. She thought the answer would burst out of its own accord but for some unknown reason, she cannot form the words, and finally, a rather timid, Oh, but yes, yes, I'm pleased... finds its way out. Opposite her, the smile is attentive now. Do you want to tell me a little bit about it? Is there a father? How are things, exactly?

Sandrine giggles. Of course there's a father. For a moment, she pictures herself as the Virgin with Child. An immaculate conception. What a question, there's always a father, and her own father knew what he thought about the sluts who ended up all by themselves with their brats. Look at that, Sandrine, fallen women we called them in my day, not to say whores. They're just common sluts. Sluts and trollops. A woman needs a man, not to be off out like that, wherever they please. She shudders, pushes the memory away, wonders why her father keeps wandering into her thoughts lately, he and her mother, when she had shut them carefully away in a tightly closed box. She excuses herself with a small wave of the hand, says I'm sorry, sometimes I think all this is making me a bit stupid. Yes, yes, there's a father.

'You're not stupid,' says the smile. 'You're experiencing something that can be a major upheaval, of course you're confused. Well. Does he know?'

'Not yet.'

'OK.'

'But it's so recent, that's why. I only found out on Sunday. Oh, and there's this...'

'Is this for me?'

'It's a letter. A letter from the emergency service at the hospital. She told me... she told me... well, she gave me a letter.'

The doctor reads, says OK… I see, OK.

The lady places the letter flat on the desk, with the test results, in front of her. Sandrine can't think of her any other way, she's 'the lady'. The doctor she used to see never did that, he never stayed sitting at his desk with an open, receptive expression, hands folded calmly in front of him, waiting for her to tell him what was the matter. With him, she always had to get undressed, Yes, down to your birthday suit, eh? Quicker this way, ah, is that cold? Well it won't take a minute, lie still, don't wince, no, lie still, no, no, this doesn't hurt, there we are, all over, you can put your clothes back on now. Often, there were questions Sandrine wanted to ask but didn't dare. Here, she can and she would dare to ask them but it's all so unexpected that they slip away, like lizards scuttling for cover beneath a stone. The lady says, How are you feeling, any tiredness? Nausea? And Sandrine says, Fine. Because it's true, she feels all right, and since the emergency doctor told her 'Get all the sleep you need', she slips guiltlessly away each night, careful only to time herself so that the dishwasher doesn't finish its cycle too late. The lady asks her some more questions, about her family history. Sandrine stares at her stupidly, her family is Mathias and his father, not the two bad people who suffered her embarrassing presence until she found the courage to leave, and so she doesn't know. She remembers that one day her father told her, You gave us enough blood, sweat and tears when you were born, and all for what, just look at you, but she doesn't tell the doctor this, an insult is not useful information, and opposite her the woman sits up so straight, her gestures so free of awkwardness or hesitation that Sandrine envies her, has no desire to report the humiliating exchange, not for anything. All this has taken a fair amount of time and Sandrine is surprised that she hasn't been shown out of the surgery. Finally, in a flash, she thinks, But yes of course, stupid cow, you almost forgot, you really are, really so— poor cow, and then she stops herself because with the little bean she cannot think or say such things any more. Sandrine says, Yes, I wanted to ask you, I had a little bit of bleeding the other day, is that a problem for the baby? The lady – no, not the lady, Sandrine repeats to herself, the doctor, the gynaecologist – says, Oh, really? What kind of bleeding? Could you feel it? How much was there, for example, compared with your period? Sandrine shakes her head, says No, nothing you could see really, just a few drops.

'Did it flow like your period, when you were on the toilet, or did you see it on your underwear?' The exchange continues. Sandrine has never described her bleeding in such detail. One day she had wanted to asked the grand, bespectacled consultant why she always bled a great deal on the fourth day of her period, and then almost nothing on the fifth, and then lots more again on the sixth, and his expression had been indifferent and slightly disgusted, as if she had offended him with her revolting questions, in his fine surgery with the paintings on the wall.

You might get a small amount of bleeding, from time to time, the doctor reassures her. If you'd like to lie down on the trolley, I'm going to examine you. She doesn't say anything about getting undressed. Sandrine is unsure what to do. She asks, Just like that, with my clothes on? And the gynaecologist, who is already on her feet and unrolling the white paper over the trolley, says, Yes, we're just going to lift your blouse up a little if that's OK.

Before placing her hands on Sandrine's belly, the doctor rubs them one against the other. My hands are always a bit cold otherwise, she explains, and Sandrine feels calm. She has always hated doctors and examinations, even before the old man and her breasts and the sinusitis. She dreads the eyes poring over her body, the judgements. But the woman doctor tells her what she's about to do, she explains, asks, touches and presses her gently, and Sandrine remains present. There is no need to seek refuge in some far distant place, as she does usually, when she is touched.

So, the woman says, very calmly, pointing to an illustrated poster on the wall beyond Sandrine's feet. At this stage, the embryo has developed to look like this. At the tip of her finger, Sandrine sees it: the little bean. I don't think there's anything the matter at the moment. So this is what we'll do: I'm going to prescribe some additional tests for you, OK? We'll check your blood sugar, iron, that sort of thing. And we need to arrange your first scan, too. And then you'll come back and see me and we'll take everything one step at a time, how does that sound?

Sandrine nods, relieved not to need any further examinations for now, relieved to be told that there's nothing the matter. But another worry tightens her stomach: the price. The grand consultant is expensive, her man likes her to see an expensive doctor in a smart surgery, he likes people to know he's taking good care of her. But what if the woman doctor is the same price and she has to come and see her every week? She hadn't thought to check the price per consultation in the waiting room, and she panics now, breaks a sweat, hopes she has enough cash. She buttons up her trousers, and her stomach ties itself in knots, and the doctor chats amiably, It's quite normal to feel tired during the first few months, you need to adjust, the body tells us what it needs and we must listen, hm? Finally, she announces a very low fee, five or seven times lower than the grand consultant with the cold hands, and Sandrine gives a small giggle of astonished relief.

The doctor is surprised and asks if she has said something funny. No, no, it's just that my partner insists I see a consultant who charges a hundred and twenty per visit so I was— I was afraid that… It's the doctor's turn to laugh now, to say Oh no, we're not like that here, this is a community surgery, we charge the standard rate... Do you have your medical card?

Sandrine hesitates. I forgot it. Ah, says the gynaecologist facing her... In that case the registration process will take a little longer, we'll have to send off a form and... it'll be a little more expensive, but Sandrine shrugs. Even if it's more expensive, it's still cheaper than before, and she is still relieved.

The gynaecologist prints off a consultation sheet, it takes a few moments, the printer is out of paper, she types a few words on her keyboard and says casually, But you know, whether you choose a male or a female doctor, it's an important decision. You'll find you have a great many questions during your pregnancy, and some scary moments, too, no doubt... If you want me to see you throughout, you must trust me.

She looks Sandrine in the eye and says very kindly, Can you trust me?

Sandrine looks away, in this moment she perfectly understands Mathias, who dreads being spoken to or looked at directly. She looks at the woman's hands, large and capable, at her neat oval nails, their lovely, creamy colour, and says Yes, of course. And she hopes that the lady isn't going to press her advantage and ask still more questions.

He does not come home at the usual time, and she's worried. Outside on the road, the woman cop is there, right on time. But not the rumble of his engine. Finally, she gets a text. He's having dinner with Christian. She gives Mathias the third toasted sandwich, going cold on its plate. The bread is a little dry after its second visit to the oven, but Mathias devours it hungrily. They eat in front of the TV like a couple of children up to no good, and stumble by chance on a repeat of the documentary they were watching last

Saturday; they munch their food and watch the cassowary birds flying among the trees in the rainforest. Mathias is happy and so Sandrine is happy too. There's no school tomorrow, she lets him watch the documentary through to the end and then they go upstairs to brush their teeth together; they have a competition to see who can make the most froth.

She tucks the little boy into bed and he says, So, is my mama coming tomorrow? Sandrine says Yes. And she tries to master the stab of jealousy that pricks her ribs when Mathias says 'mama'.

'Is she going to remember… more new things?' he asks, and of course what he wants to know is whether she will remember *him*.

Sandrine says, You know, Mathias, the doctors said we will have to be very patient but there's something *you* mustn't forget. It's that she came back because they told her she had a little boy. She came back for you. He is soothed by her words, gives a smile full of missing milk teeth, and curls up in a ball under his duvet.

She leaves the door ajar and lingers in the corridor for a moment, phone in hand. He hasn't sent another text, it's unusual for him to stay out like this, though it happens, of course, from time to time, for his work. But mostly, he's out during the day on weekends, for his tennis, or lunch appointments, because he likes to spend the evenings at home, with her, with them both.

She walks into the bedroom with the red shelves, where the first woman did her sewing and kept her books. She has taken over some of the shelves, but cannot quite make this room, this space apart, her own. Sometimes, she even feels a slight shiver when she steps inside, like a cold breath on the nape of her neck. But she doesn't believe in ghosts, and anyway, Caroline isn't dead any more.

Sandrine moves across to the window: outside, across the cul-de-sac, the woman cop is sitting in her car. What is the matter with that woman? she thinks. She should take care of her own life, if she has one. And then Sandrine thinks that yes, perhaps the woman cop has children, and yet she stays here rather than be with them, and the thought makes her feel sorry.

She walks all the way around the room. Beside the table with the sewing machine, there is a very big, very tall, round basket, with no handles and no lid. She looks at the fabrics inside. She never learnt how to sew but he insisted she keep the machine and the offcuts because he thinks she'll learn one day. She thinks there may be a piece with a pretty pattern that she could use to make something simple, perhaps a bib, she ought to be able to stitch one quite easily, or just cut out a bib shape, for when she tells him the news. Yes, that would be nice, that would be a good idea.

She wants to lift up the basket but it's heavier than she expected, and she drops it straightaway; the woman doctor told her she shouldn't lift anything heavy. Instead, she sits down beside it, on the floor, and takes out the pieces of fabric, one by one. Almost without thinking, she sorts them into different piles, plain, and patterned, and white. There are some pretty motifs, she recognises one with little hot-air balloons in red and blue. Mathias had a pair of pyjamas with that design, he's wearing them in one of the photos she saw in his bedroom the other day. One of the pictures he took from the albums in the garage. There are pieces of wool cloth, too, heavier and stiffer, and then, about two-thirds of the way down, a sort of quilted, yellow fabric folded into a square that she lifts out with one hand before realising there's something odd about it, something tucked inside. A piece of board, perhaps? She brings her hand and the fabric down onto her lap to inspect it, to feel it. There's something hidden between the yellow fabric and the synthetic foam backing.

139

She turns the fabric over. There are a few stitches to rip open, and the backing will reveal its secret.

Passports. Two passports. One for Mathias, another for Caroline. Both issued on the same date, a few weeks before the day on which the first woman disappeared. Sandrine sits cross-legged, surrounded by the piles of fabric, holding the two small booklets in her hand. She herself has no passport, she's never travelled far enough to need one, never travelled at all, in fact. She opens them and looks inside. Both are spotless and unused, still stiff, she can scarcely prise them open to leaf through the pages. In the photographs, Mathias is visibly younger and Caroline is very serious, two pairs of dark eyes staring fixedly at her.

She doesn't know what to do. She doesn't know what to do with these two passports, warming slowly in her grasp. First, she gets to her feet, carefully, and glances out through the Velux window. The woman cop is still there. Sandrine turns, glances around the bedroom. This is Caroline's room, her shelves, her boxes. It's clean and tidy, but now with two concealed passports in her hand, Sandrine realises the room is full of hiding places. Caroline hid things. Caroline was hiding things. Sandrine thinks again about Caroline's gesture, the way she opened the cupboard under the sink so naturally, automatically, to fetch the hand towel. Caroline hides things.

She hears the sound of an engine outside, and when she looks out of the window once more, the woman cop's car has disappeared at last. Sandrine feels no sense of relief. In her hand, the passports feel like lead weights. What to do with this, what can she do that will not set another apocalypse in motion? Another engine revs out on the road. It's him. He must have watched the policewoman leave, perhaps from the entrance to the football pitch that forms another cul-de-sac on the way into the housing estate. His return so soon after her departure is no accident. Sandrine stares around her in panic. She is lost, hesitates, and finally she slips the passports back inside the yellow quilting and puts them back in the basket. If he asks, she'll say she hadn't taken that piece out yet, hadn't felt anything, hadn't seen anything. She takes one of the other piles of fabrics and puts it on top of the quilted square, then stands stock-still, to listen.

He is parking the car, and there is a longer interval than usual before the sound of the keys in the door, the grunt he always gives as he bends down to take off his shoes. A little more weight in the tread of his feet up the stairs. He stops to open Mathias's bedroom door wide, then continues down the corridor to Caroline's room. His eyes are red and Sandrine catches a sharp, acid smell on his breath. He has been drinking.

What're you doing? he asks, and there's a hint of reproach in his voice. Again. She doesn't know what she's done wrong. He always says she should take up sewing, or knit, that she should tidy up, that she should give up work. He ought to be pleased to find her rummaging through the fabrics, but not, apparently, in the right way, at the right time, and she tells herself once again, Not tonight, my little bean, breathing slowly and calmly so that he will not see something is wrong, that she has found a secret, that Caroline is lying, that Caroline told lies. She says, You can see what I'm doing, I'm sorting out the fabrics, I thought it would be a good idea if I made some new curtains for the sitting room, so I was looking to see what there is. She's played her trump card – he likes everything to be neat and tidy, it soothes his anxieties, plays to his project to keep Sandrine at home with him, attending to him. He says, Yesshure 'fyou like. He's very drunk. She wonders if she's ever seen him quite so drunk. Probably not. He likes to stay in control, so much so that he would find the approximations

141

and confusion that come with being dead drunk completely unbearable. She wonders why he's been drinking but doesn't ask, she simply says, I'll just finish putting this away, I won't get it all out tonight, I'll come along in a minute. He leaves the room. He drove home drunk while a policewoman has been staking out his house every night for a week. As if he were asking for trouble. What was he after? Perhaps just a moment to do exactly whatever he wants. The first woman has landed like a bombshell in his life, too. He, too, has had to put up with an invasion – his parents-in-law, the dead woman's return – and been unable to say or do anything. Perhaps, in his place, Sandrine would drink too much. She tidies the room. The secret is perfectly concealed in the yellow quilting. And she goes to find him. He is snoring, fast asleep, in his trunks, pyjama bottoms and socks, his clothes in a pile at the foot of the bed.

She picks everything up, folds it away, gets in beside him. He doesn't move. She falls asleep.

In the middle of the night he wakes up, turns on the light, goes to the bathroom next door and drinks noisily, like a thirsty animal, from the tap. She hears him, half asleep, but doesn't open her eyes. The lady said, Listen to your body, and her body is sleepy. She pulls the duvet up over her face. She's a diligent pupil, completing her assignment.

10

SATURDAY IS ODDLY just like the previous Saturday: waking up while he sleeps; breakfast for just the two of them, Sandrine and Mathias, who quivers with impatience. He asks, Will I go and sleep at Papi and Nini's again tonight, with Mama? And Sandrine says, I don't know, Mathias, it will depend on your father. The little boy snaps shut again. She smiles and wants to say something to reassure him, but stops herself. It's not her decision, and his father seems so raw these days, so lost, that she's afraid to say anything that means Mathias might be disappointed. She suggests they make biscuits, because everyone is coming at coffee-time, just after lunch.

She doesn't let Mathias mix the ingredients, his father doesn't like to see him at work in the kitchen, but she gives him a round-ended knife with which to cut the shapes in the rolled-out pastry. Handling a knife is all right, that's different, it's not women's work. The biscuits are in the oven when he comes downstairs, treading heavily. He has showered and dressed. She sees the redness in his eyes, but that's because she knows him off by heart. To anyone else, she's quite certain he looks exactly as he does every morning. He asks for aspirin and a glass of water, asks Mathias, who has set his school books out in front of him, if he's doing his homework. The little boy nods and waits. Questions like these never come alone, but in volleys, quick-fire and precise. For a time, Sandrine had thought he took no interest in his son's schoolwork, but she could not have more mistaken. He expects Mathias to do well, that's different. That goes without saying, that's the bare minimum, there is no need to check on it every day. This morning, he sits down beside Mathias at the kitchen table and talks to him gently, takes an interest, looks through his exercise books, even his drawing book. Mathias completes the preset exercises with great care, but his free, creative work is all, still, those strange birds with razor-sharp beaks who spread their wings right across the page. He congratulates Mathias, compliments him, then suggests they go and play football in the garden. Normally, this time on a Saturday is set aside for fine-tuning the silhouettes of the box trees, the height of the grass. But not this morning.

Sandrine listens as they play ball, in the background, while she busies herself in the utility room. She knows he would like a livelier, more capable, confident son, a man's boy. When he plays with Mathias it always ends badly, in disappointment with the little boy who shows no aggression, no drive, who never tries to tackle or score points off a trick shot. He wants to encourage him in sport, where the winning counts, though the urge to annihilate an opponent, humiliate the loser, seems quite alien to Mathias. But this morning his father is patient, and Sandrine hears Mathias cheep with laughter once or twice, through the open patio door. The weather is still warm enough to air the house, and this ordinary, happy morning soothes her spirits.

They eat lunch all together on the terrace. Mathias dips his shortbread biscuits in the chocolate cream pudding that Sandrine doesn't feel like eating, and the peaceful silence is interrupted only by the boy's contented slurps and swallows. His father stares at the garden. She's afraid he'll find something that's not right, a weed, something out of place, something that will ruin this moment of peace, a moment she has longed for since they saw the first woman on the television screen, two long weeks ago. She places her hand on her belly, tells herself now would be a good time, but the sound of a car engine is heard out on the road, and he stiffens straightaway.

The cops enter first, ahead of the parents and the first woman, and a stranger who steps inside and makes no attempt to disguise her inspection of the sofa, the kitchen table, the chairs, the book-case, everything. It takes Sandrine a moment to work out who she is, some kind of social worker, perhaps. The woman shakes her hand, her grip is formal and cold.

'Doctor Benassa,' she says. And Sandrine thinks, Doctor of what? but doesn't dare ask. Doctor like a medical doctor? Why has the first woman come with a doctor?

He ushers everyone inside, his voice is bright and cheery, he's making an effort and Sandrine knows it. He says, Please, sit down! Then looks at Sandrine with a slightly surprised expression and says, Coffee? She says, Sorry! and heads for the kitchen. Mathias is already on the sofa, glued to his mother, who seems a little less hesitant than before.

Sandrine makes the coffee and tells herself that tonight is the night when she will tell him about the little bean. This evening. His manner is a little forced, but he seems to be trying to put on a good show, perhaps it will be all right. In the sitting room, it turns out the doctor is a psychiatrist, one of the handful who work with the police on occasion. She's going to help Caroline a little, until she finds someone who can take her forward over the longer term. She says they will explore various avenues together, including hypnosis, but above all, Caroline needs to spend time in familiar settings. He says, Yes of course, I understand. Sandrine hears the absolute silence that follows, and she turns to face the sitting room. She can half-see his face, his amiable expression, the thin blade of his smile and the gleam of a canine tooth. And sitting opposite him, the woman cop, the one who sat guard every night that week, the one he called a bitch under his breath, and who opens her eyes wide in surprise now. I want whatever's the best for Mathias, he adds. I think we can agree, my son is the top priority in all this. The little boy is perched on the sofa. Beside him, Caroline strokes the back of his hand with her thumb, the hand he has slipped into hers. And their two pairs of dark, unfathomable eyes remind Sandrine of the passports hidden in the quilted fabric in the red bedroom. She brings the coffee tray through and the woman cop says, Thank you so much, Sandrine, with an open smile, and Sandrine wonders why this woman keeps tossing her smiles and looks, like lengths of tow rope, while her features morph into a hard stare, almost a grimace, her mouth set in an expression of cold neutrality, every time she addresses Mathias's father. While she watches them each evening. While she ruins their life. This room is full of pretence, she realises. All the grown-ups telling lies. The only person who doesn't lie is Mathias. He doesn't talk enough to tell outright lies, but even he is pretending, hiding something. She thinks, for a second, *You should just take the kid and go*, a thought that comes out of nowhere, and which she doesn't really understand. Why would she leave when her man loves her, wants her, why would she leave when she's about to start a family, when she *is* a family, why would she leave the thing she's longed for all this time? It's the pregnancy, she tells herself, it's knocking her off course. It's perfectly normal, the hormones, obviously. That's it. She remembers he told her one day that during pregnancy, women's brains shrink by up to ten per cent. And then he had laughed and said, Well, for starters… and then she was cross and he said, Oh, come on! And she had forced a smile because she knew that he would be cross, too, at her mock outrage. Besides which, he had been talking about someone else, about Christian's wife, who'd been completely useless for weeks after their last kid was born, just whimpering and staying in bed, until finally she cut her hair very short all over and demanded a divorce. He often talked to her about Christian's wife, a ball-breaker who was never happy, but Sandrine had never met her and was very unlikely to, now. He always spoke of Christian in pitying tones, perhaps even with a hint of scorn: no man whose wife walks out on him can call himself a man. She has no opinion about Christian himself. When he invites his friends for dinner, she's too busy making sure everything is all right; she knows he's cleverer than her, better educated, that he has a more important job, above all she tries not to be an embarrassment to him. And then one evening, Christian had offered her a cigarette and she had accepted, just like that. She had drunk a couple of glasses of wine and suddenly, the idea of herself as one of those women who blow smoke so elegantly on a warm summer night had seemed unexpectedly seductive. Like a theatrical improvisation, she had played the role of the new woman, a little younger than the first. She had felt sexy, singled out, but he hadn't liked it and later, when everyone had gone, he had thrown a fit of rage, raised his voice – no, shouted. He'd shouted so loud that she was afraid Mathias would wake up. She never drinks now but he still mentions it from time to time. She catches him watching her attentively when he says, I'm going to knock a few balls about with Christian, as if the name was a magic word that could spark a reaction in her, as if he was exposing something, when the only thing she and Christian had shared, once and for all, almost two years ago now, were a few dozen Hellos and, on that evening in particular, a 'Would you like a light?' and 'What a lovely evening.'

147

'Yes, and it rained just before you got here, so the lavender's smelling lovely.'

'Ah, so it is, I was wondering what that gorgeous scent was.'

There she goes again, her mind wandering off to unexpected places. He's absolutely right, pregnant women are far more stupid. Meanwhile, the woman cop says, Ah, good, very good, in a thoughtful, doubtful way, and her man's smile widens still further, broad and sincere, he's hooked her with his show of goodwill and Sandrine can see this has reassured him, calmed him down, that he feels at home once more, and in control of events.

Caroline makes a tour of every room in the house with the psychiatrist, and Mathias hanging on to her hand. His father goes with them. For the moment, no one has said anything in front of Sandrine about what will happen on that score. Will they get divorced? Is the marriage annulled, or upheld? She doesn't know. She hasn't dared ask, it would seem so selfish, and he's the one who needs her here, to support him, not to make things worse. The woman cop goes too, crashes the group, tags along. Sandrine watches her and sees a dangerous animal, with her dark hair, her supple, well-worn leather jacket, her stubby nose. The woman is like a bat – the kind she saw in a documentary one day, with Mathias, the ones who cling to cattle at night and suck their blood. A vampire bat.

Sandrine remains in the sitting room with Caroline's parents and the male cop. They exchange a few pleasantries, because Sandrine is well-versed in the art, taking a compliment on her shortbread biscuits, saying thank you and Oh, it's nothing really, then adding that the oven is a very good brand which makes all the difference, that she made them this morning and they're best eaten on the day they're baked, but soon enough Anne-Marie cuts in and Sandrine senses that things are about to get complicated. Caroline's mother is not about to let her pursue her half-formed back-up plan in peace – quite simply, to stay here in this house with Mathias and the little bean. Quite simply to live a peaceful life with the man who cries. Anne-Marie has things to say, of which she, Sandrine, will have to take account, and she is on the brink of saying, But why are you doing this, why speak to me, I'm stupid, I have no opinion, I don't want people to say complicated, difficult, dangerous things to me, just carry on as if I'm *not here*! But that won't work, of course; now that Caroline is alive, Anne-Marie constantly oversteps the mark, taking dangerous liberties, and Sandrine knows that if Caroline comes back to the sitting room right this minute, with her train of escort, and that if he sees her, Sandrine, being secretive, and covering things up, then everything will come off the rails and she— all she asks is

one
evening
in peace
fuck
please

but of course, no. Anne-Marie begins to talk in a low voice, says, Sandrine, listen to me, the police have reopened their investigation, as you know. They would like to know— But, well, he's going to tell you. I'm sorry, I mean the detective is going to tell you how things are progressing.

Beside her, the male cop indicates that there's nothing to worry about and Sandrine realises that Anne-Marie is very comfortable around him, that she probably talks to him often and that she considers him a person of trust, almost a friend. And when the cop begins by saying, You probably know that my partner and I were very closely involved in the case, Sandrine is not surprised.

'We've been keeping in regular contact with the Marquezes…
And my colleague filed detailed reports on the national and
European databases, which is why we were alerted straightaway
when our Paris colleagues identified Caroline.'

The cop explains: now that that they know where Caroline
ended up and was rescued, they have begun investigating from
that end of things. The trail from here to Italy is cold, so we're
tracing it back from Italy. From the hospital where she was looked
after all those months, until she began to speak in French, to
the great surprise of the care team. The CCTV footage on the
emergency ward where Caroline was taken and treated. The
work rotas of the nurses who brought her in when a motorist
called to report a woman stumbling through a field. An Italian
woman motorist saw the unknown, dark-eyed woman wandering
as if lost, across a field beside the motorway. A call for witnesses
was put out, because a woman wandering naked as the day she
was born through the rice-fields of Piedmont was unlikely to be
a sight anyone would forget. The location was a long way for a
stark-naked woman to walk from the border, but a short drive.
They checked all the service stations within a 300-kilometre radius
and now they are questioning the managers, employees, and ex-
employees. It's taking a great deal of time, with cross-border and
European coordination. They must be patient.

At the mention of her daughter, treading barefoot and naked
through the rice-fields, Anne-Marie wraps her arms across her
chest as if to keep warm, but she does not cry. The cop continues: We recovered the medical records compiled by the Italian
hospital, when the Pitié took charge of her. It's a substantial
case history. In the silence that follows, the cop and Caroline's
parents all stare at Sandrine as if expecting her to reply, and all
she can think of to say is, But isn't this confidential? Why are

you telling me all this? And Anne-Marie lowers her gaze, with a barely perceptible movement of her head, a sign of surrender, or disappointment, or disapproval, perhaps.

Sandrine hears the murmur of voices returning from the garage. Caroline and Mathias and his father, like a proper nuclear family, followed everywhere it goes by a woman cop and a shrink. What people call an extended family. And the first woman is the first to enter the sitting room, the little boy still hanging on her arm. Sandrine stands up and says, Shall I make some more coffee?

Caroline is speaking: It's OK, no really, it's OK— And the psychiatrist answers, Well, let's go then. And it's clear they're going to go upstairs. Sandrine holds the half-full cafetière in her hand, and he stares at her was he walks by, looking for all the world as if he wished he were anywhere else but here. He stares at the male cop, the parents, and then he says to her, Do you want to come with us?

She feels saved. He has sensed her discomfort and found a way to get her out of the room, transformed for the moment into a police interrogation cell. She wishes these people would leave, but if she must suffer the unwelcome invasion, she might as well be at his side, and not alone under the gaze of an unknown cop and Mathias's grandparents. She is flattered, reassured that he has called for her to go with them, that he needs her. But the psychiatrist wrinkles her nose and says, Actually, I think the presence of a person unknown to Caroline might negate the process. But he says, very calmly, Sandrine is my partner, and she's a true mother to Mathias, this is her home. He has placed his hand on the nape of Sandrine's neck, in that proprietorial gesture she found so comforting at first. She feels his warm fingers and cannot help but look Caroline straight in the eye – a bold, challenging stare – as if to say 'You see, you see, I have a right to be here, too.' And in the first woman's eyes, for the first time, something flickers, and Sandrine tells herself, She's jealous.

Standing at her side, her man awaits the verdict, though with little doubt. He has decided that from now on, Sandrine will go with them, this is his house, he's the one in charge. The psychiatrist appears to think for a moment, then says, Of course, shall we? And this time the procession climbs the stairs, and the creaky step signals the passage of all six of them in turn: Caroline and Mathias, the father, Sandrine, the shrink and the woman cop.

Caroline visited Mathias's room the week before, but they step inside all the same. The shrink says, It's so neat and tidy! As if this was a bad thing. And standing next to Sandrine, he replies, in a proud voice, Mathias is like me, he's very organised. He likes to keep things in order. Then he stretches out a hand to ruffle his son's hair. He seizes the moment to move closer to the little boy and hug him with one arm, while he keeps his other hand on Sandrine's neck. The three of them stand facing the psychiatrist. He smiles at her, and at Caroline. Caroline says nothing, in fact she is noticeably silent when they file back out into the corridor and move on, to the bedroom and the room with the red shelves. Sandrine, for her part, keeps a close eye on the first woman's every step, her every breath, she wonders what will happen when Caroline sees the big basket full of fabrics. But nothing happens. Caroline walks into the red room, stands motionless facing the window. Sandrine cannot see her face but nothing in her movements suggest recognition, her posture is composed and unaffected by any hint of emotion. The first woman takes a few steps, turns around, but nothing seems to catch her eye. Then she stops in front of the bookcase. At last, something seems to grab her attention. She draws closer to the books, bends forward to read some of the titles, then points to one with a blue spine and says, I remember this book. I read it at school, in lycée, when I was about sixteen.

The psychiatrist smiles encouragingly and says, Very good, Caroline. Carry on, take your time. Caroline reaches out to touch the book, then draws back, looks up at them all waiting outside in the corridor and asks, May I? Like a shy little girl invited to someone else's house. Everyone turns to Sandrine, and Sandrine turns to her man, who says, Of course! in a voice brimming with kindness. The little pocket paperbacks are crammed in tight and Caroline must press against the entire stuck-together row while she prises the book out with her finger, then grasps it between her thumb and forefinger and slides it away from the red-painted wood. Caroline reads the back cover, then holds the book close to her face and takes a deep breath. Like a child to whom the five senses have recently been explained, and who decides to check each one methodically – perhaps she will lick it next, Sandrine thinks. The psychiatrist nods gently all the while, and Sandrine tells herself that they have planned this together, that Caroline is doing as she has been told, like a diligent pupil. How odd that she should think this, that they should have that in common, then she remembers that they both love, or loved, the same man, at some point in their lives, and she thinks, Two. Two things in common, without really knowing how she feels about that fact.

Mathias is standing in the corridor. He seems to understand that what Caroline is trying to do is important. He agrees to let go of her hand each time she enters a room. Gently, his father touches his head and draws him close, presses the boy against his legs. Sandrine is conscious of the image they project, the three of them against all the rest, a little sad for Caroline, perhaps, but she feels relief at their closeness, their solidarity. The boy's father holds her tight against him and the heat she feels through her trouser leg, warming her thigh, fills her with empathy for the first woman. Caroline is alone in the red bedroom, alone without even her memories, just a rather worn-out book that she kept from her days as a *lycéenne*, and it seems to Sandrine that whatever the first woman was plotting before her disappearance, she cannot remember it now. Or is she play-acting? Sandrine remembers the kitchen sink, the tea towel that's kept inside the cupboard. The little bean has filled her thoughts since that day, but she remembers Caroline's unhesitating, natural gesture as she opened the wooden cupboard door to wipe her hands on the towel. And yet today, right in front of her now, the dark-haired woman is utterly alone, standing inside the room, so plainly unfamiliar with the space that was once her own, that Sandrine forgets the business with the tea towel, the kitchen cupboard. She pities her and says, You can keep it if you like, with a small gesture to the book, and Caroline clutches it tight against her and says, Really? Thank you! And Sandrine says, But of course, it belongs to you, anyway, and at the nape of her neck, her man's fingers tighten a little: a sign of approval, a reward. Caroline has finished with the room. The psychiatrist asks, Do you want to stay a little longer? But Caroline answers no, she's beginning to feel tired.

Everyone goes downstairs to the sitting room, where the male cop and the grandparents are waiting in the conspiratorial silence that follows a private, interrupted conversation. Sandrine makes more coffee while everyone sits down. Moments later, Caroline and the woman cop go outside to smoke. The shrink explains that she has high hopes these visits will unblock something. Sandrine notes the word 'these'. There will be more to come. She sneaks a glance into the sitting room, watching for a flash of anger, but no, her man is sitting calmly in one of the armchairs, holding Mathias firmly on one knee. Caroline and the woman cop come back inside and reclaim their seats. Of course, I understand, he replies, as I explained before, the priority for us all is to make sure everything goes as smoothly as possible for Mathias. He places his hand between the boy's shoulder blades and adds, insistently, My son is the priority here.

Caroline's dark eyes are expressionless, and Sandrine wonders again – an umpteenth variation on a thoroughly irritating tune – Who is this woman? What is she thinking? What does she want? Sitting or standing so still, at times, but with careful, measured, reptilian movements, at others. She is sitting on the edge of the sofa, her back not touching the leather, ready to get to her feet, ready to leave. When he stroked the boy's back and, finally, rested his fingers around the tiny neck, exactly as he does with Sandrine at times, Caroline had folded her arms across her stomach, suddenly, sharply, accentuating her resemblance to a terrified lizard caught between freezing on the spot, and flight. The first woman says, Yes, of course, but she looks away, does not speak the words to his face. Reptile, Sandrine thinks again.

There is a small silence while she pours the coffee into each cup, then Anne-Marie asks in an overly bright and casual voice, How about Mathias coming to sleep with us tonight? As if the idea had suddenly occurred to her. The fingers tighten very slightly around Mathias's neck and he holds him closer still, says Hm. Sitting on the kitchen chair they have pushed into the room so that everyone can have a seat, the woman cop taps her fingers on her knee. The gesture is silent but plain to see, and irritating; Sandrine tries to ignore it and look at Anne-Marie and Patrice instead, but the small, brittle movements are there, she can see them in the corner of her eye. It's highly annoying, she would prefer it if the woman stopped. She turns a little on her stool, to get the woman cop out of her field of vision, but she can feel the gesture continuing and is surprised to discover that her own breathing has quickened. She focusses her attention on this, while everyone waits for Mathias's father's reply.

My son works hard at school, he says at length, he's a good pupil. Weekends are a time for him to rest with his family, and straightaway Anne-Marie says, We are his family, too! in an aggressive tone that Sandrine has never heard her use before. Its only visible effect is the transfer of Mathias from one knee to the other, rather heavily, like a large ventriloquist's puppet. Hm, he says again. Anne-Marie clears her throat and says, I'm sorry, it's— it's not, I mean, it's just that we love Mathias very much, too.

Sandrine knows this, of course. Everyone knows that Anne-Marie and Patrice love Mathias. Even if they hadn't adopted Picasso the wonky-faced dog for him, everyone would know, it shines out in the way they look at him, in the way they find everything Mathias does so interesting and terrific: the drawings of the birds with teeth, the way he eats chocolate ice cream, ties his shoelaces, breathes. But they have no automatic rights over him, Sandrine knows that too, he has told her over and over: If they want Mathias they come through me first, I'm the one with the authority to decide. And every lunch, every outing, every night that Mathias spends with his grandparents is negotiated, most often by Anne-Marie in her rather querulous voice, sometimes by Patrice who calls and says, We'd like to have him on Sunday, but most often the answer they get is: Come over here, it'll be easier. Yet Sandrine knows that the little boy loves sleeping over at his grandparents' place, even before they got the ugly dog. It's a rare occurrence, nonetheless. And now, two weeks in a row, that's a lot, and that's what he says, unsurprisingly: 'That's rather a lot, Anne-Marie,' in a calm, patient, instructive voice. The woman cop fidgets, the shrink clears her throat and says,

But surely the simplest thing is to ask Mathias what he would like to do? And Sandrine thinks Oh no, no! That woman has no idea what she's doing, Mathias isn't the one in charge, he's not the one who decides, she doesn't realise what she's putting the little boy through. Mathias's father has a very clear vision of what a child may decide, which is: nothing. So long as he lives under his father's roof and follows his rules. And now this shrink comes crashing in on all this, talking rubbish, putting them all— putting Mathias in an impossible situation, because there is no right answer. If he says he wants to go, his father will take it badly, and if he says he wants to stay here... But he doesn't want to stay here, in any case, obviously he wants to be with his mother. Obviously. Sandrine doesn't know what to say. Sitting in her armchair, the shrink grins as if she's proud of herself, as if she's the one who had a really great idea. *Stupid bitch, you too, can't you just fucking leave us in peace?* Seated on his father's knee, Mathias looks up and across at her, and for once Sandrine is the only person in the room, the only one to understand what that look holds. And so she says, But just for one night, hm? Perhaps you could bring him back tomorrow morning? And she looks up and past Mathias, at his father, and she sees that she has made a mistake, that she should never have spoken. Mathias says, Yes! And he wriggles out of his father's grasp, slips down from his knee with the agility of an eel. Sandrine thinks he's going to cling to his mother, but he comes towards her and puts his arms around her, Sandrine's, neck. She's so unaccustomed to signs of affection from the little boy that she doesn't even think to return his hug. His 'Thank you!' rings in her ear, and then Mathias races upstairs. This time, no one needs to tell him to prepare his things.

When the step has squeaked and the boy is upstairs, the shrink says, Excellent. The male cop says, It's a good decision,

Monsieur Langlois, and the woman cop says, Every show of goodwill will stand you in good stead when you're up before the judge. And the Monsieur Langlois in question shoots her an appalled look.

'What judge?'

The woman cop answers, delightedly, 'Oh, we'll see how things go, but one thing's for sure, custody arrangements will have to be settled. Parental authority doesn't reside solely with the father, hmmm? There's the mother, too. Madame Marquez has every much right as you to see the boy.'

He says, I don't see what my mother-in-law has to do with this. As if Anne-Marie wasn't in the room. The woman cop answers with the voice of someone having a very good day indeed. She is near-jubilant when she replies: 'Madame Marquez. Not Mathias's grandmother, here. I'm referring to Caroline.'

But Caroline is Caroline Langlois, Sandrine thinks, and here we are again, back to the status and position of Caroline, a woman who was missing, presumed dead but is dead no longer. When a dead woman is resurrected, does she revert to her maiden name? She sees the angry vein beating furiously at his temple as he begins to grasp what the woman cop is saying, that Caroline is here, that she's the boy's mother, that if he doesn't want her around, perhaps she doesn't want him, it works both ways, and they'll have to get a divorce, and that in a divorce there is always a winner and loser. The vein pulses, huge and wild, and Sandrine knows that it is costing him a superhuman effort to remain calm as he says, I understand what you're saying, but I think that Caroline and I can come to an amicable arrangement, once her condition has stabilised. Meanwhile, I don't believe it is desirable to entrust my child to the care of a woman who has no recollection of who he is. Don't you agree, Caroline?

Caroline is visibly startled, as if she had been woken suddenly. Is this the first time he has spoken directly to her, even looked at her, since she arrived? The first time he has spoken her name? Sandrine can't quite remember. But yes, it's possible. The first woman is so silent, almost mute, she has barely said a word today. She must find it hard to speak to them both, to Sandrine and to him. Perhaps she can remember it all perfectly, the passports, the subterfuge. What was she planning, with her twisted, serpentine postures, her cold-blooded pretence?

Don't you agree, Caroline? he asks again, louder, as if addressing someone stupid, and Caroline says, Yes of course, in an empty, joyless voice, apparently unforced, and her manner resembles Mathias exactly, disconcertingly. Feet are heard running down-stairs, the little boy is ready. The woman cop says, Excellent, you'll bring him back tomorrow, say before 3 p.m.?

Three o'clock in the afternoon is not tomorrow morning, she's pushing it. Sandrine feels a sudden wave of nausea, excuses herself and hurries upstairs to the toilet. She hopes she can hold out as she climbs the steps, hurriedly, then rushes to the bathroom and throws up in the washbasin. She presses the stainless-steel tap to run water and cover the noise. Some has got onto the floor, the bathroom mat, her blouse, but nothing serious. She puts a dab of toothpaste in her mouth, changes her blouse – fortunately she has another one in the same colour, perhaps no one will notice the difference – then drops the mat into the laundry basket, sponges the floor, the washbasin. She tries to work quickly, she's just rinsing the sponge when the front door slams shut. She breaks a cold sweat and is afraid she may need to vomit a second time, but this is different.

She takes a few steps out from the bathroom and looks out of the bedroom window. Caroline, her parents and Mathias, the two cops and the shrink, are standing outside on the road. They've all left. She's alone with him.

She thinks he'll call out to her but there is no sound coming from the ground floor. She looks around her, in search of something, though she's not sure what. Outside, Caroline sits Mathias in his car seat, her parents put the small rucksack in the back of the car, shake hands with the cops. The first car drives away. Sandrine watches while the cops talk to the shrink, who sits at the wheel of her own car. Then she, too, drives away.

Finally, the two cops climb into their vehicle and pull out of the cul-de-sac. The sound of the engine fades into the distance.

Silence falls instantly over the house. Then Sandrine hears footsteps, no, the pounding of a runner's feet, then the staircase groaning, he is hurrying towards her and the icy shiver she felt a few moments ago returns and she knows she is afraid. She is afraid of what is about to happen, afraid of what she has done, afraid of what he will do. She has a few seconds in which to find something but her mind is blank, empty, white-hot; and when he bursts into the bedroom, his face twisted with rage, she cannot even move. He reaches her in three short strides and all she can do is count the steps, the steps that keep her from being destroyed, one, two, three, he's there. He opens his mouth to holler WHO THE FUCK DO YOU THINK YOU ARE, YOU FILTHY BITCH, EH? WHO DO YOU THINK YOU ARE, THIS IS MY HOUSE, MINE, YOU DON'T SAY A FUCKING THING, NOT A THING! He grabs her by the neck, and there is no tenderness in the gesture. In a blinding flash Sandrine realises that there never was, that this does not say 'I love you' but 'You belong to me'. His grasp is tight and she begins to suffocate, it hurts, but that's only a secondary concern, she doesn't think of the pain, all she can think about is the air, the air that isn't coming any more. He yells SINCE WHEN DO YOU DECIDE IN MY PLACE, SINCE WHEN DO YOU SPEAK FOR ME, YOU'RE NOTHING, NOTHING, JUST A FAT SLUT, YOU SHUT YOUR MOUTH, YOU SHUT YOUR MOUTH! WHY DID YOU SAY THAT, FILTHY BITCH, WHY DID YOU SAY THAT? and she doesn't understand, everything is absurd; he's done this before, ordered her to explain herself from time to time – when she was home late, or dinner wasn't ready, a text she hadn't shown him, but never, never has he been so furious and she cannot understand what she's supposed to do, what she's meant to say, does he want her to answer or shut up? She doesn't understand what she must do to make it stop, and finally she whispers 'Hel… Help…' and he loosens his grip, just a little, and she gasps, I wanted to help you, I just wanted to help you! He releases her further. She is pressed up against the wall, she repeats, I wanted to help you, I just, I just wanted to help you. The woman cop, the shrink, they were talking about a judge, custody, I just wanted to help you, they were saying if you— if we didn't make an effort, if we didn't go along with them… I wanted to help you.

She sinks down the wall, her legs are jelly, she's so afraid, so scared, that she has forgotten to cry, she clutches her knees to her breasts, as tightly as possible to protect her belly, the little bean, the little bean. And the image of the little bean brings tears pouring out of her eyes, and sobs, and when he sees her crying, sees that she is genuinely sorry, he crouches beside her, and apologises, puts his arms around her, kisses her, almost drinking her tears, and his kisses taste salty. He says, Stop, stop, stop crying, it's them, those women, and the other one, almost threatening me in my own home. Stop crying, I didn't want— I didn't want to get angry, but you see, why did you do that without asking me.

I hear you saying what you said and I think, she's with them, but I didn't want— look at me, it's OK, it's OK, it's OK, come on, I love you, I didn't want— you mustn't do things like that, all right? Me, I won't get angry any more, I won't get angry, not any more, I promise, if you don't do that again, promise, never again. It'll be all right, I love you.

He helps her to her feet, says, Come, come downstairs, it's just the two of us, we'll make the most of it, all right? We'll go and sit in the garden, come on, come with me, shall we go out in the garden?

Downstairs, the coffee table in the sitting room is still clut- tered with cups and saucers, the empty plate of biscuits, spoons. He says, I'll see to that, huh? He smooths her hair, tucks a stray lock behind her ear, as she wonders if the new, tight knot that burns high up between her shoulder blades will be there forever. He slides her sunglasses onto her face and says, Go on, you've done so much, I'll take all this through, you deserve a rest, wait, wait... and he releases her, just long enough to open the slid- ing door to the garden and take two garden recliners out from the shed behind the big box tree. He unfolds them – they're designer pieces that cost a lot of money and mustn't be left out in all weathers – then comes back to her with the air of a contented little boy. He says, Wait, hold on! then walks past her and returns a few seconds later, his arms loaded with cushions from the sofa. See how comfortable you'll be. She follows him, on autopilot, feels the cool breeze drying her damp cheeks. He sits her down on one of the recliners and says, There! You stay right there, I'll clear up.

From inside, she hears the clatter of cups and saucers, he busies himself for a while then comes out to join her, carrying the book from her handbag in one hand and, rolled up under his arm, one of the magazines he likes to read, something about cars – fine, expensive cars. He settles down beside her and the afternoon passes like that. He, reading and turning often to smile in her direction; she, staring blindly at the words in the book, and turning a page from time to time, to stare at something different.

When evening falls, he says, How about going to the cinema? It's been a long time since we saw a film, just the two of us. It's true, she used to go a lot on her own, and had looked forward to the prospect of going as a couple, of leaning against him, the awkward armrest, kissing in the dark, the way she never did as a teenager. But he doesn't really like films and thinks no woman should go to the cinema alone, so she has stopped going. He's suggesting it now, to be nice. He recites the titles of the films, down to one she remembers seeing on a poster. She says, Yes, that one, why not, and he says, Are you sure? It doesn't look great… How about this one? She says, Fine. She doesn't mind. All that matters for now is that he has become his old self. His original self, his kind self. He cried with her just now, he's the man who cries, once again.

They drive to the cinema, watch the film, he puts his arms around her. On the screen, a woman holds a cute, cuddly baby against her chest, and she tries not to think about anything. After the film, they go to a restaurant, he orders paella for two, serves her himself, refills her plate, she eats as best she can, hoping she won't feel sick. He often does that, orders for two, insists that she eat, as if to tell her she's beautiful the way she is. Sometimes he even gets angry, asks her why and for whom exactly she wants to lose all this weight. She doesn't want a row this evening, she just wants everything to be all right and for them to go home and sleep, she wants to forget this day. That's allowed. She does that sometimes, some days don't count.

11

THE NEXT MORNING, he calls Christian and talks to him for a long time, outside in the garden, wearing a thin sweater because the weather is cooler now. She stays indoors. The windows are closed, she can't hear his voice. Christian is a lawyer. There were times when she'd tried to give her man some advice, but he prefers to talk to Christian, his friend, and anyway, being a secretary in a law firm is obviously worthless. Obviously she knows less than he does.

Almost an hour later he ends the call, takes his jacket, says he's going to see Christian straightaway, it'll be easier. She asks if he'll be back by 3 p.m. and he says, I don't know. Perhaps he doesn't want to face the scrutiny of all those strangers, the two cops, and the shrink, who knows. She may come again too, she's the last straw, Sandrine can see that – he loathes shrinks.

She stands motionless, patient. She understands, she didn't like the way the shrink looked at them both yesterday either. He has collected and checked his ID, his wallet, driver's license and car keys, as he does each time before he leaves the house. He is about to leave but she's still standing there, rooted to the spot. He smiles, turns and takes her in his arms, says, Listen, I don't think I'll be here. I don't want to see them. I'll be back later, about 6 o'clock.

When he's gone, she stands by the door and stares at the empty space in the driveway. Then she clears away the lunch that she had prepared but which neither of them has touched because the quick call to Christian turned into a long call to Christian. If he plans to stay out until 6 p.m., there's no point keeping lunch out on the table. She puts the salad in a Tupperware box – lucky she hadn't dressed it, it will keep. She puts the cheese in the refrigerator, cuts a fennel bulb into sticks. She eats, staring out though the glass in the front door; he doesn't come back. The knot between her shoulder blades loosens a little, her breathing is easier. It's almost 2 p.m.

She goes upstairs. A ray of sunshine brightens the corridor, tiny grains of dust float on the air and twinkle in the light. She did a big clean this morning, everything is vacuumed, dusted. These specks are all that remain, floating away.

She hesitates for a moment on the threshold of the bedroom with the red shelves, then goes in and opens the window. She turns on the spot, imitating Caroline yesterday as she looked all around the room. There are boxes of cotton reels and buttons on the shelves. She opens them, pushes the bobbins aside with her finger. But if Caroline was concealing passports inside the lining of a padded piece of fabric stuffed inside a basket of off-cuts, she would never have left anything important in a box that could be easily seen and reached on an open shelf.

Sandrine turns to the bookcase. When she made space for her own books, she hardly touched Caroline's. She places a chair in front of the red shelves, thinks for a moment, then gets up again to fetch some cleaning fluid, and one of the special cloths she must use for dusting. Only then does she sit down and begin to empty the shelves, one by one.

There are eight shelves. The bottom one, which Sandrine has never really touched, is full of paperback classics, rather worn – old set books from school, no doubt. It's clean and tidy, with just one empty space for the book Caroline took away yesterday.

Above this, crime novels, their covers all black and red, or black and yellow, or black and blue. And on the next shelf up, thrillers, their covers embossed with shiny or blood-soaked letters. She'd like to read them, but the truth is, she cannot make Caroline's books her own, she avoids them, keeps clear. Above these are books of assorted shapes and sizes, which Sandrine knows she will never dare touch because these bear all the marks of personal favourites, books that have been read over and over again, their pages cornered, damaged, their spines stuck back together. A book can be such an intimate thing, sometimes, once its pages have been handled and turned. And to open Caroline's soul, arranged here on the shelf, always seemed a kind of sacrilege to Sandrine. Above these, on the shelves within easy reach, are her own books, the ones she loves, the ones she has set aside, the ones she plans to read.

The small available space means she must choose carefully which to keep, the more so because he much prefers her to buy books and then throw them away. He loathes libraries, the filthy books touched by so many hands, the implication that he might not be able to pay for Sandrine to have her own books. She never throws them away, of course, no one should do that. She leaves them in the laundrette near her office, takes them to second-hand stores, the halfway house in the middle of the commercial zone near the supermarket but far away from everything else.

She starts at the bottom, breaks apart the compact block of paperback classics. The opening left by Caroline the day before makes her task easier. Then she goes through the books, checking each one with care. They must have gotten damp, some of the pages are stuck together. She persists, it takes her a few seconds to realise that the pages aren't simply stuck, they have been *glued*. Inside the first book, between two pages stuck together around

166

the edges, there are banknotes. She takes the second book. There are notes hidden here, too. She does not remove the notes from their envelopes of literary classics. She checks the remaining books, counting up the amounts as she goes. Several hundred at the final count, almost a thousand. She wonders how Caroline managed it. She wasn't working. She had access to the joint bank account, Sandrine knows this, but she knows, too, that he keeps a close eye on all expenses. That money is not a subject taken lightly. He talks about it a great deal, especially when he brings up the subject of her salary, that pittance, repeating once again that she would do better to quit her job – she doesn't get on with her colleagues anyway, those little minxes, chattering all day. And at her firm, virtually all the lawyers are men, he doesn't like that. But Sandrine's 'pittance' is important to her, she values her money, her work, her guarantee that she will never have to go home to her father. It means a lot, but he insists, and she knows already that she will give in eventually, that she will be the one to surrender in this silent but omnipresent war of attrition. She finishes adding up what Caroline had hidden away – a lot. Not a vast amount, but a lot. What was she planning to do with it? *You stupid cow, of course you know what she was planning to do with it. Money and passports, she was going to leave.* Caroline was going to take Mathias and leave. Sandrine checks her watch. It's past 3 o'clock. Hurriedly, she puts the books back on the shelf, wipes everything with the duster. It's spotless.

She fetches a cardigan from the bedroom, then goes downstairs to wait for them to bring Mathias back. She checks the cul-de-sac several times, peering out through the small glass window in the front door. It's Sunday and the weather has cooled, this is the first true Sunday of autumn, people are at home, digging weeds in their gardens, or watching TV. There are no cars entering or leaving.

She waits a long time. Ten minutes past three, then twenty, then forty. No one pulls up outside. At ten minutes to four, she opens the door and walks along the short driveway to the road. She stands and looks towards the rest of the estate. She knows she shouldn't bother him, that goes without saying, but still she sends a text to say *They aren't back yet,* then waits.

When he gets back she is sitting on the doorstep. He says, Get up, since when do you hang about on the front steps like some gypsy woman? And they go inside. He takes off his shoes and jacket. She looks at his hands as they undo his laces, at his forehead; she watches for the angry vein. You have to read the small signs. It's like a very important book that you need to read letter by letter, to find out what the end of the day will be like. He runs his hand through his hair and says, I'm hungry. Of course you're hungry, Sandrine says, you went out without any lunch.

He takes a step towards her and the slap comes all at once, she doesn't even understand what has happened. It's not the pain that takes her by surprise so much as the sound of it, and then comes the familiar burning sensation, her intimate knowledge of the pain that comes just after the surprise, a nasty, strange heat. When her father hit her, it was after the shouting, she saw it coming, she knew. But just now, the slap was his answer to her, quite simply. She knows she has said something wrong because she can see him speaking to her, see his lips move, what is he saying? The loud, sharp noise that muffled her hearing, on the side that took the slap, subsides. She can hear again, he is telling her that this is his house, that he'll do as he likes, that he doesn't have to justify where he goes, or when he eats. That's what she's here for, does she understand? He asks again. Do you understand? Do you understand? Is that clear? She nods. She understands very well, she understands perfectly that he has misunderstood, that she wasn't reproaching him in any way, that she reproaches herself for asking a stupid question, but yes, this time it's quite clear, 'Yes yes yes,' she nods, and she goes to the kitchen. Her gestures are precise, efficient, though she is still trembling a little. She begins by putting ice cubes inside a tea towel, then sets to work with one hand, holding the improvised ice bag to her cheek with the other. She takes out the salad from lunch, the potato-and-carrot mash and the stuffed meat rolls, they'll be a little dry once they're reheated but she'll add some cream, and it'll be fine. He calls Christian again, says No, no, they haven't brought him home. No. No. Yes, I'll call tomorrow... Oh, I'm going over there, absolutely. I'll eat and then go. I've got to go over there.

He chews his late lunch with stern concentration. Before the second meat roll, he shows her the chair opposite him, and she sits down. She hasn't taken out the bottle of wine, for his glass with lunch, and he hasn't asked for it. He is thinking. When he pushes away his plate, there is a cream stain on the front of his polo shirt. She moves the cheeseboard towards him, but he doesn't touch it. I'm going over to the Marquezes' place, he says. He reaches out and takes the damp tea towel from her, examines her cheek. Sandrine is tense. Her shoulders are hunched. He says, My love. It doesn't show. Do you forgive me? You forgive me. Sandrine makes no reply.

He stands up and moves closer to her, places his hand on her neck. The long knife between Sandrine's shoulder blades burns once again, paralysing her spine. I've spoken to Christian. He recommended someone, a family law specialist, but he says it'll be complicated. Sole custody is very difficult to obtain. Caroline can play the victim in court. We should try to secure an arrangement by mutual consent. He kneels beside Sandrine's chair, and speaks very softly: Sandrine, Sandrine. Until she looks at him. We're all at a loss in this situation, completely at a loss, she comes back and wants to lay down the law, she wants to steal my son, do you see? Can you see what that's doing to me? Sandrine nods, but by dint of understanding everything, she feels she understands nothing at all any more. Her cheek feels hot and cold all at once. He says, You're going to come with me.

There's the table to clear, the salad to put away a second time, a clean polo shirt to fetch from upstairs. Her cheek is a little pink, nothing much, she applies powder. It is just before 6 o'clock when they pull up outside the Marquezes' apartment building. A car drives past as they park, and Sandrine thinks she recognises the profile inside, but there's no time to identify the driver with any certainty.

He takes a deep breath then turns to her and gazes attentively at her face. He raises a hand, and she jerks away, but he tucks a lock of hair behind her ear, and smiles. I'm sorry, Sandrine. I— they want to take my boy away, do you see? That's why they didn't come back today. Your blouse is undone, by the way.

She fastens the top button. He frames her face in his hands and gazes at her. He says, But you're on my side, and he kisses her, very softly, and when he pulls away she sees his eyes are bright with tears, and she grasps his hand. Her fingers squeeze the fingers of the man who cries. There it is, he's back, this is the man she loves, and now she understands everything all over again.

They stand beside the entryphone. He presses the buzzer, she waits.

A silhouette approaches along the side of the building. The woman cop. She's changed cars, that's why Sandrine wasn't sure, and she searches her memory to see whether the new car was parked somewhere in their road this afternoon. Yes. Perhaps. So she followed them. Sandrine doesn't dare speak, she stares straight ahead at the mottled glass of the building's main doorway, at the dark red brickwork. He buzzes again. Then he leaves his fingers pressed against the call button. The entryphone must be buzzing in the apartment. And they are home; they saw a light on as they arrived.

The cop climbs the two steps to the entrance. Her mannish shoes are silent on the concrete slabs, but he turns around immediately, on the alert. The vein is pulsing and Sandrine has no idea whether she should step forward or back. Finally, she backs down to the second step, very slowly, and when the cop says 'Monsieur Langlois?', Sandrine steps down again to the pavement. Monsieur Langlois, says the woman cop, a second time, Mathias will be staying with his mother for a while.

He stuffs his hands into his trouser pockets. He does that sometimes, in situations when he mustn't get angry. There is a buzzing sound, and the door to the apartment building opens. The male cop emerges, he has come downstairs. He says 'Monsieur Langlois' as well, then repeats 'Monsieur Langlois...' as if that might achieve something, anything.

He says, I've come to fetch my son. I was very worried when we had no news.

The exchange begins, in the failing light. They form a triangle, the male cop blocking the entrance, his colleague standing to one side, her man fighting his corner. Sandrine stands apart. She doesn't want to make the triangle a square, she has no place here, would leave if only she could, but he needs her, he chose to bring her with him. She watches the scene from a far greater distance than the space that lies between them. Their roles are very clear: the nice male cop and the nasty bitch. His calm, soothing voice, while she stands too close, her chin thrust forward as if to say, 'Fuck you, eh? Pisses you off when I get under your feet, doesn't it?' The two police officers have been playing this game since the start, Sandrine realises – cat and mouse, good cop bad cop, with no understanding of the consequences, no recognition that it was they who lit the touchpaper, set off the chain reaction, ignited the blaze. And they're at it again this evening. The male cop says quietly, Monsieur Langlois, Madame Marquez has as much right as you to be with her son. He is domiciled with you, but while we wait to go before the family court, and in light of the reopening of the investigation into your wife's disappearance, the Marquezes and their daughter think it best the boy stays with them.

The vein pulses furiously, and his hands are stuffed deep into his pockets, but his voice remains calm. He says it's tantamount to an abduction. It's a scandal that the police should permit, even facilitate such behaviour. He says, too, that he doesn't understand why, that it's bad for a child to be removed so suddenly from his home environment. He says a great many very well-considered things and the woman cop's grin becomes a menacing leer, and the fists are thrust deeper still into his trouser pockets. He steps back, down to the pavement, apparently in retreat. He walks past Sandrine, looks up at the windows. And then he shouts in a hoarse voice, hollering his son's name. Once, twice. And then over and over again, just as he pressed the entryphone before.

The male cop walks down the steps and across to where he stands, tries to calm things down. The woman cop joins them, the triangle re-forms, round and round they go, he says Monsieur Langlois, Monsieur Langlois… and she answers his rage with a sly, mocking smile. Sandrine has no idea what to do, whether to come forward or hold back. She takes a few steps in the direction of the car, tells herself that whatever happens, they'll end up driving away. She will wait by the vehicle. They drove over in his big, shiny car, on which he lavishes care and attention. They left Sandrine's little two-door at the house. He wants her to sell it, tells her it's too small, a poor man's car, that it isn't 'safe'. The last time they had the conversation, she said, But, but I need it to get to work… and he laughed. He knows she'll give in, soon enough, there's nothing for her there, her colleagues don't like her, he's sure they say nasty things about her behind her back, about how shy she is, and stupid. Her bosses couldn't care less whether she's there or not, he's known that from the first, why can't she see it, besides, on that first day, when she stayed away from work, did anyone bother to find out whether she was really ill or not? Had anyone missed her? No, you know very well not. He's right, he's always right, every day, and he's right again now, about the car. Sandrine wonders if she will find the strength to say No, a reason to say No. How can she, the pathetic, weak, feeble one, dare to contradict her man?

He hollers again. There's no sign of movement behind the windows on the second floor. Other windows light up, bright rectangles in the dark of the evening. Other curtains twitch, curious heads poke out, but nothing in the Marquezes' apartment.

Mathias's name rings out, the voice is hoarser still, a bestial roar. This man is screaming for his son, and the windows are trembling, and something else, too, deep inside Sandrine, between the bars of her ribs. The woman cop says, OK, that's enough, and she moves closer to the father in distress.

That's enough now. Oh! Do you hear me?

She spoke to him using the familiar *tu*, and on a reflex, Sandrine crosses her wrists over her belly. No stranger speaks to him that way, no one disrespects him. He withdraws his fists from his pockets. The woman cop looks at his hands and puts up her own, as if in celebration, as if she had been waiting for this moment for a long time.

Come on then, come on, please yourself, punch me, try and land one on me, that's what you want, isn't it? But I'm not your wife, you crazy bastard, if you lift a finger against me I'll smash your head in.

The male cop is close beside them. He's given up reciting 'Monsieur Langlois, Monsieur Langlois…' And Monsieur Langlois tells the woman cop, Don't you threaten me.

I'm not threatening you, *Monsieur Langlois*, I'm warning you. You may be the king of your pathetic little cul-de-sac house, you might think you reign over your private universe, but out here in the real world, it's all over. The investigation is moving forward, we've got the tapes from Italy. And she remembers. Hear what I'm saying? It's all come back to her.

He smiles, calm and composed. Sandrine knows that smile well, and thinks he's bound to raise a hand against her. He will punish this outrage, the threats, the lack of respect. But instead he says, I have no idea what you're talking about, I just know that you have threatened an innocent member of the public and abducted his child, and then he turns on his heels, unlocks the car with a flick of his wrist, gripping the key fob, and says to Sandrine, Get in.

Sandrine pulls herself up into the passenger seat. The woman cop yells, And if you lay one finger on her, I'm warning you! If you touch one fucking hair on her head! But Sandrine pulls the door closed and the two of them are shut inside the soundproof cabin.

He fires the engine and drives off at speed, though they're in a slow residential zone. Out on the motorway, he powers up through the gears, revs the engine, searches for Christian's number in his contact list.

When Christian picks up he says, Right, I'm on my way home. No, just like you said, the anxious father. That's not the problem, it's that other fucking bitch. You've got to arrange a meeting with that lawyer you mentioned, the one we talked about… He glances in the rear-view mirror, frowns, then says, Hold on, I've got the cops on my tail. How the fuck should I know if it's the same ones? Call him! Call him now.

It is the same ones. In the new car, the one Sandrine failed to recognise earlier. He says, This is a fucking joke! And he tosses his mobile into Sandrine's lap. On a reflex, she lifts her hands away from the device as it lands on her thighs. She doesn't know what to do. She is never allowed to touch his phone.

He brings the car to a sudden halt on the hard shoulder. Behind them, the two cops get out of their vehicle.

Well now, Monsieur Langlois, says the woman cop, when he winds downs his window. Breaking the speed limit, are we? Using a mobile phone when driving?

He says nothing. She is exultant, it shows, and he's seething, and that's beginning to show too. She says, Keep your hands on the steering wheel, please, and he replies, This is looking increasingly like police harassment. What have I done apart from be worried about my son?

Ah, *Monsieur Langlois*, the list is long. For now, we'll start with the speeding offence, and using your phone at the wheel. He interrupts her – OK, I was going a little too fast, but I wasn't using my phone. We saw you, she says. He objects: I don't even have my telephone with me, I left it at home. We left in such a hurry, I thought perhaps my son and his grandparents had been involved in an accident on their way over.

She says, Oh yeah, so what's that? She points to the smartphone, half visible, clutched between Sandrine's thighs.

That's my partner's phone.

Go ahead, Sandrine, unlock the phone, says the woman cop, and of course Sandrine cannot. He has the codes to her phone but she is never allowed to touch his and she hasn't the faintest idea what his code might be. She tries Mathias's birthdate, and his father's, and her own as a last resort, but of course nothing works. She turns to the woman cop and says, I'm sorry, my mind's gone blank, it's because, it's— I was scared, by the siren. The woman cop says quietly, It doesn't matter, Sandrine. The main reason is, this isn't your phone. Sandrine says, But it is… in a voice she had hoped would be much steadier than it sounds. But the woman cop isn't listening, she's too busy staring down the man sitting next to her in the car, an almost greedy smile playing at her lips. She says, Get out of the vehicle please, *Monsieur Langlois.*

Outside the car, on the hard shoulder, Sandrine shivers as the woman cop pins his arms behind his back. He glares at her, with an expression of pure contempt. But she tried her best. She says, What do you want me to do? and he spits his reply: Nothing. As if this all was her fault.

Take the car home, he adds, just before he is pushed into the back seat of the cops' vehicle. She is alone.

She's never driven the big car, it's not hers. He has never talked about how they would organise things if she ever did leave her job and sell her car. She adjusts the seat and the rear-view mirror, turns the key in the ignition.

176

The car is huge and she dreads the journey home, but the imposing machine is solid all around her, and responsive. She drives smoothly back to the house. She doesn't know how she came to think she was a bad driver. She, who was so proud to have passed her test with ease, with special congratulations from the examiner; her years of driving without incident in the little poor-man's car, as he calls it, whose handling she mastered with capable care. But yes, she remembers now. He saw the marks left by a bump to the left wing, one Saturday, when he came back from tennis. And others, on another Saturday. There's no room for her car in the garage, she leaves it parked in the cul-de-sac, and often he points out that she's jutting too far from the kerb, that she hasn't performed the manoeuvre correctly, that she shouldn't be surprised if she wakes up one day to find one of the wing mirrors missing – a good excuse to sell that heap of junk for scrap. She opens the garage door and calmly slides the car forward out of the rain that has begun to fall. She is relieved to have completed her mission successfully, and about something else, too, something she hasn't felt for a very, very long time: she is pleased with her own actions. And she says so, says it out loud to herself, or perhaps to the little bean. Not bad, eh? And she gets out of the car.

Inside the empty house, she pauses to think. He has alerted Christian, who has alerted a lawyer. The last thing she must do, in any case, is call Christian. She must never mention Christian's name again. Christian is the bringer of bad things. He had been so jealous after the dinner when Christian had offered her a light, she had spent days justifying herself. He had lost his head, become a different person. He had questioned her for whole evenings and nights at a stretch, asking what they had said, whether she had flirted with him, if they were seeing one another, if she was sleeping with him, if she opened her fat thighs to get fucked by Christian or if she went down on her knees to suck him off with her fat whore's mouth, until she had wept with exhaustion in bed, her brain in tatters, saying No, absolutely not, I promise, why do you say that, why? And then he had decided that unfaithful women were bitches, and bitches sleep on the floor. He had recovered himself at last, forgiven her at last. *Forgiven what?* the small voice had asked, the one that still spoke audibly to Sandrine back then. *You've done nothing!* He had forgiven her, she could get some sleep, she was allowed back into bed, but it was since then, perhaps, that the stiff rod had driven itself between her shoulder blades, the rod that was always there, scarcely felt at times, burning hot at others. She will not call Christian. What she would like to do is call Mathias, hear Mathias's voice, know that Mathias is OK. But he will check her calls. And he always asks for an itemised bill for the house phone that no one ever uses.

The only telephone he doesn't check day in day out is his own, but Sandrine doesn't have the pass code. She takes it out of her bag and places it on the kitchen table, just as the house phone rings. She is startled, unsure whether to answer. It will stop. She wants it to stop. Then she tells herself that perhaps it's him, perhaps she had better take the call.

At the other end of the line, the male cop tells her they'll be keeping him in for twenty-four hours at least. Maybe more, but they will keep her informed. Did she get home all right? She says, I could hardly answer the house phone if I'd turned the car over in a ditch on the way back, could I? Then regrets it immediately, she has no place talking that way, and certainly not to a man, but he gives a small laugh and says OK, OK. Listen, we'll keep you updated.

He doesn't have to do that. Her legal knowledge tells her they're under no obligation to call, to be kind and considerate. To put her in danger. Perhaps he's calling in front of her man, perhaps he heard the cop laugh, perhaps he heard what Sandrine said. She feels her heart shrink, her ribs tighten. She knows she shouldn't, but she asks, Is he with you now? The cop is surprised, he says Huh? No. Ah, no. I'm calling from my office. He's in the cells, *Madame*. And that's where he'll stay until tomorrow evening, 7 p.m.

The rod between Sandrine's shoulders softens to wax, warm and soft. She thanks the cop and cuts the call.

She turns on the radio, hears music. She recognises the piece: it's Mendelssohn's 'Spinnerlied', the theme tune to a literary programme she used to listen to on Sunday evenings, before coming to live here. Searching for the title of the piece, she had discovered Mendelssohn; and then Lully, and then Marin Marais. She used to do that a lot. Give herself permission to be curious, to feel her attention was not unworthy or ridiculous. In the same way, she had read books at school, and then the ones recommended to her by the librarian at the lycée. She isn't a very cultivated person, not at all, he tells her so, often enough: she comes from the gutter and she'd better not get ideas above her station, but there had been a time in her life when her liking for such things felt legitimate, when she savoured them quite simply, did not deny herself the pleasure. That was before. This evening she relaxes her shoulders as far as she feels able, turns up the radio and tells her belly, Listen to that, little bean, isn't it lovely?

She opens the freezer and searches for the spinach. She loves spinach, she's only one here who does. Mathias, who could never be accused of being difficult or prone to tantrums, had forced himself to eat some the first time, but she saw that he was struggling. His father hadn't even tried, then declared that spinach was off the menu. She eats the spinach leaves now, lightly fried in a little olive oil, with a pinch of nutmeg and salt. She finds the soured cream he insists on pouring over everything more and more indigestible now, and she devours her big plate of spinach, asking her belly from time to time, So! Delicious, isn't it?

At 9 p.m. she has finished, and everything has been washed up and put away. His locked telephone remains on the kitchen countertop. She is unsure what to do with it. It vibrates, and she doesn't want to look, but the screen is within her field of vision. She doesn't want to read it, but the words sear themselves on her retina and she makes sense of them in spite of herself. The beginning of a text message from 'Charlie': *You must have been held up… could you*

Sandrine knows of no one he calls 'Charlie'… But then she knows hardly any of his acquaintances. He has little liking for people as a rule. Occasionally, he invites people he wants to impress, to show them the house, the smartly laid table, his young, well-trained, unobtrusive partner. Three of them come sometimes, including Christian, whom he continues to invite with the others, so as to observe his interactions with Sandrine. She dreads those evenings, when there is no right answer, no appropriate way to be. Each is a test whose unknown rules ensure she loses every single time. And then he shouts, he gets angry and suspicious, he accuses her, she sleeps on the floor, he follows her around, it goes on for days and days, more days each time, during which she waits for Monsieur Langlois, who calls her a slut and a fat sow, to go away and for the man who cries to come home. Among the three men who occasionally come to dinner, there is Christian, to her lasting sorrow, but no Charlie. She tells herself, Well, it must be someone texting about something else. She looks around at the spotless kitchen then goes upstairs to shower.

Stepping out of the cubicle, she looks at herself in the mirror, wonders if the little bean is starting to show. She thinks her breasts have got bigger. Her cheek still hurts a little but there are no visible marks. She smears herself with moisturising lotion and gets into bed. She hopes she'll be able to sleep. Sometimes, he has to travel for work and the noises around the house are different when he's away, it grinds and cracks, she can hear the boiler more clearly, and she's afraid she'll hear the front door open. But Mathias is always there with her. She has never slept alone in this house.

A few seconds after turning out the light, she is sleeping like a baby.

12

S HE WAKES SUDDENLY, very early. It's still dark. She thought she heard his voice downstairs, in the sitting room. At the base of the nape of her neck, the knife burns red-hot. Hurriedly, she gets up and goes down, but there's no one there, and the door is shut fast, with her key in the lock. She goes back upstairs to wash and get ready. From to time, she rolls her head slowly from left to right, to loosen the knot.

She's hungry, and decides to eat. Or rather, she's hungry so she eats. Since the discovery that she is nurturing the little bean, eating has ceased to be a decision, something that is thought about, undertaken, or snatched like an act of violence. She is no longer on a diet, not 'watching her weight' any more, she's been told to eat what she needs and so she eats, sublimely oblivious. This morning: half a banana, an unsweetened yoghurt – for a few days now she has relished the delicate, sharp, slightly chalky taste of the white semi-liquid – and then a small tin of sweetcorn, because she feels like it. Whatever next? she asks the little bean, out loud, then realises that what with her feelings of revulsion, or the times she just forgot, or her containers only half emptied, she has perhaps never eaten such a varied and satisfying meal, and quite without thinking. So delicious, such freedom! Is this what they mean by a 'balanced diet'? She knows, of course, but as someone who is also quite capable of devouring two packets of biscuits and several bars of chocolate in under five minutes, then gasping with shame and self-loathing, this is a completely new and different world. A world where food takes a comfortable back seat. She decides what to wear, leaves aside things that are too tight, without hating herself, without calling herself a fat cow, a fat, stupid bitch. It's not me, it's the little bean, he needs feeding. She applies her foundation, decides to leave her hair loose, it's lank and straggly, but so what. In any case, he won't see her this morning and when she comes home tonight, there will be other things to think about besides her hair. Her cheek isn't hurting, which is just as well, she cannot think about that. But there are dark red, almost wine-coloured, marks on her neck. The male cop said 7 p.m. So by the time he reaches the house… Will he call? Will they accompany him? Or perhaps Christian? She takes a scarf to cover her neck. Autumn is here.

She is coming downstairs, her mouth fresh and smelling of mint, when the doorbell rings, loud in the silence.

Not him. It's the two cops.

May we sit down? the male cop asks. She wants to say No, but instead she says, I'm about to leave for work. Well, we won't keep you long, he says, but we'd like to interview you. Would it be easier during the day – at work, for example? Are you able to get away? Sandrine doesn't know what will infuriate him most – that the cops have come to the house, his house, while he's away. Or that she might see them far from here, in a place to which he has no access. She says, Isn't he with you? And the woman cop says No, he's being detained until this evening and I promise you that if he's bailed before then, I'll call you immediately. No! Sandrine protests straightaway, unthinking. It would take too long to explain that he checks her call history, and if he sees a number he doesn't know… Instead, she adds, It's OK, no need.

We really need to talk to you, Sandrine. We can come with you to work afterwards, if necessary, that way we can talk to your employer. No! Sandrine cries out once again.

No. Work is a place apart. Impossible to explain, but it's a place apart. And so she relents, and signals for them to sit on the sofa.

They take their places in the sitting room and Sandrine notices that they have, quite naturally, returned to the seats they occupied on Saturday. You're a legal officer, is that right? asks the woman cop as she sits down. Legal secretary, Sandrine corrects her, then asks: What about Mathias?

Mathias won't be coming back today, the male cop informs her. He chooses his words carefully, but there are no illusions he can shatter now. Since her last visit, Caroline has recovered one or two memories, Sandrine. For the moment, there are still long stretches of time of which she remembers nothing. But she can remember her childhood, in part. And she has remembered snatches of more recent events, too. Still nothing from the day she disappeared. But we're getting there. The psychiatrist is pleased with her progress. Things are coming back to her quite quickly. More quickly than anyone hoped.

Sandrine, the woman cop addresses her in a kind voice, the memories that Caroline has recovered are violent memories. Memories from her marriage to Monsieur Langlois, memories of her everyday life. I told you that she wasn't allowed to drive. In the weeks before her disappearance, Monsieur Langlois stopped her eating, too. She didn't simply disappear into the woods. It's not possible. Because he he never let her out, except with Mathias, for school.

Sandrine listens and she feels as if she's floating, somewhere, off to one side. She hasn't even gone there on purpose; it's just the place she goes when things get too hard, too complicated, too painful. She looks at that other Sandrine, talking to the cops.

Which she shouldn't. Other Sandrine will regret it, there'll be trouble. But what they're saying is ridiculous, it makes no sense. He makes Sandrine eat, force-feeds her, then tells she's fat. That's she's repulsive. That no one else would want her, nobody, ever. That he's the only one who loves her, who could ever love her. Starve her? Absolutely not, that's absurd.

I told you that she wasn't allowed to use the car, do you remember? Sandrine mumbles something, the woman cop leans closer, says I'm sorry? And Sandrine forces herself speak clearly. But she drank. It was dangerous.

Facing her, two pairs of eyes open wide. She *what*? says the woman officer. She drank… Sandrine says again.

They stare at one another, there's something they cannot believe but Sandrine doesn't know what it is. Everything they thought they knew so far? What she has just told them? Her intelligence? The woman cop says, Who told you this, Sandrine? Caroline didn't drink, there's isn't a bartender within 50 kilometres of here who recognised her when we showed them her picture. We searched the bins. The house. The only alcohol we found was in the drinks cabinet.

'That doesn't prove a thing.' Sandrine thinks the words very hard, she may even have spoken them out loud.

Drink costs money, Sandrine. It had been years since Caroline had access to the bank card. There are no grocery stores any-where near here on foot, you'd have to walk several kilometres. The supermarket checkout staff recognised her, though. They all told us she paid in cash, and if he was with her, he paid with the card. She never bought spirits. Never bought alcohol of any kind, including when she was alone.

True, there's nothing in the house: one bottle of brandy in the drinks cabinet, another of cognac, and whisky. In all of them, the level goes down very slowly. There's some wine in the garage, he drinks that, a little. Thinks of himself as something of a connoisseur, likes to bring out his finest bottles when Anne-Marie and Patrice come for lunch, or Christian and the other two, the people he wants to impress.

I can't think why he told you that, the woman cop insists, shaking her head. Why would he tell you that? Sandrine thinks that for the first time, she looks unsure of herself. The woman cop adds, But no, we've been through everything. There was literally no way she could have drunk. Heavy drinking requires planning, logistics, and she had to make every journey on foot.

That's absurd, too, thinks Sandrine. She has her own car. She was even allowed to drive the big, expensive saloon, last night. Nothing they say makes any sense.

Why are you telling me this? she asks, and her voice comes out twisted, wheedling, so much weaker than she would like.

Because we're investigating him, Sandrine, says the male cop. Because we are going to question you, officially, about what you know about Caroline's disappearance. You must be prepared.

Sandrine… The woman cop leans forward and places a hand on Sandrine's knee. Sandrine moves her leg, pushes the hand away like an unwelcome cat. The hand retreats to where it came from, and the woman rubs her temples. The man takes over.

Sandrine, I told you we've been able to see Caroline's medical notes. Do you remember?

Sandrine nods.

The medical notes are those of a woman who has endured very violent treatment, and not only in the period immediately before her reappearance over the border in Italy. Caroline shows signs of several historic fractures. A lot. Do you understand what I'm saying? The male cop leans in and says quietly, My colleague

186

wants to make sure you've been clearly warned, *Mademoiselle*. She knows you don't much like her, we don't know why, and in fact we really don't care. But listen to *me*, Sandrine. Please. Has he hit you already?

Hit, hit, Sandrine hears the word and it's like when she was small and people called her things she didn't want to hear, d-i-r-t-y, m-i-s-t-a-k-e, l-i-t-t-l-e s-h-i-t, she breaks it down, spells it out, h-i-t. Then she shakes herself, feels that for weeks her life has consisted of nothing but reaching out to catch hold of thoughts that escape her, and she says, What do you mean, hit? And she sees herself, the accessory with the tow-coloured hair, and she tells herself, Stupid, stupid fat cow, they must really take you for some kind of idiot, of course she knows that word, it's what goes with it, the entire question that escapes her, what are they saying, that this man, her man— What are they saying? Hit, the cop repeats again, has he ever hit you? Has he ever hurt you? The psychiatrist who came on Saturday watched Monsieur Langlois very closely, the way he was behaving with you, with Mathias. We are genuinely concerned.

Sandrine is adrift, cut off. Each time they say 'Monsieur Langlois', she tells herself that yes, perhaps Monsieur Langlois is violent. Perhaps Monsieur Langlois is the sort of man who would beat his wife. But she, Sandrine, does not live with Monsieur Langlois. She lives with the man who cries. The man who cries hasn't been around much lately, often Monsieur Langlois is the one who comes home from work, but the man who cries always comes back in the end. Like on Saturday, when Monsieur Langlois shouted, and did what he did, and the man who cries came to console her. Monsieur Langlois gets cross with her because she's stupid, and gets things wrong, because she hangs on to her point- less, rubbish job, because she's incapable of making vinaigrette when he's told her a thousand times that it's the vinegar first, that she dresses like a slut to seduce those bonehead lawyers at work, that she gets back late because she's been screwing one of them, that she's been lying to him when she says there was a road closure. Monsieur Langlois pushes her around, throws plates on the floor, forces her to pick up the pieces and tells Mathias that's the way to treat filthy sows like her. But the man who cries always comes back and he's sorry, he's always *so* very sorry that he had to do that, that she made him angry, that her stupid mistakes spoil their life together when he wants them to be so happy. The man who cries caresses and cajoles her, crowns her with carefully woven wreaths of tender words. He is sweet and attentive, makes her feel like a queen, and then she forgets Monsieur Langlois, because Sandrine doesn't like Monsieur Langlois, because she's in love with the man who cries.

Sandrine? *Sandrine?* The woman cop is speaking to her, the woman who thinks Sandrine doesn't like her and she's absolutely right. Sandrine, there's nothing keeping you here, you know that? And Sandrine thinks, Stupid bitch. But this time she's not thinking about herself. She can't leave. Leave – to do what? Go back to the hideous loneliness that lies in wait, ready to swallow her whole? Go off and raise the little bean by herself, like a worthless single mother who couldn't say no, because she's one of those women who can't keep a man? And even if she wanted to, even if she wanted to be a family of two, she knows – because he tells her – that women and children can't just go anywhere and do anything they like, they need a man, a child needs a father. He says it so often that Sandrine asks herself sometimes if she thought it, or he said it. But not lately. Lately, she doesn't think any more. Nowadays – whether it's because Caroline came back, or because of the little bean – she can't form any answers, or any

188

questions, and so she says nothing, she sits silently in front of the police officers, empty-eyed, her mouth half open. They don't understand, they don't understand how kind and gentle the man who cries can be, how much they love one another, how badly she wants the man who cries to be the father of her little bean, how she cannot imagine any other life, any other place, a different reality. They don't understand that even if she wanted to leave the man who cries, Monsieur Langlois would never let her. She sees a bean shape floating before her eyes, and she shakes herself.

They have to leave. She must find words to make them leave. She searches for an answer to their question. Something plain and simple.

She shrugs, feels the impossible weight pressing down on each shoulder, and says, No, he doesn't hit me. She pronounces the words clearly. And you don't understand. You don't know him. Now, I must get to work. Please.

The male cop says, Yes, of course, as he gets to his feet. His colleague stands up, too, with her narrow thighs and her chewed nails, bitten till they bleed. That's what Sandrine saw on the hand that placed itself on her knee. Those fingernails. She, Sandrine, has nice nails. She has a body pockmarked with a thousand tiny scars, silent witnesses to all the times she searched her skin, looking for vile, repellent things to excise, to sacrifice, so that she would be pure and light and happy at last. But she has nice nails. Opposite her, the woman with the ugly, chewed nails says, We're trying to see if we can keep him in for longer, Sandrine, but he's got a good lawyer on his case. We're still plugging one or two gaps, we're going to make things hard for him, as hard as we possibly can with his speeding offence. But he'll be here tonight. Are you sure you don't want to leave now, Sandrine? Don't you want to— We can help you, there are hostels, emergency places... There are... things we can do. But we can't set anything in motion unless you talk.

She works all day, concentrates hard. The two cops had let her leave, lock and bolt the door, climb into her car. They didn't follow her, and she had arrived at work, her haven of peace. They won't come to the firm's offices. Nor will Monsieur Langlois. Even those times when she really angered him, even when he thought there was something going on between her and Christian, even when she makes mistakes, gets things wrong, he never comes here. He has waited for her in the street a few times, to make sure she doesn't speak to anyone, that she is hiding nothing, but he has never come up to the first-floor offices, he's too clever for that. And he's not down there now, in his saloon. He's with the cops. They promised. They said, Legally, we have until 7 o'clock this evening. From time to time she straightens up, bends her neck to one side and then the other. She feels stiffer and stiffer. Seven o'clock, she tells herself, glancing at the time in the corner of her screen.

When she pulls up in front of the house, her neck feels knotted and painful once again. She sits for a few minutes behind the steering wheel. She doesn't need to fetch Mathias from school, so she's home early, in fact. She glances at the clock one more time.

She hesitates, then turns the key in the ignition once again and drives the familiar route. The bell for the end of the after-school study period will have rung by now, a few minutes ago, he will have gone already. Outside the buildings, she peers at the gate, at the pavement, then drives away slowly. There.

She stops, double-parked. Anne-Marie is getting into a car, taking her seat. The car belongs to Anne-Marie and Patrice. Caroline is helping Mathias attach his seatbelt in the raised car seat he will soon no longer need. Patrice stands beside the open driver's door, looking up and down the street. Sandrine waits for them to leave, for Patrice to complete his manoeuvre and pull away. The car drives off and all she could see of Mathias is the top of his head, silhouetted against the light. They are talking all together in the car, she can see their heads moving. The sight warms her heart. Mathias is all right, she tells the little bean.

She goes back to the house. She wonders how it would be to live here alone, without him, just her and the little bean. An alternative reality, but one that is closed to her, far off and alien. She takes a shower and changes. She irons the flowery shirt, the one she hated that summer, so badly cut. It never suited her – it cut her under the arms, gaped across her chest, pulled slightly too tight across her stomach – so it won't make any difference, even if she has put on weight, and he'll be pleased to see her in it. She buttons the front and discovers, somewhat to her surprise, that she's slimmer now, and the shirt – though still as ugly as ever – is less painful to wear. She wonders whether to redo her make-up, but she's afraid that he will ask Christian to accompany him back home, and decides against it. If he suspects she has made an effort with her appearance for someone else, it will— It will... She won't think about it, she leaves her make-up as it is. She goes downstairs and busies herself in the kitchen. She makes vinaigrette, at pains to make sure she gets it right. There's a lasagne in the freezer. He likes lasagne. She warms the oven, lays the table for two, and waits, her neck frozen like stone. Time passes, it's a long wait. She would like to call someone, say something, but it's been months, or longer, since she had anyone to speak to. And so she stays where she is, waiting for him to come back, making an occasional tour of the ground floor to check that everything is clean and dusted, that everything is all right.

He shows up at 9 p.m. in a car she doesn't recognise, driven by a man she doesn't know. He gets out of the car and it turns around. He smells of beer. In the hallway, where she comes to greet him, Sandrine wants to ask who the driver is, how he's feeling, and what the police said, but none of these questions are safe. Besides, it's not her place to ask questions, this is his home, he can come back any time he wants. Even after a stint in the cells, under observation. But saying nothing is just as suspicious, it means she's trying to hide something, and so, after a moment, she says, I've made lasagne. He looks at her, says nothing, and closes the front door. He performs his usual ritual, down to the last detail, the last sigh: he bends down to undo his laces, takes out his wallet and leaves it on the little hall cabinet, hangs his jacket on the coat-hooks. Then slides his feet into his slippers and heads for the garage without a word. Sandrine follows, her spine stiff with expectation. He checks his splendid motor car, inside and out. It takes some minutes.

He is satisfied. He takes her by the shoulder and they walk back to the sitting room, the kitchen. His hand is on her neck. He asks, Where's my phone? She points to the countertop.

She takes the lasagne out of the oven. She has covered it with tinfoil so it won't dry out, it looks good, he'll be pleased, everything will be all right. Sandrine takes up her silent, inner refrain: the vinaigrette will be fine, everything will be all right. When she places the dish on the table, he is holding his phone and staring at her suspiciously. He asks, What were you doing last night at 9 o'clock? She removes the thick cotton glove that protects her against the scalding dish. He's trying to find out if she saw the text messages. She says, I think I was taking a shower,

I went upstairs early, I couldn't concentrate on the TV, I was worried about you. He watches her closely. She tries to steady her breathing, to behave as if nothing is wrong. Everything will be all right. She asks, Are you hungry? How much lasagne do you want? Did you get anything to eat?

He lays the phone down on the table, takes his seat. He believes her. He believes her. Everything will be all right. He says, Give me a big plateful. I'm starving. All I got was a miserable meal-tray. Disgusting.

Sandrine feels the floor sinking beneath her feet, she hurries to serve his food and sit down, so that he won't see her legs shaking. She has lied, and nothing happened. She didn't just *hide* something, she *lied*, and he believes her. She hasn't lied for months. He watches her so closely, scrutinises her expression so intently, he gives her hell even when she's telling the truth, like with Christian. But there have been other things, too: what she said or didn't say to Patrice and Anne-Marie, how long she spent at work, and who she was with, her car journeys, what she eats, what she buys, who she calls. Every time, all she tells him is the truth, right from the start of their time together, when she still believed that was enough, that telling the truth was all she needed to do. But it's not enough now, it hasn't been enough for a very long time, he demands proof, wants access to her phone, insists she share her location with him, all the time. He wants her to show him her bank statements. Sometimes, if something isn't right, or he just wants her to remember that he's the one in charge, he's the one who decides, then he insults her, wakes her up at night and insults her again, and she finds herself confessing to imaginary offences, and then she must take the punishment they entail. She must ask forgiveness, of course, on her knees. Tell him she's sorry, that she's rubbish, a big fat shit, that she won't do it again. He's torn up some of her books already, broken two phones, and he has pushed her, pinched her, pulled her lank, straggly hair. And since the first woman came back it's gotten worse, he loses control, drags her down with him. His rage on Saturday, hands on her throat, he has never squeezed so tight. And the slap on Sunday, just a day ago, the first one, and the last, he promised, the man who cries had come home and he had promised. And today is only Monday, and already he's suspicious, and already she's afraid that Monsieur Langlois is back. But she *lied* and he *didn't see it*.

She lifts a fork loaded with pasta and tomato sauce, and smiles at him. A sincere smile of relief. He frowns and says What's the matter with you, you're acting strangely, and she says I'm relieved, that's all. And it's true, she doesn't need to pretend this time; she is genuinely relieved. A possibility is emerging, a reality in which he doesn't know everything. And if he doesn't know everything, perhaps other things are false, perhaps the other things he says are false too. That if she leaves him, he'll kill her, that in any case she's far too ugly, much too stupid to find someone else and who'd want her apart from him? That if she's living with him, it's by his rules. That he wants to see her leave that shitty job by Christmas, and sell that rust-bucket of a car, that her place is here at home and that he won't wait much longer because why would she want to carry on working if it's just to go and smile sweetly at the boneheaded lawyers in her firm. Why would she want to keep a car if it's not to go and get screwed God-knows-where.

Are you listening to me?

His voice is tense, anxious, the moment's absence is over, *Careful now, come back down, listen to him, listen to him and everything will be all right.* Sandrine says, I'm sorry, my mind was wandering, I was so worried about you. And then she searches for something safe, something utterly free of danger, one of the few permitted questions – there are a couple, like 'Are you hungry?' for instance. But this is a new situation, she feels like she's walking on quicksand. She opts for 'I hope they treated you all right?' And he says he doesn't want to talk about it. They eat in silence. She stops eating before he does, she's not hungry any more. He stares at her plate and seems about to say something, probably that she should eat, that it's very good, or perhaps, Why aren't you eating anything? Who are you trying to get thin for? And if he says that, Sandrine knows how the rest of the evening will go. But when he looks up at her, she is feeling her cheek with the tips of her fingers, without thinking, and her man reaches out and strokes her forearm, kindly, gently. She jumps as if startled. Again, she hasn't been listening. *Careful now, come back down, listen to him, listen to him and everything will be all right.* She says, Do you want dessert? There are yoghurts, and fruit compote.

He says, Listen, I've been very stressed since, since she— I need you to be nice, OK? It's hard, it's very hard. And that woman cop, that… what a bitch, what a fucking bitch.

His fingers tighten around Sandrine's arm, and it stiffens as the pressure on her flesh increases.

The guy Christian sent me is very good. Expensive, but very good. It'll be all right, I'll get the kid back. She'll see she can't do that to me, no one is going to steal the kid, least of all her. And then we'll be here, the three of us, we'll be a family. But I need you at my side, I need you to be there for me.

She nods, thinks that just a few days ago, a speech like that would have made her cry tears of joy. Asking her to be there for him, telling her clearly how much he wants her. Her and his son, and that word, *family*. A word that flushes her cheeks pink. The pressure on Sandrine's wrist disappears, and now, at the end of the outstretched arm, there is the hand of her man, who cries.

He has barely slept since the police took him away, just a few hours that morning, and he suggests they go upstairs early, to bed. He is the man who cries when he comes out of the shower, his tousled hair making him look like a dreamy-headed little boy. He is the man who cries when he takes her in his arms. And then he starts talking about her again, that woman cop, and her, Caroline, and despite her silent pleas, her attempts to change the subject, her eyes that pretend to close and sleep, Sandrine feels the anger return, until he is brimful of vitriol. She tries one more time to change the subject and Monsieur Langlois asks her just who she thinks she is. The man who cries is a long way off, and Monsieur Langlois orders her not to interrupt him. His diatribe takes flight, like an evil bird, a scavenger that stinks of the flesh on which it feeds, railing against all the bitches and whores of this world, that bitch of a cop, that bitch Caroline, and Sandrine herself, bitch, how does he know she was here on her own last night? When Monsieur Langlois turns her over and presses her face into the pillows to show her what he does to whores like her, she tells herself that at least it won't last long – the angrier he is, the quicker it's over.

13

S HE HAS AN APPOINTMENT with the gynaecologist today, and she's happy to go, the first time in her life that she's been eager to get to a doctor's surgery.

She looks around as she leaves the office during her lunch break, but the saloon is nowhere in sight. She takes a deeper breath. She isn't meant to go to the doctor without him knowing. She isn't meant to do anything without him knowing.

In the waiting room, music plays softly and the same delicate aroma of eucalyptus floats on the warm air. She likes the smell. When they first began seeing one another, she told him, My favourite bouquet? Hm, white flowers, I think. And eucalyptus? She had picked those almost at random, no one had ever bought her flowers. And her small, single girl's apartment had smelt of eucalyptus for months, he never showed up empty-handed, she'd had to buy vases, three of them: two for the bouquets that were still fresh and a third, huge one in which she placed the stems of eucalyptus when the flowers had surrendered and died. She felt she was accumulating love, making a huge bouquet out of her good fortune, that the scent of eucalyptus was the scent of happiness, the happiness that had come to her, for which she no longer sat waiting.

She thinks about all that and suddenly, there are tears in her eyes. She cries often and hardly ever, both are true: never when she's alone, or rather, never when he isn't there. At first, crying was enough to calm him down, as if he had achieved what he set out to do, succeeded in capsizing something inside her. But for a long time now, crying has not been enough to stop him. Now she has to be red-faced, dishevelled, pleading, a mess. That was why he wore her out, insulted her, pinched her, pushed her, pulled her lank, dead-straight strands of hair. She remembers the broken cognac glass, his attentive, apologetic care after she smashed it, and she tells herself *that* was effective, that worked, the blood. Perhaps the logical conclusion is that he will only calm down now if he sees her bleed.

Something mutters to her: the small, muffled, furious voice that has slowly made its way into Sandrine's head these past few weeks, after months of silence that tasted of dead ends and defeat. It's faint, far off, but Sandrine makes out the words: *Of course, you stupid cow, of course he's going to hit you.*

At that moment, the gynaecologist appears. She has a new hairstyle. Thick braids draw dark rows across her scalp. She looks beautiful. Sandrine would love to have hair like that. Hair that *has* something. Life. Determination. Sandrine would love to be someone else.

The woman does not signal her to move; she comes forward, leans in, even crouches on her heels, says Hmm, you don't look so well. Are the hormones playing up? Sandrine takes out a paper handkerchief so as not to ruin her make-up and says No. I don't know. Maybe.

Well, let's see, says the lady doctor. Shall we? You can tell me all about it.

Sandrine sits in the chair and says nothing. She can still hear the angry voice that echoed inside her in the waiting room, but it's muffled now, almost comical. The same voice that hollered at her to leave the first time he asked her to show him her text messages. He thought she was texting her boss, she swore she wasn't, he said, Prove it. The voice had hollered loud and clear then. It said, *Nothing, you have nothing whatever to prove. Why did he ask you to come and live here if he doesn't trust you? To live here with him? And with his son?* But Sandrine wanted to be nice, wanted to please, wanted to hold on to her brand-new happiness. By the time he was demanding her phone codes, access to her bank account, her email inbox, the voice was barely audible, a faint, far-off hiss.

So. What's the matter? Sandrine shakes her head, she doesn't know where to begin, she has only just allowed herself to understand how this is bound to end: badly. And still she cannot put anything into words, because she cannot form her own thoughts. What's happening, what might happen, who she is, and where, or why.

She forces herself to breathe deeply, to dry her tears. Facing her, the lady doctor is calm, patient, but a small, anxious furrow has wriggled between her eyebrows. She asks questions, gently. Any nausea? Tiredness? No, I'm OK. Sandrine speaks slowly, carefully, feels calmer.

Have you done the other tests? Sandrine says No, I'm sorry, I didn't have the... any...

She doesn't know if she means to say time, courage, opportunity, she doesn't know how to explain that she hasn't told him she's pregnant because the man she lives with follows her, spies on her, times her journeys; that she has to spend her lunch breaks working in front of her PC screen because she can't arrive home even a minute late; that she didn't dare disobey his rules and instructions because now that the first, dead woman isn't dead any more, everything is getter worse and worse.

Not to worry, says the gynaecologist, can you get them done before the end of the week?

Sandrine nods.

Good, then. All sorted. Good. And the father – have you told him?

Sandrine shakes her head.

But... He's still around? You do live together, don't you?

Sandrine nods.

A very long pause follows.

At length, in the warm silence, the doctor asks, May I examine you today?

Everything is warm here, warm and smooth and round, here is all the time in the world. The paper on the examination table isn't soft under her bottom, and there are no paintings on the walls, just framed posters, but it's calm and quiet, and nothing happens without asking first. And so, Sandrine says Yes.

'Can you undress down to your bra and pants? Or you can keep your blouse on, if you prefer... Could you lie back? No, keep your top on for now, we'll examine you in stages. First, you're going to lie down flat on the table, there, that's it. I'm going to touch your belly... I'm going to move further down. There. Now this might feel a little cold... No? All OK? Good, now then...'

Sandrine gazes up at the ceiling. Textured white squares. Textured with what? It's meant to look like... marble? No. Rough plaster? The woman says something and Sandrine, who, as so often when she is touched, has floated away, emerges from her thoughts. I was saying, I can feel some scratches, some roughness here. Do you want to tell me how they got there? For a moment, Sandrine thinks the woman is asking about her scars, the endless, destructive work-in-progress that she inflicts on her own body, its cruelty all the more intense when the rest of her life slips from her grasp. And then she realises that's not it, that the doctor is talking about the marks left inside her by

Monsieur Langlois. She can tell he hurts her. Sandrine thought nothing would show.

Sandrine is ashamed. On a reflex, her legs snap shut, but the gynaecologist has already let go of her knees, removed her gloves and rolled her stool level with her patient's face. How should she answer the question? What can she say, that she doesn't notice such things any more, that it's not always like that? *But it is,* says the voice. *It's been like that for months!* Shut up, Sandrine thinks, and why answer anyway – to the voice, or the doctor, why justify herself. Why are all these women poking their noses into her life? Sandrine feels her cheeks flush, she cannot believe she's going to have to talk about it with her cunt exposed for all to see. She swallows, and the lady says, You can get dressed first, of course, if you prefer, I understand – it's not the most comfortable of positions! Here, lie on your side before sitting up. She cuts off a piece of white paper and offers Sandrine an improvised apron. Take this. I'm sure if you asked me to put my bum on show and then talk, I wouldn't feel too comfortable either! And she smiles again, but this time the smile is a little tense, a smile that forces itself to carry on smiling.

Is the baby all right? is all Sandrine can say, wrapping her arms over her stomach, because that's what matters to her most, that's why she's here, the rest is her business. The woman opposite nods her heads and rises slowly to her feet, then sits down behind her desk.

Sandrine pulls on her panties and jeans, hoping the doctor won't insist too much.

The gynaecologist doesn't insist. But when Sandrine sits down opposite her on the plastic chair, she waits. For a long time. Sandrine feels like a naughty schoolgirl. Like she will be handed down some kind of punishment – another one. And then the woman says, I have a patient who's very wealthy.

Out of nowhere, just like that, a statement laid out there on the table, on the doctor's blotter. And Sandrine thinks: nothing. Her brain is empty.

Very wealthy and... chic, you can picture what I mean? Or rather, perfectly groomed. Always beautifully dressed. Like you. This is the second time I've seen you. You're always very carefully dressed. As for me... She waves a hand, smiles like someone who has no trouble laughing at herself. Sandrine doesn't smile, because she thinks the doctor is beautiful. Her clothes suit her. Her braids give her a very regal air, today. And she has no idea where the doctor is going with this, nor why she's lying to her – Sandrine isn't elegant, she knows that. The doctor continues: And she has an important job. One she's very good at. She helps a lot of people. And of course, I'll never, ever tell you her name, but what I'm about to tell you is more important than her name. This woman is so rich, so elegant, and so effective in her work, yet for years her husband mistreated her. Was violent towards her. She was one of my very first patients. She came along more or less by chance, to the surgery where I was starting out... But she's been my patient for a long time now. Years. There was always a good reason, it seemed to me at first. She had walked into a glass door, missed a step on the stairs, she hadn't seen the open cupboard door. And there were lacerations, like the ones I've just seen on you. I'm going to say something very important to you. If you do not consent to have sex, it's rape. If anyone, your partner, your husband, penetrates you when you've said No, that's a crime. Theoretically, he could go to prison for it.

Why are you telling me this? Sandrine spits the words out far more angrily than she would have liked. There is another silence, even longer than the first, and then the woman says, No reason. To talk. To tell you that when the woman was ready to tell me what was really happening, when she decided to leave, I helped her. Lots of people helped her. The police. A refuge. Her lawyer. There are women who manage to get away, and manage to heal. Can I pay for this visit now? asks Sandrine, who doesn't want to be here any more, doesn't want to talk any more, doesn't want anything any more. Yes, says the gynaecologist, and when Sandrine puts the money on the desk, in cash, the doctor adds, There are women who choose not to leave, too, Sandrine. Because it's very hard. Because it's very, very hard to leave. And sometimes the men kill them. Sooner or later, the men kill them. They decide to kill them. Take this.

Sandrine has put her jacket on already, she's about to slip the strap of her bag over her head and around her neck. The woman pushes a booklet – just a few stapled pages – towards her, says Please, take it. Please look after yourself. And come back and see me with the test results. All right? For the baby. It's important. Please?

Sandrine stuffs the booklet into her bag without looking at it, and leaves. In the waiting room, the young man behind the reception desk signals to her, suggests a date and a time the following week. She says, Yes, fine, without thinking. She just wants to get away. We can send you a reminder by text the day before, he says. He smiles, he looks nice, a kind face. Sandrine can't stand any more of these nice-looking people who do nothing but cause trouble, she says No! Absolutely not. I've written it down, OK? I've written it down. The young man looks surprised but says, All right, see you next week, then.

Sandrine leaves. Out on the street, she breathes more easily, knows her face is crimson, but from what? Shame, no doubt. And panic. At least she didn't give the woman her medical card, just like the first time. He won't see the cost of the visit reimbursed on her account.

Late that afternoon, she shuts herself in a toilet cubicle with her bag. She will dispose of the booklet in the unit for used sanitary towels. What else can she do with it? She can't keep it in her bag, which he inspects every evening. She hasn't dropped it in the street, of course – she can never be sure he isn't there somewhere, spying on her. That he won't pick it up and think she's been talking to somebody. She can't leave it in the wastepaper basket at work. What if someone was to see it, and ask questions? She holds it in both hands. It's printed in pink, green and white, on quite thick paper. She reads the title: *Is Your Partner Controlling?* Followed by a long list of affirmations. The aim is to see whether they apply to your situation, yes or no. The list begins with:

> *My partner belittles my projects and opinions.*
> *My partner is always jealous.*
> *My partner doesn't approve of my cooking, my housekeeping, the way I dress, the way I behave when we're out in public.*
> *My partner calls me frequently at work, he comes to my workplace unannounced, to check that 'everything's OK'.*
> *He makes jokes about my shape, finds fault with my appearance (too much... not enough...).*
> *My partner makes me feel I can do nothing right. Everything I do is always 'not quite right'.*
> *Nothing I do is ever good enough for him.*
> *My partner makes me feel like I don't support him enough, or at all. That I don't love him enough.*
> *My partner never encourages me. When he compliments me, it's always double-edged: 'That was a really nice supper, for once.'*

My partner hates it when I speak to new people I've met, he
accuses me of being unfaithful with people I see socially.

He reads my phone messages and emails.

My partner tells me I don't need to work, he will take care of me.

My partner says he takes the family decisions, because he's the man.

I have to account for my spending in detail, he makes me justify
the money I spend. He demands or has found the log-in and
passwords for my personal bank accounts.

When my partner is annoyed or angry, he stands very close to
me, and his body language is threatening (clenched fists,
sudden gestures).

Arguments often or always end with me backing down; I'm afraid
of what he might do to me so I keep quiet, I let it go.

My partner throws things around and breaks things at home:
plates, ornaments, small accessories or pieces of furniture.

My partner damages, throws away or destroys clothes and objects
I am fond of.

My partner stops me from sleeping.

My partner insists on sex acts that I feel uncomfortable with.

He makes me put on clothes he likes but which I feel uncomfort-
able wearing.

He insists I wear clothes he finds 'sexy', but which make me feel
uncomfortable.

And on it goes, over the page, line after line, each with a little
white square to tick 'if this applies to you and/or your situation'.
The list ends with:

My partner will never agree to me leaving him.

My partner throws things at me.

My partner pinches me, squeezes my neck, my arm, etc. tightly.

My partner pulls my hair.
My partner hits my head against the wall.
My partner tries to choke me.
My partner kicks me.
My partner pushes me, makes me fall over, trips me up.
My partner hits me.
My partner forces me to have sex: he rapes me.

Sandrine reads everything; she thinks: *Yes, yes, yes, yes, yes, yes, no,*
yes, yes, yes, yes, yes, yes, yes, yes, yes, yes, yes, yes, yes, yes, yes, yes, yes,
yes, yes, yes, yes, yes, no, no, yes, yes, yes, yes, yes, yes, yes, yes, yes, yes,
yes, yes, yes, yes, yes, yes, yes, yes, yes, yes, yes, yes, yes, yes, yes, yes, no,
yes, yes, yes, yes, yes, yes, yes, yes, yes, yes, yes, yes, yes, yes, yes, yes, yes,
yes, yes, yes, yes, yes, yes, yes, yes, yes, yes, yes, yes, yes, yes, yes, yes, yes,
yes, no, yes.

She thinks there are things he doesn't do: force her to have sex
with other men, flirt with her girlfriends or members of her family,
threaten her with weapons, tell her it's her fault if he drinks, tell
her he'll kill himself if she leaves. Because he is much too jealous. Because she no longer has any friends, or family. Because he
doesn't own a weapon. Because he doesn't drink. And because if
she leaves he won't kill himself, he'll kill her, Sandrine.

Some of the lines are about financial dependence; reading them, she can say No. Because he keeps a close eye on
everything, but she still has a bank account of her own, and
a job. Even if, sometimes, he punishes her by confiscating her
bank card. And there's a section that reads: *He cheats on me*
but says it's because I've let myself go, that I make his life impossible,
that it's my fault if he's forced to look for sex elsewhere, and she tells
herself, No, not at all, and someone says loudly *Dammit, still so*
happy, then!

206

Sandrine looks up. The toilets are quite small, just two cubicles installed in what was once the bathroom of the grand, bourgeois apartment in which the firm has installed its offices.

Who's there? Sandrine asks, but no one answers. There was no one when she came in, and she hasn't heard footsteps. *So are you going to stay there*, says the voice, *do nothing?* The same voice, and Sandrine recognises it now. It's her own, inner voice. Speaking plainly this time. Loud and clear. The voice that knows how to get angry. The voice that burst out unexpectedly in the waiting room, the one she could barely make out any more, until now.

She finishes the leaflet. She looks at the helpline – free, anonymous, nationwide – and repeats the numbers to herself. She repeats the numbers.

When she gets back that evening he's already there. No: he's still there. She can see he didn't go into work. The kitchen table is littered with empty cups, a plate, crumbs of food. A notebook, its pages dark with words. He's talking into his phone, outside in the garden.

She clears the table, puts the dirty dishes in the dishwasher, sponges the coffee cup rings. She leaves the notebook untouched, of course, wipes around it, she's not allowed to touch his things without permission. His handwriting is bad but she can see some of the words, notes and reminders. About the house, the accounts. And then *Psych. assessment: Caroline. Demand sole custody Concealment removal of child grieving father SOS Papas Past memories suggested by shrink Damages compensation Moral damages.*

He wants to take Mathias back. He wants to take back Caroline's child. For the first time, her thoughts arrange the words in that precise order. She thinks, he's going to take away Caroline's child, which is not the same thing, for example, as: He wants to carry on seeing the child he had with Caroline, or He wants to prevent Caroline from taking Mathias away. Caroline is Mathias's mother, and he doesn't want to share. Because everything here belongs to him.

But he doesn't give a shit about the kid! hollers the voice. She places the sponge in its little metal basket on the side of the kitchen sink and sits down. The voice ringing inside her head is like an old acquaintance that shows up unannounced; Sandrine doesn't know if she's pleased to hear it. Sometimes people you haven't seen for a long time only come back to wreck everything. She thinks again about the unexpected tenderness shown by Mathias's father, the brusque caresses of the boy's small back, the big, possessive hand on his neck, in front of the psychiatrist, in front of them all.

They eat in front of the television. Exceptionally, because he thinks that's bad behaviour, that meals should be eaten at the table, but he doesn't want to miss the tennis and that suits Sandrine very well, no point trying to distract him, he's completely absorbed in the match. When she takes their plates back to the kitchen, he asks for a beer.

She is handing him a tall glass filled with *bière blonde* when his mobile rings on the coffee table. He pauses the match and takes the phone into the garage. Sandrine sits and stares at the frozen image. She has no interest in tennis, the players' savage grunts make her shudder with disgust. She takes her book out of her bag.

He returns from the garage, clearly annoyed. She is not surprised. She tries to gauge the extent of his irritation, to read the latest episode, and what lies ahead, in his face. But he's not angry at her. Not yet. The very good very expensive lawyer has delivered bad news. He had been confident of success, but the cops have done some real damage. The lawyer came 'this close' to a charge of police harassment but is now banking on the good father strategy.

He says this, he actually speaks these words to Sandrine as he reaches for the glass of beer on the coffee table. They are banking on the good father strategy. And Sandrine looks at this man. Who is he? Someone she doesn't know, not the man who cries, and not Monsieur Langlois, or perhaps a cold, still more terrifying version of him. Monsieur Langlois is angry and cannot control himself, he cannot help the things he does. Monsieur Langlois is never calm, that's why he's Monsieur Langlois. But the man beside her is very much in control, almost detached. He takes a sip of his beer.

Sandrine tries to concentrate on the pages of her book. He says, You're going to help me, we need to draft a sworn statement. She looks at him, uncomprehending. Don't look at me with that stupid face, he says. A sworn statement that I take very good care of the kid, his homework, the— he gestures vaguely with one hand, the… All that stuff.

He takes another sip of beer, sets down the glass on the table, refocuses his attention on the match.

Sandrine's voice, the one that has been shouting in her head all evening, hollers louder than ever now. Since Sandrine came to live with them you can count the meals he's prepared for his darling boy on the fingers of one hand; and the bedtime stories he's read; and the games they've played together. Mathias is there to do as he's told, to be seen not heard, to be a good boy on the rare occasions when visitors come to the house. The rest of the time, he has to put away his toys. Do his homework somewhere else, out of the way. Be quiet. Stop bothering them. Yet he talked a lot about Mathias at first, in his text messages, when they saw one another at her apartment, my son, my little boy, my little one, my little man, she remembers, he was full of talk about Mathias, his role as a father, his solitude, how he needed a woman, and how Mathias needed a mother. *That's how he got you – ball and chain*, says the voice, and Sandrine thinks, Yes. And again, Yes, and how easy I made things for him, and she feels ashamed. Sandrine is often ashamed, deeply ashamed, of her body, of course, but of what she does with it, too, what he does with it, what the men before did with it, or tried to; the clumsy path she has forced it to follow through life, but the furious voice brings with it the echo of a time when she could still say *So? So what? It doesn't mean you're worthless, it doesn't mean you're stupid, it doesn't mean you're rubbish!* But the voice had so little time to gather strength, from the moment she escaped her father to the moment she began to feel alone, to dread being alone, to dread being alone so much that she had ended up entirely alone. She had girlfriends. Her colleagues were... they had got along well, at first. She was never the life and soul, the confident, self-assured one, but she'd had her place. A small place.

Do you hear me? he says, shaking her shoulder, and his gesture is so much that of a small boy seeking attention that she cannot help but smile. He has moved closer to her, he's insisting, he's lost, he wants to know if she will help him, he says he needs her. His voice is pleading and she says Yes, of course. His eyes are bright, and she tells herself that she dreamt the flash of cold calculation, the proprietorial reflex; the voice doesn't agree but Sandrine ignores it. He is reassured, presses a button on the remote. And only then does Sandrine realise he has paused the match just long enough to persuade her, his eyes shining with tears.

14

H E IS 'ATTENTIVE', 'at her service', Sandrine tells herself several times throughout the rest of the week; expressions that spring to life before her eyes. Monsieur Langlois is nowhere to be seen. They sleep in each other's arms, Sandrine's neck feels almost supple. On Saturday morning he even goes out to the bakery for her: two *pains aux raisins* oozing custard cream. She manages half of one, smiling at him throughout. He's concerned, insists she eat more, and she comes very close to telling him about the little bean. He's been so kind. Then he says, I went out to get those specially for you, so you'll eat them now, and he crushes her face roughly into the second of the two pastries, still on top of its paper bag on the table. Then he gets up from his chair and goes to take a shower.

She straightens up very slowly, wipes her nose, her mouth, tells herself simply, I was right not to say anything, and the voice answers *You said it*. She cleans her face over the kitchen sink and dries herself with the little towel from the cupboard. She remembers Caroline and her knowledge of the hidden places where things are tidied away, the automatic gestures that she herself is performing now, with no apparent nerves, though with a little more force he could quite easily have broken her nose against the hard wooden tabletop. She tells herself that sometimes the body dances on when the head has forgotten the steps.

He comes back downstairs. His clothes are clean and fresh. He says nothing, heads for the garage and slams the door behind him. She cleans the house. The servile ritual takes all her attention, she works the vacuum cleaner a good long time, hoping it will drown out the angry voice that speaks louder and louder, more and more often.

The cleaning is done, she sits down.

She's alone in the empty house in the middle of the afternoon. This hasn't happened for a very long time. No. This has never happened at all, apart from the day when she waited in vain for the Marquezes to return their grandson. He is always there with Mathias, or she and Mathias are together. There is a special quality to this silence, it has scope and texture. She wonders what would have happened if she had never met the man who cries. If she had never seen him on the television. If she had never gone on Patrice and Anne-Marie's White Walk that day. She touches her belly, tells the little bean, Except of course, there's you.

She wants to do something, be someone, gain some measure of control. The voice tells her she must. But each time Sandrine lets her thoughts stray somewhere else, somewhere different, a small noise startles her and she turns to the door, convinced he's come back, that she's missed the sound of the car on the driveway, that he's here to punish her for daring to listen to the angry voice, for sitting there doing nothing, for thinking without his permission.

He doesn't come back. It doesn't happen very often, but sometimes it does. It's getting dark already when she receives a text message. She makes soup – for the first time that autumn – and eats it while watching a film full of explosions, asking herself if this is something she's missed, eating alone. She turns off the TV, hears a noise at the door. The empty soup bowl leaps from her grasp and smashes into pieces on the tiled floor. Her legs are shaking and her head burns. She struggles to control her breathing as she walks towards the door.

It's not him, but the woman cop, which is almost worse. When she opens the door and the woman facing her breaks into a smile, Sandrine tells herself that perhaps, perhaps she could— but no. He'll be coming back, he always comes back, and then she would regret it.

Her visitor hasn't even asked to come in, but Sandrine is already shaking her head. No, no. He won't be coming back tonight, says the woman facing her, straightaway, without even a 'Good evening', and Sandrine says, How do you know? And that's how their conversation begins. No one says 'Good evening' to anyone. Instead, the woman cop tells Sandrine that her colleague is staking out the house where— is watching Monsieur Langlois where he is. And that if he gets into his car, she'll know straightaway.

The question that occurs to Sandrine is not, What house? Whose house?, but 'What if he leaves on foot, what if your colleague misses him?' and the woman cop says No, he's thirty kilometres away from here, he won't set off on foot. Well, they're talking now, too late, she may as well come inside.

Thank you, says the woman cop once she's taken a seat. Sandrine apologises and picks up the shards of crockery on the floor, wipes away the remains of the soup. Do you want some help? the woman cop asks, and Sandrine says, No, it's OK.

When she's finished, she sits on the sofa. The cop says You're sure you don't want some help?

Sandrine faces her in silence, perhaps a little less hostile than usual. The policewoman speaks slowly, asks if Sandrine knows where he is. Sandrine shakes her head.

He's with a woman.

What? screams the voice.

I'm sorry? says Sandrine.

Monsieur Langlois is with his… his mistress, I suppose, even though you're not married. Charlotte. Do you know a Charlotte?

Sandrine shakes her head.

Well, he certainly does. It's been going on for about eight months.

Sandrine shakes her head.

But it has, Sandrine. I'm sorry to have to tell you, but it has. And before that, there was Sandra. And others before her, no doubt, but that was in Caroline's time.

Two women. Two.

The woman cop tells her some things, what's been happening over at the Marquezes' apartment, where Caroline now remembers and has recognised her son, and about what Monsieur Langlois's choice of the very good very expensive lawyer means. About what happens when a woman requests sole custody of her child and why this time, this time, she hopes that it won't happen that way because they've got a file on him. But Sandrine isn't listening. Because there have been two women.

Two other women, the very definition of choice. Two other women means love is impossible. Because sometimes, Sandrine thinks, love can surprise you. You can love someone and want to be faithful to them but suddenly, completely by surprise, you might see someone else, and feel your heartstrings pulled, feel yourself hooked by something too big and powerful to resist, and find yourself, quite by surprise, loving more, at the same time, somewhere else. And that's love, and it can't be helped. She herself met a man who cried and there was nothing she could do.

But two women.

Two women, two, that's not love: that's a choice, that's a cruel habit, a deliberate insult, that's bile spat in your face. That says, You stupid, fat bitch, I could not care less, I don't give a fuck about you, I'm fucking somewhere else. I'm cheating on you, you've been cheated. You're a woman whose man is cheating on her.

She thinks about the nights spent on the floor because that's where bitches sleep, she thinks about how she was forced to beg his forgiveness because he thought she was sleeping with Christian, with her bosses, with the intern he saw leaving the office behind her one day when he had come to spy on her at work, with the cashier at checkout 32, with the trainer at the sports centre, with the head teacher at school. She thinks of all the vile things he's said to her, about her fat whore's thighs that she opened for anyone, her filthy cunt that got wet for total strangers, she remembers the actions that accompanied the insults, the brutal fingers and scavenger's claws that split her apart so that he could examine the scene of the imaginary crime, sniff her sex and declare it guilty, delve ferociously into her flesh for proof; she remembers everything that Monsieur Langlois did to her while *he* was fucking someone else. The images are precise, distant, like a film of terrible things that happened to someone else. And throughout all this, she, Sandrine, meek and well-behaved, performed scenes of quiet, spotless domesticity, Mathias doing his homework, dishes of food steaming on the table. And *he* was sleeping with *other women*?

The voice hollers very loud, *You stupid bitch!* It's deafening. And then again, in the seething hiss of a commiserator, an ally, *And as for him, that bastard.*

Sandrine? Sandrine? The woman cop is talking to her.

Sandrine recovers herself. She is here. *I'm here*, says the voice, which has risen now to a new place inside her. As if it was her own voice. As if Sandrine was the one feeling furious, though she cannot be sure. She has never felt furious on her own behalf, only ever furious with herself. She cannot be sure. Of what? Of that woman. The one facing her, with her pale, faded jeans, her hard-bitten fingernails.

Sandrine, do you hear what I'm saying?

Yes, says Sandrine. Well, no. But now I do, yes.

When the woman cop leaves much later that evening – 'You must be very careful, but I'll be here, OK? I'm here' – Sandrine feels a knot loosen, as if something is opening inside her, perhaps, and she smiles at her. The woman cop holds out her hand and says, Please, call me Lisa.

Sandrine takes a shower, dries herself with careful, decisive gestures. She fetches the moisturising cream, the one that costs quite a lot and smells so lovely. Diligently, she anoints herself, resisting the urge to scratch her scabs, the desire to gouge her skin. The desire that has disappeared since the arrival of the little bean, but which returns this evening, as it does every time her body fights with itself and her mind wanders. Breasts. Shoulders. Arms. Bottom. Belly. Thighs. Legs. She is plastered in cream, she smells delicious, she has taken care of herself. She looks at her skin, speckled with tiny welts, dug with her own nails for so many years. It will probably never heal. Perhaps. She'll see in time.

She lies down in bed, an empty space beside her. She cannot concentrate on her book, but not because she is tired.

She falls asleep at last. Furious.

15

S HE WAKES A FEW MOMENTS before her telephone buzzes. The alarm is set for 6.45 a.m. and outside, it is still dark. She remembers the first mornings, this time last year, in this house, when she had to leave her bed before daybreak. It was different then. She lived for him, for Mathias, she was still… was she still? Happy, even joyful, at the prospect of returning home each evening, keeping house, waiting for the little boy at the school gate, when the after-school study period finished, cooking for the three of them. Yes. Mathias filled her with joy. But had it started already, last year at the same time? Yes. Yes, of course it had started already. It began the moment she came to live in this house.

He needed her.

He loved her.

More than anyone else.

More than her friends, with whom she had more or less lost touch – a text now and then is not friendship.

More than her colleagues, who didn't seem to like her very much: had she not told him several times that she was too shy to fit in with the group? But the problem wasn't her, it was them. Or perhaps it was her, after all, he began to suggest. You make other people feel uncomfortable. He had said it outright, after a time. You do know that, don't you?

And that was how it had begun, or perhaps even before that, when he would be the one to decide what they were going to drink, when he ordered for her in restaurants.

When he chose the film, when he switched channels.

When he interrupted her that day, the day of the White Walk, insisted she tell him things even she didn't want to tell, in the forest, with its hint of the wild.

When he said, Everyone's gone that way, into the woods, come with us.

When he saw her, dripping with good intentions and eager to please, desperate to count for something, that day on the doorstep.

She gets up, and she is furious.

This is a new sensation – the heat rising in her throat, a ball of energy that makes her lift her chin and hold her head high. She has slept only fitfully, but her eyes are wide open. She does her morning wash, and talks to her belly, to herself, in almost confident-sounding tones. Almost. Almost is something. Well, almost, it's better than nothing.

She leaves for work. She is *not* afraid. In fact, she is terrified. But for the first time she doesn't feel frightened or lost. This is different. It's frightening, too, but in a new way. A purposeful way. Different. *Focussed.*

The policewoman's appearance at her work is uncomfortable. It's awkward to watch her talk to the partners in the main conference room. Sandrine is there too, listening to a policewoman explain to the rest of the firm that she is in danger. That the man she lives with is a suspect. That if they see him, if he tries to gain entry to the offices, he must not be left alone with Sandrine. An awkward, almost humiliating moment, but by now Sandrine has forsaken so much that only a top-of-the-range humiliation could accomplish that, cut and finished just for her, like a precious jewel. It takes more than this to annoy a woman who has been called a bitch and treated like a dog, made to sleep on the mat beside the bed, and covered all over with spit as payment for an imagined affair.

The men around the table are ill at ease. Embarrassed that they didn't know. The tangibility of Sandrine and her case begs unspoken questions that itch and irritate like a coarse, too-tight woollen sweater. The idea of women like Sandrine is easy to put to one side. Her solid physical presence, seated opposite them, is trickier to avoid. They clear their throats and assure her of their support. Except one who doesn't care and decides it's no concern of his, that this is... a private matter. He doesn't say 'women's business' but that's what Sandrine hears, the woman cop too. Sandrine says nothing, but the woman cop speaks up, and when she has finished addressing the man who doesn't care, he gets up, red-faced, and leaves the room.

It's a morning of talk. They talk to Béatrice, too. Or rather, at first, the policewoman speaks to Béatrice with Sandrine sitting in. And then Béatrice turns to Sandrine and says, Shit, we knew there was something the matter, why didn't you tell us? And Béatrice gets cross, she gets really cross, and then suddenly she bursts into tears. It's very strange. Sandrine isn't crying but Béatrice is. Béatrice the big talker, the one who always speaks her mind, the one who keeps her man thoroughly in line. Because she suspected, but she had no idea, because she didn't know enough about what was going on, or perhaps she did and now she is completely overwhelmed by feelings of guilt. And plus, this is such a selfish way to react, says Béatrice, who is sorry she's sorry but not in the right way. She wants to understand, show empathy, but instead she feels guilty and angry until finally the policewoman says, Just so we're all completely clear, the three of us: you, Sandrine, feel angry with yourself, and you, Béatrice, feel angry with yourself, too, and I just want to know whether at any moment at all, either of you is planning to feel angry at the *man* who's the cause of all this, and Béatrice blows her nose and laughs.

Béatrice carries out her appointed task: her and her big mouth. She warns everyone, informs them of the situation. Now everyone knows what Sandrine's man looks like and if anyone sees him parked in the street they must tell someone straightaway, and why.

At lunchtime, Sandrine and Lisa go to the doctor's surgery. The doctor frowns when she sees a cop sitting next to her patient in the waiting room.

Of course I can provide a medical certificate, the gynaecologist assures her once the cop has finished her explanation.

Your testimony will be crucial, Lisa tells her. And you'll be facing other experts – the lawyer Monsieur Langlois has hired to act in his defence has a whole network of colleagues every bit as expensive and unscrupulous as he is. If you aren't cross-questioned by him, you'll be questioned by someone who uses the same methods. And I've seen him at work before. He'll stop at nothing.

The doctor says, Don't worry about me, I can stand my ground and fight, I assure you. But I'd like to hear what you have to say, Sandrine. I want to know what happened to you, in your own words. If you can.

Sandrine takes a deep breath, she hopes the angry voice hasn't disappeared, she hopes that it will speak out. She has silenced it so many times; smothered it so often, when it told her *Leave, just go, get out of this. Call social services, Take the kid and live your lives. Save him, save both of you, save yourself, save yourself,* and Sandrine had been too afraid to listen, when even the thought of running away was dangerous. She opens her mouth and, oh, thank goodness, the voice is there. And the angry voice fills her entire being.

When he comes back that evening, everything is exactly, meticulously, precisely as usual. The sitting room, the kitchen, the painful, scalding rod of terror in the nape of Sandrine's neck. He comes in and she tries not to stare him in the face, not to show the grin of disgust she can barely suppress. It's not that difficult, in truth. He has terrified her too much, for too long, for her to look him in the eyes; he has to cajole her, even order her to do that. Or cry, of course. The man who cries still moves her as much as ever, no, *moved*. *Moved*, he moved her back then, the unfaithful cheat who threw himself onto, into other women.

He comes into the kitchen to see what she's making for supper. It doesn't suit him, of course, sausages and mash, make an effort at least, and she explains that the sausages were in the fridge and almost past their date. She wants to add, And since Mathias isn't coming back, but she keeps the words carefully shut up inside her mouth because 'Mathias' is one of the forbidden words now. The list has grown like a tumour, unobtrusive, painless, but it eats at Sandrine's thoughts: what am I allowed to say, and what will start an argument? Sandrine uses a very special language when she talks to the man she lives with; there is no 'Why?', no 'You're home late', still less 'No' itself, except of course in answer to a question which she cannot answer 'Yes'. In any case she always gets it wrong and then there are sparks.

Sandrine concentrates on the salad leaves in the kitchen sink, she tries repeating to herself what Lisa and the gynaecologist told her. That she is *not wrong*. That she is *not* the one who starts the arguments. And that an argument is when you talk and disagree.

It's not when someone says, That's very kind but I'm not hungry, and then they get their face crushed into a custard-and-raisin pastry. And above all, that *she doesn't start anything*. He is not angry, he just wants to frighten her, remind her who's in charge. Petrify her. Immobilise her. That nothing frightens *him* more than the prospect of Sandrine as a free woman, somewhere else, leading a different life, out of reach, *no longer in his possession*. She repeats this carefully to herself, she's a good girl, always did as she was told, and now this will work to her advantage, she doesn't really believe it but she tells herself over and over again, because the woman cop and the doctor said Please, Sandrine, please, say it, say it as many times as you need, it's his fault. It's *his fault*.

She places the salad leaves in the yellow plastic wringer and says, Do you want me to make something else? He comes over to her and puts his arms around her waist. The rod in Sandrine's neck burns. His breathing is short and quick, she tries to stay calm, he seems in a good mood despite the mashed potato. He kisses her neck and she feels a shiver of disgust run through her. He says, Kiss me? She obeys, turns around. His mouth is too narrow, dry and slightly scratchy, his lips are dry and chapped, and his early-evening stubble feels like sandpaper. She breathes his odour and detects more than just his aftershave. Is her brain finally connecting the dots? The sharpened sense of smell that seems to come with being pregnant. An illusion, perhaps. She smells another scent, not his aftershave, something feminine, sugary, and something else, something organic, carnal, a whiff of butchered meat. He smells of sex and suddenly she feels sick, she needs to vomit, and she turns quickly to throw up into the sink.

He is revolted, steps back, mutters, What the hell's the matter, that's disgusting! And she flutters a hand to tell him everything's all right, but when she straightens up, he's not looking at her.

He's checking that Sandrine's vomit hasn't marked his pale blue shirt.

Sandrine rinses her mouth and runs water into the sink to wash away the acrid, acid-smelling pulp.

It's not enough. He makes her scour the sink with bleach. She doesn't object, simply says, Two girls at work have gone down with a vomiting bug, I think I may have caught it.

How? How could you catch it, you don't speak to them.

That's the rule. She mustn't speak to her colleagues. Especially not the men; no more than the bare minimum (by his definition). If she followed his instructions to the letter, she'd have been fired long ago, and that's clearly what he wants.

You can catch it from toilet seats, door handles, anything, she reminds him. He has a horror of falling ill, and stares at her in suspicion and disgust. He says, I'm not touching that, jerking his chin in the direction of the food she had been preparing, and he picks up his phone to order pizza.

When the pizza arrives, he settles himself on the sofa to eat, and Sandrine realises he has no intention of sharing. Something surges in her stomach, something from very far away, that she hasn't felt for a very long time, her cheeks tremble uncontrollably. What's happening? The corners of her lips hurt, and a tiny pinch of pain warns her that she has broken into a smile: she is actually laughing.

Laughing silently in front of this man, this little, mean-minded man, with his shoes stacked discreetly at the heels (so he thinks), his poorly camouflaged bald patch, revealed by the movement of a stray strand of hair. And she takes a few very indiscreet strides over to the pantry, where she hiccoughs with laughter, her face buried in a roll of kitchen paper, praying he won't hear but incapable of stopping, tears streaming down her face, it goes on and on, and when she turns around he's there, framed in the doorway, staring at her suspiciously, and he asks, Whatever's the matter with you?

Sandrine's laugh disappears instantly, her body tenses, remembering the fear. She wipes her eyes and says, I'm crying because I thought you'd be happy with what I made for supper.

It's a risk. The time when the sight of her tears would calm him, make him stop, is behind them now. Anything she does may annoy him, unintentionally. The little box in the pocket of her jeans, with the button to press in an emergency, isn't there for this. She mustn't provoke, mustn't put herself in danger. The cops want to catch him in the act, red-handed, but Lisa said, Not so that you put yourself in even more danger, Sandrine.

Whatever the cops can prove will not be enough. Everything that Caroline remembers now will not be enough. They all know that, the man cop, the woman cop, the doctor, Patrice, Anne-Marie, Caroline, and now she knows it too. That it's never enough, that men who hit women still get visiting rights, still get to remain in their homes, still get to see the children. And they take advantage of that, to kill. It's dangerous to stay, but it's dangerous to leave, too. They think that Caroline wanted to leave, and that he wanted to kill her.

That's what Lisa, the cop, explained to Sandrine. That Caroline has recovered everything, or almost: the isolation, the humiliation, the punishments, the beatings, the rapes, but not the day he decided to kill her.

The first woman doesn't remember either, what happened after her husband killed her. But that, everyone hopes, may never come back to her. All the two cops have is the firm belief that she survived by a miracle, that she climbed out of the ravine where he left her, that she was wandering, confused, with no idea

224

where she was going, and that one or more men picked her up naked, disorientated, and with her memory a blank – a fragile silhouette covered in mud and dead leaves – and that they kept her for a time, in a van or perhaps in the boot of a vehicle; which is how they crossed the border. Perhaps she escaped, eventually, or perhaps they did everything they felt like doing to her, and then got bored. They have some leads on those men – vague and slippery, they need more time.

But as Lisa assured her the day before, Caroline has plenty to say about all the rest, Sandrine. About everything he did before killing her.

'That way he has of holding you by the neck: that released quite a few memories for her. She said it's like a slot machine. The dials are turning constantly, backwards and forwards, and then suddenly a small memory will drop, and then nothing for hours, days. And then it churns around and around again, there's a smell, a colour, Mathias makes a particular – or just a very ordinary – sound, and a whole lot will come tumbling out. But when she saw you with his hand on your neck, she remembered that he would take her like that, and grip tight, and throw her to the floor, or shake her while holding her by the neck. And now, Caroline remembers that she wanted to leave.'

'I know that,' Sandrine told Lisa. 'Are you sure he can't come back without your colleague knowing?' Facing her, Lisa was quite sure, and so Sandrine had pulled the scarf from around her neck, to show the bruises Monsieur Langlois left in his rage the Saturday before, and then she took her upstairs to the red bedroom to show her the money and the passports.

Sandrine and Monsieur Langlois face one another in the pantry. She doesn't wipe her cheeks, she wants him to see the tears, to believe that she was crying, that she's sorry she disappointed him, that she's well-trained, and servile. That she is what she thought she was, the image he cultivated with pleasure: a stupid, fat bitch, ugly and stupid, stupid, stupid, who will never leave because who else would want her? He says, That's enough. Stop crying.

Sandrine's vision of the pathetic little man has disappeared. As if shifting shadows had altered the face of the man standing in front of her, as if she had imagined it all. He makes her afraid again, with an immense fear that tightens her throat and turns her stomach to water, and again her neck is tense and painful. He walks back to the sofa to eat his pizza.

She comes out of the pantry, closes the door, feels the wood with her hand, the place where three screw-holes once held a lock in place. The day she'd asked him about it, he said, It was because of the bleach, all that stuff. It was down at floor level, it was safer for Mathias. When she first came here, the cleaning products were kept in a cupboard under the kitchen counter, and Mathias was past the age at which child safety is an issue. Perhaps he had lied. If Lisa was telling the truth, if he starved Caroline, if she was unable to get to the food, then he had lied. He says simply, Come and sit down. It's an order. She does as she is told.

She sits beside him. She has finished her plate of sausages-and-mash, cheating like a small child, hiding the industrial, processed meat that tastes sugary to her in the mess of white purée. He doesn't offer any of the pizza, and when he's finished, he wipes his mouth with a serviette that he drops onto the slices he hasn't touched. Her punishment. For being sick, or for something else, there are always so many reasons. She doesn't care. He has no idea how little Sandrine cares about the pizza. She is concentrating hard on her tightly knotted neck, her relief that she did not tell the woman cop everything, that she had not agreed to leave right then, earlier today.

Are you sure? Lisa had asked her. And when Sandrine said, Yes. No, I don't know, Lisa had given her the emergency alarm and said, I will be nearby, I promise.

He takes her by the neck, then pushes her cheek down against his thigh. She thinks he's going to open his zip, but this isn't that sort of evening. It's an evening when Monsieur Langlois is absent or hasn't yet appeared. It's up to Sandrine to make no mistakes, on the slippery path that crosses the shifting, uncertain terrain over which she struggles day by day, skirting the abyss into which he will drag her when he's angry. She slides her bottom up and around onto the sofa, getting settled, unresisting. If he wants her to lie down, she'll lie down. They watch a film. Or rather, he watches a film and she lies there, under his hand, while he strokes her like a huge cat. His vision of a peaceful evening, watching whatever he wants while Sandrine says nothing. At first, his automatic gestures provoked nothing but happiness. Snuggling beside him for hours filled Sandrine with simple, wholehearted joy. Now she realises how he hated to let her read, that he didn't like hearing her talk; when she tried one more time to give her opinion on a film or a TV programme, he would stare at her in surprise, like someone who watches a child stumble over the same reading word again and again, when it ought to know by now what happens when it doesn't *try*.

Stretched out on the sofa, she loses herself in the pixels on-screen, not really watching, wondering what would happen if— If she got to her feet and said something impossible, like I'm bored with this film, I'm going to read instead. Would he hit her straightaway? Or would he shout first? And if he shouted, how loud would he have to holler, before she pressed the button? Is

Lisa really as close by as she says? Sandrine blinks. *Lisa.* No, the woman cop. She's alone with him, here, and 'Lisa' is not there. Sandrine blinks again. She's the one, she, Sandrine, who said, No, I don't want to leave. All she had to do, all she had to do was say the words, all she had to do was nod her head. But no, it's too dangerous, and why should she trust this woman? Here is what she knows. She knows this man, this house is her home, her life is here, her reality, here all around her, she can't— she doesn't know— A high wall stands between her and everywhere else, a wall that stops her from imagining *a different life.* There's no way out. Today, she had a moment of madness, she strayed into danger, but that's over now.

In a way, she feels released from the need to choose, from feeling guilty. All those people who looked at her and pitied her this morning, asking themselves, But why doesn't she just leave? Their faces fade, their condescending looks disappear. She doesn't leave because she doesn't want to. She sighs with relief and regret. The man's fingers are in her hair. She was so right to choose to stay. She cannot imagine leaving, she cannot conjure an image of herself, suitcase in hand, turning the key in the ignition and pulling out of the driveway for the very last time. But there are vague, violent images, too, of what might happen if she *did* leave. She sees herself drawn into a great red and black mass, heavy, razor-sharp, brutal. Why are you breathing like that? he asks. And she only says, I like it when you stroke my hair.

When they go up to bed, he lets her use the lubricant and she tells herself, It will be all right, it will probably be all right. He is kind.

16

S HE SEES THE WOMAN COP'S CAR next morning as she leaves
for work. She spots it in a neighbour's sunken driveway, at
no. 12. Clever. Not so visible from theirs, but with a good view
of the upstairs windows, and easy to see whether the lights are
lit on the ground floor, or in the garage.

Driving past, just below the speed limit, she sees a hand raised
in the driver's seat, but does not respond.

The car follows her, and Sandrine drives on. Perhaps if she
ignores it, the vehicle behind will disappear. Perhaps by the time
she reaches work, they will have given up.

They do not give up. When she parks, they park. And when she
steps out of her car, Lisa the cop is there, walking towards her.
Is everything all right? Sandrine could burst out laughing again,
the question seems so absurd: nothing is all right and it's her
own fault, and their fault, the fault of the first woman, everyone,
all of them, why, *why* can't things, people, why can't they just
disappear, cancel themselves, leave her alone, leave them both
alone. In a blank, empty world there would be nothing to justify
Monsieur Langlois's appearances, in a blank, empty world she
would make no mistakes and they could live happily together,
she and the man who cries.

She says, Leave me alone, please, leave me alone.

Lisa says, But Sandrine, yesterday you were ready to file a
complaint, to corroborate Caroline's statements, yesterday you—

Sandrine says Please… And she steps to one side, tries to walk around them. The male cop raises his eyebrows, then frowns and says Now listen, I'm beginning to— but Sandrine doesn't hear what it is he's beginning to, because his colleague presses his arm and shakes her head.

They let her pass and climb the stairs to the office.

On the staircase, she breathes again, at last. There. They just need to disappear.

That evening, he comes back early and smiles at the sight of the new potatoes roasting in the oven. He pokes a finger into the salad bowl, in which she has just finished making the vinaigrette, and says Ah, you see, that's how it should be!

They eat dinner. He talks about his work. He is happy.

After dinner, while she's clearing the table and putting everything away, he takes a printed sheet of paper from his briefcase and says, You just need to copy this out and sign it.

The table is still damp where Sandrine has wiped it with the sponge. When she comes over to look, and picks it up, the sheet of paper is already slightly sticky and soft. She reads. It's a sworn statement, a statement made by her, Sandrine. In it, she swears a great many things. That Mathias's father is devoted and gentle. That he looks after his son every day, and shows all the commitment and involvement of a responsible parent. That he finds life without his son very hard, even impossible. That the mother's decision to remove the boy without discussion or warning is not only illegal, but agonising, unbearable.

Something drops onto the paper. It's him. He is bending over her and eating a biscuit. The crumbs land on the sheet. She knew he was close behind her, of course, she always knows where he is, but absorbed in reading the words that tell so many lies, she hadn't heard him searching in the pantry for a packet of biscuits. You need to copy that out by hand and sign it, he says. Yes, of course, says Sandrine. Now, he adds.

She goes to fetch a piece of paper, a pen. He watches her copy it out. She signs.

Then they watch television.

When she emerges from the shower, she looks at her body, lumpy and repulsive. She feels cowed, her breasts droop even further, and the fat of her belly rolls slightly over the top of her thighs. She begs the little bean to stay hidden. Just a little longer until— she doesn't know. Until something.

They go to bed. He's tired, he doesn't get hard. Today is a day without Monsieur Langlois. Days without Monsieur Langlois are good days.

17

THE WEEK GOES BY, and Monsieur Langlois doesn't re-
appear. She wakes with the rod stiffening her back, but
nothing worse.

At work, everyone keeps well away, as if she were contagious.
The man who declared that this sort of thing was none of his
business casts hostile glances in her direction. Béatrice suggests
they go for lunch, several times, but Sandrine declines, her refusal
is discreet. Discreet, then terse, and Béatrice steers clear, too, as
if bitten.

She should never have let the woman cop warn them all. She
is immune to humiliation, and indifferent to pity, but because of
the police, the narrow path she treads on the precipice of danger
has become narrower still. If he comes to wait for her down on
the street, and sees people from the office staring, he will know,
things will occur to him. Each time the thought crosses her mind,
a cold sweat drenches the small of her back. At lunchtime, she
eats at her desk and avoids the break room. She isn't hungry,
anyway, her wastepaper basket fills up with salad and cold rice.
Normally, everyone disposes of leftover food in the kitchen, but
no one says anything. She is grateful for that. Perhaps no one
will ever say anything to her ever again, perhaps she'll be able
to work in silence, in the blank, empty world where everything
will be plain and simple.

The days go by.

She copies out more letters, more papers. He is planning something, consolidating his case. She tells herself that Caroline doesn't stand a chance. She signs documents for a joint bank account. He doesn't want her to have her own bank card or chequebook. He has decided. He's made an appointment at the bank so that she can close her savings accounts and transfer the money to the new account. He says it's 'for us'. She wonders what it's like when people fall in love and live together and open a joint account to build a life together. Perhaps it's like this. A feeling of immense emptiness and fear. She doesn't know. He places his hand on her neck and speaks calmly. It's worse than when he hollers. She signs.

Each time she obeys, she gets something in return: an unspoken contract, like a dog that's rewarded for its increasingly complex tricks by not being beaten. He eats a meal without criticising. A peaceful evening. He lets her read her book beside him while he watches television.

The following Saturday, when she closes her bank account, he takes her to a Japanese restaurant, all the while stressing how much he hates raw fish. She hesitates at first, thinks he would rather go somewhere else, that they could eat something different, that she doesn't really feel like fish anyway, but when he says, No, I'm doing this for you, she thanks him profusely, repeats that he's being very kind. It's what he wanted all along. He wants someone to say thank you while he eats meat skewers with soy sauce and she eats makis with cucumber. When he pays, he leaves the bill lying open conspicuously, so that she will thank him again. Perhaps, somewhere deep down inside her, the buried voice is muttering: *Are you kidding me, he's just robbed you of all your money and you're thanking him for spending 20 euros??* But Sandrine doesn't hear it, or hardly at all.

They stock up at the hypermarket on the way home. At checkout 32 the young man has been replaced by a young woman and she can fill the boot of the car without suffering his questions or suspicion. He always insists on using the same checkout, but the ritual had become a horrific ordeal, with the youth on the other side of the conveyor belt, and then having to repeat for hours afterwards that she doesn't know him, that he means nothing to her, they were not exchanging secret signals, there is no secret rendezvous. Now, she no longer greets other men when they're out together, just a tilt of the head, not even a direct look. But a small acknowledgement is better than nothing, because then, he suspects she's hiding something, that her detachment is exaggerated.

'So now you won't have to go out again this weekend,' he says, as he turns the key in the ignition, before leaving the car park.

That afternoon, she does the housework while he watches TV. He is quiet.

When they go to bed that Saturday night, he says, Well, good night, and turns away. She has given up her bank account, he has given up taking her by force. Win-win.

She dreams of a much younger Sandrine, a little girl who screams silently, red and dishevelled, locked away somewhere, out of sight.

18

O N SUNDAY MORNING, alone in the kitchen, she makes a cake. Her mind is blank, it's like a ritual she can perform without thinking. No tiny finger comes to steal raw mix from the tin. Since she signed the papers, all those papers, she doesn't even know which any more, he has stopped talking about his son. It's as if the boy never existed. She gazes out of the window. The tree at the bottom of the garden is turning yellow. She places a hand on her belly.

He comes downstairs already dressed, says he's off to play tennis.

When the car leaves the garage, she stands for a long time in the hallway, her eyes resting on the sports bag he has left behind, with the handle of his racket sticking out. Perhaps now that he's got everything he wanted, he will stop lying. Almost everything. She thinks of the job she still holds. The car she still owns. The bank account she has lost.

The oven rings. Time to take out the cake. The sugary smell makes her feel nauseous.

There is no news from him at lunchtime, nor at teatime. He gets back late. The dark that eats at the day has long since fallen, and he wears his jacket all done up. It must be cool outside, even cold. He asks if she's been out. No. The right answer, if he believes her.

He unbuttons his jacket and continues the questioning. No one came to the house? No, nobody.

He picks up Sandrine's phone, flicks through the call history. Does the same on the house phone handset.

He is satisfied. She is granted a kiss she hasn't asked for, a kiss that smells of another woman. This time, she manages not to throw up, but says she's going upstairs to take a shower. He says he hasn't eaten.

This, too, is a test she must get right. It's up to her to figure out what this means: that she should cook a meal, and eat dinner with him whether she's hungry or not, sleepy or not. She takes a Tupperware of soup out of the freezer, the soup she made that afternoon, the containers cooling slowly on the kitchen countertop in the silent house, while he was somewhere else. He wants something different. She warms up a cordon-bleu chicken dish that fills the kitchen with the smell of fat.

For dessert he eats a slice of cake. Says it's dry. She doesn't answer. She feels tired, achey, almost feverish. The tension in her neck is exhausting and all she wants is to take a hot shower.

While she clears the table and loads the dishwasher he tells her: Your stomach is getting fatter.

The words reach her as she is bending over, her nose just above the basket of cutlery. She hopes the slight tremor in her voice may be attributed to her posture, bent double. She says, Oh, maybe, and prays that's enough. She doesn't know if he'll pinch her thigh and call her My Little Piglet, as if that were a compliment, or if he will say, You should make more of an effort, I'm ashamed to see you filling out like that, or if he will scream suddenly, And why would you want to lose weight, you filthy whore, so you can sleep with who?!

Finally, it is none of these, and Sandrine hears a far-off, angry voice – or perhaps it's just the blood rushing in her head – that says the other woman must have pumped him dry for him to let it go so quickly. She stands up, and the buzzing in her ears disappears.

19

O N MONDAY EVENING, he is at the house when she returns from work. He is reading a magazine. He has eaten lunch there, the dirty plate is still on the kitchen table.

She will have to choose between resigning from her job, or just not going into the office any more. Because he will not allow it. He says this quite calmly, she is lucky. He warns her that one day she will no longer be allowed to work. He does not say when, she doesn't know, perhaps he doesn't either. But she has been warned.

It seems to her that things are gathering pace. That there are more pitfalls to avoid, more responses to second-guess, more and more difficult tricks to perform, but with fewer and fewer instructions from him. She feels herself trying to figure things out, like a confused dog that doesn't understand what's being asked of it.

She doesn't answer, nor – most especially – does she object any more. He is satisfied by her defeated silence, and strokes her back. And so everything is perfectly all right.

20

FRIDAY NIGHT, he does not come back and she dots her breasts with multiple tiny scars. There is always something to dig out, something to purify; she spends an hour extracting tiny, almost invisible hairs, all over the fine skin of her chest; digging out suspect pores with the tip of a needle stolen from among Caroline's things. Her body releases a drop or two of sebum, lymph fluid, and blood. She hurts herself and feels bad but her hands keep on until she is puffy and disgusting. At least now he has good reason to go sticking his dick into women he doesn't know. At least now she is *truly revolting*, there's a reason for all this.

When she manages to stop, at last, and throw the needle into the bin, she sits down on the floor and cries. There is no excuse, no reason, no consolation. She takes out the healing cream and forgives herself. She begs unspecified forgiveness from an invisible entity. She is sorry, she's a battlefield. She goes to bed in the silence of the house. She is still not used to it. But there it is, and she's had no news from the cops, no unfamiliar car is parked on the road. The emergency alarm is still in the pocket of the trousers she has folded on the chair at the foot of the bed. Perhaps it's been deactivated now, but in any event she won't use it. Because everything is all right. Everything is terrible, but everything is all right.

He comes back the next morning with that smell on him, the smell of another woman's sex. The reek of carrion.

Sandrine wrinkles her nose, involuntarily, and he takes it as a reproach. She has said nothing, but her nose wrinkled. He doesn't shout, but he slaps her. Three times. Very hard, very simply. Until she huddles over and lets herself fall to the floor. It's very simple. This is how it is, now. Very simple. The new rules. She takes note. He leaves her there on the floor for a while.

Sandrine thinks, This is my fault.

She stood up too straight. She wasn't careful enough.

She stays on the floor, because she doesn't know if she's allowed to get to her feet. In her pocket, she has the emergency alarm, pressing against her groin. She doesn't touch it. Now, when she wrinkles her nose, he hits her three times. Who knows what would happen if she pressed the button. If the cops came. If they didn't come.

When he comes down from his shower, he picks her up off the floor and says he's sorry. He says he wants to take her out for lunch at a restaurant, but he can't take her out like that, she smells bad. She should go and wash, and then they'll see, OK? See what they might do? But they'll do something together, the two of them. His voice is kind. She goes upstairs and takes off her clothes. She took a shower the night before, but he's right, she stinks. She was very afraid when he hit her, and she stinks. She sniffs her clothes with detached curiosity. It's her, but not her at the same time, an unfamiliar version of her own smell, because this is a different fear, a new fear. Perhaps her body will produce a different sweat each time something new happens.

Monsieur Langlois never used to hit her quite like that before; he pushed her, a lot, pushed her up against the wall, sometimes he pulled her hair, and there was the first, angry slap that came suddenly out of nowhere, but he has never hit her in such a matter-of-fact way, so simply, right on the face, three times on the same side, and she looks for a long time in the bathroom mirror at the cheek that has puffed up. A small blood vessel has burst in her left eye, her cheekbone is red and shiny like an apple. The apple of his eye, she thinks. Right where he hit her, on her face, on the left.

She puts on one of her pairs of jeans, one of her shirts, a black gilet; these are the clothes she likes. At least these protect her. Her armour.

She comes back downstairs, fully dressed, but with no make-up. There is no make-up that can hide that cheek, except perhaps the slice of a knife: a cruel, fairy-tale solution, like the one invented by Cinderella's stepsister, in the story by Charles Perrault, who cuts off her own toe so her foot will fit a slipper of sleek, red squirrel-skin. When he sees her, he puts the match on pause and comes to meet her, arms open wide, his mouth trembling. He says, Oh Sandrine, oh my love, oh my love, look at you… And the man who cries takes her in his arms. She resists a little, she hates these moments when the man who cries drags her out from the soft, cottony cocoon where she has gone to hide. She is far away, in another place, and he draws her to him, back into the here and now, where she hurts and feels ashamed, so that he can take her in his arms, stroke her back, her face, her neck, hold her tight, be sorry. He cries on her shoulder, she feels his wet tears staining her clean blouse. He takes them both over to the sofa, sits them down forcibly so that he can cry and cry at his leisure. She does not resist now, the heat of the man who cries warms her body, she is here, now, and he slips down to the floor, at the foot of the sofa and presses his face into her knee, clutches her, kisses her. He is repentant, begging forgiveness, the man who cries is sorry, and his face is tearful and twisted.

Of course, they do not go out, she cannot be seen like that, but after fetching a tea towel filled with ice cubes to bring down the swelling in her cheek, he drives to the Japanese restaurant for sushi. She looks at the strips of raw, red fish and wonders if this is a test, if he's understood about the little bean, if he's trying to force her to tell him.

She doesn't want to remember, but the memory is there. What the woman cop told her. That often, violence begins or gets worse when a baby is on the way or is born. That possessive men aren't loving but jealous, and full of self-pride. That a woman with a child is a woman who loves another human being. She doesn't trust the woman cop. Under the table, she places a hand on her belly.

She eats the raw sushi.

The man who cries stops crying, but stays with her until the evening. Until dinner. Until nightfall. He takes her tenderly in his arms, cradles her until she drifts into sleep, lulled by his soft voice and its sing-song round of apologies. You understand, you see, you've understood, there are things not to do, and when she doesn't do them, see how everything goes OK? Isn't everything easier that way? Aren't they happy? Does she understand what she's done? What she started? How stressed he is right now? How much pain the cops, the Marquezes, their daughter are causing him, right now? How they are all against him? How unfair this all is? And she falls asleep, late, in the desolate wasteland of the man who cries.

On Sunday morning, he tells her to leave her hair loose around her face, and comes with her to the hypermarket to do the shopping for the week.

Then he busies himself in the garden while she turns on the heating indoors, where it feels cold, and sets about preparing meals for the week ahead. At lunchtime, he's surprised to see no biscuits or cake for dessert. She avoids pronouncing Mathias's name at the very last second, swallows the syllables just in time. Instead, she says she's sorry, that she will make it up to him this evening and asks what he would like? He says, that walnut thing.

That morning at the supermarket, he filled two entire bags with walnuts. She said nothing but watched the manoeuvre out of the corner of her eye. Normally, she's the one who does that; he doesn't like selecting the loose produce, taking the bags, weighing everything, it bores him. He's just there to keep her company, watch over her. That's why she watched him in surprise, this time. She likes these furtive moments when, amid the shifting sands, some small thing makes sense. When two tiny pieces of the giant puzzle slot into place. He wants a walnut cake. The one she made several times back in the beginning, before Mathias whispered to her that he preferred chocolate. She had always made it with powdered walnuts, sold in plastic sachets, the result was the same and it was much easier. He says, It's better with real walnuts.

After lunch, she stands at the kitchen counter, nutcracker in hand. After a quarter of an hour, her wrist aches and she needs to sit down. He comes in from the garden to ask for a coffee, and while he sips at it, before heading back outside to trim the box hedge, he says, Why don't you do all the rest straightaway? That way it's done. You can keep the nuts in a Tupperware box.

He bought several kilos, the loose walnuts were on special offer.

Sandrine doesn't know if the suggestion is an order and she does not want to take the risk. It takes her two hours, or more. She rubs the tips of her fingers raw on the fine but hard casing around the nut kernels.

When she finishes, her hands hurt.

At dinner, he says the cake is not bad, but a bit tasteless. In the palm of Sandrine's right hand, where she held the nutcracker's metal legs, a large pink-and-white blister has formed.

She hopes that the man who cries will still be there when they go to bed, but he's gone, and Monsieur Langlois has got hard.

21

WHEN HER ALARM SOUNDS the next morning, she waits
to see if he says something, if he orders her to stay in the
house. But when she lets it ring, he just turns over and mumbles,
Turn it off.

She is still allowed to go to work. Perhaps he will change his
mind. Perhaps the rules will be altered again. Sometime. Perhaps.

It takes time to apply her make-up. She cannot hide the marks
completely. She leaves her hair loose so that it falls around her
face. Her cheek is still swollen, and a little yellow, and the burst
blood vessel in the white of her eye will be there for some time
to come. No way that can be hidden with make-up.

She arrives at work, a little later than usual because of the swollen apple-cheek. Béatrice is already there. Béatrice addresses her
with a small nod, not exactly curt, but cautious.

Sandrine takes a small step, a tentative half-step, the merest suggestion of a step in her colleague's direction. At her desk, Béatrice
straightens up, raises her eyebrows questioningly, and says, Yes?

And then Sandrine changes her mind, what's the point, it
won't change a thing. Unthinking, she tucks a strand of hair
back behind her ear. Béatrice's brows are low over her eyes now,
observing, then horrified. She has seen the cheek. Sandrine panics,
steps back, she mustn't show anything, it's always so much worse
afterwards, when she says— When she does, or thinks anything
at all. But Béatrice stands up and comes close.

Béatrice insists on looking, and finally, she does something that takes Sandrine quite unawares: she touches her. Béatrice takes her chin in her hand, makes Sandrine look at her. Sandrine feels like a naughty little girl, but there is something in Béatrice's gesture, in the way one action leads to another, that stops her from pulling away or protesting. In the raw neon light of the main office, where the secretaries work, she allows Béatrice to examine her face. The human contact is unexpected, a way of being touched that she has never known, or had forgotten. She had a friend at nursery school, a little girl called Christelle who was too small while she, Sandrine, was too fat. They were alone together, and until Christelle moved away there were games, and line-ups in the playground which meant they had to hold hands. Later, when she was about thirteen, there was another girl, Cassandra, even taller than Sandrine, and dark, coal-black. Until Sandrine's father forbade her – yet again – from going anywhere near her friend. Sandrine has filed these memories away carefully, the memory of physical contact suffused with— with, how can she put it? What is it? Something so old, from so long ago, yes: tenderness. Sandrine liked to feel an arm around her shoulders, the touch of palms patting in rhythm, foreheads pressed together for whispered secrets. Cassandra's hair was arranged in neat, wave-like rows, tight against her scalp, and curly-headed Christelle wore a very short, practical pudding-basin cut; Sandrine remembers her two friends' fascination, one after the other, with her own fine, long hair, their natural curiosity as they reached out to touch it, their fingers braiding the strands. She hasn't thought about either girl for years, decades. An eternity since anyone touched her that way, in friendship, with consideration and concern, not wanting to rob her of anything, or to snatch anything away. Sisterly, physical contact, like puppies who take the proximity of kindred skin completely for granted.

She knows that Béatrice has a child and a partner, that there's no fooling her. And when her colleague turns her cheek towards the neon lights overhead, firmly but carefully, without animosity, and asks, What's this?, Sandrine relents and allows her head to follow the movement. Béatrice's warm fingers on her chin bring tears to her eyes. Have you told the woman cop? Béatrice asks. And Sandrine shakes her head, her colleague's fingers still clasping her chin, determined not to release her, not to abandon her, not to let her sink down and collapse.

When the woman cop arrives, Béatrice greets her in reception. Sandrine sits alone in the glass-walled meeting room, where everyone can see her, a curious creature, a case for the social services, a battered wife. Everyone present at the office that Monday will have an appropriate label nestled comfortably in their mind. Sandrine doesn't care. From time to time, she shifts a little in her chair, and the pain, distant and faint, reminds her that last night, Monsieur Langlois was hard. When she moves, the tiny scabs on her breasts rub against the fabric of her bra and she remembers the hours she spent turning all the things she holds against him, against everyone else, in upon herself, in the unending battle that leaves her exhausted, each time, but strangely, still very much alive. The same thing, perhaps, that makes her love the man who cries, the same thing that makes her take out the healing cream and tell herself that this was the last time, each time. Suffering and survival. She has told herself so many times, in a vague, unformed way, that she is far from innocent in all this, that she *goes looking* for it. But since allowing Béatrice to touch her, first her chin, then her hands, then her shoulders, she has begun to tell herself that the man who cries is not the healing cream. Perhaps he's the needle. She doesn't know. She has decided to trust Béatrice. She tries to focus on this idea. That she should leave it all to Béatrice. And Béatrice has called Lisa, the policewoman.

Lisa does not come alone. Her colleague is with her, the man who's beginning to… And as Sandrine discovers when he stands aside, to let the slim, dark-haired woman through in her jeans and blue sweater, they have brought Caroline with them, too.

Sandrine watches them as they approach. They walk towards the meeting room in single file. She is curious. A little surprised. It's like the pain in her lower belly, the pain in her breasts: distant, because she holds it at bay, but she could let it all go, if she dared. If she had the energy. To shake herself out of it is to suffer. Sandrine has learnt to find safety in stillness and silence, in giving up. A blank, empty world where no voice rings out inside her head, because if the voice spoke, if Sandrine let herself listen, the voice would ask her to account for herself, demand she get moving, take action. And very probably the voice would say: *Well now, what's she doing here?*

The male cop is the first to speak. He apologises, in the tones of a lesson well-learned, and Sandrine realises they are surrounded, he and she both, by women who have taken charge. When he has finished explaining that he regrets his thoughtless misstep, that he realises he still has a lot to learn about cases of coercive control, that his colleague has explained to him how extremely difficult and dangerous it is to leave a manipulative, violent partner, he looks Lisa in the eye and sees that Lisa is satisfied, and so, therefore, is he. Sandrine thinks of Monsieur Langlois, and what he would say about men like that, with their sweet, faggoty, limp-dick ways, their non-existent pride. How a man who lets women walk all over him is no man at all. Then she sees the look that Béatrice is giving the male cop, a look that speaks loud and clear of her colleague's designs on the dick in question, limp or otherwise, and she tells herself that right there before her is another reality, another way of being, one she knows nothing about. A world beyond the scope of anything she has been taught to understand. *Trained*, she thinks suddenly. Trained to understand. The word slips through her consciousness like an eel, while Béatrice asks if Sandrine would prefer she left the room? Or we can go somewhere else, Sandrine, suggests the woman cop— Lisa. We can do this somewhere else. I mean, without your colleagues, or anyone.

Trained. *I was trained to think that way.* Trained to think and say nothing, to shut up. Like a dog turning tricks, a she-dog, a filthy bitch, as Monsieur Langlois would say.

Sandrine? Would you prefer we go somewhere else? If you don't feel comfortable here, where your employers can see us?

Somewhere else.

Sandrine says, Yes, OK. Somewhere else.

She fetches her coat, her bag. Along the way, she fetches Béatrice, too. Their hands touch and again, the contact opens doors somewhere inside, doors to a place where she can touch people without being misunderstood, where hands can reach out gently, kindly, because sometimes human beings need to touch one another to keep warm or find their way.

They are in a café-brasserie. Mid-morning. People stand or sit at the bar, sipping espresso, cappuccino, coming and going. The room is large, quiet. They are sitting at the back. In peace.

It's been a very long time since Sandrine set foot in a café. She would come here for lunch with her colleagues sometimes. On a Friday, the day without Tupperware. They would take a whole hour. That was when she was allowed to go to a brasserie. When she still felt a little at ease with her colleagues; a time before she felt tainted by the distinctive odour of solitude, when she tried her best. She says this as she sits down – that it's been a while since she came here, and Béatrice says Yes, we never knew why you stopped coming with us… But that was even *before* him. But that doesn't matter now, she adds quickly, discarding the issue with a wave of her hand.

Sandrine is grateful. She cannot summon the strength to ask that particular question of herself today; the question of the path along which she became the Sandrine who thought her life had begun when the man who cries first laid eyes on her. That question needs time, and resources. Things she no longer has.

The first woman is silent. She sits up straight. Her shoulders quiver almost imperceptibly, and Sandrine realises that just like her, under the table, Caroline is tying her fingers in impossible knots, pressing tight against the base of her nails. Her mirror image. Sandrine rests her nervous hands on the Formica table and, with an effort, looks straight across at the first woman. Caroline does not look away. There is something there. Her eyes are not bottomless wells. There is light, you just have to see it. And a smile. Caroline smiles. She places her own hands on the table, her fingers are nervous and entwined. Two women tied in knots. *Vous*— Caroline begins, formally. Then the familiar *tu*… Shall we call one another *tu*? Sandrine nods.

How is Mathias? Sandrine asks, unsure whether she has the right to know. Caroline reaches forward and covers Sandrine's hands with her own. Her fingers are warm, dry, tense, and she squeezes Sandrine's fists. She says, He's fine, he's fine. I want to say thank you. For looking— for taking such good care of him. He's very fond of you, I hope you know that.

Sandrine says, Thank you, I— Thank you. I'm very fond of him, too.

You're wondering why I'm here, aren't you? I'm here to tell you what happened. What I remember.

And so Sandrine asks, What do you remember?

The bartender appears, places the coffees on the table. A decaf for Sandrine. The spoons tinkle in the saucers.

Everything, says Caroline, and her voice is lower, quieter now. I remember everything.

There are things Sandrine already knows, in what Caroline has to say. Things that her parents, Anne-Marie and Patrice, have told her before. That she was good at science. That she was going to study to be a vet. There are things they never told her, too, because they didn't know. The evening when a boy Caroline knew and trusted had insisted on seeing her home because she'd had too much to drink, then forced his fingers inside her, saying 'You like that, don't you, you like it, you slut.' How something broke inside her then, how it changed the way she walked, and carried herself, out in the street. The insomnia, and the important entrance exam she could not finish, because the boy was there among the other candidates, in the room, staring at her and mouthing the word 's-lut' when she walked in. How she gave up.

The years when going out of the house, talking to other people, breathing the smell of a man was painful to her. The efforts she made to mend and start over. The start of nursing school, feeling proud. And then the man.

'The man who cries?' Sandrine asks.

'He didn't cry when I first knew him. But he was a *man*. Eight years older than me. He was a man. All around me, the nursing students were like kids by comparison. But he had… he was a proper man. He shaved every day, he had a job, a career plan, grown-up things. I don't know what it was he sniffed out in me, perhaps just the fact that I never said anything. I walked into a tobacconist's to buy cigarettes, and a drunk said something. Something with the word "slut" in it, and I— I froze on the spot. And then he came in. He stood between me and the other man. He dragged him out of the shop by his collar and hit him. Really hit him, hard. Too hard. But it was so… reassuring. You know my father.'

Sandrine nods her head. She knows Patrice, even though Caroline's husband never wanted them to be close. And nothing about Patrice suggests fist-fighting.

'My father— I'd never seen him hit anybody,' Caroline continues. 'I never thought I would want a man who was capable of that, but there he was, he had protected me, and I agreed to the date he suggested there and then, because he had protected me, because he looked as if… as if he could take care of me.'

Very quickly, they moved into a brand-new house. She had very little money, and the disparity was a source of shame for her. She insisted on contributing to the mortgage repayments. A small amount, but it was important. That was when she still thought he was happy for her to study, to have a career. She was passionate about her studies, they demanded a great deal of hard work. Gradually, as the months went by, she felt his resentment grow, at the time she spent revising or covering the emergency shift at the veterinary surgery, where she worked to pay her fees. He seemed to have thought that once she had found a man, she would give it all up.

'Give up what?'

'My— my studies. My girlfriends.' The few evenings out she still allowed herself. Her work. Everything. That she would stay at home, waiting for him and cooking his favourite meals. She had thought he was joking.

He was not joking.

I became pregnant with Mathias in the third year of vet school. It was an accident. I took my pill every day at lunchtime and I can't see how he could have tampered with the pack, but I did wonder… He insisted we keep the baby. He wore me out. Until I said Yes, OK. And I thought he'd be— that he'd be content. That it would be enough. A child is a big step. Two things happened when Mathias was born. The first was that he refused to take care of him. The baby was mine, it was up to me to take care of it. He never prepared a bottle, not a single one. I don't even know if he touched Mathias during the first months. Maybe longer. The second thing was that he started hitting me. It didn't happen overnight. We had been arguing a lot since moving to the house, I felt he wasn't helping, that it wasn't fair that I was the one who managed everything, the housework, the washing, the— everything. He would take care of the garden, because that was a man's thing, but that was all. He had this way of presenting things, at the end of every argument, so that I was the one who felt guilty. Selfish. Beholden. He was the one who went out to work every day. Who was paying for this house? He was. One day, I said No, I'm working too, and I give you money, the house belongs to me, too, and that's when I learnt my name was no longer on the deeds. That I was not registered as one of the owners. I felt I'd been taken prisoner, but that was also when I found out I was pregnant, and so the discussion moved on, there was something else to talk about, except they weren't discussions, they were like— battles, endless exhausting battles. All I could do was give in, that was what worked, every time, I would give up.

And feel guilty, all the time. The pregnancy went well, it was… a quiet, peaceful time, at first. Until my gynaecologist advised against having sex, and that drove him crazy, he wouldn't stand for it. He said it wasn't up to some quack bitch of a female doctor to tell him whether or not he could have sex with his wife. I was… I was seven-and-a-half months gone. I felt huge, I was sweaty all the time, my legs had swollen. He got me all mixed up in my head. He persuaded me I was repulsive, but that he still wanted me because he was being generous and kind. I didn't want it, but I felt almost grateful.'

Caroline digs the sharp edges of a white sugar cube into the pads of her fingertips.

'He was raping me and I had to say thank you.'

The signal is given, and the bartender comes over to ask if everyone has everything they need. Same again. The first woman drinks a little water and runs her hands through her hair. Sandrine notices the fine streaks of white. She doesn't remember Caroline having so much silver the last time she saw her. She wonders if hair can turn white in just a couple of weeks, if a person's hair can turn white because certain memories have resurfaced.

'Where was I? Yes, Mathias's birth. He began to hit me. Not straightaway, but I remember the first time it happened, Mathias was still bottle-feeding. The first time it was because… Because I said "five minutes." He had come back from work, and Mathias was crying… dinner wasn't ready, I was going to cook pasta but it wasn't ready and the sauce had burned… He came back and asked me to fetch him a beer. Sixteen-year-old Caroline would have told him to piss off! She would have said "Fetch your own beer." But by that stage I knew it was up to me to serve him his glass of beer. I— it was, I just didn't bother

254

arguing any more. It would have gone on for hours, he was the one who was going out to work, he was doing everything for me, and me, I couldn't even be bothered to get him a beer? The beer or something else, whatever, when he wanted something he was always right, and I was always wrong. But I... the tomato sauce was boiling and spattering everywhere. Because he had come back later than expected, again. He came and went without ever telling me his plans, but the food had to be ready the instant he came back. And Mathias was hungry... So I said "Give me five minutes." And he slapped me. I had Mathias in my arms. I could have dropped him, I could have fallen over, tripped over onto the boiling saucepan... And then he said he was sorry, sorry, sorry. He said, "I'm sorry, but." When he said sorry, it was always "I'm sorry, but..." And the "but" was always because it was my fault.'

Caroline speaks for a long time, and her words are slow, calm and terrifying. Mathias was born, she loved him, and the man in the house hated that. He hated that this tiny, vulnerable human being needed care and attention, and that Caroline gave him those things. He never hit the child, but he never agreed to take care of him. Until Mathias became 'interesting', when he was about three or four years old. Until he was big enough to start learning how to build things, play football, become a man. One day she heard him talking to Mathias, telling him that girls always said the opposite of what they were really thinking. That proper men had fights with other boys and they always won. She watched her baby boy, his still-pudgy fingers closing around the toy bricks and answering his father's question in his gentle, piping voice. What are girls like? They tell lies. What do real men do? They like fighting. Do you want to be a real man or a little girl? A real man. The words were repeated, almost chanted like a nursery rhyme, and she took the child in her arms and carried him upstairs to his room and when she came back down again she said, What on earth's the matter with you, teaching him things like that?

He said, I'm sorry? What did you say? in a very soft voice, and she knew that she had better shut up, but she was so angry, for the first time, so very angry, for what she could see him doing to her baby boy, for what she could see he was doing to Mathias, for the poison he was pouring into her son's ear, into his warm, round head with its crow-black, downy hair. And so she spoke out. And her voice was shaking with rage: 'I don't want you to talk to him like that.' And at first he laughed, a nasty, cruel laugh, and then he hit her very hard.

She thought she was going to die.

When he had finished, he pulled her into the pantry because she really wasn't fit to be seen, and then he took Mathias out to the cinema, to see a film he was far too small to watch, and eat a pizza that upset his stomach. That night, she had to drag herself into Mathias's room to save him from a nightmare, and a flood of pizza that he had thrown back up, acrid and foul-smelling. Carrying him to the shower had been almost impossible. She was so broken that the pain of moving had made her vomit, too, into the shower pan. But she had to change the sheets, change Mathias into clean pyjamas. All while her own body cracked and suffered with every breath.

To begin with, when the little boy woke from being sick in his sleep, he had cried because he didn't recognise her. She told Mathias she had slipped and fallen down the stairs. Finally, he said 'Mama…' because he recognised her voice.

She stayed shut away in the house, hidden, for several weeks. She was black, purple, then blue, and green. And finally, yellow.

'Like that, there,' she adds, pointing to the glossy green-and-yellow apple of Sandrine's cheek. 'But all over.'

And when she was fit to be seen in public again, daily life resumed. She went shopping. She cooked food. She went running. She took care of Mathias. At night, in bed, he penetrated her, and the degree of violence depended on his mood, and how his day had been.

She was silent, obedient, discreet. One thing only had changed: she had decided to get away.

This was the period when he still allowed her to go shopping. When she still had access to the car. That was how she put the money aside. How she managed to arrange the passports. She knew about the other woman. He was capable of going wild and inventing affairs on her part, but he was sleeping around. At regular intervals. Intervals that aided Caroline's plans. It took a long time, a very long time indeed.

When she was ready to go, all she needed was the courage to make it happen.

When she says this, Sandrine wants to interrupt, to say that thinking about it meant she was already brave enough to resist. But she remembers Monsieur Langlois, who interrupts her all the time, and she holds back.

She just needed to find the courage, and that took time, as well. Several times she told herself, Today's the day, and then faltered at the last minute. Sometimes, it was because he'd been nice, and the unspoken terror was just a faint buzzing in her head. Sometimes it was because he hadn't been nice at all, and she was paralysed with fear.

And he sensed something. She had no idea how, but he sensed something was up. He altered the pattern of his nights away, and then he didn't sleep over at all. He became stricter, too; her punishments were delivered for smaller and smaller missteps. She had less and less to eat. He took the car keys. It was a long walk to Mathias's school. Sometimes he would wait for her to get back from taking the boy to school, and shut her inside the house for the day, with nothing in the fridge, and the pantry shut with a big padlock that he placed on a metal bolt. Sometimes he told her she had been good, though she had no idea what she had done differently from usual, and she would be free to go out for a run, to organise her day, the pantry would be left open. But the punishment days fell more and more often.

She kept silent, never looked up, was submissive, but he knew, he felt something. Caroline was building up her courage. She never thought it would be harder to amass than the small stash of money she needed to get far enough away.

One morning, Mathias had spilt his breakfast bowl of hot chocolate. He caught the little boy by the wrist, and with his other hand, his big man's hand, he had slapped him with the same determination, the same openness he showed when he hit her. Proprietorial indifference, like stinging a horse with a riding crop, because the creature has to learn, because he can.

Mathias did not cry. He was too shocked. Suspended above the floor, at the end of his father's arm, he looked like a baby chimpanzee hanging from a vine, his huge dark eyes fixed on Caroline, and she realised that she had been lying to herself, that she could not protect him, that he did not believe the falling-downstairs and the walking-into-cupboard-doors, that he understood everything. And that he, too, was in danger.

What did the man see in her eyes when she turned to look at him that morning? What secret loathing, in the impassive gaze she had cultivated so carefully? Caroline does not know.

When she came back from taking to Mathias to school, he was there. She remembers that he waited while she closed the front door behind her and took off her shoes. And then he came towards her, quickly, confidently, and she saw that this was something new, something final, this was her own end approaching, and she ran. Through the sitting room, into the kitchen. They stood frozen for moment like that, the two of them, and the kitchen table was all that stood between her and death, and then he threw the table over, he pressed her up against the countertop, and he hit her, but less hard than usual, as if that was not his purpose, not this time, and finally he put his hands around her neck and he squeezed and everything went white, then red, then black.

'After that, I woke up in the field. But I don't want to say what happened then,' Caroline adds, before drinking a glass of water, gulping it down.

Sandrine knows what happened then. Caroline wandering naked, picked up by unknown men, then set loose, wandering again. Sandrine hopes that Caroline does not remember *everything*. Lisa tells the first woman, 'There's no need,' and then Caroline finishes her drink and places the glass on the table, and says to Sandrine, 'I'm here to tell you that it will never get any better. Sandrine, he won't change. He won't stop. I know you can't— that it's, that, I know it's just so *hard*. But it's not impossible.'

Sandrine doesn't know what to say, she doesn't know where to start, Caroline has said so much to her. And facing her, the first woman asks if he knows about the baby. The woman cop gives a small gesture of her hand, indicating to Sandrine that she, Lisa, has said nothing. Caroline tells the male cop, I heard you talking on the phone. Lisa sighs, the male cop says he's sorry.

259

'No, not yet,' says Sandrine. 'I think he knows something. That something's changed. I wanted to tell him and then, and then you— Well, he…'

'What have you got there, at the house, Sandrine? Do you still have your papers? Your accounts?' Caroline is precise, efficient. She lists the things she no longer had herself. When Sandrine confirms she has signed for the joint account, the admission comes in a whisper. She feels so ashamed. Poor, stupid bitch, stupid, fat, fat, *fat* bitch, filthy bitch. But no one reproaches her for anything. Caroline asks if they can go to the bank that afternoon, and the cops say, Why not. Caroline says, It's still less than fifteen days… it should be possible to open a new account, no? Lisa's partner replies that they're cops, not bankers, that he has no idea, but it's worth a try.

'What else is there? At Monsieur Langlois's house? Any personal valuables? Photos you treasure? Jewellery?' Sandrine says no. She doesn't have much, and nothing of that sort. She came with the big cardboard boxes, not all of which she has unpacked. He was the thing she treasured, the man who cries, and Mathias. She has a tiny fabric pouch in the bathroom, with a few bits of cheap jewellery. And a handful of precious items, one or two nice art books that she loves, some letters from her grandmother… But they're in a box in the garage, because there's no room for them anywhere else.

'Does he know which things are precious to you?'

Sandrine thinks not. Because the truth is, he really doesn't care.

'You don't have to go back there,' Caroline says.

She doesn't find fault with anything. She states the facts, explains, and Sandrine knows she's right. Because she, Sandrine, never had items of family jewellery, never really had a family, never anything of value, because she placed no value on her own self, and Caroline says, I think I know what you're thinking, and I want you to know how wrong it is. He makes us feel stupid, but you've been careful, that's all. Perhaps you don't realise it. But you've been careful. You can leave this evening. Right now.'

'He knows where I work.'

'So do we. We know where you work,' says the male cop. 'He's putting his case together for custody of the boy, and that's not going to be easy for him. He knows we're following him. Behind closed doors, he can still do what he likes, but out here, it's not in his interest to cause trouble.'

'There's one very important thing,' says Lisa. 'You need to know that you are not alone, Sandrine. That he has no rights over you.'

Sandrine mutters something, and everyone leans in and says, Hm?

'It's his baby.'

'As to that,' says Caroline, 'I can't decide in your place. But you still have time to think.'

Think what? Sandrine doesn't understand, at first, and then gradually, the idea dawns. Caroline says again, 'You must do what you want. But you're young. You're pretty. There'll be other chances'

Young. Pretty. Other chances. The words mean nothing to Sandrine, and Caroline can tell. She changes the subject.

'Well, you can see about that. What's important now is that he doesn't know about it. And he doesn't care one bit about Mathias. I know that. He wants him because it will hurt me, that's all. He wants him because I left, and because this is a way to steal something from me. He wants him because he's my son.'

She's right, and no one disagrees. Perhaps somewhere, deep down inside, amid all the cruelty and pride, the possessive thirst he mistakes for love, the man who wanted to kill Caroline has some grain of affection for Mathias, something pure that has escaped the wickedness, the power games. Perhaps. But no one around the table has any time to lose over that.

'If he finds out about the baby, he'll try to use it,' says Sandrine, and nothing in her tone suggests regret or fear, she herself does not know what she thinks any more.

The woman cop says, Let's take this one thing at a time.

And that's what they do.

They carry on talking for a long while, and from time to time Lisa looks at Sandrine and asks, Are you OK? But it doesn't mean, Is everything all right? Because of course everything isn't all right. What she means is, Are you with us? Are you here? Do you agree? Because Sandrine must decide to leave. She must *want* to leave.

And Sandrine does her best. She does her best to want it. To be there. To picture this new reality, one in which she will not go back to the house tonight. In which she leaves Monsieur Langlois. Little by little, the image forms in her mind and she clings to it. It grows, it is warm and alive, she can do no better, she has no strength left, she focuses her whole mind and body on this vision of herself, pushing open a different door, that very night. At first, it's the door of her old apartment, but that's absurd, of course, someone else is living there now. They're telling her about a shelter, and she tries to picture it, she really tries. The cops talk about beatings and wounds, coercion, violence, rape, sexual assault, acts of torture, but the flow of words subsides because all around the table, everyone can see her state of shock, her struggle. Lisa signals a pause and asks the waiter for the lunch menu.

They need a breather.

Lisa goes outside to smoke. The male cop heads for the toilets. Béatrice goes too.

Caroline has said nothing for a long while. She and Sandrine are alone at the table: the first woman, the second woman, the one who was murdered, and the one who is utterly lost. Caroline stares at her. Perhaps she foresaw, or perhaps she is seeing only now, how hard Sandrine finds it to picture herself in a different place, a different life. Or perhaps it's not that at all, perhaps it's a sudden impulse that drives the dark-eyed woman to say, Do you want to come to our place?

Sandrine repeats the words, with an effort: Your place? She's trying her best, really, but she is just so exhausted.

'My parents' place. It's small. But we can manage. I mean, for a few weeks. Until he understands you really have left, until the investigation… I don't know, while things take their course. I can sleep with Mathias, I'll leave you the sofa. My parents are—they'll agree to it. They don't want you to come to any harm.'

Sandrine thinks about Anne-Marie and Patrice, their kind deeds, their quiet thoughtfulness, she wonders what they think of her, if they know she did her best to take care of the little boy. One part of her resents them, resents them for taking Mathias away from her. But no. No. She tells herself they've done nothing wrong, only their best, she must remember that. They had no rights over the boy, and they knew nothing, they were just afraid. That something would go wrong. That Monsieur Langlois would stop them from seeing him. Caroline's recovered memory has broken them into tiny pieces. The discovery of what she endured all those years, without ever daring to tell them, has left them in bits, just a few scattered shards. Caroline said earlier, I didn't tell them everything, but even without knowing, they know enough, too much.

Patrice and Anne-Marie are incapable of hatred, Sandrine knows that, and powerless to enact revenge. Their only weapon is the all-consuming tenderness with which they surround their daughter, and her son. Caroline jokes about it. She says, It would do me good to have them fret about someone else, and Sandrine sees that she really means it. That she really is suggesting she stays at the Marquezes' apartment. It's a place she knows, a little. The place where Mathias is now. She can see herself push open the door. She can see herself sitting down on the blue sofa, surrounded by Patrice's plants – he has green fingers but no garden, and each room has been transformed, patiently, by instinct, into a quiet jungle of gently rustling leaves. She thinks of the perfectly trained box hedges flanking Monsieur Langlois's terrace, cut with his secateurs, stripped back Saturday after Saturday. She says, Are you sure? And Caroline's dark eyes are filled with warmth when she says, 'Well, that's settled, then.'

Lisa raises one eyebrow very slightly, but agrees. She says, Good, she can remind you how much of a crazed bastard he is, in your moments of doubt. Or words to that effect. They order lunch. Béatrice must get back to work. Before leaving, she places a hand on Sandrine's shoulder and again, the miracle occurs: the discreet, affectionate gesture draws Sandrine back to the present, to a place where everything will be all right, where she can be forgiven, and where women like Béatrice love men who do not smash their faces into plates of scalding-hot mashed potato for breathing the wrong way. An alternative present. A present that holds a future.

The waiter serves their food – simple, well-made dishes. Sandrine eats a piece of fish that she asks to be cooked right through, with runner beans and fries. Before leaving, Béatrice says, Keep your strength up, Sandrine. And she does as she's been told.

That afternoon, they go to the bank. The cops are patient. Sandrine's former contact at the branch – a very young deputy manager – fails to understand at first, but remains very polite, very helpful, then makes the necessary changes. Sandrine has her own account once again, in her own name. When they ask for the address, to send her bank card and chequebook, Sandrine hesitates but Caroline smiles and gives the Marquezes' details. It's done. All sent off. She can go. Just like that. After months when nothing changed and everything seemed impossible, something has changed, and she can start again. Yesterday, just a few hours ago, that was out of the question. She needs a moment. That moment is now.

Sandrine calls the office. She takes a few days off. Lisa takes the phone. She gives clear instructions: if Langlois shows up, they must be informed. On absolutely no account should they tell anyone, anyone at all, where Sandrine is, or when she will be back. If anyone asks, say she has resigned. When the cop is done giving orders, she cuts the call and slowly puts down the phone, as if handling something very delicate, or dangerous.

Sandrine's phone lies on the brasserie table. She reaches for it but Lisa wriggles her nose, leans forward and covers the device with her hand. Sandrine hesitates. For some reason she can't have her phone back, and like a good, well-brought-up girl, she does as she is told, doesn't dare protest, or make a grab for it, or question why. I'm sorry, says Lisa, as if speaking to a child whose only toy she has taken away, I'd like to— She turns to her colleague, then back to Sandrine, I need to make sure this phone is safe. Can we check that out? Sandrine nods. The request for her permission, the acknowledgement of her right to her own things, feels strange, unfamiliar. Thank you, says Lisa, and when she slides the phone across the table to her colleague, Sandrine sits still, watches as her phone is switched off and disappears into the male cop's pocket. He stands up and says, I'll meet you there.

They drive to the Marquezes' apartment, Sandrine at the wheel of her own car, Lisa beside her, up front. Caroline in the back seat. In her rather husky voice, the woman cop congratulates her, encourages her, tells her, 'Bravo, well done, Sandrine, really well done, I hope you realise what a good thing you've done, for yourself, for your life, for your… pregnancy, I mean, if you decide to keep it. It's a strong decision, you are very strong.' A sweet refrain that accompanies her all the way to the Marquezes' building.

Anne-Marie has come down to open the ground-floor garage. Of course, Sandrine thinks: Caroline must have texted them en route. Sandrine parks her car inside. She understands that the Marquezes' five-seater will sleep out in the open so that she can hide her car in their garage. Theirs is a quiet neighbourhood, no fear of vandals, but all the same.

She emerges from the garage and apologises to Anne-Marie: 'I'm so sorry for the disruption.' And she is startled when Anne-Marie takes her in her arms and cuddles her, cradles her like a mother in a TV commercial.

Sandrine had always allowed herself to be influenced by Langlois's coldness towards his parents-in-law. He didn't like them, he tolerated them with a show of politeness. The cops think he was keeping up appearances. He had cut her off from Anne-Marie and Patrice, steeped in their grief and kind-heartedness, just as he had cut her off from everything else, everyone else. And now Anne-Marie hugs her tight against her generous, soft bosom, and apologises, too. She says she is sorry. That she should have spotted the signs sooner, that she should have helped her. She says, My poor girl, my poor, dear, little girl. Anne-Marie smells of remorse and a fresh, flowery, delicate perfume. No one has ever embraced Sandrine so tenderly, with such obvious determination to protect her, to wrap her in warmth, no one since her honey-sweet grandmother. Sandrine puts her arms around Anne-Marie's waist and cries. It begins all of a sudden, something gives way, completely, in the aroma of maternal love that surprises her and quenches a thirst she has never recognised, never slaked. Sandrine says, No, it's me, it's me, I should have, I should... I tried to protect Mathias but I, but I was— I was, I'm sorry. Caroline joins the hug, they are all three of them so very sorry. Sandrine is surrounded by a wall of tears and sorrow. Finally, Anne-Marie says, Well, here you are now, that's what matters, and thank goodness I brought some tissues down with me, eh?

Sniffing, they climb the stairs.

Inside the Marquezes' apartment, Patrice trembles with emotion and doesn't know what to do with his man's hands, his man's arms, he wants to hug Sandrine but holds back, he's afraid she'll be afraid, he's afraid to hurt her, he holds her against him timidly, awkwardly, briefly, but the gesture is dripping with good intentions and Sandrine, who knows it, says, Thank you. Thank you for everything. He says, Well now, listen, I found my old folding camp bed, it's a bit basic for now, but we'll go and buy you a proper mattress tomorrow, all right? We thought it was... that it was important for you to have your own bed, even if it's just a small one. I hope that— that it'll do, and you can stay as long as you like, of course, as long as you like.

On the bed, there are clothes. Clean. Folded. On top of the pile, a pair of trousers and some shirts in black, and plum. Sandrine recognises Anne-Marie's clothes, things she has complimented in the past, because they reflected her own taste. Her throat tightens again. The kindness of these people, to whom she means nothing; the people she kept at a distance, showing mere politeness, all this time, even when they needed her, needed to talk to her. Their kindness overwhelms her. Everyone wipes their eyes, while the police officer waits patiently.

When it's time for Patrice and Anne-Marie to fetch Mathias from school, Lisa calls her colleague, asks if he'll be finished soon, then listens for a few seconds while Caroline's parents put on their coats. Sandrine cannot hear what the male cop is saying, just the deep sound of his voice. Lisa walks a few steps, tearing at her already bitten nails, her phone pressed tightly to her ear. When she rejoins them, the tips of her fingers are damp and gleaming. One of her nails is bitten almost to the quick, exposing the pink flesh beneath, raw and livid. He'll meet the grandparents outside the school, Lisa explains. Then he will accompany them back here. There's something we need to discuss.

Patrice and Anne-Marie leave the apartment. Caroline says, We were afraid he would take Mathias, at first, but he's never come to the school gate. Sandrine asks Lisa, But does one of you go every day? How long will you do that for? A simple enough question, she thinks, but Lisa's reply is deadly serious. Sandrine's alarm button: does she still have it?

The truth is, Sandrine, you're entering a phase that will require a great deal of strength on your part. That man has a hold over you, and it can be difficult to break free. We've been watching his movements for weeks now. For the moment, it seems he's chosen to proceed along the official channels. To take it to the courts, play the good father, use Mathias to punish Caroline, and you, too. We'll do everything in our power to prevent him from getting custody of the boy. I've warned Caroline already: it is very, very rare here in France for fathers – even violent men, even men who have committed incest, men with criminal records – to be denied access to their children. He's contesting the case through the family courts. But we've been working on Caroline's case for several weeks now, and that will go before the court, too. The problem with our system – and let me be very, very clear about this – the problem with our system is that unless something very serious occurs, it's immensely difficult for us to support victims of conjugal violence. But in this case – and I'm sorry, Caroline, for what I'm about to say – but in this case we've been lucky. Something very serious *did happen*. He killed his wife. She remembers. And she will testify.

Lisa rubs her forehead.

He's hired a family lawyer, a specialist who doesn't come cheap. Clearly, he's got the money to pay for the very best. He's found someone who can get him out of being taken into protective custody. Listen to me, Sandrine: there's a chance he won't be detained before, or during the hearing. And that's when you are going to have to be very, very careful.

Careful in what way? Sandrine asks.

Very careful.

Sandrine feels the moment with frightening, even painful intensity. Here and now, on the sofa, beside Caroline, facing Lisa. She feels the warm leather against her legs. She smells the two women's scent, the faint odour of cigarettes, and the leather of Lisa's jacket. The sun is out today. Sunlight pours through the window, warming Patrice's plants. The sitting room looks like a tropical conservatory, luxuriant, carefully tended, but without the stuffiness of a glasshouse.

Be very careful. OK.

When Mathias comes home from school and finds her there, he opens his eyes wide and smiles. An immense smile that she scarcely recognises. Mathias is just the same, and completely different. He stands up straight and his gestures are broader, more expansive. Less than a month has gone by, and Sandrine could swear he is half a head taller, or half as tall again.

Lisa's colleague is with the boy and his grandparents. He enters the apartment, and Sandrine sees her phone in his hand. He seems tired, but then she cannot remember either of them ever looking anything but exhausted. Patrice and Anne-Marie set out a snack for Mathias and carefully, quietly close the kitchen door.

Can you change your phone? the male cop asks. And again, Sandrine cannot grasp what is happening. If she felt stronger, she would hate herself for being so stupid, for staring dully while people repeat or explain themselves, but it takes all the strength she has to sit and breathe and survive from one moment to the next, while the day crumbles slowly around her. Sandrine doesn't understand. Lisa rubs her forehead, this is a long day for her, too. And then she explains.

He installed a program on your phone that tracked your movements, your precise coordinates – far more accurate than your location-sharing app. He texted and called to check where you said you were, but he knew all along, thanks to this. The male cop waves Sandrine's phone. It's something we see more and more often in abusive relationships. Easy enough to do. He runs a finger across his unshaven cheek and adds, I've reported it, and uninstalled the program, but I was pressed for time… He sits in the Marquezes' sitting room now, playing absently with the device, tapping it against his thigh. Best get rid of it, he says. I need to get back to the office, to ask for— You know. And Lisa nods. He gets to his feet, says, Oh, sorry! as if suddenly remembering something he'd forgotten to do, and finally hands Sandrine her phone.

She turns it on. The device bursts into life, vibrating and pinging again and again. Texts, one after the other, from him. The buzzing in Sandrine's palm fills her with terror, she can almost feel his hand on her neck, his fingers squeezing her throat. She drops the phone onto the coffee table.

A heavy, fascinated silence fills the sitting room. Everyone stares at the phone. It buzzes again, then goes silent for a few seconds more. Sandrine feels an overpowering urge to reach for it. To grab it, to read, to answer, to beg and to cancel everything out, to erase it all and go back. But she does not. Somehow, she finds the strength to cross her arms and sit motionless on the sofa, the phone vibrating and her not answering.

She knows now that she has decided to leave, to get away once and for all. The Sandrine who would go back would be incapable of not answering. It would be too dangerous, draw down too many punishments. Lisa asks, Is it him? But of course she knows it is.

Sandrine nods, neither looking at her phone nor offering to show it to the other women. The texts keep coming, relentlessly, every few minutes. With each new message, she does nothing, avoids looking at the screen, and moves a little further from the possibility of going back. To do nothing is a giant step. She has taken several giant steps this morning, though it doesn't show.

Nothing shows at all, and Sandrine apologises again and again for her failure to react, for sitting there, limp and useless. But Lisa and Caroline reassure her. Caroline understands, above all. She knows how hard Sandrine is fighting, despite her silence, her stillness, despite being bundled like a sack from the café to the Marquezes' apartment. Caroline knows that Sandrine's muscles are tensed, her breathing short and fast, her heart racing. She knows Sandrine's mind is racing too, as she pictures what might happen, what will happen, what could happen. She knows the agony of painful memories or, quite the opposite, like daggers to the heart, the torture of gentle, loving moments, stirred up like silt at the bottom of a swirling lake. And how those images can make her question everything. And then Sandrine comes back to the present, inevitably, and that in itself is painful, and then it starts all over again, and all this time she must listen, and try to decide, and sit up straight. Everything is a struggle. Everything is a mighty achievement.

'You are very brave,' Caroline tells her. 'Everything you're doing, it's so hard, I know.' She smiles at her. The corners of her dark eyes crease with concern, but her expression is warm and encouraging. Sandrine feels stronger when Caroline looks at her like that. How strange that Caroline should inspire such confidence in her. Strange that her expression should say 'It will be all right, you can get through this', when this is the woman who went down, when Caroline herself was killed. But now everything about the first woman reassures her, everything comforts her, Caroline's very existence is a source of strength and Sandrine needs all the strength she can muster.

So we need to keep all his text messages, Sandrine, OK? Lisa is speaking to her. It's up to you to decide how you answer, if you answer, but we need to keep them all.

Do I have to answer, what do you think? Sandrine asks.

The woman cop falls silent for a moment. Then she says, He's going to play the grieving father. The harassed citizen who knows his rights. He'll very likely try the 'anxious partner' act, too. If you make it clear to him, in writing, that it's over, tell him not to come after you, not to try and contact you, then the forty texts you get straight back will constitute harassment. Do you see what I'm getting at? The minute you tell him you've left, things will change. But… I… You really must be careful. I can't decide in your place.

Caroline explains: Sandrine, what Lisa's trying to tell you—what she isn't saying, because she doesn't want you to give up hope, is that now is when the danger really begins.

They look at one another, and out of nowhere, they smile. And that's the worst of it, the creases at the corners of Caroline's eyes seem to say. Really the worst: that *now* is when things can become more dangerous than ever. When you leave the man who's been hitting your head against the wall, starving you, strangling you. It's even, tragically, rather funny, don't you think?

Lisa is uncomfortable. She cannot lie, makes no attempt to disguise the reality they face. It's true. The moment is now. She takes refuge in figures, confirms that statistically, the moment of the separation is the riskiest time, and Sandrine gestures to say that she doesn't want to know, she doesn't want to hear, too bad. That's it. Over.

And she taps a reply into her phone: *I've left.*

It's finished.

It's over.

He mustn't call her any more.

Do not call me again.

Her fingers tremble and the few words take a long time to write, her phone suggests *fun* when she tries to type *finished*, and *Do not call plumbers.* She fumbles to override the autocorrect.

She presses 'send' and places the phone on the coffee table. She hoped she would feel a sense of relief, but she feels sweaty, ice-cold and feverish. She finds it hard to swallow and wonders, just for a second, if this roller-coaster of terror will ever leave her. She remembers a life without fear, without endless anxiety. But she cannot project herself back into that memory, her body cannot recover the absence of tension. She has just sent a simple text message, yet she feels she might faint, she feels suddenly light-headed, and Lisa says, Sandrine, you've gone very white.

Sandrine hears the voice, as if muffled through headphones. Sandrine? Sandrine? You're here with us now. You're here. It's just a text message. He isn't as powerful as you think he is.

What does she know? Sandrine shakes her head, slowly, unsure whether she wants to refocus on hard-edged hyperreality or, on the contrary, slip away forever to this soft, unfocussed place where nothing can reach her. And for the first time, the idea of death slips into her mind. Perhaps that's the best of all possible victories, to kill herself and deprive him of the pleasure of doing the job. Kill herself and escape him for good? Something grips her, pulls her back. Caroline's hand is on her hand, Caroline's short, nervous fingers. Sandrine— I know, I know. Be brave. Be strong.

They stare at the phone for a long time, still as statues. It stays silent, and dark.

It's Lisa's phone that rings. She says, Yes. Good. No, I won't be long.

OK, so, we've been granted a bit of extra time and my colleague is outside Langlois's office. He'll stay right there, so we'll know if he decides to come and look for you. Sandrine, have you decided? About the phone?

Sandrine thinks about the other things it contains: some music, photographs, especially of Mathias. She shakes herself, says, Yes… but her voice is small and almost hoarse, and she has to clear her throat and sit up straight and repeat, Yes. Such a small thing, again, yet it takes her to the brink of exhaustion, just nodding and agreeing, saying she will do it, she will save everything and get rid of the phone; she wishes she could be different, she wishes she could be like Lisa or Caroline, steely, strong-willed, capable, she wishes she could be someone else, but the two women greet

274

her capitulation with such awestruck approval, she cannot understand why, it seems overdone, but she remembers what they've
been telling her all day, the endless refrain, that it's not easy, that
she's brave, that it takes time and courage, and Sandrine almost
believes it, almost. She says again, Yes, I'll do it, and her voice is
louder, and almost firm; it's the best she can do, she's doing her
best and that will have to do because it's all she has. Lisa leaves
them. She needs to go and get some sleep, and then she'll be
back this evening, nearby, when Monsieur Langlois leaves work.

Caroline sits down at Anne-Marie's ageing computer and
saves the handful of memories from Sandrine's phone on a USB
key, the texts in a separate file. Then, together, they destroy the
SIM card, uninstall the apps, turn off the device, like a couple of
trainee spooks. Sandrine pays careful attention to each action –
concrete, palpable, useful.

Sandrine is glad to focus on straightforward, practical tasks.
When they've finished, Caroline calls out and Mathias emerges
from the kitchen, his homework already done. He smiles at his
mother and Sandrine. He doesn't question her presence.

He is much more talkative now, even has to be asked to let
the grown-ups finish what they're saying. He wants to show her
what he's been doing at school. He opens his drawing book. His
birds are fatter, round-bodied, they lie sleeping, or stand proud.
Their teeth have vanished.

Lisa spends the first night outside, at the foot of the building.
Monsieur Langlois does not come.

22

T HE APARTMENT is a little cramped, but the days slip by. During the day, Caroline and Sandrine busy themselves together, helping Patrice and Anne-Marie. Sandrine learns to take care of the plants. Caroline is looking for a job, and Sandrine helps her write a CV on the Marquezes' rather slow computer, scarcely able to believe that she, Sandrine, the useless dead weight, knows how to do something that Caroline, the survivor, does not.

Mathias's timetable dictates theirs: he leaves for school, comes home from school, they eat dinner with him, they go to bed. Sandrine summons all her energy to appear calm and serene when she is with the little boy. The effort leaves her exhausted. When she lived with Monsieur Langlois, she struggled to hide the fear that held her prisoner, and now she concentrates her efforts so as to not poison the atmosphere with her flashes of terror, her endless doubts. The weather has turned cold, it is late autumn now, but still, in the afternoons, she sits on the small balcony terrace with Caroline, and they talk. Caroline smokes. Sandrine talks.

They sit outside so as not to pollute the air in the apartment.

It's been four days, and now five. The apartment is filled with bodies and Picasso the ugly dog is in heaven. He carries his huge, clumsily drawn head from Mathias to his grandparents, to Caroline. When it comes to Sandrine's turn, he rests his jaw on her knees and gazes at her with big, loving eyes.

On the first evening, they all went to bed early. Mathias told the dog, Go, Picasso! Go to Sandrine! And the ugly dog sneezed enthusiastically and did as he was told, eager to obey. Picasso lay stretched out beside the folding camp bed. When Sandrine turned over in the night, he looked up at her, kept watch, and she told him, Everything's all right, it's all right, so that he would rest his head once again on his crossed forepaws.

Sandrine was exhausted that evening but lay on the bed for a long time with her eyes open, telling the dog at intervals that everything was all right, everything was all right. She thought of their neighbours' dogs, lips curled in snarls of hatred whenever Monsieur Langlois came near. Poor, stupid bitch. No. No. No. It's not my fault. She repeats the words to herself. She did not believe them, at first. But she repeated them all the same.

The day after she left, Sandrine went to the police station with Caroline. Patrice took them in the car and waited for them outside. No one pushed Sandrine to file a complaint, no one asked her to justify her silence, her blindness, her choices. It's as if they have given up. She is there simply to help Caroline. But that has changed everything. She confirms that there was an extra lock on the pantry door, that it had been unscrewed before she arrived but that she had seen it, tidied away in one of the plastic boxes in the garage. She talks for a long time and now there is an official statement. In which Sandrine confirms his violent nature. The controlling. The money stowed in the red bookshelves. The passports. Yes. She confirms all the things that she was forbidden to do, and the punishments she received if she did. She confirms the beatings, the nights when she was granted no sleep, forced to lie on the floor, the sworn statements that she copied and signed with Monsieur Langlois's hand on her neck, the attempt to rob her of her financial independence, the threat of being locked up.

There is an official statement in which she confirms that she was the one who took care of Mathias. That if they ask the teachers at school, his class teacher, the after-school study invigilators, they would all confirm that since she came to live with Monsieur Langlois, he had not taken Mathias to school, nor come to fetch him, one single time. That he never cooked a meal for the boy. Had no idea which were his favourite toys. His favourite pyjamas. Never bathed him. Never kissed him. Never listened to him. She states everything. She states everything that Monsieur Langlois is. She says it all because she's not speaking for herself. She is speaking for Caroline. Sandrine knows how to act for the good of others.

When they left to go home again that day, Lisa said, When you're ready to file your own complaint, let me know, Sandrine. Sandrine doesn't dare. She is still so afraid. She wonders if one day she will stop feeling so afraid. But she has managed to record her victim statement. Lisa said, It's important, Sandrine. If something happens one day and you can't reach me, we need a written record, something, anything. Sandrine knows that if not, there are cops who will dismiss the case as a lover's tiff, who never turn out for 'domestics'. That women die because some cops will never turn out for a domestic fight. She knows all this. She has understood the implication, that Lisa or her colleague will not be able to keep watch outside the Marquezes' apartment forever, that she cannot stay there indefinitely. But in these days of waiting, when time itself seems suspended, she takes tiny steps, and each step carries its own immense weight, and she is very proud of her victim statement, even if by night, when the dog is asleep, she regrets it, tells herself that it looks like provocation, that it's an absurd, even dangerous thing to have done.

She has a new, cheap telephone. She even felt a little afraid of it, at first, because it seems that being afraid of everything is her life, now. She told herself he would find the number. Then Caroline saw her, lost in thought, with the cheap little mobile in her hand, and said, Remember, he doesn't know everything. Remember, he's not omnipotent.

But Sandrine receives no texts. When she did not go back to the house, that first night, she had moaned from sheer dread, in the toilet at the Marquezes' apartment, for the call that was sure to come, perhaps on their landline at the thought of having to hear Monsieur Langlois's voice again, or worse, the voice of the man who cries. What would she do if the man who cries called her? But the telephone stayed silent.

He is nowhere to be seen. He does not hang around outside her office. He doesn't wait at the school gate. He is nowhere inside her phone, nowhere in the neighbourhood around the apartment. Since the first day after Sandrine's departure, Lisa and her colleague have taken turns in the cul-de-sac outside the house with the yellow kitchen. Monsieur Langlois leaves for work in the morning and comes home again at night.

Sandrine practises being present, in the here and now. Practises fitting herself into her own body, into this new, temporary life. No one in the Marquezes' apartment talks about letting her go. Mathias seems delighted to see her each evening, and indifferent to the oddness of the situation. He is with his grandparents, his mother, and Sandrine, and that's good, he is happy. Sandrine, too, is happy, in a way, in the fraction of a second between a deep breath of anxiety and a heavy sigh of dread. She is surrounded, warmed, by three generations of Marquezes. Like sparrows on a branch, their chatter soothes her, their proximity reassures her. Timidly, the week goes by. She goes out very little, and never alone – Caroline insists.

Sometimes, Sandrine has bad, small-minded thoughts. That they're being kind to her because she's helping Caroline – quid pro quo. That he hasn't come looking for her because she is nothing to him, that he never loved her. That thought, in particular, is a hard one to make disappear, even in the loving eyes of the ugly dog, even in the warmth of the small apartment.

Because you have to remember, each time, that it wasn't love. That's not what love is.

And then Mathias comes into the room, or Anne-Marie places her hand on Sandrine's back, and she shakes herself out of these acid thoughts, and repeats to herself that this, this is true and real. It's small, almost nothing, but it's real. The Marquezes are a tactile family, it shows in tiny, minuscule things: tender, delicate touches, a stroke of the little boy's hair when he's doing his homework, a hand placed on a shoulder, a forearm squeezed, a bump on the hip, laughing, when everyone is busy in the kitchen. They touch Sandrine but never hurt her. Sometimes, she feels as if she's in some unknown land, surrounded by creatures of alien, unfamiliar habits.

23

A FTER A WEEK, she goes back to work. Béatrice is kind and attentive.

Sandrine has no idea what instructions everyone has been given, but no one questions her, everyone treats her as usual. The way they did before her private life was laid bare for all to see, shared around, dissected. The only difference is that on Friday, when it's time for lunch and everyone is heading for the brasserie, Béatrice stands waiting with her bag over her shoulder, and refuses to take No for an answer. She has lunch with the other girls, the conversation is noisy and messy, she likes it, she even likes the slight headache she feels when she comes outside afterwards, the product of the echoing interior, the voices, the life all around her.

Each morning, she waits until she sees someone from work walking along the street towards the big gateway, before getting out of her car. In the evening, she never leaves the building alone. She likes her little car. It's the closest thing she has left to a space of her own, a space that's properly her own. She congratulates herself on keeping it. To have left before he forced her to give it up. Though in truth, the congratulations are delivered by the voice inside: *Well done.*

24

A FEW DAYS AFTER Sandrine's return to work, they arrest Monsieur Langlois. She and Caroline knew it would come to this, but still. They heard Lisa's voice down the telephone, telling them, We're going round there tomorrow morning, 6 a.m., and they held one another tight, and their hands trembled just a little. That evening Picasso, who had gone back to sleeping in the other bedroom, with Caroline and Mathias, lay down on the sitting room floor beside Sandrine and gazed at her with deep concern. She said, Good boy, everything's all right, it's all right, until finally, she believed it herself. Enough for them both to go to sleep.

Next morning, the male cop comes to find Sandrine. Langlois is in temporary custody. Lisa is with him. The cop has come to fetch Sandrine, so that he can go with her to collect her things.

Entering the house is difficult. Caroline offered to come too, but Sandrine said No. She's afraid, she feels sick, but Caroline died within these walls and Sandrine cannot make her relive the experience, now that the memory of it has returned. The house is crowded. People in white protective suits are inspecting every room.

Sandrine fetches her clothes. A few books she had left on the red shelves. Along the way, she makes sure the hidden banknotes are photographed, then puts them in an envelope that she stuffs deep inside her bag, for Caroline. It's her money. The fabric pouch with the bits of costume jewellery that belonged to her grandmother has gone. She gives up the search. She wants to get out of here as fast as possible. He had allowed her to unpack so little that she was ready in under an hour. Only the boxes in the garage are left now. The boxes filled with her silly treasures: photographs, the handful of letters from her grandmother.

The boxes are nowhere to be seen. The male cop scratches his head then remembers that Langlois took a load of boxes to a second-hand book place, a few weekends ago. Sandrine tries not to cry. Since living with the Marquezes, since she has learnt to live without fear, she cries easily, as if the red-hot rod that paralysed her back had released a torrent of tears as it shrank away. As if the thing that held her prisoner had also kept her upright, hard and tight. The cop asks the two guys with the huge camera, in their white astronaut suits, busying themselves back and forth between the kitchen and garage, if they have moved or taken any boxes. No.

Sandrine moves across to the patio door that opens onto the terrace. Autumn rain is falling on the subjugated box hedge, the garden shed, the barbecue. She feels her stomach twist. She walks out into the garden. It's cold and the grass is waterlogged, soaking wet underfoot. The cop follows her, signals to one of the astronauts to come too. They stop in front of the barbecue and the technician lifts the domed metal cover. The camera clicks. A scrap of Sandrine's grandmother remains among the ashes, a half-consumed photograph in shades of purple and grey.

Wearing his white latex gloves, the technician lifts the photograph, almost three-quarters of which have burned away, then searches the ashes that have congealed to a greyish paste. He extracts a metal chain and a brooch, its brass structure empty of the paste stones that have melted away. A brooch shaped like a bouquet of flowers. A thing of no value. Except to Sandrine. She presses her hand to her mouth. She's afraid she will be sick, but the feeling passes.

Methodically, he had opened the boxes, sorted her things. He burned the worthless bits and pieces that constituted her personal treasure. She thought he'd forgotten, that he wasn't listening when she told him about these meagre souvenirs. She was wrong. He had committed to memory every means at his disposal to hurt her. She asks if she can take the smoke-blackened chain. The cop and the technician shrug their shoulders, it's of no importance. She rubs it carefully with a paper handkerchief and puts it in her jacket pocket.

She goes upstairs. She takes Mathias's favourite books. She fills a suitcase with his favourite toys. Finally, the belongings she moves out are mostly the little boy's.

An hour later, she has finished.

On the ground floor, everything is upside down. The cameras click around the door to the pantry, the traces of the screws that held the bolt in position. There is nothing for her in this house now. She leaves, walking quickly. She had waited so long to feel at home in this place. She never wants to come here again.

She watches the white housefront recede in the rear-view mirror. A great wave of relief engulfs her. It's kind of you to come with me, she tells the male cop. Then it occurs to her that this is the first time she has been alone with another man for a very long time. He explains that Lisa insisted he drive her.

She does so much for us, says Sandrine. For Caroline and me, I mean.

The cop is silent at first, then he says, The truth is, Sandrine, all that time we spent watching the house, quite a lot of it was of our own accord, unofficial. Especially Lisa. Women who—

He flicks the indicator, seems to have left the phrase hanging, then says finally: This isn't the first woman she's buried. I mean, as a rule, they don't come back.

A touch of dark cop's humour? Sandrine is unsure. She just nods her head.

She comes back to the Marquezes' apartment with a suitcase and bags. Mathias's things. And the necklace. Her whole life. Next to nothing. *Even that's something*, says the voice.

The Marquezes are waiting for her. Her papers have come from the bank. She is once again the holder of an account in her name only. Langlois will be held until 6 a.m. tomorrow. Sandrine invites the Marquezes out to dinner.

It's a strange evening, a moment of peace. Tonight, for one night only, they are in no danger. Monsieur Langlois is behind bars. They go to a restaurant in a vaulted cellar, with fine white tablecloths. Mathias is very well-behaved.

What a strange family, Sandrine thinks when she sees them there, all together. Then she corrects herself. This is not her family. This is a temporary arrangement. Then Anne-Marie pats her hand and says, Thank you for Mathias's things. You do know how brave you've been, to go back there? To that house! Anne-Marie says nothing more, but Sandrine knows exactly what she means. That house.

They climb the steps and emerge from the restaurant, out onto the street. Sandrine's telephone buzzes over and over again. In Caroline's pocket, and in Anne-Marie's and Patrice's pockets too. Mathias looks up at the adults standing all around him, checking their texts, listening to the voicemails.

Monsieur Langlois is out.

They turn to the little boy. Their smiles are tense. They try to reassure him, but Sandrine sees only too well the anguish and fear in the expressions that mirror her own. Lisa's voice in her ear: 'His lawyer came to collect him. One other thing, Sandrine. I, I wasn't— I couldn't follow him straightaway. And now, he's not at the house. Be careful. I'll call you back, OK?'

In the car, with Mathias's small, warm body squashed between Caroline and her, Sandrine taps a message, says she's received the news, that they were out at a restaurant. That they are heading back to the Marquezes' apartment. That she will be careful.

Be very careful.

When Caroline enters the Marquezes' apartment, the front door makes its usual, distinctive sound. The old mail slot, with its metal frame, clatters slightly in the draft. In the autumn, they seal it up with sticky tape. The sticky tape is hanging loose. The sticky tape had been firmly in place when they left. The sticky tape should not be unstuck like that.

Picasso? Picasso!

Mathias's high-pitched voice rings out in the empty apartment. Usually, the dog is waiting just behind the door, cheerful, madly excited to see them, especially when he knows the little boy is coming back, too. But the dog is motionless in his basket.

Something is wrong.

Picasso?

A sharp, unpleasant odour floats in the kitchen. Mathias crouches over the dog's basket, not daring to touch him. He says Mama? Picasso's been sick.

Very quickly, four anxious silhouettes cluster around Mathias and the basket. Picasso is still a young dog, barely more than a

286

year old. He isn't supposed to fall ill. Caroline bends to touch him, tells the others, He's warm, which is another way of saying 'He's not dead.' She bends closer, then straightens up. Her voice is urgent, she says, He must have eaten something bad.

Glances shoot here and there. The cupboards are all closed. There are no chewed remnants of a toy, a ball, that the dog might have ripped apart. In the moist, viscous substance that has fouled his mouth and part of his muzzle, that stains the cotton lining of the circular basket, there is something white and round.

Sandrine knows that smell. Mothballs. How could the dog have got hold of mothballs? She's not even sure that Patrice and Anne-Marie use them. It's a distinctive smell, and she has never noticed it in the apartment until now.

She suggests that perhaps Anne-Marie should take Mathias to clean his teeth? When they have left the room, she crouches beside Caroline and points to the white ball. Carefully, Caroline moves the dog's head, which had obscured her view of the small white sphere coated in bile. She lifts her large eyes to look at Sandrine. 'What the hell is this?'

There is no time to waste figuring out how or why. Patrice picks up the basket with the dog in it and Caroline opens the door for him. Together, they disappear down the stairwell. Carefully, Sandrine shuts the door tight behind them.

Mathias calls to her. Sandrine goes to the small bedroom.

The little boy is in his pyjamas, in bed. He smells of toothpaste. He's worried. Sandrine knows the signs. She tells herself, It's so easy, so quick. The immediacy of the switch to a state of anxiety. And with it, for her, the switch to the pretence she showed before, the soft, reassuring tone she always used to talk to him when they were still living at Monsieur Langlois's house. Everything's going to be all right. Don't worry.

There's a knock at the door. Anne-Marie says, Oh, they must have forgotten something, and leaves the room. Sandrine watches her go, waddling slightly as she hurries off. Anne-Marie is a dynamic, energetic woman, but when she forces herself to walk faster than is comfortable, her hips waggle in a particular, rather comical way. Sandrine watches her leave, and is seized with dread, with an appalling feeling of apprehension. She hears Anne-Marie's footsteps along the tiled corridor, heading for the door. Panic overwhelms her, she opens her mouth, she is short of breath, gasping painfully like a fish out of water. With difficulty, she gets to her feet. Something is wrong, she wants to shout out loud, but each word is like a lead weight in her mouth, and she struggles for air. At last she makes it to the bedroom door, out into the corridor, it takes seconds, hours, and she yells NO!! But too late, Anne-Marie has opened the door.

It's not Caroline. Not Patrice.

It's Monsieur Langlois.

And Sandrine has no doubt. This is not the man who cries. Nor that other man she lived with, the one she survived, the controlling entity who ruled her daily existence but did not, ultimately, threaten her life: his cold, calculating nemesis, the one who made her sign the statements, grant power of attorney and access to her accounts. No, this is Monsieur Langlois, this is raw violence and cruelty, she knows the look in his eyes. She sees the arm rise and shoot forward, she sees Anne-Marie crumple to the floor. He has punched her, very hard. Sandrine takes a step back from the corridor, into the bedroom. She turns, looks at Mathias.

The boy is silent and his eyes are wide. He knows. He can smell it. His father's rage reaches them on the air. Sandrine has got to— she must, she absolutely must, she has to— but panic fills her belly, seizes her throat, and the burning rod is there once again, in her neck, her back, and nothing moves, she is petrified. She hears the sound of footsteps in the entrance. Slow. Confident.

He is taking his time.

Sandrine swallows, and the simple reflex action is so painful that she thinks something is broken inside her. *MOVE YOURSELF! FUCK!!* the voice shrieks in her head, the angry voice, the voice of survival. Sandrine manages to move close to the bed. She speaks to Mathias, very quietly. 'Hide. Hide yourself.' *LISA. CALL LISA.* She takes her phone from her pocket. Her fingers are trembling, she can't unlock the screen. She tries again, it's the same code, she didn't change it, the date they met, 0310, 0310. She gets it wrong. And again.

What will she do if the boy doesn't move? She can hardly breathe, let alone hope to be able to pick Mathias up and hide him somewhere. But Mathias reacts. Mathias moves, fast as an eel, he wriggles to the bottom of the bed and slips into the tight space under the divan. She lets her phone drop to the floor, reaches into her jeans pocket and finds the emergency button Lisa gave her. Mathias's feet disappear under the bed. Amid the clutter of objects, travel bags, the spare quilts in their big plastic storage bags. *Lisa, Lisa, Lisa.* Mathias wriggles and disappears. Sandrine moves forward once again, how can the bed be so far away. *Lisa.* She presses the button, again and again, nothing happens, she hoped there might be a noise, something, but nothing, is it even working? The button is grey, unchanging, it doesn't light up. She feels the floor slipping from under her feet, and when her hand touches the bedsheets at last, ten years have gone by. He is in the sitting room. A few metres more. The moment stretches out to infinity. The footsteps are approaching. But she's there, she's reached the bed. She lies down on the sheets, extends her arm and hides the useless box under the duvet. He's coming. *GET YOUR HAND OUT FROM THERE. HE'S COMING.*

He enters the room. Monsieur Langlois enters the room. She is lying on the bed, her hands tight around the cheap chain necklace, cleansed of its smoke stains and ashes.

She sees him and thinks, Wild with rage— no.

He is brimming with rage, she feels the heat of his fury as it breaks over her in burning waves, but he is not wild. On the contrary. This is the Monsieur Langlois who crushed her face into a custard pastry, quite simply and deliberately. Because Monsieur Langlois has that ability – to make everything, life itself, very simple. When he's there, there is only him and his violence, contained or unleashed; his decision to strike a blow, or not; pain, or the absence of pain; the moment before striking the blow, the moments after the blow hits home, and the blows themselves. Blows that beat time, blows as a measure of time. Sudden, quick-fire, infinite.

He enters the room and looks at her. He looks at the bed, says, Where is he?

She sits up, with difficulty. There are short, stabbing pains in the nape of her neck.

Lie.

Who?

The kid.

Lie.

He's sleeping at a friend's tonight, a neighbour in the building, it was all arranged. We left him at Ismaël's apartment after we came back from the restaurant.

She hopes, she hopes so hard that he was watching them from outside. That he was not inside the building already, not counting the stops made by the elevator, the footsteps on the landing. She affects a stupid expression of bovine placidity. Stupid, fat bitch, poor bitch, stupid, stupid, all those years people treated her like a dumb animal, a halfwit, that must be how she looks to the world, after all. Her cheeks sag, her eyes are glassy. She slips into her familiar suit of limp resignation and defeat. The Sandrine who never dared tell lies. He seems to believe her. She doesn't move. Her fingers are tight around the chain.

He comes closer.

She recoils, on the bed. He is almost calm. Almost. His breathing is a little fast. His forehead a little damp. He doesn't shout. She is terrified. He reaches out and runs his hand through her hair. She huddles into a ball, she feels the rage mounting, she knows the gesture is a lie, that something will happen. She curls so tight to protect her head that she feels her neck disappear, she is nothing but a coiled, tightly balled, burning-hot spine. The man's fingers are hot on her skull. No, she mumbles, though that's one of the forbidden words. A few weeks ago, he had stroked her hair, in another house. He looks at her and balls his fist. No, Sandrine says again, begging this time. Her scalp is flame. He pulls, pulls, and Sandrine's head follows the direction of the movement. Her elbows move under the quilt, she moves, by reflex, seeking out the angle, the elevation that will interrupt the pain. He pulls her out of bed, not hurriedly, but decisive, purposeful. He drags her along with him and when she falls from the bed to the floor he doesn't lower his fist. On the contrary. She struggles to get to her feet, she is screaming now, bent double, her scalp on fire, he is heading for the sitting room and he begins to speak. He doesn't scream, he just talks, he says, You see, you see what you've done, you are the cause of all this, you poor, stupid bitch, you fat bitch, you filthy whore. Sandrine screams, she screams very loud, she yells, No! NO! The door to the apartment is still open, Anne-Marie is lying on the floor, motionless, perhaps dead, poor woman, Anne-Marie never did anyone any harm, and Sandrine understands, she understands what's about to happen, and she screams, and begs, she calls for help. Her screams echo on the landing, in the stairwell, someone will come, someone will come, she calls and calls again, someone will come, someone must come. Monsieur Langlois pauses in the sitting room, the luxuriant sitting room where the plants sprout leaves by the thousand under Patrice's care, where they have made space for her, where Picasso the dog came to watch over her and where Sandrine repeated, Everything will be all right, everything will be all right. Monsieur Langlois opens the door to the balcony with one hand and pushes her outside. She trips, falls forward. The little terrace is paved with rough-textured tiles. They are wet, it is raining. Her hands are burning, her head is burning, her knees are burning. It's cold outside and her breath rises is desperate clouds, she is panting. She begs once more, says No! No, please! Please! She sees Monsieur Langlois's feet stepping over the bottom of the sliding door, testing the floor outside, in the rain, first one, then the other. And he says, This is your fault, IT'S YOUR FAULT. He bounds towards her. She screams NO! But nothing stops him, he kicks her, he kicks her hard with his foot, in her belly. The pain cuts her in two and she thinks of the little bean, she thinks, *no, no, no*, and she curls tight into a ball, as tight as she can, all around it, to protect what's left. Someone will come, someone will come. She is groaning, she says, Please! Please, no! But he strikes her again with the tip of his shoe, he strikes her buttocks, then again higher up, in the small of the back, she doesn't think she has any breath left, but she screams, the pain is appalling and she thinks, *Someone will come.*

You see? You see what you made me do? You see what's

292

happening because of you? What is it, you saw that other slut and you thought you could be like her? Thought you could leave? Who the fuck, who the *fuck* do you think you are?

He pushes her with his foot, she stays balled tight as a fist and screams, Stop! Stop it! I'm sorry! I'm sorry!

He crouches down and grabs Sandrine under her armpits; the wire in her bra scrapes against her ribcage, he pulls her up, stands her on her feet, presses her against the balcony rail. He says, Look, see. See what you've done! And facing him she says she's sorry, so sorry. Stop, stop, I'll come back if you want, I'll come home, I'll never leave again, I'm so sorry! But he isn't listening, he's talking to himself, he lists everything she's done to him, the humiliation, her audacity, when she's the one who's less than nothing, a piece of shit, what was she thinking, that she'd find someone else, fat sow that she is, poor, stupid bitch, and anyway who did she leave him for, who's been screwing her, who's been fucking her? He says, I've had enough, enough of being humiliated by whores and sluts, by you, you fat sow, I'm going to finish you right here. He tightens his hands around her neck and Sandrine's screams are exhausted. She feels the damp concrete of the balcony wall against her back, the backs of her legs, she feels the round metal rail that stops the pots of flowers from falling, under her shoulder blades. She wants to say No, one more time, but the words do not come, she whispers, she feels hot, she feels the blood beating in her face, searching for a way out, she gasps, she tightens her fists around Monsieur Langlois's wrists, tries to scratch him, all she can hear is the frantic beating of her heart, in the veins at her temples. Clawing at him doesn't work, she begs with the last shred of air that remains, she says, she tries to say No, but nothing comes, everything is very red, and the light dims, something is moving in the sitting room and she cannot keep her eyes from turning to look at the small, pyjama-clad silhouette, she tries one more time to say No! But this time it's not for her.

No, not him, not him, not Mathias.

Someone will come. The man sees something in her eyes and his hands loosen a little, Sandrine gasps desperately for air, a rasping, animal noise rises in her throat. He turns, curious to see what she has seen, and his eyes alight on Caroline's son.

Sandrine falls to the floor. She coughs, splutters. Mathias. You have to look up. Keep your eyes open. *Keep your eyes open. Mathias.*

Monsieur Langlois enters the sitting room and moves towards the boy. Petrified, Mathias is consumed by Monsieur Langlois's shadow.

Sandrine drags herself forward. *Mathias.* She feels nothing. No pain. *Mathias. No one will come. Mathias.* She drags herself on all fours over the metal frame of the glass balcony door, her legs are paralysed, she is unable to stand, but she moves forwards, an animal, reduced to nothing, to this one thing, she moves forward. *Mathias.* Mathias is so dark, his unfathomable eyes and his soft, sweet skin. Mathias, Caroline's son. Does the man see something else as he moves towards him? Does he see anything but the first woman's child, the baby she loved, the baby that turned her away from him? This man murdered Caroline but that wasn't enough, now he will destroy the first woman's child, hurt him and kill him and tear all she has from her grasp, he is going to kill Mathias and no one is going to come. Sandrine stretches out her arms, clutches at anything within her reach, Mathias is frozen, silent with terror, only Monsieur Langlois speaks, repeating that this is all their fault, those sluts, those bitches, those unfaithful, ungrateful women, he insults and curses the females who have humiliated him and dared to defy his will, he says no one leaves him, no gets to leave him, If you leave me I will kill you. Sandrine begs him, begs the empty void on the landing, the neighbours behind their silent walls, begs the building in which not one single door has opened, she begs and pleads, they are going to die, he has come to punish them, he has come to kill, his hand is around the boy's slender neck, Mathias's eyes are huge and their deep, dark black contains nothing but terror, a trickle of wet soaks the cotton of his pyjama bottoms, and Sandrine smells the acid reek of ammonia. And she, the second woman, the friend of no one, the pathetic prey, the pretend mother, is breathless, with no strength remaining, she wants to fight, to protect Mathias, to hold back the man who kills, but her arms are limp and her tears are scalding hot, no one is going to come and someone comes.

Someone comes.

Lisa is here. Lisa has come. She is not alone. Suddenly, Monsieur Langlois is down on the floor, too, his arms twisted at improbable angles, knees pressing his back. Someone is speaking to him, using the familiar, disrespectful *tu*. Someone is talking to him the way he talks to women, someone is saying YOU MAKE ONE MOVE, YOU SHIT-BRAINED BASTARD, *ONE MOVE*, I TELL YOU… and his face is crushed into the sitting room floor.

Lisa glances sideways, repeatedly, in Sandrine's direction, she has come with people in navy-blue jackets, the emergency team, people who are feeling Mathias's head, his pulse, and Sandrine's head and pulse, too, people who are handling Anne-Marie in the doorway. Instructions are shouted, Anne-Marie must be brought to the hospital, and Sandrine thinks *The hospital is for people who need treatment*, just as, earlier, Caroline said, He's warm, meaning the dog was not dead. If Anne-Marie needs treatment then she is not dead either.

Sandrine tries to drag herself up from the floor, and all around her voices say *Madame!* Don't try to move, wait! But she moves along, she crawls, obstinate as a wild beast, towards the little boy, and she touches him, holds him, smells his skin. Mathias is warm, too, Mathias is alive, and she cries into his crow-black hair. She says, Don't look, Mathias, don't look, I'm sorry, I'm so sorry. Oh, Mathias, Mathias, it's over. It's all over. Mathias clutches her tight, very tight. His thin arms are around Sandrine's neck. The smell of washing powder and urine reaches her in waves, and the acrid stench of terrified sweat.

Sandrine's senses are sharp and alert, she can smell again, clearly, precisely; she can feel again, the pain is coming back, she feels her aching back, her tightened belly. Her jeans are wet, and she wonders if what she can feel is blood. Her hands are filthy, her head is burning, and across the room, strewn over the floor, beside the door to the balcony, she can see strands of hair, her hair.

They are separated, strapped and wrapped up. Sandrine croaks, Lisa, Lisa, my telephone, I need to call, I need to warn…

Lisa says, Don't worry, Sandrine. All right? And she goes to the bedroom and picks up Sandrine's mobile phone. Her radio crackles, she speaks a few words into the heavy black box. Lisa comes back and slips Sandrine's phone into her hand, the telephone she could not unlock. And she says, They're downstairs, Patrice and Caroline. They're downstairs, they'll come with you to hospital. Sandrine? Sandrine…

Sandrine is trembling. The phone is in her hands. She is shaking all over. She cannot stop, cannot control it. Soaked in adrenaline, her body shakes and shudders, and Lisa moves away to allow the emergency team to take her pulse, feel her painful limbs.

Monsieur Langlois is pulled roughly to his feet. Sandrine would rather look away but they are examining her neck, feeling her vertebrae, checking for damage to her trachea, and they turn her head in his direction. So she sees.

She sees Monsieur Langlois, stunned and dripping with sweat. His eyes are tiny, pig-like, moist and red. She sees the man, the man who came to kill her, who failed; the man who is crying now. She sees and she understands. She understands the pretence, the lie that was there all the time, she understands her blindness, her mistake. The man who cries only ever cries for himself. He cries out of hatred, hatred in his own image – small, and miserable. He cries for the loss of his own pride. His mouth gapes wide and twisted like an angry, needy child. He cries out of the meanness of his own emotions. He cries because they are taking him away and he can see that she has escaped. He cries because she is alive and because she is free.

In the stairwell, the witnesses huddle and whisper, all the neigh-bours who called the police and the emergency services. The building's residents are shaken but relieved. Lisa carries Mathias in her arms – he screamed when her male colleague tried to pick him up. She holds him close against her, oblivious to the urine soaking his pyjamas. Mathias has placed his arm around her neck, and he looks at Sandrine as she lies on her stretcher, as they take her carefully, expertly, down the stairs. His dark eyes bore into hers and she ventures a crooked smile. She tries her best.

The little boy blinks slowly, huddled like a baby crow, and then he returns a crooked smile of his own. He's trying his best, too.

Outside, the first ambulance takes off with a roar, carrying Anne-Marie, and Patrice at her side. Caroline is there, standing in the rain, her fingers knotted in anguish. When he sees her,

Mathias wriggles frantically, shakes his legs and feet, moans with impatience. Lisa passes the boy into Caroline's open arms. He huddles tight against her body. Their black heads of hair blend into one and they hold one another so close, the first woman and her son, that it's impossible to say where Caroline ends and Mathias begins. Sandrine thinks of the warm, liquid stain soaking her panties and jeans, and she hopes— but what, she doesn't know.

Caroline comes over to the trolley where Sandrine lies strapped into place. She reaches out a hand, the emergency team object, she's getting in their way, but she doesn't care. Caroline clutches her precious child tight against her, reeking of piss, and shoulders her way through. Sandrine extracts her arm from under the shiny gold blanket and holds out her hand. They need to touch, to squeeze, to prove they're alive, that it's over. Caroline says, Thank you, thank you, Sandrine. Thank you. Her voice is ragged with the first tears Sandrine has ever seen her shed, and her short, muscular fingers are hot and full of life. Thank you, Sandrine, thank you. And Sandrine keeps that with her, holds it tight as they shut the ambulance doors, on the journey to the hospital, the memory of Caroline's grateful hands, the shared imprint of their women's fingers, tightly bound like tendrils of ivy: perennial, determined and powerfully alive.

Author's note

Coercive control is often compared to an iceberg: we may try to quantify the instances of physical violence, the femicides, but these are only the visible tip of the phenomenon, the product of a campaign of psychological violence that builds slowly, over time.

The articles I have read on the subject all describe an initial phase of narcissistic seduction, followed by alternating violence and displays of affection. The controlling man will give his female partner compliments and pleasant experiences, followed by seemingly minor acts of aggression, violence, or unpleasant remarks. If the woman objects, her controlling partner accuses her of a failed sense of humour, or claims he is telling her unpleasant truths for her own good.

Psychiatrists suggest that these alternating, contradictory messages have a paralysing effect on the brain. The alternation persists and becomes more exaggerated. Typically, this particular form of violence is perpetrated well before the controlling partner's aggression turns physical.

To say that the partner experiencing this behaviour (most often a woman) 'should just leave' is to deny the overwhelming importance of this hidden aspect of the phenomenon. 'Just leave' also presupposes that leaving is an easy thing to do, that adequate systems are in place to help and accompany women whose partners have been violent. This is not the case.

In the UK:

- Almost one in three women aged 16–59 will experience domestic abuse in her lifetime.
- Two women a week are killed by a current or former partner in England and Wales alone.
- In the year ending March 2019, 1.6 million women experienced domestic abuse.
- On average the police in England and Wales receive over 100 calls relating to domestic abuse every hour. This has increased to more than 40,000 calls during the first three months of the Covid-19 restrictions. One in five offences – more than a quarter of a million – recorded by police during and immediately after the first lockdown in England and Wales involved domestic abuse.
- For the year ending March 2018, only 18% of women who had experienced partner abuse in the last 12 months reported the abuse to the police.

In the US:

- On average, nearly 20 people per minute are physically abused by an intimate partner. Over one year, this equates to more than 10 million women and men.
- On a typical day, there are more than 20,000 phone calls placed to domestic violence hotlines nationwide.
- Intimate partner violence accounts for 15% of all violent crime.
- Only 34% of people who are injured by intimate partners receive medical care for their injuries.

- 72% of all murder-suicides involve an intimate partner; 94% of the victims of these murder-suicides are female.
- 1 in 15 children are exposed to intimate partner violence each year, and 90% of these children are eyewitnesses to this violence.

If you feel threatened, isolated, or endangered by your current or ex-partner, you can call Refuge on 0808 2000 247 (UK) or the National Domestic Violence Hotline 1-800-799-7233 (US). British pharmacies operate the 'Ask for ANI' scheme: anyone asking to speak to Annie ('Action Needed Immediately') will be taken to a secure interview space and given help to escape their abuser.

AVAILABLE AND COMING SOON
FROM PUSHKIN VERTIGO

Jonathan Ames

You Were Never Really Here

A Man Named Doll

Olivier Barde-Cabuçon

The Inspector of Strange and Unexplained Deaths

Sarah Blau

The Others

Candas Jane Dorsey

The Adventures of Isabel

Martin Holmén

Clinch

Down for the Count

Slugger

Elizabeth Little

Pretty as a Picture

Maxine Mei-Fung Chung

The Eighth Girl

Louise Mey

The Second Woman

Joyce Carol Oates (ed.)

Cutting Edge

John Kåre Raake

The Ice

RV Raman

A Will to Kill

Amy Suiter Clarke

Girl, 11

Tiffany Tsao

The Majesties

John Vercher

Three-Fifths

Emma Viskic

Resurrection Bay

And Fire Came Down

Darkness for Light

Those Who Perish

Yulia Yakovleva

Punishment of a Hunter